About the Authors

Coming from two generations of journalists, writing was in **Fiona Harper**'s genes. As a child she was constantly teased for having her nose in a book and in a dream world. Things haven't changed since then, but at least in writing she's found a outlet for her runaway imagination! She loves dancing, singing, reading and watching a good romance. She lives in London with her family. Visit her online at: www.fionaharper.com

Christy Jeffries graduated from the University of California, Irvine and received her Juris Doctor from California Western School of Law. But drafting court documents and working in law enforcement was merely an apprenticeship for her current career in the relentless field of motherhood and romance writing. She lives in California with her patient husband, two sons, and one sassy grandmother. Follow her on or visit her website at www.christyjeffries.com

Between walking her Jack Russell-beagle mix, petting two cats and driving her two kids all over creation, **Amanda Berry** writes contemporary romance novels (with a supportive husband). A Midwest girl stuck in the lowlands of South Carolina, she finds inspiration in her small-town upbringing. A list of her current releases and backlist can be found at amanda-berry.com

Summer of Love

Summer of Love: Once Upon a Wedding

FIONA HARPER

CHRISTY JEFFRIES

AMANDA BERRY

MILLS & BOON

DUDLEY LIBRARIES

000003088770	
Askews & Holts	13-May-2021
AF ROM	£7.99
2GL	

Waking Up Wed © 2016 Christy Jeffries
One Night with the Best Man © 2014 Amanda Berry

ISBN: 978-0-263-29964-9

MIX
Paper from
responsible sources
FSC® C007454

This book is produced from independently certified FSC™ paper to ensure responsible forest management.

For more information visit: www.harpercollins.co.uk/green

Printed and bound in Spain
by CPI, Barcelona

ALWAYS THE BEST MAN

FIONA HARPER

For Dad, who likes sailing much better than
he likes reading romance. x

CHAPTER ONE

IF DAMIEN STONE had been a woman, he'd have become a bit of a standing joke by now. Three times a bridesmaid was unlucky, apparently. Double that number would have knelled the bells of matrimonial doom. Clucking aunts would have reminded him of that at every opportunity, told him to get a move on before he was left on the shelf.

But no one had ever made the mistake of thinking Damien was a girl, and he hadn't been a bridesmaid once, thankfully. Nobody seemed to mind he'd been a best man so many times. If anything, other men clapped him on the back and congratulated him for such an accomplishment. No, Damien didn't think there was anything unlucky about it.

It meant his friends respected him, thought him a stalwart ally. It took a certain kind of person to stand beside a friend at the front of a church, as that man prepared to utter the most life-altering words of his existence. Someone who was reliable, who knew how to get things done. Someone with a little dignity. He supposed he should be flattered.

But more than that, he was thankful—because he was going to need to draw on all of that experience if he was going to survive this day.

Six times now he'd worn a buttonhole as he stood beside a good friend. Six times he'd stood at the front of a pretty stone church in the hush just before the bride made her entrance.

But never before had his palms been so sweaty or his heart run around inside his ribcage like a wind-up toy gone mad.

However, never before had the woman of his dreams been standing at the doors of the church, about to make her way down the aisle towards him.

He turned and looked at Luke, his best friend, and Luke gave him a fortifying smile and clapped him on the back. Damien swallowed. He was glad it was Luke standing here beside him. He didn't think he could have made it through the day if it had been anyone else.

He tried to smile, but a nerve in his cheek made his lip twitch. Humour flashed in Luke's eyes and Damien thought his friend was about to make one of his usual wry remarks, but just at that moment there was a ripple of movement behind them. Row upon row of heads turned towards the back of the church, like some nuptial Mexican wave, and the organ began to play.

He couldn't look back at first, had to prepare himself for what he was about to see. This was it. No turning back after this. The future would be set in stone.

It was only when Luke nudged him in the ribs that he sucked in a stealthy breath through his nostrils then looked over his shoulder.

She was perfect.

He didn't really look at the dress. Just her.

But then Sara Mortimer always had been pretty wonderful in his eyes. He'd thought so from the day he'd seen her across the room at a crowded bar, laughing with Luke, and had felt as if he'd been hit by a truck. Side on.

After today the rest of the world would be left in no doubt about her perfection, either. The white satin dress was pure class, and her soft blonde hair had been caught up in a twist of some kind behind her head. She wore a veil and a simple tiara and held a bunch of lilies, tied together with a thick white ribbon.

Sara was poised and elegant, intelligent, kind. He couldn't find one fault with her—apart from her taste in men, maybe.

He let go of the breath he'd been holding and grabbed another while he had the chance.

It seemed to take ages for the bridesmaids to waft past in a cloud of dull gold. Well, *most* of them wafted. The maid of honour had too much of a wiggle in her step to do anything as graceful as waft.

It wasn't just Sara's taste in men that let her down, then. Damien had never really understood why Sara was friends with Zoe. Another one of the bride's glowing qualities to add to his list, he supposed.

Where Sara was slender and cool and sophisticated, Zoe was too...everything. Not in the same class—and that didn't refer to her parents' wage brackets. Damien wasn't a snob. No, Zoe was too loud, too uninhibited. Too busting out of her bodice, if his eyes served him right. Was it even legal to have that much cleavage in a bridesmaid's dress?

For some bizarre reason, just her presence jarred his senses and irritated him. Or was that just the eye-watering perfume? She caught him looking at her and her expression took on a saucy glimmer. She *knew* she got under his skin. Couldn't she have left it alone for just one day? And today of all days? He was sure she did...whatever she did...on purpose, just to goad him.

And now Sara was almost at the front and he'd been distracted, which only served to exasperate him further.

Thankfully, at that moment the last of the bridesmaids peeled away, leaving him with a vision of only Sara. He forgot instantly about bulging necklines, saucy glimmers and ginger curls popping out of their grips. In comparison, Sara was like a cool stream on a hot summer's day. As she approached, she even gave him the smallest and softest of smiles. Sadly, he didn't manage to return it; that nerve in his cheek had gone into overdrive. For a moment, though, their eyes connected and something flashed between them. Something bittersweet he was sure would haunt him on restless nights for years to come.

Because then Sara's gaze was on the man standing next to him, and her father placed her hand in Luke's and stepped away. Now it was Damien's turn to be forgotten, to be totally pushed out of someone else's mind by another.

The bride and groom stepped forward, eagerly looking at the minister. All eyes were on Sara and Luke, the happy couple, but all Damien could do was close his lids for a second, let his fingers close around the ring in his pocket.

Luke's ring. For Sara.

No, if it had been anyone else, he couldn't have made it through today. He couldn't have stood there and watched Sara marry anyone but Luke. He equally couldn't have refused when Luke had asked him to be his best man. Luke would have wanted to know why, and if there was one thing Damien was determined about it was that neither Luke nor Sarah would ever find out about his feelings for her, how they'd grown in strength, side by side with Luke's, as he'd fallen for his best friend's girlfriend.

He'd hidden those feelings successfully for the last eighteen months and he wasn't going to slip up now. No, Luke would never know. Even if it killed Damien to make sure of that.

Today of all days, Damien Stone needed to be the perfect best man.

As the congregation mumbled their way through 'Love Divine, All Loves Excelling', almost completely drowned out by the rabidly enthusiastic organist, Sara's cousin Tilly poked Zoe in the ribs with the stalky end of her bouquet.

Okay, maybe 'poked in the ribs' was a bit of an exaggeration. There was a bit too much *squish* where floristry met torso to accurately describe it as contact with bone. Zoe tried to ignore her, but Tilly leaned forward and whispered behind her lilies.

'Best man's hot,' she said, sneaking a glance across the aisle. 'Lucky you. As chief bridesmaid, you get first dibs.'

Zoe couldn't help glancing across at the man in question. How did he do that? Manage to look all grave and heartfelt as he sang, while other people just buried their noses behind their Order of Service and hit a few right notes in the chorus?

'If you like that sort of thing,' she mumbled back to Tilly.

If you liked tall, dark and handsome. If you liked long legs and good bone structure and that irritating sense of aloofness. Even now, with his mouth wide open, singing one of the long notes of the hymn, he looked good. Untouchable. And Zoe had never been interested in anything that was too good to be touched, one step removed from life, as if it was something behind glass on display in a museum. Life was for getting your hands dirty, for jumping in one hundred per cent.

'What?' hissed Tilly, forgetting to shield her mouth with her bouquet. She earned herself a stern look from the mother of the bride. A woman who managed to scare the pants off the normally irrepressible Zoe St James. If, as the old wives' tale threatened, Sara was going to age into a gorgon like that, she'd have to find herself a new best friend once she hit forty.

'Are you blind?' Tilly added, ignoring her aunt's stare. Obviously the black sheep of the Mortimer family—which, funnily enough, put her a few notches higher in Zoe's opinion.

Zoe just rolled her eyes and shook her head ever so slightly. It was still enough motion, however, to send yet another curly tendril tumbling over her face. She was about to blow it out of her way when she caught the Gorgon's eye, and resorted to delicately tucking it behind her ear while the other woman's eyes narrowed.

She looked away, and her gaze was drawn inexplicably to the subject of their discussion.

No, not blind. Just not stupid.

She knew he couldn't stand the sight of her. Oh, he tried to hide it, and he actually did it rather well, but she'd been on the receiving end of similar treatment ever since she'd been old enough to open her mouth to recognise disapproval when she saw it.

Disdain. That was the word.

And that *disdainful* glimmer in Mr Perfect's eye when he glanced her way just made her want to deliberately provoke him. And Zoe wasn't one for resisting an urge whenever it hit. Life was too short. Just once she'd like to see him lose his cool, to see fire in those pale blue eyes instead of ice. In the past she'd got close a few times, but close wasn't good enough. What Zoe really wanted to see was the whole firework display.

Not today, unfortunately. She wouldn't do anything to upset Sara, and the poor deluded girl thought Mr Damien Stone was wonderful. Not as wonderful as the lovely Luke, obviously, but Zoe reckoned he came a close second in Sara's eyes. She turned to Tilly and made a silent gagging motion, to show just what she thought of her fellow bridesmaid's suggestion.

Whoops! The Gorgon was staring at them openly now, her mouth thinning. And Zoe really didn't want to see tiny snakes popping up all over her head and burrowing their way up through the stiff and elaborate dove-grey hat. She turned to face the happy couple again, clutched her bouquet and started singing sweetly.

Mr Perfect must've caught the sudden motion out of the corner of his eye, because his head turned slightly and he glanced across. Zoe ignored him. Ignored the flicker she saw in those eyes before it was quickly hidden again. She put on her best angelic face and sang loudly, all the while warmed by the imagination that she could hear Damien Stone's blood hissing faintly as it boiled in his veins.

Oh, how she wanted to see that firework display.

But not tonight, Zoe. Keep a lid on it. Sara and Luke had decided they didn't want fireworks at the end of the reception, saying that everyone did it now and it seemed a bit of a cliché, so she guessed they wouldn't welcome a similar display of the interpersonal kind. Damien Stone's fuse would have to go unlit—for now.

But that didn't mean she couldn't mess with his head a little, did it?

'Aren't you going to eat that?'

Damien stared at his half-finished individual pavlova for a second. He remembered taking a bite, but he didn't remember pushing it around his plate so much it had disintegrated into Eton Mess. He flexed his shoulder muscles slightly. His morning suit jacket felt as if it were shrinking.

'What's wrong with yours?'

He turned to look at the maid of honour sitting next to him at the top table. Ridiculous seating plan. He'd never been sat next to the maid of honour before, not in six other weddings.

'Nothing,' she replied sweetly. Too sweetly. 'It was stupendous...but rather small. That's why I want yours if you're not going to do it justice.'

Damien glowered at his plate briefly, as if the ravaged dessert somehow held some of the blame in this situation, and then shoved the plate in her direction, nobly resisting the urge to say anything about overfilled bodices.

'Knock yourself out.'

'Thanks.'

She dug in straight away, he noticed. Somehow that irritated him. He focused on a rather ugly pink hat somewhere else in the massive marquee and tried to will the minutes to go faster. Only a short time now and his official duties would be over. Soon he'd be able to slink off and find a good single malt to lubricate his petrified facial muscles. They'd set into a stupefied smile earlier in the day. Right about the time Sara had said, 'I do.'

Always the best man...

It was starting to sound like a joke to Damien now—and not a very funny one. While he enjoyed helping his friends out in this way, he was beginning to feel like the odd one out. So many of his friends were all settled down and happy now, just as he wanted to be. Damien felt as if he was the unlucky jockey in a horse race, whose starting gate had failed to open while all the other riders were racing away from him. And now his best friend had snapped up the one woman Damien had considered a viable candidate for being Mrs Stone, it was even more disheartening.

'Mmm. You don't know what you're missing,' Zoe murmured next to him.

Damien braced his aching shoulders to stop them sagging. Unfortunately, he knew *exactly* what he was losing out on today. How could he not when she was sitting only three places away? He made the mistake of glancing to his right, the opposite direction from the pavlova-devouring machine on his left.

He must have momentarily forgotten the granite smile, because he snagged Sara's attention for a second. She made the most adorable face, asking him what was wrong by pulling her lips down and creasing her forehead into a little frown.

He shook his head, shrugged one shoulder and resurrected the ghoulish grin he'd been fooling everybody with all day. Blast that Zoe. Her dessert stealing had made him lose focus. Why couldn't he have been seated next to Sara's mum? He could have distracted himself from this train wreck of an afternoon by charming her socks off.

Sara noted his changed expression and gave him a soft smile before turning her attention back to her new husband.

Damien wanted to sigh, but his ribs were too tight under his skin to allow his lungs to expand that fully, so he made up for it by huffing out an exasperated little snort through his nose.

'Calm down, tiger.' The words were slightly muffled through a layer of whipped cream and raspberry coulis. 'There's still a bit left if you're regretting your generosity.'

He turned to look at Zoe as she nudged the almost empty plate his way. A lump of soggy meringue with a single berry on top was all that remained. Her mouth was pressed together in a knowing little smile and her eyes glittered with unsaid words.

Regretting your generosity *to me*, they seemed to be saying.

He shook his head, not trusting his tongue to remain civil.

'Sure?' she asked, as she began to move her spoon into position to capture the last morsel. 'I'm sure I could pilfer one for you from somewhere, or sweet-talk one of the waiters...'

'I'm sure you could,' Damien replied dryly.

That saucy glint again. Now his suit was three sizes too small instead of two. And all that shrinkage was making him feel hot and jittery.

'Oh, well,' she said and popped the now full spoon into her mouth, turning it upside down at the last moment so she could suck every square millimetre of the silver clean. She closed her eyes and murmured her appreciation deep down in her throat.

Damien experienced a quick, hot jolt of something unexpected. Something he didn't really want to identify. Especially when it was prompted by Zoe St James's mobile lips sliding along a spoon.

Thankfully, Sara's father chose that moment to stand up and clink his dessert fork against his glass. All heads turned towards the top table and Damien instantly sat up straighter and put his game face back on.

In fact, he was so busy making sure he wasn't giving off any unwanted non-verbal cues to more than a hundred guests that he didn't even hear the opening sentences of Colin's speech. He couldn't let anything slip. Not a facial twitch, not a glance in the wrong direction. No one must guess that he was anything less than the perfect best man. But all the while the guilt, the frustration, the slow, glowing flicker of rage kept building inside him until he wished he had a giant version of the metal cages that went round champagne corks. If he wasn't very much mistaken, his head was about to explode from his shoulders, and that wouldn't do before the toasts were over.

More words. They floated past like yachts in a stiff breeze. Words he'd heard a hundred times before at occasions like this. Until the end of the speech, that was…

'So…' Colin Mortimer beamed at his wife and then his daughter '…Brenda and I decided we wanted to do something special for our little girl.' He paused for dramatic effect as his only daughter smiled back up at him. 'We know you'd planned a simple honeymoon sailing Luke's pride and joy down the south coast, but we decided we'd like to upgrade you a little…'

Damien sat up straighter. Uh-oh. Luke had planned the perfect honeymoon for himself and Sara, one Damien would have given his right arm to have. A fortnight on *Dream Weaver* with no one but Sara? It sounded like heaven. Oh, Luke would smile and thank his new father-in-law if he produced tickets for an all-inclusive break in some slick hotel, but his dream holiday would be ruined.

Always the one to take charge, to make sure all the details were ironed out and perfect, Damien started composing a speech in his head, one he'd have with Colin afterwards, to try and help Luke back graciously out of this latest development.

The father of the bride handed Luke a wallet. 'Two plane tickets to the Virgin Islands—'

Damien began rehearsing that little speech in earnest.

'—and the use of a luxury yacht for three weeks!'

There was a collective gasp from the guests and then people started to clap and cheer. Damien was frozen. For some reason he couldn't move. Hell, he couldn't even think straight.

Sara was hugging her father and Luke was pumping his hand enthusiastically.

No wonder. Luke had dreamed of sailing those turquoise Caribbean waters since he and Damien had both been racing little Laser dinghies together at summer sailing school. However, since Sara had put her foot down about a transatlantic crossing for a honeymoon, Luke had had to settle for West Country cruising instead.

Why hadn't Damien thought of doing this for them? He should have done. After all, it was sailing that had bonded him and Luke as friends all those years ago.

You know why.

Damien closed his eyes. Yes, he did know. He'd let his guilt at having feelings for his best friend's woman cloud everything.

And the jealousy too. Don't forget the jealousy.

No. I tried so hard not to let that happen. I don't want anything but the best for them. At least, I don't *want* to want anything but the best for them.

But he had been jealous. As much as he'd tried to outrun it, he had.

And it made him lower than pond life. Which was why, when one hundred and fifteen guests rose and joined Colin Mortimer in toasting the happy couple, Damien began to shake. Not on the surface—he was too well-practised at being the textbook best man for that—but deep down in his gut. He was almost surprised the untouched champagne glass in his hand didn't rattle.

And then the father of the bride turned to him, a beneficent smile on his face, nodded and sat down.

Damien rose, his legs propelling him upwards suddenly

so he hit his thighs against the table top and made the silverware jiggle.

His turn now. His turn to spout and toast—and lie. He swallowed, knowing he was about to open his mouth and prove himself the biggest hypocrite in the world.

CHAPTER TWO

THE whole room went quiet. Zoe felt a familiar and almost irresistible urge to blurt something shocking out, just to inject some life into the dead and faultless silence. Instead she rested one elbow on the table and twisted her head round to hear His Highness say something pompous.

Only he didn't say anything. Pompous or otherwise. He just stood there, staring at everyone. The only movement was a Jurassic Park-type mini-tremor in his glass of champagne.

He opened his mouth. A few wedding guests leaned forward. Damien Stone was famous for his best man speeches. People joked about crashing weddings just to hear them. He closed his lips again.

The silence began to get awkward. Children began to fidget.

Damien Stone cleared his throat.

Zoe seriously considered jumping up and shouting, *Knickers*!

But just in the nick of time a noise came from the back of his mouth, so quiet she was probably the only person who heard it. But she saw him tense, push the sound forward until it grew and words followed it.

'I haven't got anything clever to say.'

People began to look at each other and smile. They knew this was just the start. It would be clever and funny and touching. It would.

He took a deep breath. 'Just that Luke and Sara are truly the perfect couple.'

Zoe frowned. She'd been all revved up to smirk inwardly at his artfully crafted spiel, but his simple sincerity had stolen all her thunder.

'And I can't do anything more than say that Luke is the best friend a man could have, and remind him he is the luckiest man in the world to have found Sara, and wish them a lifetime of happiness together.'

He paused, raised his glass to the bride and groom.

Zoe held her champagne flute up, but her eyes were on the best man. Had that really been a catch in his voice when he'd said his best friend's name?

'To Luke and Sara,' he said simply, and suddenly the whole marquee was on its feet, clapping and cheering and marvelling at how, once again, the best man had outdone himself.

Damien knocked back his fizz and sat down, exhaling heavily. If Zoe hadn't known any better she'd have thought he was nervous. But that would have meant he was feeling an emotion other than smug superiority, which was clearly impossible.

She took a sip of her own drink and sat down beside him. Now, she'd never been one to want to cause Damien Stone's head to swell any bigger, but for some reason she felt she needed to say something, to tell him how perfect his words had been.

'That was—'

His head snapped round in surprise—as if he'd totally forgotten she existed and had been occupying the space beside him—and he fixed her with those cold blue eyes.

His voice was low and hoarse. 'Just don't, Zoe. Not right now.'

'But I wasn't going to—'

The glare he gave her made her shut her mouth abruptly. And if he hadn't been concentrating on being just so fierce and condescending, he might have realised what a miraculous feat that had been.

And then, while all eyes were on the bride and groom, while the happiness seemed to be spilling out of the other guests and pooling around their feet, Damien rose stiffly from his chair and headed out into the twilight.

Zoe sat back in her gold-sprayed, velvet-seated chair and crossed her arms. Not even good enough to offer the precious Damien Stone a few words of congratulation. She had obviously sunk to a new low in his eyes. But Zoe didn't let that cold feeling settle deep down inside like it wanted to. She couldn't. She'd promised herself that never again would a man like that make her feel this way. And if crumbling in defeat wasn't an option, she had no alternative but to go the other way. So, by his actions, the best man had decreed tonight would be all-out war, and the evening reception would be their battlefield.

Look out, Damien Stone, because all those snotty comments you've ever dished out are coming back to bite you on that finely toned rear end. Tonight, Karma is wearing a bridesmaid's dress—and she's in one hell of a mood.

'Those ballroom dancing lessons really paid off in the end.'

Zoe smiled into the face of the man who had just twirled her into his arms. He really was looking particularly handsome today. And so he should.

'I beg to differ, Luke. You've trodden on my foot twice already, and we both know why.'

He gazed above her shoulder, looking every inch the dashing groom. 'I have no idea what you're talking about.'

At that point Zoe did a little bit of toe-crunching of her own. 'Really?' she said innocently. 'And there was me thinking all those last-minute work emergencies on a Thursday night were merely a ruse so you could cry off and go down the pub with your mates.'

Luke's smile spread wider. 'No,' he said. 'Still no idea. You must have the wrong person.'

The smile wavered momentarily, however, when he misjudged a step and almost sent the pair of them flying. Thankfully, Zoe rescued them with quick thinking and even quicker feet. There was a reason for that, too.

'You owe me,' she whispered in his ear as she clutched onto his sleeves. 'You knew Sara wouldn't want to go to those lessons on her own. You knew she'd drag me along as a substitute.'

Luke just beamed as if he was on a TV ballroom dancing contest, fixing his eyes beyond her. 'And just look how well you can waltz now,' he said. 'You have me to thank for that.'

Zoe wanted to punch him. Or tickle him. She wasn't sure which.

Luke saved himself by having the decency to look just a little repentant. 'Okay, I do owe you. And I've just had an idea for a very fitting peace offering…'

He paused while he concentrated on changing direction so they didn't plough into the four-tiered cake.

'I know that all the wedding craziness has meant that you haven't had the chance to have a proper holiday this year.'

He *should* know that, Zoe thought. She'd moaned long and hard about it often enough.

'Well, *Dream Weaver*, thanks to the generosity of my new father-in-law, is now going to be sitting idle and unloved at her mooring for the next two weeks. Why don't you make use of her?'

Zoe laughed so hard that the couple next to them lost their timing. 'Don't be daft, Luke! I don't know the first thing about sailing.'

'From what I remember, the few times you have made it on board, the highlights were sunbathing on the deck and sipping wine in the cockpit while the stars came out.'

Well, there was that. It had all been *awfully* civilised. And she could almost imagine herself using the twenty-year-old yacht as a base for a relaxing holiday. She could explore the surrounding countryside and the nearby village of Lower Hadwell, wander down narrow streets lined with ice cream-coloured houses. She started to dream of long pub lunches and enough time to read the stack of paperbacks that had been gathering dust on her bedside table.

She must have looked as if she were weakening because Luke added, 'I can always arrange for my friend Matthew to take you out on a couple of day trips—up and down the river, or round to one of the little beaches near the estuary that can only be reached by boat.'

Zoe stopped turning and looked Luke straight in the eye. 'Matthew? The Matthew who has the shaggy blond hair and the cute, tight little rounded—'

Luke burst out laughing.

She half-closed her eyelids. 'I was going to say "nose".'

'Of course you were. But, yes, *that* Matthew.'

Well, that sounded like the perfect recipe for a last-minute, spontaneous holiday. Fit, toned surfer-dudes and throwing things into a suitcase were definitely her thing. She instantly forgave Luke for the further three times he would tread on her feet before the dance was over.

'In that case,' she said, dipping low as Luke very bravely swung her into a pose, 'you might just have a deal.'

The music changed to a slow, sweeping tune, but Damien hardly noticed it. He was tired. Bone-deep, soul-weary exhausted. Which was odd, because if anyone should have built up a best man brand of stamina by now, it should have been him.

He checked his watch. Nine-thirty.

It couldn't be long now before Sara and Luke left the grounds of this smart country house hotel to begin a new life together. And once the car had disappeared, even while the tin cans were still clattering down the drive, he planned to slip away.

He had a room booked at the hotel, but he wasn't going to use it. He needed to go back to his flat, be by himself, not extend the aftermath of the wedding with nightcaps with the other guests or jolly communal breakfasts the next morning.

Just before he looked up from his watch he became aware of someone standing in front of him. A quick glance downwards revealed his worst fear—white satin and a pair of matching shoes.

'Come on, you…' Sara said in that gentle, clear voice of hers. Damien transferred his gaze to his brogues. She was too close. If he looked up now, really let her see into his eyes, she might guess.

Slim fingers tugged at his jacket sleeve. 'We can't have you moping about in the corner on your own. You've got your pick of the bridesmaids, you know. Once upon a time that would have excited you.'

He looked up without actually looking *at* her, and shook his head. Why settle for second best?

'Well, you'll have to make do with me, then. Dance with me, Damien?'

He pulled air in through his nostrils and pushed it out again through his teeth. He stood up, unable to refuse this bride anything. Besides, she would think it odd if he refused, would probably send Luke to wheedle the secret he could never tell out of him.

Sara grasped his hand and pulled him towards the dance floor. So much for *slipping away*.

When she stopped, turned and waited for him to take her in his arms he almost bolted, but instead he stoically took her hand in his and drew her close. Not too close, however.

Imagine it's someone else, he told himself.

And it seemed to work, because they started to move their feet and he still felt relatively normal. There were no fireworks where they touched, no unexpected jolts or hot flushes. This was good. He had things under control.

'You've been fabulous today,' Sara said as he led her round the dance floor. 'Perfect.'

Damien smiled. A smile of duty. 'It was easy to do this for Luke,' he said. His words were plain, slightly evasive, but not devoid of truth. It *had* been easy to decide to support his best friend all the way when Luke had announced—in his own words—that he was going to marry the most wonderful woman in the world. Damien couldn't have done anything else. It wasn't in his bones.

But where the spirit was willing, the flesh had been weak. He hadn't been able to eradicate the growing feelings for the woman he was now holding in his arms. He'd tried. God, he'd tried.

Sara attempted to chat as they danced, but her efforts clanged off him and fell to the floor between their feet. He'd always been able to jest and banter with Sara before now, but after the emotional marathon he'd run today he found himself searching frantically for something to say.

Conversation would be good, Damien! Conversation would distract him from the feel of her waist beneath his fingers, the light touch of her hand on his shoulder, the rose-scented perfume that was flooding his nostrils and drowning his lungs.

He looked down, breaking eye contact. 'Your ring is beautiful,' he said.

Sara lifted her hand off his shoulder to inspect it, twisting her hand one way then the other. 'Yes, it is, isn't it?'

Damien looked at the elegant curve of white gold studded with diamonds that was wrapped around Sara's fourth finger. It suited her perfectly.

She smiled wide and replaced her hand on his shoulder. 'Zoe really outdid herself this time.'

'Zoe made *that*?'

He must have blurted that out in a rather uncharacteristic

fashion because Sara burst out laughing and nodded. Damien looked again at the shiny, pale ring against the charcoal of his morning suit jacket, not quite able to get his head round what Sara had just told him.

He knew Sara and her girlfriends went wild for Zoe's jewellery but, from what he remembered of her pieces, they were chunky, asymmetric things, involving not just stones and settings, but shells or wooden beads or feathers. Sometimes all three. To be honest, he didn't get it. Must be a girl thing. He had always thought the simple chain and diamond pendant that Sara always wore was much more classy.

He felt a tap on his right shoulder. 'I think you owe me a dance,' a deep voice said. He twisted his head to find Luke grinning at his new bride, Zoe in his arms. Sara let her hands slide from Damien's shoulder and back as Luke moved towards them.

Let go, Damien told himself. It's time to let go…

It felt as if he had to peel himself from her.

'Not *her*,' Luke said, nodding towards his wife. 'I meant *you*, my fine figure of a man.'

They all laughed at the joke, the way Luke held his arms aloft in invitation to Damien, before using them to scoop Sara closer so he could nuzzle into her neck. And off they went like that, joined from forehead to toe.

That left Zoe and Damien without partners and staring at each other.

He knew what the polite thing to do was. Problem was that, right at this moment, he wasn't feeling particularly polite. He hesitated a fraction of a second too long, though, and one of Zoe's mobile eyebrows twitched in recognition of his predicament. A wry smile pressed her lips together. Not an expression of humour, but of challenge.

Damien recovered quickly and held out his arms, just as Luke had done a moment earlier, as if that tiny transaction had not just occurred between him and the maid of honour.

Pretend it's all fine. Bury the uncomfortable feeling. That was what normally worked.

Zoe stepped into his hold, but the naughty twinkle in her eye told him her memory would not be so easy to erase. It also told him she would make him pay. Thankfully, the song was almost over.

But, as they started to move, the band segued into another tune, something in a four-four time with a bit of a Latin beat. He could hardly pull away now, thank her politely and head for the fresh night air outside the marquee, could he?

Damien growled inwardly. Now he had a whole song to get through. With a woman who—for no apparent reason—had not only decided she didn't like him, but had made it her mission in life to wind him up.

What a perfect way to end the evening.

Pompous ass, Zoe thought to herself, grinding her teeth gently as she held her smile in place. She'd show him.

You'd think, on a day like today, when they were both here to support their best friends, he could have let up a little. But, no, Mr Holier-than-thou Stone had to ramp up the superiority factor even further.

Well, thanks to all those ballroom dancing lessons Luke had skipped out on, Zoe knew how to rumba just fine. At least on the dance floor she'd show him who was top dog.

Despite the urge to clench all her muscles ready for a killer right hook, she made herself breathe out, concentrated on relaxing into the rhythm so her hips and waist twisted and flowed. The bridesmaid's dress was perfect for it. Sara had chosen well. Satin, the colour of old gold, skimmed her hips and flared from her knees in a bias-cut skirt, and it moved sensuously with every step.

They danced in silence, but after a particularly tricky bit of footwork she glanced up at Damien to find him staring down hard at her.

'I thought the man was supposed to lead,' he said, his voice expressionless.

Zoe shrugged. 'This is a rumba. I'm just dancing the steps. Not my problem if it's beyond you.'

His grip on her hand tightened and he pulled himself up straight, bringing their bodies closer together. Zoe feigned nonchalance.

'Whoever said it was beyond me?'

Damien continued to stare at her, a slightly devilish smile kinking the side of his mouth, and his feet began to move in a pattern that had become horribly familiar to Zoe over the last couple of months. Rumba steps. Oh, hell. Of course Mr Perfect would be able to do this. Just another superpower to add to his vast collection.

At first they moved mechanically, stiffly, but as the song continued they both seemed to melt into the rhythm. None of those peacock-like, ostentatious moves from a ballroom competition for Damien Stone. His movements were slow, measured, restrained yet fluid—a style born more of the streets of Havana than from Gertrude Glitz's Ballroom Academy. Zoe adjusted her moves to match, no flinging arms or swinging feet; just the feeling of the teasing, back and forth rhythm snaking up from her core and moving her limbs.

She'd been so lost in the sways and pauses, the feeling that her muscles were turning to marshmallow, that it took a few moments to realise their gazes were still locked. His smile had gone now, replaced by a look of concentration that was at once unnerving and—dare she admit it?—sexy.

She swallowed. Her mouth had suddenly gone very, very dry.

They were closer now too, and she wasn't quite sure how they'd got that way, their torsos a hair's breadth from touching.

The bridesmaid's dress, which had been a little on the snug side up top already—thanks to a failed pre-wedding diet—

now seemed to compress her ribs, making it hard to do anything but grab oxygen in short bursts.

No, no, no.

She was not going to forget just how up his own...backside...Damien Stone was just because he knew how to rumba, just because the slow swaying, the leashed feeling of power in his movements, made her think about *other* superpowers he might have.

Men like him were trouble. They said they liked girls like her. They might even believe it when they promised that quirkiness and a unique take on life were enchanting, but sooner or later they changed their minds.

She couldn't let this lazy rhythm lull her into a stupor and forget all of that. In fact, she needed to do the opposite. Men like Damien Stone needed to be reminded that, actually, they *weren't* God's gift, and that maybe they should climb down from their impossibly high horses now and again and remember that they were just like everyone else: flawed, clueless... human. That was all she was asking for. Surely that wasn't too much?

He must have a weakness, this man. His own personal brand of kryptonite. She just had to find out what that was—and then use it against him.

CHAPTER THREE

DAMIEN felt the muscles of Zoe's torso tense quite clearly, even though his fingertips were only lightly resting on her shoulder blade, and it pulled him out of whatever delightful bubble he'd lost himself in. For a moment he'd been totally focused on the dancing, neither regretting the past—of what might have been had he met Sara first—or yearning for a future that would never be his. How odd, that it was with this woman he'd found a sense of calm in this nightmare of a day.

No more, though. The unusual softness that had been in Zoe's eyes was gone, replaced with the more familiar hard, cheeky, taunting one, and he mentally kicked himself for forgetting he was dancing with an unexploded bomb.

'I'm impressed,' she said, but the look in her eyes told him this compliment had a sting in its tail. 'I didn't think a man like you would be any good at something like this.'

Ouch. There it was. But gentler and more skilful than he'd expected.

A man like him. What was so wrong with that?

He found he couldn't let her remark go unchallenged. Dancing had been a good momentary distraction, but now she'd ruined that he'd resort to a bit of one-upmanship with Zoe, if that was what she wanted.

'A man like what?' he said through his teeth, still smiling, as he flicked his wrist and spun her out to the side.

She didn't miss a step, her hips moving like molasses, accentuated by the clinging fabric of her bridesmaid's dress.

'Oh, you know...' Her voice was light and breezy. 'Uptight. Buttoned-up.'

He ignored the comment, even though he noticed the movements of his torso became less fluid with each step, despite his efforts to the contrary. He bunched his shoulders, one after the other, and let them drop again. 'I'm not uptight.'

Zoe didn't answer—not with words—but her smile hitched to one side, giving her an impish air.

Oh, no? the smile said.

Damien shook his head, narrowing his eyes. And he *made* his lower half move more freely, just to prove her wrong. It wasn't quite the same as when he'd been truly relaxed a few moments before, but it was better than nothing, and he threw in a few dips and turns, just to keep her from noticing the difference.

She kept up, of course, adding her own brand of spice to each shift of weight, each wiggle. Grudgingly, he gave her silent credit.

But Damien didn't want to notice just how easy it was to dance with Zoe St James, didn't want to admit they complemented each other in any way at all, despite the growing sense of heat travelling up his body or the skipping of his pulse in his veins, so he tore his gaze away from hers, looked beyond her shoulder.

And instantly regretted it.

Without wanting to, he sought out the bride and groom on the crowded dance floor. They'd finished with any pretence of doing proper steps now and just clung to each other, her head resting on his shoulder, eyes closed in a state of bliss. A horrible emptiness settled on Damien.

Since his partner was probably the lesser of two evils, he switched his gaze to her and found her studying him. Without letting him lead, she released his hand, stepped out, free arm raised, and then moved back in again, coming close. Much too close.

Sara would never have danced with him like this, not even if they'd been a couple. And suddenly he was angry with Zoe for causing him to make comparisons, for making him notice who she *wasn't*, because that ache was growing now, filling his chest, catching his breath.

No, this wasn't Sara. She would never be Sara. And, on some entirely primal—and completely unreasonable—level, he wanted to make her pay for that.

He caught her in a ballroom hold, using slightly more pressure than normal, and saw her eyes widen in response. Surprise, however, was quickly doused by defiance.

Damien turned, letting her have the unhindered view of the happy couple, but unfortunately, the nature of the dance meant that every few bars he was faced with the sight of them again. And he couldn't help torturing himself by looking, by wondering *what if…*?

When he looked at his partner again she blinked slowly as a mischievous smile played on her lips. 'I'd thank you for the pleasure of dancing with you, but it would be a lie,' she said.

Damien knew he shouldn't rise to the bait, but his defences had been eroded by the acid of this happy day. 'Believe me,' he replied, 'the feeling is entirely mutual.'

Zoe smirked, and Damien's blood rose a few degrees in temperature. She wasn't supposed to be *enjoying* this. He wanted her off his back. Avoidance had failed. Charm had failed. The only artillery he had left in his current state of mind was the blunt truth.

'Look, I don't like you and you don't like me, but let's just get through this dance—for Luke and Sara's sake—then we can go our separate ways.'

And then, because looking at Zoe made him feel clammy and out of control, his gaze slid inevitably back to Sara.

Zoe twisted her head to follow his line of sight and then whispered in his ear, 'I've seen you watching them.'

That got his attention. That got his focus one hundred per cent back on his partner. An icy electric shock arced from his chest down to his stomach. She hadn't guessed, had she? Because, if Zoe knew his secret, there was no doubt in his mind that she would broadcast it far and wide.

'I'm happy for them,' he mumbled, and his feet suddenly felt like bricks, causing him to miss a step.

Zoe's smirk grew, enveloping her in an aura of smugness. 'It's more than that,' she said and then her eyes widened a little—a penny dropping into place somewhere in the back of her head. 'There's something about what they've got, about *that*—' she pulled her hand from his and waved it in the direction of the bride and groom '—you can't keep your eyes off.'

Damien held his breath while Zoe began to laugh.

'Who'd have thought it? Damien *Stone*, not living up to his name, actually having an emotion other than pride for once.'

Pride? What was she talking about? He was a stand-up guy, someone to depend on in a crisis. What was proud about that? And how dare Zoe St James judge him?

'Well, at least I have some pride,' he countered. 'Having no sense of shame isn't considered an asset by most people.'

Her mouth dropped open and a little gasp slipped through her lips.

Damien couldn't hide his slow smile. Now he understood just why Zoe enjoyed firing off her little verbal darts so much. There was a lovely glow of satisfaction to be had when one hit home.

Her eyes narrowed. 'You stuck-up...unbearable...'

Now he was tempted to laugh, never having seen this woman without just the right sarcasm-laced word for any occasion. It was oddly gratifying to see her speechless, even for just a few seconds, because he was sure her talent wouldn't desert her for too long.

Unfortunately, his plan to silence her, to get her off his, backfired. It was then she decided to pull out the heavy artillery, get really personal.

'What is it about Luke and Sara that gives the great Damien Stone that faraway look in his eyes, I wonder? Just what is it that turns him into a big-eyed puppy dog with his tongue lolling out?'

Pins and needles tingled up Damien's spine. He knew she was spouting nonsense, just hunting for ammunition, but if she kept talking—and Zoe St James would *always* keep talking—she might just stumble onto the truth. He had to get her out of here. Out of earshot of any of the other wedding guests and especially Luke and Sara.

They weren't far from one of the entrances to the marquee now and, with a bit of nimble footwork, he spun her in that direction, then hauled her through the muslin-draped doorway. Once they were out into the cool night air, he dropped all pretence of dancing—dropped *her*—except for one hand, which he kept firmly clasped in his as he dragged her towards the formal gardens, ignoring her squeals of protest.

He marched down gravel paths edged with low box hedges towards the sound of running water. When they were far enough from the marquee not to be heard, or even to be stumbled upon, Damien put on the brakes and turned to face Zoe, throwing her hand back to her as if he'd been contaminated by its touch.

'What exactly is your problem?' he said, his voice thin from the effort of keeping a lid on his temper.

She held her hand to her torso with the other one, rubbing it furiously. 'Ow!' Her mouth stayed open as she searched for more words. When they came they were worth the wait.

'What's *my* problem?' She shook her head in disbelief. 'This, from the guy who is so far up his own backside he can probably see his tonsils!'

There it was. Zoe gold—although its properties were closer to those of petrol as far as Damien was concerned.

'That's enough.' Far too much. She'd do well to heed the silky tone that had crept into his voice. When his employees heard it, they scarpered.

But Zoe, as always, didn't know when to stop, didn't know when too much was too much. She just battled on, pointing out his flaws, circling round the undiscovered truth, but getting closer to it every second.

He tried to shut her up by various methods: further warnings, ignoring her. He even tried to reason with her, but that runaway mouth just kept on jogging.

'I don't know what's got you all churned up today,' she said finally, her hands on her hips, her breath coming in short pants, which was emphasising the rise and fall of her breasts in a way Damien was trying very hard not to notice. 'Maybe you're just jealous because Luke has Sara and you've got no one. But until you can climb down off that self-made pedestal and act like a human being instead of something carved out of marble I doubt any woman would say yes to you anyway!'

Oh, Damien was feeling very human at this moment, thank you very much. Nothing cold and dead about his racing pulse, or the jumpy feeling that reminded him of a pressure cooker just about to pop its lid. He needed to move, to shout, to run, to do *something* to release whatever was building inside of him. And that sensation seemed to grow with every syllable spilling from Zoe St James's mouth.

She opened it again, and Damien decided he couldn't take another second. He had to shut that smart mouth up. And only one way came to mind.

It was stupid. Reckless. But the cocktail of stress, disappointment and adrenalin egged him on until he had no other option but to slip his hand behind Zoe's neck, drag her to him and kiss her.

* * *

Damien had marched her down a path that led to a large stone fountain with a wall surrounding it. Zoe grabbed onto it with one hand as the other made a mess of Damien's shirt, bunching it up so hard she doubted the creases would ever be erased. That flimsy grip on the cotton and his hand at the back of her neck were the only things that were preventing her from taking a swim.

Apart from his lips, of course.

She should pull away and slap him, shouldn't she? Who the hell did he think he was? But she didn't pull away. She didn't slap him. Because, unfortunately, Mr Perfect was living up to his name in the kissing department too.

It started out hot and hard and...hot some more, but after a while it changed, slowed. The kiss became more about tasting and exploring than competing and raging. Zoe stopped gripping onto the fountain and placed that hand on his chest too, snaked it round his neck, matching him, as his long fingers uncurled and began to explore the fine hair that curled into ringlets at the base of her skull.

Damn her impulsive nature. It was entirely responsible for starting all of this. First of all, it had got hold of her mouth and had run away with it, then it had poked a stick at a caged tiger to see what it would do. And now it knew just what the tiger was capable of, it wasn't particularly inclined to stop!

This was Damien Stone, remember? Pull away.

He's not attracted to you. He doesn't even like you. And it shouldn't matter just how good he tastes or exactly what he's doing with his lips. Save yourself the humiliation and end this. And if you want to salvage some of that non-existent pride of yours, you need to end this first.

But Zoe had never been one for listening to advice. Especially her own.

And the kiss, although it was still slowing in tempo, was building in intensity. In fact, she thought the tops of her ears might have just caught fire. What was more, she really didn't care.

Damien had been kissing her for quite some time now, and he certainly seemed to be enjoying himself just as much as she was, seemed to be immersed in the moment. Of course she could be wrong. This could just be him on autopilot. But, crikey, if all this slow expertise was what he managed when he was only halfway invested, imagine what the full blast would be like! Forget the tips of her ears—she'd have to throw her entire body in the fountain.

She let go of his shirt, now creased beyond all hope, and explored his torso, running her fingers between jacket and shirt, letting her palms slide across his back.

Perhaps he did find her attractive after all. Maybe all that pent-up aggression and haughtiness had just been the Stone version of pigtail-pulling. She knew she shouldn't let it, but that thought burrowed deep inside her and started to glow. She couldn't stop it, not when she'd spent a lifetime being invisible to most men like him, men who were way out of her league. She sighed as Damien's lips left her mouth and headed towards her ear.

It was then they both heard footsteps on the gravel path. They both froze, not even coherent enough to pull hands and lips away from each other, ending up stuck together like a parody of Rodin's famous statue.

'Damien, there you are. Sara was looking for you a moment ago and, oh…um…sorry.'

It was Luke's voice. Zoe tried to shrink herself sideways. Not easy when you were as generously proportioned as she was. But at present Damien was shielding her from Luke's view, and for some reason he didn't want Luke to find out who he was with, and that was fine by her. She didn't want this moment of temporary insanity being reported round the wedding reception any more than he did.

But trust Damien to choose this moment to stop doing the

perfect thing. He found the strength to move, stepped back and stared at her. The heat rushed from the top of her ears straight into her cheeks.

'Oh! *Zoe…!*' Luke was frowning and smiling at the same time, although the smile was starting to win. 'Sorry… Just didn't think you two… Like I said, I'll come back—' he grinned '—later.'

Footsteps on gravel again, getting quieter. And then it was just a trickle of the fountain, the rasp of their breath and the noise of the party from the marquee, otherworldly and muffled.

Neither of them spoke. Not with words. But Damien's face began to get very eloquent, and the emotions on display were not what a girl wanted to see after a kiss like that.

Shock. Confusion. Even a little bit of guilt, if she wasn't mistaken, although she couldn't guess why. His mouth pulled down and she felt as if he'd taken a huge step backwards, even though he hadn't actually moved. It was that last emotion that really put the cherry on top.

Disgust.

That was when she slapped him.

Damien was still rubbing his cheek as he ran back over the lawn towards the marquee. He wasn't sure if he'd deserved that slap or not. Surely, the time for hand to face contact would have been when he'd lurched towards her, not five minutes later when her arm had been hooked around his back, pulling her closer to him, and his teeth had been at her earlobe?

But, then again, maybe he should have saved her the bother and slapped himself first. What had he thought he was doing? Really? *Zoe St James?*

He shook his head, trying to put it down to some kind of mental breakdown, brought about by weeks of stress and then having to endure the worst day of his life, but his attempt at reasoning with himself kept getting side-tracked by thoughts of Zoe's supple lips, memories of how complete and unfettered her response had been. She certainly knew how to more than talk with that runaway mouth of hers, he thought wryly.

Okay, so he was attracted to her. They had chemistry. Weird things like that happened all the time. It was all down to pheromones and brain chemistry and strange evolutionary throwbacks.

But a girl like Zoe St James wasn't part of the picture he'd painted of his future, the one he'd been slowly piecing together like a jigsaw for the last decade. It didn't matter if they had enough chemistry together to power the New Year's fireworks in London—she just wasn't part of the plan. And Damien Stone always stuck to the plan.

'Luke!'

He caught his friend just as he was about to go back inside. Slightly breathless now, he pressed a hand to his chest. 'You said you wanted a word with me?'

Luke shook his head. 'I said *Sara* wanted a word with you.' Sara.

A wave of guilt washed over Damien. He felt as if he'd been unfaithful, which was ridiculous.

Luke was grinning at him, waggling his eyebrows.

'Shut up,' Damien said.

Luke just grinned harder. 'Well, I can't say I wasn't surprised. I mean…Zoe… But it's good to see you being less of a hermit where women are concerned. You've been working too hard for far too long.'

Luke was wrong. It wasn't work that was the problem. Yes, Damien put in long hours occasionally, but Luke was under the impression that things were worse than they really were, because that was the excuse Damien trotted out when spending an evening with Sara and Luke at his house would be just too cosy to bear.

He pulled a face. Just when had he become this person? A person who skulked around hiding from everyone, lied to his friends and, yes, launched himself on unsuspecting women, even if the woman in question had deserved a bit of a comeuppance?

'So...' Luke clapped him on the back then gave him a one-armed hug '...are you going to see her again while we're away on honeymoon?'

Damien shook his head. He'd rather set himself on fire.

But there *was* something in what Luke had said. He'd spent too long pining for a woman who wasn't his, too long shutting himself off from all the other possibilities out there. Okay, Sara fitted perfectly in that ten-year plan of his—owning his business, buying a decent house, wife, kids—but that didn't mean no one else could ever fit that gap. He needed to read-just, and he could do it. He could.

It was time to move on.

What a pity he hadn't quite been able to let go of the *idea* of Sara before now. Maybe if he'd done it sooner, he would have been here with someone today and, instead of struggling on his own, feeling like a volcano that was trying to stop it-self erupting. He might have enjoyed himself.

He tried to imagine what it would be like...

A faceless girl. Brunette—not blonde, like Sara—in a styl-ish dress. A woman who reached for his hand during the ser-vice, squeezed it as the vows were said.

But it didn't work. The fantasy morphed into a picture of him out by the fountain, taking Zoe by the hand, leading her back into the hotel, a slow, knowing smile on both their faces...

No.

Get a grip, Damien.

Luke's right. It's been too long. Those pent-up hormones are driving you screwy.

'*Relax*, mate!' His friend's hand was still on his shoulder and it began to knead the tense muscle there rather painfully. 'You know what you need?'

'A stiff gin and Angelina Jolie's phone number?'

Luke laughed. 'Nope. You need a holiday.'

Damien shook his head. The last thing he needed was endless days on his own, nothing to do, too much time to think. No, work was the answer. Work was always the answer.

And coming up with a new plan. A better one. An achievable one.

That thought stopped him in his tracks.

He'd fallen into the same trap as his father had, hadn't he? And he hadn't even realised it. If anyone should understand how much damage yearning for the impossible did, it was Damien Stone.

'So where's Sara, then? I thought you said she was looking for me?'

Luke nodded towards the inside of the marquee. 'Talking to her father at the table in the corner.' His smile became sappy. 'You can't miss her—just look for the most beautiful girl in the room.'

This morning a comment like that would have been a slap in the face, but Damien let it bounce off him. Time for a new plan, remember? And this time he wasn't going to let himself get derailed.

He would walk over to Sara and her father. He would listen to what she had to say, and then he would say goodbye.

To Sara. And the idea of Sara.

CHAPTER FOUR

NOT many drivers were on the road at one in the morning to witness the sight of a bridesmaid shooting down the motorway in her car, foot to the floor, flowers in her hair. Zoe wouldn't have noticed them if they had. Her efficient little runabout didn't go much above seventy, but pressing the pedal all the way down gave her a small sense of satisfaction, something to counteract the growing sense of shame.

She'd never been so humiliated.

The look on his face…

As if he'd just committed some heinous crime. Even the thought of fit, blond Matthew as her own private deckhand for the next two weeks didn't cheer her up. Maybe she'd send him away and stay moored in the marina for the holiday, hiding out in the cabin and saving the other holidaymakers from her obviously disgusting presence.

But if there was one thing Zoe liked to do it was change her mind, and she did just that when she saw the bleary-eyed Matthew waiting for her in *Dream Weaver*'s cockpit.

Her wheel-along case had been making a terrible racket on the pontoons and must have woken him up. Along with the rest of the residents in the tiny marina halfway up the River Dart. She checked her watch—four-fifteen! Eek!—then tried to haul her case over the edge of the boat, but it was obvious her lightning-speed packing method—just throw everything she owned in—made that impossible. Matthew very gallantly hopped out of the boat and dealt with her luggage, giving her ample time to admire his fine physique.

'Sorry,' she said blithely, skipping on board and showing none of her guilt. 'I got here as fast as I could, but my car is a bit past it.'

Matthew shrugged and handed her the keys. He even smiled. 'No problem. Luke said he'd let me take *Dream Weaver* to France and back later in the summer if I helped you out. So for the next two weeks I'm all yours. Ready to fulfil your every whim.'

For the first time in six hours Zoe smiled. Now *that* was the kind of response a girl liked to hear.

Matthew looked her up and down and laughed softly. 'Not sure about your sailing clothes, though.'

Zoe looked down, and then she laughed as well. 'Well, I suppose satin and trainers aren't the usual attire, but don't worry—' she patted her hundred litre case '—I've got more appropriate stuff in here.'

Matthew laughed even harder. 'I'll bet!'

He ran a hand through his delightfully tousled hair. 'Do you want to go out tomorrow? Maybe round to a beach?'

Zoe patted her suitcase again. 'Swimming cozzie is packed,' she said, and noticed a glitter of interest at that fact in the skipper's eyes. 'Why not?'

He checked his watch and frowned. 'What time do you want to get started?'

She waved a helpless hand. 'Oh…whenever. I like to go with the flow.'

Matthew nodded and grinned. Zoe grinned back. Kindred spirits. Oh, this holiday might just be what she needed after all. A summer fling, maybe, to restore her confidence in life, love and men in general.

However, thinking of men in general led to thinking of one man in particular. Her ears burned with shame while other places burned with something else entirely.

We're not thinking about him, she told herself. He's two hundred miles away, polishing his halo, probably, and the next two weeks is all about forgetting him and that…unfortunate…kiss ever existed.

Matthew handed over the key to *Dream Weaver*, a small square-ended piece of metal with a squash ball-sized piece of cork on a key ring, and then clambered off the boat and on to the pontoon.

'See you in the morning,' he said with a relaxed wave.

'Not *too* early, though,' Zoe added quickly.

Matthew nodded, one night owl to another. See? Kindred spirits.

Once she was alone again Zoe realised she was actually quite tired. She headed below decks. However, she'd forgotten that there weren't proper stairs leading down into the cabin, but what was more like two wooden boxes stacked on top of each other, with an extra little foot platform bolted onto the top one for those with shorter legs. She managed to man-handle the giant case down into the cabin without smashing it on the floor, then wrestled it past the seating area, past the tiny toilet she'd forgotten how to work, and into the two-man cabin at the front of the boat.

She plopped the case on one side of the V-shaped bunk and took a long hard look at the two narrow berths, separate at the head end, but joined together near the feet. Not a lot of room, and Zoe liked to sprawl. It was also a long way down to the hard wooden floor if she rolled out of bed during the night.

But then she remembered there was an extra section of wood that fitted between the two berths, making them one giant triangle, and a matching wedge of mattress to complete the jigsaw, and she went in search of it.

Once that was sorted, she rummaged through her case for her PJs, leaving her underwear and clothes where they fell, then squeezed herself into the tiny bathroom to get ready for bed. Thankfully, the instructions for the toilet were written on a plaque on the wall—but it still took her three attempts before she got it to work properly.

Within twenty minutes of getting on board, she was climbing into the soft cotton-lined sleeping bag that had been left out for her. Probably by Matthew. She smiled as she closed her eyes and stretched her mouth wide in a silent yawn.

Oh, yes. This holiday was going to be just what she needed.

Dawn was just breaking as Damien hauled his soft sailing bag, compactly filled with everything he would need for the next week or two, down the steep jetty that led to the pontoons of Lower Hadwell's marina.

After weeks of being cooped up in a city office, or in the dust and noise of a construction site, it was blissful to feel the cold dawn breeze on his face, smell the salt and seaweed in the air. Even better would be the bacon sandwich he planned to make himself on board before setting off. Two weeks on board Luke's beloved boat, no one to please but himself.

It was the perfect plan. He'd be busy the whole time and he wouldn't have to talk to a soul if he didn't want to. And by the time he got back to his office in London he'd have made progress in wiping his best friend's wife from his mind—at least in any capacity other than 'family friend'.

He'd also do his best to forget that it had been Sara's idea to use the boat now it was free. She'd square it with Luke in the morning, she'd said. But he knew his friend wouldn't mind. He'd taken *Dream Weaver* out many times before when he'd needed a bit of space and solitude.

The boat was quiet when he arrived but, strangely, unlocked. He found the key on the table in the middle of the seating area in the main cabin and threw his sailing bag down on one of the long benches that doubled as a berth. Probably that flaky Matthew who kept an eye on *Weaver* when Luke wasn't around. He'd have to have a word with him about that when he got back.

But for now…

Well, Damien was standing on a boat with the key in his hand and a whole river, then the Devon and Cornwall coast waiting to be explored. Why wait? He could sort out the bacon sandwich later. What he really wanted to taste right now was salt on his tongue. He couldn't wait for that moment of perfect silence when he got out to sea, winched up the sails and cut the engine.

Not wasting a second, he ran upstairs into the cockpit, turned the engine on and set about casting off.

A distant rumble lulled Zoe as she dozed, and the gentle side-to-side movement of the boat rocked her back into a deep slumber. When she woke the sun was high in the sky, streaming through the glass hatch in the roof, and her face was squashed against the wall of the cabin. She was also pinned beneath her bright pink case.

Huh?

While she'd slept somebody had messed with the earth's gravity. Instead of everything heading straight down, the world was tilted at forty-five degrees. It was also very bumpy, and every few seconds her cabin would bounce off something and a hollow noise echoed round the boat's hull.

Was there a storm? The weather forecast had been good. Well, at least she'd imagined it was good because it had been bright and sunny for the last week, and Zoe wasn't the type to check that kind of thing religiously. If at all.

Large drops of water sprayed onto the hatch as the boat did its biggest lurch yet. Definitely a storm, then. But a strange kind of storm because, apart from those dull echoes from the underside of the boat, it was completely quiet. And why was the sun still shining?

She rubbed her eyes, got out of bed and braced a hand against the wall to stop herself from falling over. Her brain struggled to make sense of the mismatched information being sent to it. She hadn't drunk much last night, so this couldn't be the hangover of all hangovers. What the heck was going on?

As she lurched her way through the cabin she glanced out of one of the tiny lozenge-shaped portholes and finally the jigsaw pieces began to come together. There was blue. Lots of it. Above and below the horizon. And cliffs. Last time she'd checked Lower Hadwell had been all about green hills covered in woods and sheep-filled fields. Not a cliff to be seen. Which left only one conclusion to stumble onto.

They were at sea. Almost. Right at the mouth of the estuary.

Matthew must be much more of a morning person than she gave him credit for. How disappointing. And she'd at least have expected him to discuss with her which beach she'd like to go to. Behaviour like this reminded her of someone she'd much rather push to the recesses of her mind and slap the label *What were you thinking*? on.

The breeze hit her full in the face and tugged at her hair as she emerged from the cabin. The cockpit was empty, and no one was at the large wooden tiller at the back end. She could hear the mainsail rustling frantically above her head as it flapped in the wind. She stepped out into the cockpit properly, stood on one of the non-slip benches and looked further down the boat.

There, clipping a sail onto the wire that ran from the front of the boat to the top of the mast, was a hunched figure. Zoe called and waved at Matthew, but the wind stole her words. She yelled louder.

And then she had another one of those *worst hangover ever* moments, because when the hunched man stood up and turned around his face was different and his hair was all wrong. In fact, it looked a lot like...

But it couldn't be!

Before she could tell her brain to start making sense, another large wave hit the boat—which she now realised had been responsible for the hollow bumping she'd heard in her cabin—and Zoe, who had not been on a yacht enough times before to know it was a good idea to hang onto something at all times, tumbled back into the cockpit.

Had that been the only thing that had happened, things would have been fine, apart from a few bruises and a general sense of embarrassment. But Zoe fell against the tiller when she landed and grabbed onto it for support, causing the boat, which had been facing the wind, to swing round sharply. The mainsail filled and *Dream Weaver* pitched sideways.

Zoe righted herself just in time to see the shocked face of the man at the other end of the boat. Definitely not Matthew.

Definitely her worst nightmare.

Definitely losing his balance from the unexpected lurch of the deck. In slow motion, he grabbed for the wire he'd been clipping the sail onto but missed. For a couple of seconds he seemed to hover in mid-air, but then there was a splash and a yell, and Zoe's worst nightmare had fallen overboard.

Zoe freaked. For a moment she was frozen to the spot, her mouth opening and closing, her hands twitching as if they were grasping for something, as if their ineffectual motion could wind time backwards so she could catch him on the replay.

Then she screamed. Then she ran. Up the deck, hardly looking where she was going, until she reached the spot where he'd disappeared. Then she screamed a second time at the sight of Damien Stone, half-consumed by the sea, clinging for dear life onto one of the metal posts that surrounded the deck.

There was no time for discussion of the surreal wormhole that had ruptured time and space to bring him here. Zoe just grabbed his wrist, anchored one foot against another one of the metal posts and pulled. For a while they seemed to make no progress. Between them, they managed to pull Damien up towards the deck, but another wave would hit *Dream Weaver*, causing him to slip back a couple of inches.

Eventually, Damien managed to pull himself up further and Zoe took handfuls of his clothes—anything she could get her hands on—and dragged and tugged and yanked until his chest and one foot were on the deck and he managed to haul himself back on board.

As soon as he hit the deck he jumped up and ran to the cockpit, where he grabbed a rope and loosened it. Zoe ran after him, and by the time she reached the cockpit the mainsail was down, hanging untidily in folds over the boom like a giant piping bag.

That was when Damien turned to face Zoe. That was also when the shouting began. Lots of words, lots of half sentences. Not a lot of sense. They both finally fell silent, regarding each other warily, ribcages heaving.

Damien's tone was low and dark. '*Please* tell me I'm hallucinating!'

Zoe's hands popped onto her hips. 'Charming! That's what I get for saving your life!'

'It was *you* who tipped me overboard!'

He wanted to cast accusations around? Fine. Zoe had plenty of her own.

'Well, if you hadn't practically kidnapped me... If you'd actually thought to inform me you were taking the boat out for a sail...' She paused and frowned. 'Hang on. What are you doing here anyway? Are you *stalking* me?'

Damien laughed so hard he almost fell overboard again. 'This really is an alternate reality, isn't it? And I should ask you what you're doing on board *Weaver*. You don't even know how to sail!'

She pulled herself up straighter. 'I *might* know how to sail. How would you know?'

Damien gave her one of his patented superior looks at that

moment. It made her wish she'd let him flounder in the waves instead of breaking three nails fishing him out.

'Believe me, it's obvious,' he said dryly.

They stood there, at opposite ends of the cockpit, radiating irritation, neither of them willing to answer the other's question first, as if doing so would indicate surrender.

Damien blew air out through his mouth and shook his head, then he reached for the rope dangling into the cockpit, wound it round something that looked like an over-sized pepper grinder and started to hoist the sail. She sat down in the cockpit and folded her arms. 'Where are we going?'

Damien looked back over his shoulder as he secured the rope. He reached for the tiller, then sat down facing her. The boat started leaning again as the wind hit the triangle of white, and Zoe was childishly pleased that she was on the upper side. At least she was until Damien turned the boat around so it pitched again, and then he was smiling down at her, his lips thin, and she was glowering back at him, her arms folded so tight now they felt like a corset.

'I'm taking you back to the marina,' he said finally.

Zoe frowned harder. 'Why me?'

Damien looked at her as if she should have been in a straitjacket. 'So you can collect your stuff and disembark. I don't know what kind of stupid joke you are trying to pull—'

'Listen, Mr—' Zoe stood up, but forgot to factor in the wonky floor and sat straight back down again. 'Luke told me I could use his boat for the next couple of weeks, so I'm not going anywhere.'

That wiped the smug smile off his face. 'But Sara told me...'

They looked at each other.

'Double booked,' they both said in unison.

Then they sat in silence, trying to cogitate what that might mean.

'You don't think they *meant* to…' Zoe said, shaking her head.

Damien was doing the same. 'No. They wouldn't. They know I don't like—'

Zoe raised her eyebrows and the rest of the sentence stayed unsaid.

'It must be some kind of mistake,' he added, having the decency to look at least a little sheepish.

Zoe looked out to sea, as if searching for answers there. 'We could always call them and ask them if…' Zoe trailed off and her gaze returned to Damien, who looked every inch the competent sailor as he nudged the tiller this way and that, every now and then checking the compass or looking out to a spot on the headland.

He lifted one side of his mouth in a wry smile.

'You're right,' she said. 'Not a good time to be phoning the happy couple, first day of their honeymoon and all.'

Damien's mouth thinned into a straight line again and he looked away.

'We're just going to have to work this one out on our own, then.'

Zoe nodded, and then she shivered. She'd been so taken up in rescuing Damien, then wanting to rip his head off, that she'd totally forgotten she was only wearing her pyjamas— a soft grey vest and a pair of pink and grey striped bottoms.

Damien must have caught her shudder out of the corner of his eye, because he turned his head and looked at her again.

'Why don't you go below deck and get warm?'

If Zoe had been a cat, the fur along her spine would have just risen straight up. She opened her mouth.

'Oh, calm down,' he said dismissively, and when she looked as if she was about to do the opposite he made an observation. 'You're a little bit wet,' he added.

'So are you,' she countered.

'Yes,' said Damien, looking her up and down, 'but I'm

dressed for sailing and I don't think that fabric you have on is very...water repellent.'

Zoe was about to argue, but then she glanced down and saw what he meant. Her vest was plastered to her, soaked front and back, and her trousers weren't much better. She glared at him. He couldn't have mentioned this sooner? Or he couldn't have taken a hot poker and burnt out his eyes?

She got up with as much dignity as she could muster, and then wobbled her way across the cockpit and down the stairs, mightily glad that after the first few steps he couldn't see her front any more, couldn't see the vest moulded to her rather impressive chest.

She didn't, however, realise that the striped fabric clung just as lovingly to her bottom. And she didn't see Damien lean over a little bit to watch her ample rear end wiggle its way into her cabin and disappear.

CHAPTER FIVE

AN UNEASY truce was established over bacon sandwiches a short while later. Damien took the boat to a little cove just near the estuary and dropped anchor. And Zoe, who was now warm and dry and dressed, fried the bacon while Damien took a quick shower and got himself into the same state.

The truce held, of course, because neither of them said much to each other. However, that couldn't continue indefinitely, so once butties had been eaten and washed down with tea, it was time to retreat to their corners and fight this thing out.

Damien had decided as he drove down that morning that sailing was just about the only thing he could think of that would keep him sane over the next couple of weeks, that sailing and sailing alone would dislodge the unwanted fantasies in his head. He really didn't want to hand *Dream Weaver* over to this woman—a woman who probably wouldn't even untie her from her mooring. It was almost criminal to leave the boat neglected like that.

But underneath that sense of indignation he also had the horrible creeping feeling that he would end up doing the chivalrous thing, even though he'd rather be eaten by sharks first. The knowledge only served to make him more irritable. He drained the last of his tea, plonked his mug down on the propped-up wing of the table and looked at Zoe.

'What were your plans?' he asked in a perfect impression of calm and reasonableness.

Zoe tucked a strand of wet hair behind her left ear. She seemed slightly unnerved by his politeness, and Damien had a flashback to the night before, when she'd kissed him without reserve or barrier, and he'd sensed a hint of vulnerability beneath that brassy armour.

But they weren't here to think about kissing—they were here to talk about sailing, remember?

She swallowed. 'Just…you know. Having a break—a holiday.'

Damien frowned. 'You weren't going to take *Weaver* out on your own, were you?'

A spike of irritation totally eradicated any hint of vulnerability in Zoe's eyes. That was better. He preferred that.

'No,' she replied, the space between her eyebrows puckering, 'I'm not that stupid, whatever you might think!'

Damien took a deep breath. He was going to stay in control. He was.

'I was going to explore Lower Hadwell and maybe Dartmouth, read, sunbathe—and Luke had arranged a skipper for me for a few days so we could go out sailing.'

Damien nodded. He knew he should do the decent thing, but the bobbing of the boat beneath him on the swell, the familiar slap of the steel shrouds against the mast, teased him. He really didn't want to get back in his car and drive all the way back to London. It had been too long since he'd had the opportunity to sail like this. Maybe Luke had been right. Maybe he *had* been working too hard.

She folded her arms across her chest, and he knew she was digging in for a fight, that he might not get her off this boat unless he tied her up, popped her in a sail bag and drove her all the way back home in the boot of his car. He allowed himself a little daydream to that effect before he made himself face reality, and a stony-faced Zoe, again.

Just looking at her made him restless and jumpy—and in two completely different ways. How did she do that? How did his body respond to those curves when his mind was yelling *No way*?

And then an idea occurred to him. Both beautiful and idiotic at the same time.

At least while Zoe had been needling him at the wedding he'd forgotten about Sara. She might drive him crazy, but she was one hell of an effective distraction. And, much as he might wish it so, she wasn't going anywhere. He knew she'd never cave and let him have the boat for the fortnight. For some reason she took everything he said or did very personally. So maybe he could make all her irritating qualities work for him rather than against him.

'Why don't I be your skipper?'

Zoe stopped moving. Her chest didn't rise and fall, her eyelids didn't blink. 'What?' she said so quietly he almost didn't hear her.

'You want two weeks relaxing in the sun—or whatever weather we get. This is England, after all—and I want to sail...'

She nodded, very softly, very slowly.

'I know we...clashed...yesterday—' He'd almost said *kissed*, but that hadn't been his intention at all. He cleared his throat and continued. 'But it was a stressful day for everyone, emotions were running high...'

His voice dried then. He went to take a sip of tea, but discovered too late his mug was already empty, and had to make do with swallowing once or twice.

Zoe leaned forward slightly, and her eyes lost that narrow, suspicious look. 'You'd be my personal deck hand?'

That wasn't quite the way he'd have put it, but he wasn't going to quibble about it. This way, they could both get what they wanted.

'I suggest we both use the boat. I can sail. You can sunbathe or shop or do whatever you want to do, and we can stay out of each other's way. Same boat, separate holidays.' It sounded so reasonable he almost believed it himself.

Zoe blinked, and Damien decided that without that hard, garish persona of hers in place—the one that made her head-butt life like a nanny goat—she was actually quite pretty.

Unfortunately, Zoe didn't stay quiet and almost ladylike for long. He saw the moment the insolence crystallised around her like a shell. She folded her arms across her front and rested back against the padded bench that would probably double as his bed that night.

'You're on,' she said with a twinkle in her eye, and Damien had to fight the urge to smile. 'To separate holidays.' She lifted her mug and toasted him with the remainder of her tea. 'And a truce. I can do it if you can.'

Ah, they were back to that—competition. Oh, well. It was something he and Zoe knew how to do excessively well, and as long as they were both trying to outdo each other being polite and accommodating, things should go pretty well.

Zoe sat in the cockpit, her feet up on the opposite bench, with a book in her lap and a large baggy shirt on over her swimming costume. It was still a bit chilly this morning to start sunbathing, which actually suited her fine at present. She was going to have to work up to baring substantial amounts of flesh now she had an audience. Once again she wished she had her best friend's figure. Sara had slender thighs, a flat stomach and an uncanny ability to say no to cake. Zoe, not so much—as her jelly-like thighs, bulging one-piece and general lumpiness bore witness to.

If only Mr Damien Stone weren't so…well…good-looking. She'd feel more comfortable stripping off if her companion had a white, pasty pigeon chest and legs like two knotted pieces of string. No such luck. Even under his jeans and T-shirt, it was obvious his body was every bit as perfect as the rest of him.

A fact you know only too well, Zoe St James, since you were freely exploring it with your fingertips not even twenty-four hours ago.

That was then, she told herself. This is now. And she wasn't going to mention that kiss, not if Damien wasn't. She wasn't going to weaken first. Bringing it up would only make it seem that she was some kind of desperate girly who had fallen under his spell. No way was she letting him think he had the upper hand.

Unwittingly, Damien Stone had engineered his own downfall. His suggestion had played right into her hands, because she was going to make him pay for that look on his face after he'd kissed her. He'd practically agreed to be her personal slave, and she was going to make the most of it. By the end of this holiday he'd know she could do *disdain* just as well as he could.

In fact, the whole situation might be deeply satisfying on so many levels. Teaching him a lesson would be cathartic, because it really wasn't about him alone. It was all men like him, who thought everyone was beneath them, who needed to be taught a lesson. Men like her ex. Well, she was going to make sure Damien Stone felt way, way beneath her this holiday. A little humiliation might just be on the menu.

They'd sailed back into the Dart estuary and up to Lower Hadwell marina. Ever since they'd tied the boat up—Zoe knew there was a proper name for that, but it escaped her—Damien had been running around the boat like a mad thing. He'd opened all sorts of hidden lockers that she'd had no idea existed, checking sails and ropes and things she couldn't identify.

He'd pulled charts from the small desk that was opposite the tiny galley by the stairs that led to the cockpit, and then had spent ages muttering to himself and poring over them, and now he was up the other end of the boat doing heaven knew what. You'd have thought they were planning a transatlantic crossing, not two weeks puttering up and down the River Dart. At least, she'd assumed that was the plan. That had been *her* plan, anyway.

'Hey, deck hand!' she called, without looking up.

Damien's head appeared through the hatch right beside her, and her book jumped out of her lap. She scrambled to pick it up. How on earth had he got down there? Last time she'd seen him he'd been up the pointy end of the boat.

'Yes.'

Zoe took a moment to reply. He'd been so absorbed in whatever he'd been doing that he'd forgotten to put on that habitual frown he always seemed to wear when he looked at her. And without the suit—Damien always seemed to be wearing a suit—he looked younger and less stuffy. In fact, that look on his face was the distracted one her brothers had used to wear when they'd got into one of their aircraft modelling frenzies, the sort that meant they looked stressed but were actually enjoying every second.

'We're not planning on heading for Newfoundland or anything, are we?'

Now the frown was back. That hadn't taken long.

'No…' he said, sounding as if he was expecting it to be a trick question.

She gave one shoulder a breezy shrug. 'Just wanted to know, that's all.'

He turned to back down into the cabin. Zoe waited until he was a couple of steps down and then said, in her sweetest, most feminine voice, 'And, oh…Damien?'

A second of silence and then she heard his foot heavy on the step and his head appeared again.

'I'm thirsty,' she said, tipping her head on one side and squinting at him. 'Could you bring me a drink?'

Damien found that funny. At least, that was what she guessed the slight quirk of one eyebrow was all about.

'What?' she said, putting her book down and sitting up straighter. 'You're supposed to be my deck hand for the next two weeks—that was the deal, wasn't it?'

'Oh, that's the deal,' Damien said, still smiling. 'But I didn't agree to be your galley slave and personal servant. You need to get your terms right before you enter into contracts you don't understand.'

Zoe's mouth dropped open.

'So,' Damien said as he turned and headed back into the cabin, 'you can get your own drink. I'm going back to doing what a good deck hand should do—getting this boat ready to sail. I reckon we can get as far as the Isles of Scilly if we get going this afternoon.'

That had Zoe on her feet and following him into the cabin. 'The Isles of Scilly?' she squeaked. 'What are you talking about?'

Damien turned round from where he was flicking switches above the map desk on something that Zoe guessed might be a radio. 'You wanted me to sail the boat for you, so I'm going to sail it. That was my part of the deal. We can get all the way down the Devon and Cornwall coast if the weather's good, stopping at different towns and villages every night.' He pointed at a chart laid out on the desk. 'Once we've rounded Lizard Point we can head for Land's End and after that the Scillies.'

'But—'

Zoe was about to argue, but an image popped into her head: wide, flat rippled sand at low tide, fringed by rock pools covered in glistening emerald seaweed. Bantham Beach.

Her aunt had had a coffee table book of Britain's best beaches when Zoe had been small. When they visited the rest of the family would come to blows over a game of Monopoly, but Zoe would curl up in an armchair with that book and imagine what it would be like to visit all those different beaches, and some of her favourites had been in this part of the world.

Now she had a chance to see them for herself—and not by trudging through sand dunes or hiking down cliff paths, laden like a packhorse with coolbags and blankets and windbreakers. No, she'd get to sail right up to them, be one of those elusive and glamorous people she'd sometimes seen from the sand, the ones on the glossy white boats who *had* to be somebody important. Okay, Luke's old boat wasn't exactly glossy and expensive, but it would do. And she'd always wanted to have an excuse to say, *Just popping back to the yacht, dahling...*

'Are you up for it?' Damien asked, startling Zoe out of her fantasy.

Zoe chewed her lip. This way, with Damien to do all the donkey work, all she had to do was lie back and enjoy it. 'Cruising round the Devon and Cornwall coast?' she said, and surprised herself by smiling. 'Yes. I think I am.'

This is the life, Zoe thought, as she lay stretched out on the deck, just in front of the mast. The sun was warm on her skin, but the pleasant breeze filling the sails stopped those rays from scorching, and the gentle slap of the waves against the hull was lulling her into a half-doze.

Damien was off somewhere keeping himself busy, which was just how she liked it. He'd told her with grave seriousness that they were going to be heading across Start Bay, round the point and into Salcombe and there they would stop for the night. Zoe didn't care particularly where they went or where they stopped as long as the sun kept shining and she'd have a glass of wine in her hand when the sun went down. Until then Damien Stone could keep out of her way.

She'd much rather pretend he was some faceless minion, there to do her bidding. And, while she doubted very much he'd play along, at least while she was off doing her thing and he was off doing his, she could keep the fantasy alive. He might be useful to her at present, but that didn't mean she hadn't forgotten that kiss—or, to be more precise, the look *after* the kiss—and she intended to make him pay at some point. Until then she was lulling him into a sense of false security, playing nice.

Zoe's lids were already closed and the world behind them was pale pink and blurry, lit up by the afternoon sun, but it wasn't long before she wasn't aware of sunshine or waves any more and she fell into a deep and lazy sleep.

She woke when a chilly breeze danced across her bare shoulders. While she'd slept she'd rolled over onto her front, and now she peeled her face off her forearm and peered fuzzily towards the back of the boat.

A dark shape was there by the tiller. Damien. The brightness seemed to have gone out of the sky. She turned her head to get her bearings and realised they had left the long pebble-beached bay behind them and had now turned round the headland and were heading into the Salcombe Kingsbridge estuary. It was windier here and the sun was much lower in the sky, skulking behind low grey clouds and blessing them with bright haloes.

She sighed. If the rest of the holiday went like this it would be perfect.

It was time to move, though, before she fused with the deck and became a strange kind of beached figurehead, stuck to the top of the boat instead of the front. She pushed herself up on one arm. That was when the pain began.

'Ow…!' Her back was tight and burning fiercely. 'Ow, ow, ow!'

She collapsed down onto the deck again and tried another approach, rolling over onto her side and then pushing herself up. More pain. None of it suffered in silence.

Zoe didn't have to look in the mirror to know what had

happened. She was sunburned. Always a risk with her col-
ouring, but she'd applied a high factor sun cream all over before lying down. Just how long had she been asleep up here?

Gingerly, she made her way along the boat and down to the
cockpit, dreading the smirk she just *knew* would be plastered
all over her sailing companion's face. She straightened up and
ignored the stinging of her back and arms, not wanting to
give him the satisfaction of seeing just how pathetic she was.

But when she stepped down into the cockpit, she was in for
a surprise. Damien had been staring somewhere far ahead of
the boat, lost in his own thoughts, but he glanced over when
he heard the thud of her foot hitting the cockpit bench and
his neutral expression quickly changed to a look of horror.

Zoe held a hand up to her face, which she was now aware
was stinging just as badly as her back. And then she jumped
down the steep stairs into the cabin, ignoring the pain it
caused, and rushed for the little bathroom and checked out
the damage in the mirror above the sink.

When she first saw her reflection she wanted to cry.
Her face smarted. Well, to be more accurate, *half* her face
smarted. The right half, which had been turned towards the
sun while she'd slept, was a bright angry red. The left side
was its usual pasty self, marred only by the vestiges of pale
childhood freckles.

She looked like a freakish Halloween mask! How on earth
was she going to go out in public looking like this? People
would point and stare—and snigger, probably. She'd be ban-
ished to the cabin for at least a few days until it calmed down.
Hardly the perfect holiday! And wouldn't Damien be pleased?
With her locked away in her cabin he could pretend she wasn't
there.

There was a soft knock at the bathroom door and Zoe
jumped and banged her elbow on the wall—it was little more
than a cupboard with a toilet, a sink and shower head above
the couple of square feet of standing space.

'Are you okay?' Damien said, sounding far too genuine for Zoe's liking.

'I'm fine,' she snapped back, and she discovered her eyes had now added themselves to the inventory of body parts that stung.

Don't let him be nice to me, she prayed silently, holding her breath in an attempt to halt the moisture threatening to breach her bottom lashes. I don't want to think of Damien Stone as being nice.

Because that would mean she'd have to like him. And if she didn't despise him, she'd have no defences against that slow-humming attraction she'd been trying to fend off since a couple of stupid rumba steps had blindsided her.

Okay, most people would say that being attracted to a good-looking man wasn't a crime, but Zoe knew better. She knew how utterly seductive attention from a man who was way out of a girl's league could be. For a moment it made her feel special, made her believe she was worth something. But she also knew how those things ended, and she was well aware of her own propensity for falling hard and fast, ignoring all her own warnings to hold back, stay safe. So she wasn't looking Damien in the eye again, no matter how nice he was being, until she had her defences back in place.

So, a few minutes later, rather than heading back into the main seating area and galley, she slunk off into her own cabin and shut the door tightly behind her. She didn't come out again until the boat was stationary and she could hear the bustle of a busy marina all around.

Damien was sitting at the map desk with a large tube of aftersun in front of him. Trust Mr Perfect to have packed the essentials. He threw it to her and she caught it one-handed, and couldn't help feeling slightly cheered at the flicker of respect she saw in his eyes.

'Thanks,' she said, and sloped back off to her cabin to put it on. Her swimsuit was cut low at the back, though, and although she contorted herself into various positions to try and reach every bit of throbbing skin, there was a patch in the middle, just below her shoulder blades, that she couldn't quite reach.

Once she'd soothed the angry skin, she eased herself out of her costume. This took at least a couple of minutes, as she avoided dragging it across her skin or letting the elasticated straps slap back anywhere too tender. And then she put on a long, brightly coloured strapless sundress with a wide elasticated section round the bust. The ruched top pinched the area she hadn't been able to reach with the aftersun, but it was worth it to not have to deal with straps of any sort.

Then she set to trying to disguise her harlequin face with half a bottle of foundation. She ended up looking like her ballroom dancing teacher did just before a competition, but at least it was an even orangeness instead of half white, half pink.

That accomplished, she ventured out into the cabin and started hunting through the small cupboards surrounding the galley. At times like these, a girl needed something sweet.

She heard Damien thud down the steps from the cockpit. 'Looking for something?'

She nodded and kept ferreting through the cupboards, although she didn't know why—there was hardly anything in them. Damien had gone shopping at the tiny general store before they'd left Lower Hadwell, but all Zoe could find was some bread, some cheese, a few tins of beans, tea bags, coffee, long-life milk...

She twisted her head to look at Damien and winced; it felt as if she were giving herself a Chinese burn. 'Where are the biscuits?'

Damien's eyebrows rose a millimetre. 'What biscuits?'

Zoe blinked in disbelief. No biscuits?

'What about the chocolate?' she asked, her voice wavering slightly.

Damien just shook his head.

Zoe untwisted her poor neck, stood up and turned to face him. He was lounging in the hatchway, one foot on a higher step, one arm resting on the roof of the galley.

'Some deck hand you are! I thought you said you went shopping.'

Damien's mouth curled at one side. 'I did. But I did tell you it was just a quick shop to get the essentials, and that we'd stock up at the supermarket here tomorrow morning.'

'Chocolate *is* essentials!' Zoe cried, her plummeting sugar levels making her sound just a little desperate.

'Like I said, we can get other supplies in the morning. A whole case of chocolate, if you want.'

Now he was mocking her. And Zoe didn't like being mocked.

'Just a little bit for emergencies is enough, thank you very much,' she mumbled.

Damien just shrugged. He didn't say anything else. Didn't pick a fight—which left them both standing there, him towering above her half in, half out of the hatch, and Zoe suddenly realised how close they were. And then she realised how difficult it was to be anything *but* this close on a boat this size.

Damn it, if her non-pink cheek didn't flame to life to match the other one at that point. Thank goodness for the relative gloom of the galley and a layer of foundation her plasterer brother would have been proud of.

Damien held out his hand, and Zoe eyed it suspiciously.

'If you're really in need of nutrition, why don't we go and grab some dinner?'

Zoe obviously let her feelings regarding that suggestion show on her face because Damien gave her a weary look.

'Surely we can be adult enough to eat at the same table without starting World War Three. I'm starving, and there are plenty of restaurants nearby. I just can't be bothered to argue about it tonight.'

While Zoe didn't really want to spend any more time with Damien than was necessary, she was feeling more than a little sorry for herself, and the idea of letting someone else do all the thinking, all the planning, was rather appealing. She was all for delegating whenever she got the chance and, since her business meant she was a one-woman operation she really didn't get an opportunity to delegate that much, and she supposed Damien's proposal was reasonable enough.

But she ignored Damien's hand, retreating further back into the cabin. 'I'm just going to…er…go and get a wrap for my shoulders,' she muttered.

No hand-holding with Damien Stone, okay?

Last time she'd taken his hand willingly was when they'd swapped partners on the dance floor, and look how well *that* had turned out.

But he can't find you too disgusting if he's willing to touch you again, even if he's just being polite.

Yes, but he might change his mind again, like he did last time, and she couldn't have that. Better to keep as much of a distance as possible, especially as whenever she got within five feet of him she couldn't help remembering how strong and sure his arms had felt around her or just how expert those lips were. So she made sure she trailed behind Damien as they got off the boat and negotiated the metal wires that ran round the deck without assistance, even though the long skirt of her dress threatened to wrap itself round them.

No, who would want to put themselves in line for humiliation twice in twenty-four hours? Definitely not her.

CHAPTER SIX

Zoe got her wish. By the time the sun was setting she was sitting on a restaurant terrace, high up on a hill above the estuary with a glass of perfectly chilled white wine in her hand. Bliss. Delicious seafood smells wafted from inside the trendy but reasonably priced restaurant and her stomach gurgled in anticipation. The breeze was soft, still clinging to the memory of the sunshine that had filtered through it all day, and the sky was a frosty blue, warming to primrose at the horizon.

Even Damien was behaving himself. He'd let her choose the restaurant, and he hadn't got all caveman-like when she'd insisted on paying her share.

Their starters arrived. Zoe had chosen a crabmeat timbale, covered in smoked salmon, but when she saw Damien's deep-fried lime and chilli king prawns she couldn't help thinking that she'd chosen hastily, and that maybe she should have perused the whole menu instead of just plumping for the thing that jumped out at her first. She couldn't help counting down the prawns as Damien worked his way mechanically through them.

Eventually, when there were only two left, Damien shook his head, glanced heavenwards and held one out to her by its tail. 'I can't eat with you staring at me like that. You might as well have one.'

I couldn't possibly.

That *should* have been the response that sprang instantly

to her lips, but she was so transfixed by the bubbly golden batter and the sweet hot chilli sauce that glistened and threatened to sully the clean white tablecloth that she completely forgot to utter it. Saliva pooled in the bottom of her mouth.

Part of her didn't want to take anything from this man, but that part was quickly clubbed over the head and locked in a cupboard by the part of her that was licking its lips.

Moving quickly—so as not to hijack herself by coming over all appropriate—she leaned forwards, opened her mouth and closed her lips round the prawn, biting it off near the tail. She couldn't quite help closing her eyes as she savoured the sweetness and acidity of the dipping sauce, then the crunchy texture of the batter, and finally the firm flesh of the prawn beneath. A perfect pairing of opposites in so many ways. She let a little murmur of satisfaction out before opening her eyes again.

When she did, she found Damien in exactly the same position he'd been when she'd closed them, hand still outstretched, the remains of the prawn tail still pinched between finger and thumb. And he had a rather strange expression on his face. What was up with him?

He seemed to realise what he was doing, because suddenly he pulled his arm back and dropped the tail on his plate. Then he stared at the one remaining curl of battered seafood before dunking it in the sauce and holding it up in front of him, looking at it as if he'd never seen one before in his life.

Was this some weird kind of delayed seasickness that had got him in its grip? Zoe didn't know. But anything that took his critical focus off her and onto something else must be a good thing.

Up until now he'd been eating the prawns and accompanying salad as if it was a task to be got through, something to be ticked off an invisible list inside his head, no satisfaction to be had until the job was done, but now he closed his eyes and chewed slowly.

She could see it in his face—the revelations brought by each new taste and texture. She could almost feel her own taste buds responding as the different flavours hit his tongue. And then it was Zoe's turn to find herself frozen in position. A warm, fizzing lightning bolt shot through her, starting at the top of her head and raising gooseflesh as it travelled down her body to her toes. She shook herself slightly to quell the feeling of bubbles dancing along her skin. She quickly picked up a fork and attacked her forgotten crabmeat just as Damien opened his eyes again.

It's nothing, she told herself. Just a residual tingle from the kiss last night. It doesn't mean you fancy Damien Stone.

She scooped the rest of her crab up and stuffed it into her mouth in one go. The cool creamy taste would eradicate the memory of that prawn, get her back to normal again. She hoped.

And more conversation would be good. Something to distract her from the ideas of eating and tasting. And, from the looks of him, Damien needed distraction too. He was staring at his empty plate as if it held all the answers of the universe.

Pick a topic, Zoe. Any topic. It's not normally a problem for you, is it?

'So, how did you meet Luke?' she blurted out, her mouth only just emptied of crab. 'I know you've been friends for years, but I don't really know how it all began.'

Probably because she made a habit of tuning out or finding someone else to talk to whenever Damien had been around before.

She had, hadn't she?

It hadn't been a conscious thing, at least not at first. But he reminded her of that love-rat Aiden, so she'd steered clear, but after a while Damien had earned the dubious honour of irritating her completely on his own merits.

He had that same kind of I-rule-the-world confidence that Aiden had. However, when—like Damien—you headed a construction company that had just won a contract to erect buildings that would change the London skyline, you were probably entitled to be a little pleased with yourself.

But it bothered Zoe. Mostly because she had personal knowledge of just what was under that layer of confidence in a man like that. Nowhere near as pretty as the packaging, that was certain.

And she should know—she'd been engaged to it once.

How could one prawn result in such a profound experience?

Damien liked good food, would have said he enjoyed it, but in the end it was just calories and fats and proteins. Fuel, basically, no matter how much you dressed it up. But then he'd watched Zoe eat that prawn, her eyes sliding closed in obvious pleasure, and he'd realised he'd eaten six of the things already and had got none of that level of satisfaction. So he'd decided to try it her way.

And…wow.

Stopping for a moment, taking time to savour the tastes and textures, had been a totally new experience, and he wasn't sure what to do about it. He decided to put it on the back-burner and let it simmer for a while. He also needed to find something to do to stop him thinking over and over again about Zoe's lips closing around that prawn.

'You wanted to know how I met Luke?'

Zoe sipped her wine and nodded.

'Both of our families used to rent holiday cottages down here—the same ones each year—at least until…' He stopped himself. She didn't need to know that. It was too personal. 'Until I was about fifteen. Luke and I were roughly the same age, so we teamed up occasionally, but it was the year we both begged our parents to enrol us in sailing school that the friendship really began. We bonded over a shared love: wind, waves, water—and finding the fastest way to travel across them.'

'So why don't you have a boat? I presume you don't, otherwise you wouldn't be borrowing Luke's.'

That was a good question. A very good question, actually. Zoe was as sharp as she was blunt. Interesting.

'I plan to,' he said. It had always been part of the plan: establish the business, settle down, buy a house, then maybe he'd think about a boat. 'It's just not been the right time yet.'

Zoe pulled her mouth downwards. 'That's a pity. You seem to love it so much. Why wait?'

Because...

Because he didn't like doing things out of order, or changing a perfectly good plan for no other reason than it might be fun. Succumbing to those self-indulgent urges was what had caused his father to destroy their family. As a result, Damien was rather suspicious of things with a feel-good factor. He weighed decisions to engage in such activities carefully. But he couldn't say something like that to someone like Zoe. She'd never understand.

'I just haven't found the perfect boat yet,' he replied finally. That sounded better.

Zoe pulled her napkin off her lap and placed it back on the table before leaning back in her chair and twisting her head slightly to take in the view.

Take in the view... That was the right phrase to describe what she did. She didn't just look at the fork of the estuary, the little sailing boats left impotent on a mud bank now the tide had receded, or the white dots of the seagulls circling above them. She seemed to engage in it, draw it all into herself using every sense at her disposal.

She turned and looked at him. 'So why not buy a "good enough for now" boat and enjoy that until the perfect one comes along?'

Hmm. He hadn't thought of that. And he didn't like admitting a different plan would be better than the one he'd already set in stone.

'I don't have to,' he said rather smugly. 'I can borrow Luke's.'

Zoe smiled reluctantly. 'It's nice that you share things. He's like a brother to you, isn't he?'

Damien nodded. Being an only child, he didn't know much about that sort of thing, but he'd imagined that was what having a brother might have been like. Thoughts of his friendship with Luke inevitably led to comparisons with Zoe and Sara's relationship. No one would ever describe those two as sisters. Opposite ends of the spectrum, maybe, but never sisters. He decided to satisfy his curiosity on that front.

'What about you and Sara? You must go back a long way as well.'

Zoe's face blossomed into the most beautiful smile at the mention of her friend's name, and Damien couldn't help letting his lips curl up a little too as they shared that particular mental picture.

'We've known each other since school. Sara was one of the popular girls…' She frowned and looked intently at him. 'Not the *mean* variety. I just meant that everyone wanted to be like her.'

'Did you?' He hadn't meant to let that question pop out, but out it had come. Too late to call it back now.

For a moment Zoe looked as if she was going to say something biting and sarcastic, but her expression suddenly softened. 'Maybe. I was in awe of her a bit, I suppose. I didn't really understand why she befriended me.' She gave Damien a sardonic look. 'I don't know if you've noticed this, but I seem to be very talented at rubbing people up the wrong way.'

'No kidding.' But he smiled as he said it, and the glitter of challenge that ignited in Zoe's eyes softened instantly into humour.

He had the oddest sense that there was more to Zoe St James's outrageous remarks than just having no filter between brain and mouth. She chose to be that way, he realised. Chose to act that way, even though she'd just come out straight and told him she knew the effect it had on others. Why would anyone do that?

Their main courses arrived and Damien jokingly pushed his plate in Zoe's direction, one eyebrow raised. She rolled her eyes and shook her head.

'I think I'll stick with my tuna, thanks.'

Damien picked up his knife and fork and began carving his steak precisely. 'You say that now, but I don't want you staring lovingly at my plate for the next half-hour. It would drive me crazy—a bit like having someone read over your shoulder.'

Zoe shrugged as she chewed her first bit of tuna. 'I never did understand why that was such a problem. I read over people's shoulders all the time.'

Damien shook his head and reached for the salt. 'Anyway... So you kept in touch with Sara after school?' He felt slightly guilty even saying her name, but it seemed their mutual admiration for Sara was the one thing he and Zoe had in common, and the lull in their sparring was actually quite pleasant.

She nodded and swallowed her mouthful. 'I suppose lots of people lose touch with friends after school, but Sara's very loyal.' She looked down at her plate and lines appeared on her forehead.

'What?'

Her bottom lip protruded slightly and she looked thoughtful.

'Odd, isn't it?' she said, looking back at him. 'The things you remember from your school days. Kids can be so cruel...'

Damien leaned forward. 'What did they say?'

Zoe gave him a lopsided smile. 'You think, with this hair and this figure they didn't have plenty of ammunition? Can't you guess?'

Damien could imagine it. Even worse, he felt ashamed he'd thought the same thing himself. Kids would pick on anything that marked someone out as different. But Zoe's hair wasn't ugly because it was different. Look at it now—the edges of those unruly curls lit up gold by the setting sun.

She flicked those very same curls back off her face and looked at him, her chin raised a notch. 'They didn't say anything I hadn't heard before. I've got four older brothers. Believe me, I can dish it out just as good as I can take it. But there was this one girl—Abigail—she always had to go the extra mile.'

'You shouldn't let it bother you, not now. That was a long time ago.'

Zoe turned her attention to her tuna and ate another mouthful before she answered. 'She said the only reason anyone would want to be friends with me was because it made them look better when they stood beside me.'

Damien wanted to say something conciliatory, but the memory of his own prejudice was lodged in his throat, preventing him. Hadn't he thought something similar? Not that nasty, of course, but he hadn't been able to help comparing the two friends and judging them on their differences. Sara did seem to shine even brighter next to Zoe, but that wasn't Zoe's fault. Or Sara's.

He put down his knife and fork and looked directly at her. 'You and I both know that nothing is further from the truth in Sara's case.'

Zoe lifted her chin even higher and looked back at him. 'I know,' she said quietly.

But deep down somewhere she hadn't recovered from that comment, Damien realised. What must that be like? To always be cast as second best or, even worse, the 'ugly one'? He'd never known comparisons like that. He'd been an only child and the golden boy at school, the one who went after what he wanted and got it.

The mood had grown far too serious. He decided to use one of Zoe's well-known tactics to lighten things up: he reached over with his fork and stole a juicy chunk of tuna.

'Hey!'

He refused to look repentant. She could take it as well as she dished it out, could she? He wasn't so sure. But, even if she couldn't, it was good to see the fire back in her eyes as she retaliated by stealing a chip from his plate, one eyebrow arched saucily high.

After dinner they walked back down the endless cobbled steps to the marina. Once back on board *Dream Weaver*, Zoe flopped onto one of the long padded benches in the main cabin, winced and sat back up again.

'Need more of that aftersun?' he asked, and headed off to retrieve it from one of the small lockers above the bench he'd be using as a berth later on before she could answer.

Zoe nodded and took the tube gratefully from him. She then spent a few minutes gently patting the cooling gel into the reddened skin at the tops of her shoulders.

'You have to be careful out on the water,' he said.

Zoe glanced over her shoulder and gave him a sharp look. 'I was careful. I was covered top to toe in sunblock.'

He squashed a spike of irritation at her defensiveness. Couldn't this woman discuss anything without turning it into a fight?

'I wasn't saying you did anything wrong,' he added carefully. 'It's just that somehow the sea and the wind have a way of magnifying the sun's intensity. It can catch you out.'

'Now he tells me,' she muttered as she contorted her arm behind her head in order to reach her shoulder blades. 'You couldn't have mentioned that up on deck earlier?'

Damien took a step forward. No way was she making this his fault.

'I had no idea you'd burn so quickly and, if you remember, my attention was taken up with sailing a boat single-handed.'

'Well, bully for you!' she snapped, her face contorting as

sore skin rubbed against sore skin when she tried to reach a spot in the centre of her back.

'Oh, for goodness' sake! Here… Let me.'

And, without asking, he tugged the tube from her other hand and dumped some of the clear blue gel into his palm.

She went very still, but flinched slightly as the chilly gel met the hot skin of her shoulders. Damien rubbed it in as gently as he could, using just the pads of his fingers, taking his time, making sure he didn't miss even a spot. After a little while, Zoe let out a small whimper and he paused, hands millimetres above her skin.

'Am I hurting you?'

'N…no,' she replied, her voice wavering somewhat.

'Sure?'

She nodded.

Damien looked at the wide elasticated band that made up the bodice of Zoe's garish dress. It rested just below her shoulder blades and prevented further progress.

'Do you want me to do…' he swallowed; all the saliva had drained out of his mouth, as if the tide had gone out there too '…lower down.' He was sure her swimming costume—not that he'd been looking, of course—had dipped lower than that at the back.

Zoe didn't answer for a few seconds. 'Erm…if you could.'

He gently hooked the elastic with one of his non-gooey fingers and lifted it away and down, revealing more tomato-red skin beneath. 'You did a really good job with that sunburn, didn't you?'

He saw her ribs move as she breathed out a little laugh. 'Well, yes, that's me. Never do anything by halves.'

He smiled, even though she couldn't see him. 'I think I've worked that out for myself already.'

He felt rather than heard the shallow chuckle that followed. And then he was quiet again, concentrating on fingers and skin, gel sliding over muscles.

That was one thing Zoe had over skinny girls—she had a nice back. It dipped in invitingly in the middle, no ribs or bones protruding, and it was all curves and soft skin, no sharp contours. He let his fingers and palms gently skim each one.

And then he realised that he'd run out of gel, and for the last minute or so he'd just been lost in following his eyes with his fingers. Exploring.

He wasn't supposed to be exploring. He was just supposed to be helping.

He pulled his hands away and very gently replaced the gathered section of Zoe's dress back where it was supposed to be, ignoring the inviting drip of gel on the end of the tube that was just begging to be used up.

She turned to face him, her hands at the front of her dress, where they'd clutched the fabric to keep it from sliding down. Her eyes were big and her lips slightly parted. It reminded him of how she'd looked in the moonlight the night before.

Had that really been less than twenty-four hours ago? It felt more like a decade. At least he felt he'd aged that much since then.

But thinking about the…incident…by the fountain made him realise he'd been remiss. There were things he should have said that he hadn't.

'I'm sorry,' he said and, before he could continue, Zoe jumped in.

'Don't be. My back feels much better now.'

'No,' he said, thinking he really should take a step back, move away. 'I meant about last night…About kissing you the way I did.'

That left Zoe silent and blinking. Not a very common sight.

'I…' She fell silent again, looked down at her brightly painted toenails.

'It wasn't a very gentlemanly thing to do.'

'No, it wasn't,' she replied but, instead of her voice being hard and confrontational as he'd expected it to be, it was low and husky.

'You had every right to slap me. I think I needed it.' He puffed out some air and ran his hand through his hair. 'Let's just say that I wasn't at my best that day, for a whole string of reasons I don't really want to go into.'

She didn't say anything else, just searched his face with her eyes. He felt as if he was an interesting specimen on a microscope slide. She was looking at him as if she'd seen nothing quite like it before.

'Thank you.' Her voice was steady and low. 'I've done plenty of things in the heat of the moment I've had to apologise for later, so I know what the genuine article is when it comes my way.' Her lips curved into the barest of smiles and he saw the sparkle of something warm and soft and gentle in the backs of her eyes. 'I appreciate that, Damien.'

He nodded.

He still hadn't stepped away, he realised. Now would be a really good time. Before he did *two* things he needed to apologise for within twenty-four hours.

Zoe's hands were still clutching the front of her dress, but she dropped them now and held one of them out to him. 'Truce?'

He slid his hand into hers and they shook solemnly. 'Truce.'

Then something occurred to him. 'Wait a minute... Didn't we declare a truce of sorts this morning?'

The softness, the vulnerability was gone now and the impish Zoe was back. 'Technically, yes, but it didn't count,' she said as she withdrew her hand from his and looked at it. 'Yuck.'

Damien mirrored her. He'd forgotten that blobs of gel still clung to the edges of his hands. 'And why didn't it count?' he asked, still staring at his palm.

She lifted her arm. 'Because I was lying.'

And then she dragged her palm across his face, wiping

the excess gel off on his cheek, before grinning saucily at him and disappearing into the cabin. He stood there, his gaze alternating between his upturned palm and the cabin door.

He had a feeling he'd just become friends with Zoe St James.

Sara and Luke would be delighted. But Damien? He wasn't sure whether he should be pleased that the war was over or just very, very scared.

CHAPTER SEVEN

WHILE the good weather continued Zoe spent a lot of time during the next few days in the sunshine, even though she made sure she was covered up. She either lounged up the front of the boat while Damien managed things down at the business end, or window shopped on her own in the little towns they visited, looking at girly things such as shoes and pretty locally made trinkets.

She wasn't avoiding Damien. They'd agreed to have separate holidays, hadn't they? And they met up each evening to go out to dinner. It was all very grown-up and civilised.

They discussed cooking on board, but Damien's utilitarian menu ideas, involving limited rations, had Zoe screwing her face up, and Zoe's more flamboyant suggestions put a look of fear in Damien's eyes. Eating out solved the problem. No fighting about food then, because they could choose what they wanted, but Zoe made sure she kept her grubby mitts off Damien's plate now. Somehow that had become dangerous territory. Mainly because it reminded her of what had happened *after* that meal. She couldn't quite look that tube of aftersun in the face any more.

She wandered along the narrow streets of Fowey on one of her daily shopping trips, and stopped to stare into a smart but quirky jewellery shop window. Just the memory of that massage had her placing a palm on the window to steady herself. She fanned her face down with her non-supporting hand and heaved in a breath.

Okay, so Damien wasn't quite the arrogant snob she'd pegged him for, but that didn't mean that having the hots for him was a good idea. He was still the same type as her ex-fiancé, and that kind of man wanted a certain kind of woman in his life, even if he said he didn't. And if there was one thing that Zoe had taken away from the whole call-off-the-wedding-because-I'm-in-love-with-someone-else fiasco, it was that she wasn't that kind of woman.

She sighed as she looked at her reflection in the shop window. One side of her face was a little more tanned than the other now, but it was almost back to normal. Nothing a little tinted moisturiser couldn't cope with.

It still pained her to think of her time with Aiden. Not so much because she'd lost the man, but more the loss of the fairy tale he'd brought with him. She'd never thought someone as wonderful as him would ever be interested in someone like her. It was as if Prince Charming has swooned at the raggedy Cinderella's feet instead of waiting until she'd got all dolled up for the ball. She'd never felt so wanted.

But somehow the story had gone into reverse. The clock had stuck midnight, the prince took one look at Cinders, had suddenly seen the rags for what they were, and had run a mile in the other direction. With one week to go before the wedding.

She looked at her reflection in the shop window again, looked herself steadily in the eye. *So no more thinking about getting deliberately sunburnt just to be on the receiving end of Damien's magic fingers again, okay?*

She nodded back at herself just as sternly.

That settled, she peeled her hand from the window and went inside to have a look round. The shop was tucked into the ground floor of a row of Georgian buildings, compact but beautifully decorated. The wood panelling had been painted

off-white and the silver and amber jewellery the shop special-
ised in was housed in glass cases that lined the walls. A bit
restrained for Zoe's tastes, maybe, but it showed the pieces
off beautifully.

She always liked to see other designers' work and she spent
ages browsing, but she found herself admiring the shop more
than its contents. One day she'd have one of these. A nice
little quirky shop with a workshop at the back and a comfy
little corner where she could talk to clients about designing
bespoke pieces. Selling her designs to other shops around
south-east England was all well and good and she was starting to make a name for herself, but it would be really lovely
to have a shop of her own. One day…

She made it back to the marina at about twenty to six.
Damien had said to be back by five, but she'd spent much
longer in that shop than she'd meant to. She walked down the
ramp and on to the pontoons, but when she came to the spot
where *Dream Weaver* had been moored she found a large,
sparkling cruiser.

She rested her hands on her hips, causing her paper shopping bags to fan out around her. Where the heck had he gone?
She carried on to the end of the pontoon and stared out across
the water.

All the while she'd been standing there, the buzz of an
outboard motor had been getting louder and louder somewhere close by. A flash of sunlight on the water drew her
attention, and that was when she saw him—Damien—coming towards her in a little grey inflatable dinghy. He wasn't
looking very happy.

Zoe put both hands behind her back in an attempt to make
a shopping trip seem slightly less successful. Why did these
little boutiques have to wrap everything in tissue paper and
put it in an oversized bag, anyway?

Don't react, she told herself as he brought the dinghy round
to the end of the pontoon and slipped its rope round a bollard.

'I said *five*,' he shouted over the noise of the engine.

Zoe bestowed her most fetching smile on him. 'What's a few minutes when we've got ten whole days to fill?'

It didn't work. He just glowered back.

'I explained that these were short-stay berths, that we only had two hours and that we needed to move to a swinging mooring by five.'

He well might have. But after thirty seconds of sailing jargon it all started sounding like *blah, blah, blah* to Zoe.

'What's the rush, anyway?'

Damien remained stony-faced as she handed the first of her shopping bags to him.

'Hey!' she said as he chucked them unceremoniously into the triangular space at the front of the dinghy, just forward of the little inflatable seat.

He held out a hand so she could steady herself climbing in, but Zoe needed both arms to keep the rest of her bags out of his clutches. She managed somehow without his help and sat abruptly down on the little bolster-shaped seat, facing him.

Damien eyed the brightly coloured bags before casting off. 'How many pairs of flip-flops does one woman need, anyway?' he muttered as he reversed away from the pontoon then swung the dinghy round to plough across the river against the current. 'If we want to get into town by seven-thirty to eat, we need to get the food shopping done by six forty-five, and I couldn't take the dinghy to do that until I'd picked you up.'

'Sorry,' Zoe said softly. She hadn't been late on purpose, just had got caught out in a little daydreaming. 'Can't we just shop a bit quicker or go into town a bit later?' Seriously, would the earth fall from its axis if they weren't sitting down and ordering by eight?

Damien didn't answer, so obviously it would.

Dream Weaver was about five minutes away, secured to a mooring buoy up a large creek near a wooded part of the riverbank, away from the noise and bustle of the marina. Damien didn't bother turning the engine off when they reached her, but let Zoe climb aboard while he held the dinghy steady. She had to post her bags through the railings into the cockpit before climbing up the ladder at the back of the boat. Once her foot was on the first rung, he was off again, speeding away in the direction of the town centre and the supermarket.

Heaven forbid the boat wasn't stocked with exactly three tins or packets of everything on Damien's shopping list at all times. He really was quite neurotic about it. But then Zoe went to make herself a cup of tea and discovered they were out of milk, and she couldn't even moan about it because she was the one who'd finished it off.

It was quiet in this spot and there was no one else to talk to, as there would have been at the marina, so Zoe reached into one of her shopping bags and pulled out a beautiful leather-bound sketchpad she just hadn't been able to resist. She then rummaged for a pencil in the navigation desk before returning to the cockpit and settling down to draw.

But she didn't draw the scenery. Well, not exactly…

She took the shape, the textures of the landscape, and turned them into designs for bracelets and earrings and necklaces. Rolling hills and soft clouds, clean sharp lines and rippling water were stylised and shaped into silver.

Ever since she'd designed Sara's ring she'd started to think about doing something different, more understated. She'd wanted to find a theme to tie some of the new collection together, and now it seemed she had it. She was so engrossed in what she was doing that she only noticed Damien had returned when a plastic carrier bag full of bread and apples came over the side of the boat and landed on the bench beside her. She put her pencil and pad down, flipping the pad closed first, and went to help.

She supposed she could have gone shopping with him, but that would have defeated the object of 'separate holidays'. Anyway, Damien didn't seem to like to sit still and Zoe did—

rather a lot—especially when she was on holiday, so she decided not to stop him if he'd silently volunteered for the job.

She put the kettle on and made Damien a cup of tea. They'd got into a semi-comfortable routine over the last couple of days, working around each other, doing their own thing, talking only when they needed to. It was working. Sort of.

Damien bounded down the cabin steps with the last of the shopping, looking far too strong and healthy for Zoe's liking, in a soft cotton T-shirt and knee-length shorts. He gladly accepted the tea she offered and took it back outside into the sunshine.

Zoe knew she ought to stay in the cabin, not go out and join that six-foot hunk of male healthiness sitting outside, all wind-ruffled and glowing from his jaunt back across the river. But it was such a glorious day... And it was ever so dingy in the tiny cabin, with only those long thin windows high up in the wall to let in light.

She emerged into the cockpit to find Damien sipping his tea and flipping through her sketchbook.

'Hands off, nosey,' she said, attempting to swat his hand away from it.

Damien didn't have any trouble fending her off, even with a cup of tea in one hand. 'A very different style for you—even from Sara's ring—which I thought was beautiful, by the way.'

She stopped her ineffectual swatting. 'Thank you...I think.'

He looked up at her, a mischievous glint in his eye. 'You think?'

Zoe fidgeted. 'Well, in my experience, it pays to be wary of compliments from good-looking men—' She stopped and blushed.

Damien's glint worked its way from his eyes down to his mouth. 'In my experience, it pays to compliment attractive women.'

Zoe, who'd been half-enjoying the gentle banter, despite her mortification, suddenly snatched her pad out of his hands and retreated to the cabin door. 'Don't make fun of me, Damien,' she said, her voice hard on the surface while her stomach quivered underneath.

'I wasn't. I was just—'

She didn't wait to hear the rest. She turned and headed back down inside and tucked the sketchbook safely away in her cabin. Then she folded her legs underneath herself and sat on her bunk.

She didn't want Damien to say things like that to her. It would make the raging crush she seemed to be developing for him *so* much harder to control. In fact, she thought she preferred it when they were bickering. At least then she was safe.

Without stopping to think whether it was a good idea or not, she stood on the bunk, opened the hatch in the roof of her cabin and stuck her head through it.

'Next time you can keep your opinions to yourself,' she yelled in the direction of the cockpit. 'About me or my work. Separate holidays, remember?'

And then she flopped down on her bunk, leaving the hatch open as ventilation.

There. He wouldn't think she was very attractive after the way she'd screwed her face up and yelled at him, and that was fine by her. She didn't need another smooth man who was way out of her league, giving her hope, making her believe in herself before whipping it all away from her again.

Remember what he's like, she told herself, when he's not in shorts and a T-shirt, when he looks all buttoned-up and rigid, not relaxed like this. That's the real Damien Stone and you'd better not forget it.

But then a shadow blocked out the sun momentarily and a soft thud on the sleeping bag beside her completely undermined her resolve. He'd finished unpacking the shopping, it seemed. Found a bag she'd missed.

A small bar of her favourite chocolate sat innocently on

the bunk with a Post-it note attached. *For emergencies*, it said in a strong, dark scrawl.

Damn that man, Zoe thought, as she ripped the foil open and sunk her teeth into it. She didn't want him to be nice to her, not when she was doing her best to put him off, because she was starting to like—really like—Damien Stone. And if that wasn't an emergency, she didn't know what was.

Zoe woke the following morning to find a huge grey cloud hanging over her cabin skylight. She did her usual contortionist's act to get dressed in the tiny triangular space. Maybe sharing it with a huge case hadn't been such a great idea after all.

When she emerged, most annoyed at having to put something with long sleeves on, she found Damien humming to himself in the little galley, cooking sausages and looking horrendously chirpy. Didn't he know that grey skies on a holiday practically required one to be in a state of mourning?

She yawned. Zoe wasn't usually an early riser but the daylight flooding into her cabin and the noise of the wire shrouds banging against the top of the mast in the wind had been a pretty effective alarm clock.

'Where are we off to today?' she mumbled as Damien shoved a mug of tea in her direction.

'Mevagissey,' he said, and carried on whistling.

'Really? I thought we'd stay here if the weather was going to be bad.'

He made a scoffing noise and looked up to the monochrome sky above the hatch. 'This isn't bad weather. It's not even raining, and the forecast says it'll hold off until evening.'

Zoe leaned forward to follow his gaze. By the looks of that cloud, it would rain sooner rather than later.

'It's perfect sailing weather,' Damien announced matter-of-factly.

Well, they obviously had very different ideas about what

perfect sailing involved. If it didn't involve a cool drink and a bikini, Zoe didn't want to know.

'You've got a waterproof coat with you, haven't you?' he asked, looking a little concerned.

Zoe rolled her eyes. 'Of course.' Even she wasn't that stupid. This was an English summer, after all.

Damien seemed to have inhaled his sausage sandwich while she'd been staring heavenwards and grumbling about the weather, and now he glugged the last of his tea down and bounded up top with all the restraint of a springer spaniel.

Zoe slid forward onto the table until her cheek met polished wood and then stared at her mug with one eye. Damien had better be right about this perfect day of sailing ahead, otherwise he might just have a mutiny on his hands.

The wind sliced through Damien's hair, lifting it at its roots, and he turned his face to the wind. *Dream Weaver* was listing about forty-five degrees, her sails full, and he stood with one foot on the sloping cockpit floor, the other on the leeward bench and both hands on the tiller.

As he'd told Zoe—perfect sailing weather. They were making fabulous progress. In fact, if they kept this up they might even make the Scillies a day early. And if there was one thing Damien liked better than sticking to the plan, it was being one step ahead of the plan.

Thinking of Zoe... Where was she? He hadn't seen her since he'd hoisted the sails and cut the motor, and that had been over an hour ago. She was missing all the fun.

'Zoe?' he yelled in the direction of the hatch. He'd go and find her, but the wind had been steadily increasing in force and he needed both hands to hang on to things. In fact, an extra pair of hands would be a godsend. He opened his mouth to yell again. 'Zo—'

A dishevelled copper head appeared in the hatchway. The face, however, was grey and her eyes were huge. He'd never noticed before that they weren't brown but a more woody olive-green. Unfortunately, the ashy colour of her complexion was bringing the colour out nicely.

'Not feeling too hot, I take it.'

She shook her head and turned to go back inside.

'You'd be better out here,' he added.

Slowly, she twisted back to look at him, her disbelief obvious.

'No, really. It's just like being car sick. Keeping an eye on the horizon and plenty of fresh air will help.'

She stayed where she was for a second, but then continued up the steps. It was then that he realised her waterproof coat had some kind of animal print on it—in luminous pink, for goodness' sake. He knew he shouldn't, not when she was feeling so rough, but he couldn't help himself. He had to fake a cough so he could cover his mouth and hide his smile. There was nothing predictable about Zoe St James.

Once in the cockpit, she shuffled over to one of the benches and turned as if to sit down and huddle in the corner. Before she could do so, he grabbed hold of her and positioned her on the other side of the tiller. 'Here, hold this,' he said, and shoved it into her hands. 'I just need to check on something.'

Zoe let out a strangled noise which could have been a scream, and the boat lurched as she lost control for a moment. Damien, however, had learned his lesson from the first day on board *Weaver* with Zoe, and was hanging on to one of the shrouds that ran from the deck to support the mast.

She needed something to do, something to keep her mind off feeling so queasy—and he could use the help when it was blowy like this.

'Hold it steady,' he shouted back, meeting her wide eyes with his own focused gaze and noting the thin line of her mouth.

'But I don't know what I'm doing,' she shouted back. The

last word was muffled somewhat when a clump of ginger curls landed in her mouth.

'You're doing fine,' he said. 'Just hold her steady. See that radio mast up on the cliffs?'

She spat her hair out of her mouth and nodded gravely.

'Just keep aiming for that. I'll be back with you in a second.'

He did what he needed to do but, once back in the cockpit, he stayed just far enough away to prevent Zoe handing the tiller back to him. She was looking better already. He just had to keep her concentrating on something other than her head and her stomach.

'Now you're here, I could do with some help. I want to change the direction of the boat. If we keep going on this course we won't end up where we want to.'

Zoe squinted at him. 'Can't we just point the boat in the direction we want to go?'

Damien opened his mouth to give a mini-lecture on the subject, but then had second thoughts. He jumped down beside Zoe. 'Try it. Move the tiller in the opposite direction to where you want to go: left to turn right, or right to turn left.' He pointed to the south-west, where the little harbour town of Mevagissey awaited them. Tentatively, she gave the polished wooden tiller a push and was rewarded with a slight change of course. When she was happy with that, she tried again, bolder this time, and *Dream Weaver* turned into the wind.

Immediately the mainsail deflated like a let-down party balloon and the jib flapped wildly. The yacht began to slow, no longer pushing through the waves.

'Oh…' said Zoe, suddenly looking very worried. 'What did I do?'

Damien smiled. 'Don't worry. That always happens when you turn the boat into the wind. The sails can't catch any of it. So when our destination is the same direction as the wind, we have to tack—or make a zigzagging path—sailing with the wind on one side and then the other.'

Zoe looked up at the flapping mainsail. 'Oh, I get it. So I just need to push this thing a bit—'

'Hold on.' Damien reached out and grabbed the tiller, steadying it with his hand. 'See this sail at the front? It's called the jib. If we're going to tack now we have to loosen the ropes that hold it in—the sheets...' he noted Zoe's raised eyebrows '...I'll explain later. We have to loosen the sheet on one side and tighten it on the other, so the jib can move over to the other side of the boat. You can help me winch.'

Zoe's cheeks were flushed pink now and the dullness had gone out of her eyes. 'Okay,' she said, smiling slightly. 'Holding ropes...I can do that.'

'Just do what I say and you'll be fine.'

She let out a dry laugh. 'Ah, so that's what this is all about! I bet you can sail this boat with just your little finger. This is your excuse to order me around.'

'Chance would be a fine thing,' he replied.

But she paid attention and followed instructions all afternoon as they criss-crossed the bay. At one point he handed the tiller back to her, pointing out the compass heading she needed to stick to, and she actually grinned at him.

'How do you know all of this stuff, exactly what to do?' she asked. 'Are there hard and fast rules, tables and numbers to learn?'

'Partly,' he said, leaning back against the cabin wall and watching her handling the tiller with confidence now. 'But you never know exactly what's going to happen until you get out on the water. No two sailing days are identical, and that's half the fun of it—pitting yourself against the wind and the waves, making it to your destination despite the obstacles, knowing that you were ultimately in control of these unpredictable forces, making them work for you rather than against you.'

Zoe frowned a little, but one side of her mouth curled up. 'Who are you and what have you done with the real Damien Stone?'

He stopped smiling. What did she mean by that?

'Oh, come on...' Zoe said, chuckling slightly. 'You? Going with the flow, dealing with the unpredictable? Doesn't really sound like you, does it?'

'Then you don't know me very well,' he said, and looked out over the grey waves. 'When you're sailing you have to be flexible, and I can be as flexible as the next guy.'

Zoe's guffaw had him snapping his head back round to look at her. 'If the next guy is a tin soldier, maybe...'

Damien stood up straight. 'I think you're making a rather sweeping statement.'

She sighed. 'Damien, I have never met anyone as structured as you. You have a plan for everything.'

'Not everything,' he mumbled. Not really. He hadn't planned to come on this holiday with Zoe St James, had he?

She did that thing with her eyebrows again. 'Oh, no? So what time are we supposed to be sailing into Mevagissey harbour?'

He shuffled a little, then took the tiller back from her. 'Three-thirty...if the wind stays like this.'

'Exactly,' Zoe said softly, and then she walked to the edge of the cockpit, rested her hands on the side of the boat and stared out towards the cliff. 'But what if we decided we wanted to take a detour?'

Damien pressed his lips together. Detour? What sort of detour? There was nowhere else to go.

Zoe was smiling at him. He didn't like that smile.

'There's a beautiful beach over there—totally deserted. Can we go and have a look?'

Everything inside Damien stiffened, and he knew that Zoe saw every muscle fibre snap to attention. He could tell it from the way that annoying little smile grew even more asymmetrical.

'You can't cope with it, can you?' she said, her voice almost a whisper, her eyes sparkling. 'Admit it.'

He was admitting nothing. He'd spoken the truth earlier on. Sailing required a man to be flexible, yes, but a sailor was always in control of the decisions—when to sail, when to stay in port, which sails to use, what compass heading to go on. And if he wanted to he could choose to go and visit a beach he'd never even noticed before, even if he'd been sailing these waters for more than ten years. Just because he'd got into the habit of focusing on that mast on the headland, it didn't mean he couldn't do things differently this time.

He pulled the tiller towards him and let *Dream Weaver's* sails out as the boat turned and the wind came full-on from the port side. And, with one last longing look at that spike of metal on the hill and with the sensation of a ticking stopwatch inside his chest, Damien pulled hard on the tiller and headed off to the strip of yellow where sea met cliff.

CHAPTER EIGHT

THEY eventually made it to the harbour village of Mevagissey, so pretty it featured on many a 'Greetings from Cornwall' postcard. The old fishing port filled a sheltered valley and was further protected by a sturdy harbour wall. The houses had spread beyond the narrow streets and up the surrounding hillside so they seemed to perch on top of each other, all vying for the best view of the bay.

'The joys of sailing, huh?' Zoe said. Her fuchsia leopard-print rain mac was plastered to her head and was making her feel very sweaty, which was no mean feat, considering it had condescended to put up with ten minutes of rain and spray before giving up and letting any moisture that landed on it in.

Damien was tying a rope round a cleat on the quay. He jumped back on board *Dream Weaver* in one smooth motion. 'If I remember rightly, it was your idea to take a "detour". We might have been here by the time the weather hit otherwise.'

Yes, there was that. But she wasn't going to tell him that sticking to the plan might have been a good idea after all. That would undo all the good work she'd done that afternoon.

And what a detour it had been! Something new to experience, all right, but not exactly what Zoe had been expecting. Oh, the beach had been fun—while the weather had lasted. They'd dropped anchor a short way away and had taken the dinghy to the shore. Then they'd walked along a virgin beach that may not have seen another human footprint in months, thanks to the remote location. Even Damien had looked as if he was enjoying himself—which had been part of *her* plan. Mr Live-by-the-timetable needed to learn how to loosen up a little, stop and smell the roses, and Zoe had decided that she was the one to teach him. It was a fair exchange for teaching her how to sail.

But the pearly bright sky had changed within ten minutes of landing. It was as if that dark cloud she'd seen that morning had been stalking them, staying out of sight until it had its chance to pounce.

Damien had told her repeatedly that it wasn't a gale and they were perfectly safe, but she felt as if, just as he'd said in his rather impressive speech, they'd pitted themselves against wind and waves on the journey into Mevagissey. Pity that the final score had been elements one, humans zero. She didn't think she remembered ever being so wet and cold.

She would have added *miserable* to the list, but she had a horrible feeling she'd almost enjoyed helping Damien sail *Dream Weaver* to her destination. Despite the hair plastered to her face and a coat with a hood that was so useless it didn't matter if it was up or down, an adrenalin surge had warmed her insides. Or maybe that had been the quiet look of approval on Damien's face every time he'd caught her eye.

Blast that rain cloud. She'd have been safer if she could have kept out of his way and sunbathed as normal.

And blast Damien Stone for being right again. Not following the rules—the handed-down wisdom of generations—would have been disastrous in all that wind and rain, she could see that now. Not the time for reacting from her gut, but for thinking ahead, doing as she was told. None of her friends would have believed their eyes if they'd seen her. She'd moaned long and hard about the weather conditions to compensate, though. Now *that* was more like the Zoe St James everyone knew and loved.

'Well, Master and Commander of the ocean,' she said in

a droll tone, casting a look in Damien's direction. 'I'm off to get warm and dry and clean.' And then she hauled her aching limbs down the stairway and into her cabin.

She bundled herself into the tiny little shower-slash-bathroom and scrubbed and soaped until her body was no longer tired and achy, until she smelled of something other than damp clothes and salt. By the time she got dressed again she started to feel more human, which meant she was more likely to act like it. Always a good thing.

Zoe emerged from her cabin just as Damien was pulling on a clean sweatshirt. The sight of a lightly tanned and muscled back sent all the words she'd had ready to say flittering out of her head. He must have heard her because he turned round suddenly and looked at her.

'Hi,' she said. Obviously one word—a very basic one—had decided not to desert her. She was very grateful to it. Then another one came back to roost. 'Sorry,' she added.

His eyebrows raised. And was that the start of a smile she could see at the corners of his mouth? She couldn't tell.

'For moaning on and on about the weather,' she added. 'I get a little tetchy when I'm soaked to the skin.'

He blinked and his face remained totally deadpan. 'You do surprise me.'

Zoe felt a little bubble of laughter rise up in her throat. She hiccuped and let it out. 'Never been known to suffer in silence, me,' she said, smiling a little. 'But with four older brothers who liked to use me for wrestling practice, there's a reason for that.'

Damien nodded and shrugged. 'I'm an only child, so I wouldn't know about wrestling or brothers. I'll take your word for it.'

Ah, of course he was. She could see it now—that telltale air of entitlement and confidence that could only come from being the apple of Mummy and Daddy's eye. Unlike Zoe, who had been an unplanned late addition to her clan of sport-loving, high-achieving brothers. Her mother always used to joke that she hadn't known what to do with a girl after all those boys, and Zoe reckoned it had showed. She'd been the tagalong kid, always trailing after her brothers to their different sports matches, always standing in their much larger shadows.

'I can teach you a few good headlocks if you want.'

She'd started talking in a jaunty voice, just making a joke to cover things over the way she always did, but by the end of the sentence her mind had flipped away from wrestling matches on the living room carpet to having her arms wound round Damien, exploring that fine back she'd just had a glimpse of, and in her daydream they definitely *weren't* wrestling. Her voice trailed away and she realised the extra layer of clothes she'd put on had been one too many.

Damien didn't have much to say to that either, so they just stared at each other for a few seconds until he moved towards her, making her jump.

He cleared his throat. 'We need to find you something more practical to wear than that…pink thing.'

Zoe glanced through the high, narrow windows of the cabin at the gloomy sky. It was only late afternoon and on a sunny day it would have been light for hours longer, but today it seemed as if twilight had already cocooned them.

'I could buy something tomorrow, but it doesn't look as if it's going to let up this evening.' She sighed. 'I'm probably going to get drenched all over again on the way to dinner.'

Damien did his own reconnaissance of the sky, frowned, then looked back at her. 'Maybe not,' he said mysteriously, then moved past her to open the cupboard opposite the bathroom. Zoe scampered out of his way, noting that as he'd got close her internal thermostat had risen another couple of notches.

No, she told herself. Not a good idea. He's not for the likes of you.

Damien returned only moments later with a bright yellow jacket on a hanger.

'I remembered Luke and Sara had some spare oilskins in the locker,' he said and handed her the hanger.

Zoe slid the waxy rubber duck-coloured coat on. The arm length was fine, but over the bust? Not even close, matey. She blushed hard and shrugged it off quickly.

What had she been thinking? Of course she wouldn't fit into Sara's coat. She never tried on her friend's clothes any more, remembering the few times she had and knowing that the results in the mirror would mock her. Not a natural clothes horse, was Zoe, because she wasn't as slender as Sara. But then there were a lot of ways she wasn't like Sara. Not as pretty. Not as clever. Not as popular. The list was practically endless.

And now Damien had seen her in Sara's jacket, he wouldn't be able to help making the comparison, just like everybody else did. She looked at the floor as she handed the jacket back to him.

'I'm not sure I'm that hungry, anyway,' she mumbled. 'Maybe a bowl of cereal would do.'

He really should look at her face, not where his gaze had slid and snagged when she'd tried to pull the coat tight across her chest. Heat flooded his torso and it took him a couple of seconds to register what she'd said, but the words finally filtered through. Move your eyes *now*, Damien, before she looks up and catches you staring where you shouldn't.

He managed it just in time. A split second later Zoe's focus flicked from the wooden floor to his face and then back again.

She had no idea, did she? Absolutely no idea that she'd brought him to a gibbering standstill, that she'd drained all his willpower away, making him question whether following through on the unacknowledged attraction between them would really be as catastrophic as he'd first thought. She wasn't his type at all.

His body begged to disagree.

He told his body to shut up.

Damien was used to taking control of every urge that was counterproductive to his grand life goals, and he squashed this one down alongside all the others. Pity he didn't notice that, just like an overstuffed ship's locker, there was hardly any more room in that place where he stuffed all those whims and desires and dreams he didn't like. Things were starting to bulge out. One day soon the lid might just pop off, exhausted from keeping all those pesky things at bay.

'What if I went out and brought back some takeaway?'

There was another one of those rogue urges now. It slid free and hit him between the eyes just as Zoe looked up at him from under her lashes and bit her lip.

Kiss it, the urge said. *Taste that lip—bite it, even.*

'You'd do that for me?' she said quietly.

He nodded emphatically. Air. Space. Those were things he needed in large quantities at present. And a cold shower, courtesy of the English summer, probably wouldn't hurt.

'What do you want?' he said, backing away, pretending he was reaching for his jacket. 'Fish and chips? Pizza?'

He saw the gratitude in her eyes, and a third jolt hit him.

No. That shouldn't have happened. This was only supposed to be a physical attraction. It wasn't supposed to happen when she looked all soft and vulnerable and un-Zoe-like for a few seconds.

But he needn't have worried. She offered him a reprieve. Seconds later the softness left her, replaced by an over-bright smile and animated hand gestures as she talked.

'You're forgetting there's one more coat in the cupboard,' she said, grinning at him. 'One that shouldn't find my physique so much of a challenge.' And before he could stop her she pushed her way into the little upright locker and had re-emerged with Luke's oilskin. She threw it on and zipped it up, battling with sleeves that were easily four inches too long, and finished it off by buttoning her hood up under her chin. Not a flattering look for anyone.

'I hear pregnant banana is in this season,' she said, giving a little twirl. And then she'd stuffed her feet into her trainers and headed for the hatch. 'Come on, you. There's a Korai Chicken in this town with my name on it somewhere.'

Damien had no choice but to shrug his coat on and follow. He wanted to reach out and stop her as she bounced along the quay in the direction of the high street. Don't do that, he wanted to say. Don't make a joke of yourself and turn that biting, acidic humour inwards.

The clear, damp air hit Damien's nostrils and he breathed it in deeply as he followed Zoe into the heart of Mevagissey.

That was what she did, didn't she? Used that rapier humour of hers not only as a weapon but as a shield. A very cunning approach. People were usually too busy licking their wounds after a bout with Zoe to look too hard at their attacker, to notice the wounds that went wider and deeper in her.

Underneath all that brashness, Zoe St James was as defenceless as an urchin without its shell, and she used her quick brain and her creativity brilliantly to make sure nobody ever guessed the truth.

As they trudged the narrow streets looking for a curry house, Damien began to wonder who'd put those wounds there and how long they'd bled.

He realised now that Zoe was at her snappiest, funniest and most irritating in his presence. It had been her default position with him since almost the first day they'd met, and he started to wonder what on earth he could have done to raise her alarm to maximum alert. What was it about him in particular that set her defences mile-high?

* * *

It was as if the weather had decided to apologise for its bad manners the next morning, rewarding them with a day that was as bright and clear as it was warm and breezy. Damien suggested setting out early, trying to round Lizard Point before the day was out, and Zoe didn't disagree for once, slightly repentant and willing to let him have his plans and stick to them—at least for one day.

Later in the afternoon the wind dropped significantly, but it gave Damien a chance to do something he'd wanted to do but had held off doing with just the two of them on board. A bigger crew was needed to do this when the wind was stronger, but now he could get the spinnaker out.

Zoe followed instructions, helping with the brightly coloured sail on the foredeck, as he dealt with what needed to be done back in the cockpit and winched it up. She was audibly impressed when the wind caught it and took it high above the bow, making it look like a captured parachute. She spent much of the rest of the journey there, sitting with her legs posted through the metal railings at the tip of the boat, dangling towards the water.

Damien stayed in the stern, smiling. He'd known she'd like the rainbow-coloured spinnaker and had actually been glad the wind had dropped enough finally to get it out for her, as a reward for all her hard work the day before, possibly. A week ago he would have expected her to throw a tantrum over the bad weather, but she'd been amazing. She'd followed every instruction he'd given her in the difficult conditions perfectly, and he hadn't had to repeat anything.

The afternoon passed with them at their opposite ends of the boat but, unlike before, when Damien had felt the resistance, like two magnets pushing each other away, it now felt easy. Peaceful. So peaceful, in fact, that Damien was shocked when he looked at his watch and realised time had been slipping away far too quickly.

It was late in the afternoon and he hadn't kept a check

on their progress. The silent sense of satisfaction that had paused time that afternoon quickly ebbed away. Rounding the Lizard would take more hours than they had before nightfall. He called Zoe back down from the bow and explained the situation.

'We're going to have to pull into Falmouth and attempt the Lizard tomorrow,' he said as she stepped down into the cockpit, looking windswept.

'That wasn't the plan. Won't it put us behind schedule?'

He kept his face expressionless. 'We've got a new plan now. It's called being flexible. See? I can do it, even without your prompting.'

Why was she laughing? Well, almost laughing. Her eyes were, even if her mouth wasn't.

She turned away and looked towards the large sprawling estuary where three rivers met and merged before pouring into the sea, a jumble of bays and creeks.

'Cool,' she said brightly. 'It looks pretty here.'

So they took down the spinnaker, furled the sails and motored towards civilisation. Unfortunately, it seemed the rest of Cornwall had decided to converge on Falmouth that weekend—some big regatta was on—and every marina space or mooring was fully booked. They ended up dropping anchor in a sheltered bay on the opposite side of the estuary, just across from the smaller town of St Mawes.

Zoe was ecstatic at their makeshift anchorage for the night. It was a truly beautiful spot. And they'd have missed it, he realised, if they'd powered straight past and headed round the Lizard. Perhaps there was something to be said for detours after all.

The sun was glowing low, just skimming the top of the steep hills, and blistering heat had given way to languid warmth. They were round the tip of the Roseland peninsular, in a sheltered little bay close to a beach. St Mawes, to the north, could be reached easily by the dinghy, and off to the east was a stately home or hotel, its elegant green lawn reaching down to a stone wall at the water's edge.

'Can we swim here?' Zoe asked, practically jumping from foot to foot. 'I feel like a roast chicken and I'm dying for a dip.'

'I don't see why not.'

Zoe squealed and ran below decks, appearing again with all the speed of a quick-change act in a retina-searing multi-coloured kaftan thing over the top of her swimming costume.

'Are you coming in?' She reached for the hem of her kaftan and headed for the metal ladder at the stern. 'It's close enough to swim to the beach.'

They were indeed only a hundred feet away, and it was a very pretty little beach. The sea was the other side of the peninsular, but on this side jagged cliffs gave way to a curved green hill, ending with a strip of woodland near the shore. A lone cottage sat between trees and sand, a low, off-white stone building that must have been there for centuries.

However, despite the picturesque surroundings, the beach was almost empty—probably because the layout of the es-tuary demanded winding roads, and this would be quite a drive from the nearest town with no bridges to speed things up. Only the most determined of beach-hunters would make it this far, leaving the casual holidaymakers to the spots with toilets and cafés and places where they could buy rubber rings and blow-up crocodiles.

Suddenly the thought of that cool water against his sun-baked and salty skin was almost irresistible. 'Give me a min-ute,' he said, and dived below decks to quickly slip on some swimming shorts.

When he returned, Zoe was nowhere to be seen. He could tell where she was, though, from the series of little shrieks coming from the direction of the ladder.

At the end of the summer the water here would be the warmest it would be all year round, but a heated swimming pool it wasn't. He peered over the railing at the back of the cockpit, grinning, and found Zoe, up to her waist in water, a look of frozen shock on her face.

'Still desperate for that dip?' he asked. 'It'll be better once you're in.'

Zoe just scowled up at him. 'Clear off and let me do it my own way,' she said.

Damien decided that was a very good idea, partly because it could be Christmas before she got off that ladder, and partly because his vantage point was giving him a wonderful view of her cleavage, even though it was encased in a modestly cut one-piece. A figure like Zoe's was impossible to hide. For which he was momentarily very thankful.

But then he remembered all the lectures he'd given himself over the last couple of days. It wouldn't be fair to either of them to start anything—well, *continue* what they'd started the night of the wedding—because it just wouldn't go anywhere. They were too different. He knew what kind of woman he wanted: a woman like Sara...

Sara. He realised he'd hardly thought of her in days. Which meant Zoe had, in fact, been doing a fabulous job as a temporary distraction, just as he'd planned. It just wasn't the kind of distraction he'd envisaged. Still, if it was working...

Anyway, since Sara, he'd decided he wasn't going to waste his time dating for the sake of it. Finding the right woman to share his life with was his focus for the moment, and he couldn't—shouldn't—let himself get side-tracked.

In which case, more cold water would definitely help.

He made his way to the side of *Dream Weaver* nearest the beach, climbed over the guard rail and jumped straight in, welcoming the way the chill drove all thoughts of Zoe from his head as he struggled to catch his breath.

CHAPTER NINE

THEY swam and explored the beach until the sun had almost set. Zoe would have continued to swim there all night if she could have, but Damien suddenly got twitchy, talking about dinner and how busy it would be even in St Mawes, so Zoe reluctantly followed him back to the boat.

He looked so tense by the time they climbed back on board that they just shoved casual clothes on over the top of their swimming things and headed straight off in search of a café or pub in the dinghy.

Just as Zoe had expected, they were fine. They found a pub that served bar snacks and, yes, they had to wait a while for their food and pad the meagre portions out with a couple of packets of crisps, but their tummies were full at the end of the evening, and surely that was what counted?

When she saw Damien scowling at the empty packets, Zoe couldn't help but make an observation. 'You really *don't* like to veer from the plan, do you?'

Damien shrugged as he drained the last of his beer. 'I don't see the crime in that. Plans help you get where you want to go in life.'

She had to give him that. He'd certainly proved that in his professional life.

'You have plans for your business, don't you?' he asked.

Zoe nodded. She had plans, she supposed, although she liked to think of them as dreams. It sounded less suffocating.

'And once you lay down your plans, you start working towards making them a reality, don't you?' Damien added.

Zoe nodded again, although this time she started thinking about her dream of owning her own premises. What exactly *had* she done to make that happen, aside from wandering round other people's shops and sighing? Not a lot, actually.

'But surely there has to be some balance,' she said. 'It can't be work twenty-four hours a day. What about room for fun, the joy that can only come from following a mad impulse?'

Damien's eyes instantly narrowed and his shoulders tensed. When his next words came out, they seemed to have been squeezed out between his teeth. 'What about the chaos that can follow? You were the first one to moan when your "impulse" to divert from the course yesterday afternoon didn't end well.'

'Okay, I admit that, but you have to step outside the box occasionally, follow your heart sometimes?'

Damien pushed his chair back and stood up, even though he hadn't finished his drink. 'That's the problem with people like you. You jump in and "follow your heart"—' he almost sneered as he said those words '—and don't even notice the trail of destruction you leave behind you.'

Zoe smiled, but it was a puzzled smile. What was he talking about? What trail of destruction? Yes, she'd knocked him in the water a few days ago, but apart from that she'd done nothing.

'Nobody said life was perfect. Sometimes it's unpredictable—' her smile grew '—you said it yourself! It's like sailing. Dealing with the unexpected challenges life throws at you, navigating those treacherous times… Aren't those victories the ones that give you the biggest sense of satisfaction in the end?'

Damien shook his head and walked off back towards where the dinghy was moored. 'You don't get it.' There was a hopelessness in his tone that snagged at Zoe's heart, sidetracking the smart reply that had been ready and waiting on her lips.

She followed him in silence until they were back in the little grey inflatable and heading back out across a moonless, glass-smooth bay. He cut the engine as they neared the stern of the boat, letting them float the last few feet, and Zoe stood up and secured the painter to a cleat. She turned to face him, one foot on the ladder, before climbing up on to the yacht.

'Who disappointed you, Damien?' she asked softly. 'So badly that you don't even want to have fun any more?'

He snorted. 'Fun! What good is fun when you've got people who love you, that need you? Pursuing fun like that is selfish...' He seemed to realise he'd said more than he'd meant to and closed his mouth abruptly.

Zoe climbed up the ladder and waited for him in the cockpit, but when Damien climbed on board he walked straight past her, up on to the deck, and sat down on the cabin roof, staring at the oscillating reflections on the water that the vibrations from their outboard motor had caused.

Mad or not, Zoe followed the impulse to go to him. She'd never seen Damien before. And, even though seeing him rattled like this had once been her chief desire, now the moment was here she found it uncomfortable. She climbed out of the cockpit and went and sat next to him. The ridge of the hand rail that ran along the top of the low cabin roof dug into her bottom.

'Who left you behind in their wake of destruction?' she asked, then fell silent. She didn't push, even though she was burning with curiosity.

Night birds that Zoe couldn't name cooed. Gentle ripples, the memory of a boat passing by somewhere else in the estuary, licked the hull. And those shards of reflection had almost mended themselves together again by the time Damien spoke.

'It was my father,' he finally said, his voice strangely scratchy. 'He followed one of those impulsive urges to have fun when I was fifteen, decided to up and leave my mother and I with hardly any warning. He just sat us down at the kitchen table one day, announced he was bored and unfulfilled, and the next day he was gone, off to do something about it.' He turned and looked at her. 'He never came back.'

Zoe laid a hand on Damien's hunched shoulder. 'You didn't ever see him again?' she asked, her voice husky.

Damien blinked slowly and stared back out at the water. 'Oh, I saw him again, but he didn't come home. My mother was heartbroken.'

Zoe swallowed. She didn't have anything to say—smart, sympathetic or otherwise. Instead, she slid her hand along his back and laid her cheek on his shoulder blade.

'So forgive me if I'm not overwhelmed at the idea of following a mad impulse,' Damien added, giving a good impression of Zoe's most sarcastic tone.

She nodded against his back. 'Did he ever find what he was looking for, your father?'

Damien laughed. A low, heartbreaking sound. 'I think he's still looking. That was the funny thing…' He turned to look at her and Zoe peeled her face from his warm cotton shirt and looked back at him. Their faces were close now, only inches away.

'He had a good job, a wife who adored him and ran around after him doing everything she could to make him happy. He had a son who worshipped him. In other words, he had a life many people would kill for. For years I asked myself why it wasn't enough.'

Zoe was finding it a little hard to speak, not only because she was so close to Damien, but because all sense of superiority she'd ever thought she'd seen in his eyes had been stripped away and behind it she only saw pain and defeat.

'Did you ever find any answers?'

Damien nodded and heaved in a deep breath. She saw him start to build the layers of protection back around himself and she wanted to yell out, tell him to stop, but this was the urge she managed to curtail. If anyone understood the need for those layers, it was her.

'My father had unrealistic expectations, for a start. He'd always dreamed of a better life—more money, more social success—and he got to his mid-forties and realised he didn't have what he'd expected he'd have, and he blamed us for it.' He shook his head. 'The stupid thing was that he couldn't see that it was his fault, not ours. He should have worked towards those things instead of just daydreaming about them.'

He gave her a ghostly smile, his teeth shining white in the darkness. 'He should have had a plan.'

Pennies dropped hard and fast inside Zoe's head now. His father's failure had been a catalyst to Damien's success. She understood now why he was so clear about what he wanted, why he pursued those dreams as if demons were on his tail and, to be honest, she couldn't really blame him for it.

She sighed and joined him in looking out to the little stone cottage on the beach, a fuzzy shape of blue-grey above a strip of silver sand.

'Plans aren't everything,' she said quietly, and heard the same emptiness in her voice that she'd just detected in Damien's. 'Even the best laid ones can backfire and blow up in your face.'

Damien turned to her, and even in the semi-dark she saw the deadness in his eyes had turned back into that one settling, penetrating focus. He trained all of it on her.

'What do you mean?' he asked, and Zoe began to regret that urge to follow him after all.

She shuffled a little, repositioning her well-padded behind on the wooden grab rail. 'I mean that you can plan all you like—dream all you like—but that doesn't mean those things are definitely going to happen.'

Damien's expression told her he'd never even considered such an outrageous notion. 'Such as?'

Zoe shook her head. She didn't want to talk about this. Not with him. Especially now she'd seen under that perfect, polished exterior to the warm, human man beneath. She was already in too much danger; she couldn't let her barriers down as well.

'Zoe?'

She grimaced, her face turned away from him. Her big, fat mouth had got her into hot water again. When would she ever learn?

'You know... Just plans... Things...'

'What sort of things?'

He wasn't going to let this go, was he? And her insides were starting to twitch, to tell her she shouldn't be such a coward, not when he'd opened up to her.

She moved away from him a little, sat up straighter. 'Like weddings...'

'You had a wedding planned?'

His voice was soft and sympathetic, delicious in the anonymous darkness. Could she? Could she confide in this man—a man so like the one who'd broken her heart?

'My love-rat groom phoned one of my bridesmaids from his stag do and confessed his undying love for her.'

There went that mouth of hers again. Really, she was going to have to get herself a muzzle one of these days.

Damien muttered his judgement on her errant fiancé in the form of a rude name.

'Thank you,' Zoe said. And she meant it. Suddenly she was very glad that Damien managed to say and do the right thing ninety-nine per cent of the time. The word had been perfect.

'What about the bridesmaid?' he asked.

Zoe sighed. 'I have better taste in friends than I do in men, it seems. She told him to grow up, and then she did the gutsy thing by coming and telling all to me.'

She leaned back on her hands and stared up at the moonless sky.

'It was a bit of a buzz kill, I can tell you. There was I at the karaoke bar, in full hen night regalia—net curtain veil on a headband, angel wings and L-plates—three verses into "Stand By Your Man". I hogged the mike a bit after that, I'm afraid, Alanis Morrisette being my artiste of choice.'

She let out a little laugh but, instead of floating away on the night air, it seemed to hit the deck.

'You don't have to make a joke out of this, Zoe.'

She breathed in sharply through her nostrils, furiously ignoring the stinging on the backs of her eyes. 'Actually, I do.'

Hold it in, Zoe. You can't let it all out.

'So, you can see why I'm not big on plans any more,' she added.

Damien swivelled round so he was facing her. 'You don't ever plan to get married or have children? Don't let one loser ruin it for you.'

One loser. Ah, if only there'd been just the one. No, Aiden had merely been the one she was stupid enough to let close enough to hurt her.

'I'm not saying I won't, just that I'm not setting my heart on it. I'll just live my life and see what happens.'

Damien nodded, but his expression told her he couldn't think of anything worse.

'Anyway,' she said, 'this is supposed to be a holiday. It's practically illegal to get maudlin.' She stood up and rubbed the grab rail dent out of her backside. 'I've found that the best way to cheer myself up is to do something new, something unexpected.'

One option was to lean into Damien and seek refuge against his shoulder again. But that would be truly pathetic, especially as he must think her a horribly sad case after her recent revelation.

The only other thing she could think of doing was to pull her cotton jersey sundress over her head, kick off her shoes and jump overboard. And that was exactly what she did.

She'd thought the water would be colder than it had been earlier in the day but, if anything, it felt warmer. Probably something to do with the ambient temperature of the air being closer to that of the water, she thought distantly as her head went under.

She opened her eyes just before she broke the surface again, kicking upwards, and at first nothing made sense. Tiny specks of bluish-green light danced around her. It was as if the stars had dropped out of the sky and had sprinkled themselves on the surface of the water like icing sugar on a cake. She laughed as soon as her mouth was above water, and then spun around, treading water arms outstretched.

'It's magic!' she yelled, feeling like a kid on Christmas morning. What was this? Every time she moved the water sparkled around her, as if she were setting off miniature underwater fireworks. She stopped spinning and swam away from the boat and the lights followed, clinging to her, dancing with her. After a few strokes, she turned and trod water, looked back to the dark shadow sitting on the roof of *Dream Weaver*'s cabin.

'What is this?' she yelled, her voice musical with latent laughter.

The shadow stood up, moved to the edge of the deck. Zoe stopped laughing, closed her mouth and trod water silently. Suddenly she felt very, very serious and she didn't know why.

Damien watched her from the deck. He hadn't planned to stand up; he'd just been drawn to her, had moved closer without even thinking. He couldn't take his eyes off her.

Sara would never have done this—jumped into the sea at night on a whim, relished in the natural phenomenon so totally and completely—and for once he was one hundred per cent glad that this wasn't Sara. This moment was Zoe's, hers and hers alone.

She'd gone still and, even though he couldn't see her face,

Damien realised she was watching him, waiting for him to speak. He gave her something better. Something unexpected.

He slipped off the T-shirt he'd thrown on over his long swimming shorts, prised his feet from his deck shoes and joined her.

She screamed as he jumped in, and then she laughed. Not the same kind of sound as a few moments earlier—this one was part shock, part nervousness—but he couldn't help but join her in that also. He didn't think he'd ever swum while laughing before, and he discovered it involved drinking more salt water than he'd wanted to. For some reason, that just made him laugh harder.

The water lit up around him too, linking them long before he reached her.

'It's phosphorescence,' he said between deep breaths when he started to tread water beside her. 'Tiny little biolumines-cent marine life forms that react to movement.'

Zoe's eyes grew wide. 'All this? From plankton?'

'Pretty much.' He moved his arm through the water again, just to see them sparkle almost neon green. He'd seen it be-fore, of course, tiny specs of light trailing behind a ship on a dark night sailing, but he'd never got down *into* the water and swum in it before—and he wouldn't have done, if not for Zoe's mad impulse to jump overboard.

She'd called it magic, and while his very logical and prac-tical brain refused such definitions, part of him was starting to agree. Maybe it was the setting: the quiet, secluded bay, the stately home in the distance. Maybe it was the water, so flat that every reflection was perfect.

He stopped watching the bright flecks dancing round his fingers as he used his hands to keep himself afloat and looked at Zoe, totally absorbed in doing the same thing.

Maybe it was this woman.

Maybe she'd brought the magic with her, because he'd

seen this phenomenon before but had never felt this sense of wonder.

He turned the next arm movement into a splash, dousing her with water.

She screamed. Loudly. But there was no one here to shush them, so he did it again.

'Right!' she spluttered. 'You've asked for it.'

He discovered Zoe was a worthy opponent. She held nothing back in trying to dunk him under. But his arms were longer, always able to keep her at bay, and without the weight advantage—which she didn't have, no matter how much she moaned about her curves—she had no hope of success.

At least, that was what he thought until she disappeared under the water and didn't emerge again. He searched for her, backing away from the spot where they'd been splashing, hoping the telltale creatures would give her away, but...nothing.

Now Zoe wasn't with him, the night air around him was horribly quiet. He started to get worried. Where on earth was—?

The next thing he knew, his head was under water and a four-limbed female limpet had clamped herself to his back, dragging him down, their combined body weight doing the job that she'd hadn't been able to achieve on her own.

He kicked hard and made some headway. She must have been holding her breath for quite some time, because suddenly she stopped fighting him and they both floated upwards.

When they broke the surface, she slid round to his side, hands locked behind his neck, ankles crossed over his opposite hip, and let him do the job of keeping them afloat. Once she'd gulped in enough air, she laughed triumphantly, letting the sound echo all the way to St Mawes.

And then there was silence again and they were staring at each other, bodies locked together, both breathing hard.

He shifted a little, brought her round so they were chest

to chest, face to face. Her eyes widened and he felt her heart start to thump beneath the hand he had splayed on her ribcage.

She didn't say anything. No quick retort to make light of the situation, to ease awkwardness. She just looked back at him, breath held now, lips parted.

This time he didn't kiss Zoe St James because she pushed him to the end of his rope, or because an unwanted attraction had raged out of control. He didn't even have to kiss her to shut her up.

No, this time he kissed Zoe because he wanted to.

She was hesitant at first, letting him lead, but gradually she relaxed, softened and pulled him closer by sliding her arms around his neck. It was still there, the chemistry, crackling between them, even though he made sure this time was different, that he slowed things down so the kiss was soft and achingly light. He was surprised they hadn't lit the whole bay up with the sparks they must be generating.

Keeping both of them afloat got harder and harder, and eventually he had to break away. She instantly unhooked her legs, slid out of his arms and kicked away, going into retreat, but he caught her hand, tugged, as he started to propel himself towards the beach.

At first she resisted slightly, but no sound left her lips, no complaints arose, and then she swam with him, kicking with her legs and flapping with her free hand as he did. It wasn't long before he found sand beneath his toes and he dug his feet in to anchor himself. Zoe floated into him and he kissed her again as soon as she was close enough, and he enjoyed the fact that, because he was a good six inches taller than her, she couldn't reach the bottom and she had to cling on to him for support.

In fact, he decided he liked kissing Zoe St James very much. Not just because of the undeniable chemistry between them, but because, when she stopped talking and let all her barriers down like this, there was an intoxicating sweetness to her.

She kissed him slowly, almost innocently, savouring every sensation as if she couldn't quite believe it was happening and that he was part of a delicious dream she might wake from at any second. He defied any man not to be rendered helpless by a kiss like that.

She was a surprise, this one, that was for sure. A mix of intriguing contradictions. But hadn't she said 'new and unexpected' was good for the soul? And when she kissed a trail down his neck and tasted the salt on his collarbone, he decided she might have a point. He could easily get lost in this, forget about everything that had plagued him in the run-up to that torture of a wedding just a week ago.

Zoe's lips left his shoulder and she leaned in close to his ear. 'This isn't part of the plan, is it? Separate holidays, remember?' she whispered.

He moved his head so he could look at her. Her mouth was set in that familiar quirky smile, but her eyes were large and questioning. Vulnerable.

He ran the hand that had been pressed against her back, holding her to him, round to her waist, delighting in the soft curves. 'Do you *want* me to stop?' he whispered back.

She shuddered underneath his hands and, while her eyes grew even larger, she shook her head.

'I don't want separate holidays any more,' he said before kissing her just below her ear. 'That was a stupid plan.'

Her voice was breathy and barely audible when she answered. 'Then what do you want?'

'I want you.' He pulled her close again, dragged his lips across hers. 'I want a holiday with you.'

CHAPTER TEN

DAMIEN lay awake on his bunk, staring into the darkness, hardly able to see anything in the cabin on this moonless night, even though the portholes weren't obscured. He checked his watch—three in the morning.

But he wasn't tossing and turning on the long berth in the main cabin, taking his frustration out on his pillow or tangling himself in his sleeping bag. He was perfectly calm and relaxed. In fact, he couldn't remember feeling this relaxed in a long time. He'd sunk straight into this serene state after the adrenalin rush brought on by kissing Zoe had worn off.

They'd eventually swum back to the boat, kissed some more, and then she'd said goodnight and retreated into her cabin, almost shyly. He got it. She was blindsided and a little scared. He supposed he should be too, but he couldn't seem to summon up the energy.

His gaze wandered over the interior of the cabin. He was starting to be able to make out a shape here, a line there. *Dream Weaver* might not be the most state-of-the-art yacht on the high seas, but she was welcoming and comfortable and he'd really enjoyed sailing her for the last week. So much that he'd started to wonder if borrowing her for a couple of weekends a year was enough.

Zoe had a point. Perhaps he didn't have to wait for his dream yacht. Perhaps he *should* get a 'good enough for now' boat, one he could moor closer to London and sail when he liked.

Ah, Zoe…

She blew him away. But she wouldn't fit in his life long-term. Probably wouldn't want to, but maybe that was okay too. He'd spent—no, wasted—over a year pining for a woman who'd never be his. That was where his 'stick to the plan' mentality had got him. He'd got so fixated on the idea of Sara he hadn't been able to shake her loose from his head, even when he'd desperately wanted to.

Where had that plan got him romantically? Nowhere. So why had it taken him so long to work that out and decide to move on? It didn't make sense, even to himself.

But he had decided to put the past behind him now, thankfully, and maybe this borrowed honeymoon had given him the perfect opportunity. He genuinely liked Zoe, and not just because of the strange, unexpected and rather explosive chemistry they seemed to have. She was good company, and she shook things up wherever she went.

Damien had an idea that maybe he *needed* a little shaking up, that maybe he'd got too entrenched in his ways in recent years, and he suspected his crewmate might just be good for him in that respect. In small doses.

So, while Zoe St James definitely *wasn't* the missing jig-saw piece in his future, maybe, if she was open to the idea, she could be his 'just for now' girl.

Oh, heck, thought Zoe, as she got dressed the following morning, sliding a sundress on over her swimming costume. But she was smiling, and she touched a fingertip to her bottom lip, then let the hand fall away again.

What are you doing? This is insanity.

You can't seriously be considering getting involved with this guy. He's too… And he's too… And you're definitely *not*.

Aw, phooey. He was hot. Seriously hot. And a fabulous

kisser. She might be mad *not* to follow this attraction wherever it may lead.

Wherever it did lead, one thing was sure: the end destination would never be an altar. And that was fine by Zoe. Thinking of Damien standing there, waiting for her, it gave her the heebie-jeebies. Too much like déjà vu. And she wasn't making that mistake again.

No, when she finally was ready to take that step she'd choose someone like her. Someone in her own league. Someone who wouldn't realise suddenly that he was punching *way* below his weight and do a flit. No. Lesson learned on that front.

But that didn't mean she couldn't have a little fun...

Be careful, a little voice in her head said as she opened her cabin door, pulse racing, a shoal of quicksilver fish darting around in her stomach. *Put some limits on it. Set some ground rules for yourself.*

Have a plan.

She opened her cabin door and went looking for Damien, still not quite sure how she was going to navigate the tricky line between fun and heartbreak. He was up already, his sleeping bag and pillow stowed away and the seating bench put back to normal, but there was no sign of him in the cabin. Her heart was thumping wildly now. She pulled in a breath and let it out slowly through pursed lips, and then she climbed the stairs into the cockpit.

Damien was leaning over the back of the boat, messing with the rope for the dinghy. He must have heard her coming because he turned round and gave her the most wonderful smile.

She felt herself blush furiously. What was up with that? She thought she'd given it up long ago, had decided one required a sense of shame to do such things. Even Damien had told her she had none.

'Hi,' she said, and found she had an almost irresistible

urge to look down at her toes. She managed not to. Which was just as well because Damien's face crinkled even further.

'Hi.'

She felt all awkward. Didn't know what to do... Should she go and kiss him? Shake his hand? What?

Damien saved her from further dithering by crossing the space between them, wrapping his arms around her and kissing her soundly. Zoe didn't mind a bit. Top result as far as she was concerned. And it proved it hadn't been some elaborate dream brought on by dodgy pub grub—that a man like him could find a girl like her desirable.

But they couldn't stay like that all day, more's the pity, and eventually they came up for air, made some breakfast, got ready to set sail for the day.

It hovered in the air around them all day, though, as if there was some intoxicating chemical in the sunshine. She found herself smiling doing the most mundane things, and every time he caught her eye she thought her heart had stopped, but it always kicked back into life double strong, and then tap-danced for a few minutes inside her chest.

She'd forgotten what it was like, this heady sensation of being totally caught up in an attraction. For the last two years she'd avoided it. Not that she hadn't gone out, but she'd always seemed to pick men who were pleasant but not heart-stopping. She was so bored with *nice* now.

She'd forgotten what she'd been missing.

They didn't round the Lizard that day. Instead Damien took them upstream beyond Falmouth and St Mawes and they tacked up the River Fal, zigzagging from one bank to the other. After the rougher weather a couple of days earlier it was easy to work alongside each other. Comfortable. They were a good team.

When they dropped the sails and used the motor to explore one of the tidal creeks they discovered a gorgeous little medieval church on the bank, set incongruously in a garden of palm trees and tropical ferns. They dropped anchor close by and went ashore to explore the parish of St Just-in-Roseland.

Sitting on the grass in the church garden, looking out over the estuary bathed in bright golden light, Zoe turned to Damien.

'What are we doing?'

He lay back on the spiky grass and smiled at the sky. 'I think it's called relaxing, but I'm new to it. I'll let you know when I've got a handle on it.'

She poked him in the ribs, then lay down beside him. 'You know what I mean.'

He rolled over on to one side and looked at her. Zoe stared defiantly at the sky, watched a little turtle-shaped cloud chase a bigger, wispier one.

'What do you want it to be?' he asked softly, and the low rumble behind his words made it sound slightly naughty. She twisted her head round and gave him a penetrating look.

'Not games,' she said. 'Not pretending it's something it's not. Let's be honest about it.'

'Agreed.' He nodded, a serious look creeping into his eyes. 'But does it need a label?'

She breathed out noisily. 'Maybe not. But I think it needs a time limit.'

He thought about that for a moment, chewed one side of his lip. She wasn't sure he'd liked what she'd said, but he saw the sense in it. 'Okay,' he said.

'We both know there's an obvious cut-off point.'

There. She'd saved him the trouble of saying it should end with the holiday.

He blinked and shrugged the shoulder that wasn't supporting him. 'That doesn't mean it doesn't mean anything,' he said gravely, those blue eyes boring into hers.

Thank you, she whispered inwardly. For being honest. For being brave. For not making me feel disposable.

'It means it's a summer fl—'

He pressed a finger to her lips. 'No labels, remember? Let's just enjoy this for what it is, see where it leads us.'

She assumed a look of mock-seriousness and laid the back of her hand to his forehead. 'I'm sorry, but this is you—Damien Stone—saying these things. Are you sure you haven't got a temperature?'

He gently peeled her hand away from his head, turned her palm towards his mouth and did something amazing with his tongue that made Zoe's toes actually, truly curl up and her eyes slide closed. Whatever fever it was, it was catching.

She pushed hard against his chest with her free hand, sent him toppling backwards and, while he was still grunting in surprise, she swung one leg over and sat on top of him. Then she kissed him slowly, sensuously. *Hello*, the kiss said, *to whatever new thing this is*. It felt as if they'd crossed some invisible barrier into new territory and it needed to be marked somehow.

Damien didn't reach up for her or pull her to him. Instead he lay spreadeagled on the grass, a slight smile curving his lips as he kissed her back. 'To answer your first question,' he muttered between kisses, 'I don't know what this is.'

Zoe ran her hands up inside his T-shirt and let her fingers explore.

'But whatever it is,' he added hoarsely, 'it's certainly working for me.'

Zoe felt like a goddess. There was something intoxicating about being slap-bang in the centre of Damien Stone's attention. And while part of her panicked every time she noticed a similarity between Damien and her ex, another part told it to just calm down please and take a breath.

She wasn't marrying this one, was she? It was safe. And they'd both been honest and upfront about their expectations. He wasn't going to leave her unexpectedly; they were going to leave each other at the end of the week. Mutual decision.

Six more days with Damien, with a man who made her heart skip because he enjoyed being with her. Six days when he'd look at her and she'd see fire ignite in his eyes. Six days to feel the comfort of his arms around her when she just needed to be close to someone.

It had been a long time since she'd let anyone close.

In fact, it had been a long time since she'd had that kind of physical contact with anyone—hugs that lasted more than a few seconds, a hand to hold, a warm body to mould herself against. The play-wrestling her brothers still attempted at family get-togethers didn't count. Really, it didn't.

With Damien it counted. And, while she knew this couldn't last, she would be forever grateful to him for that. He was healing something inside her. Something she hadn't even known had been broken.

It was a blustery, sunny day and, rather than heading round Lizard Point and making progress to the Scillies, Damien had suggested sailing up the neighbouring Helford River to have lunch. Nothing fancy, just sandwiches and salad and a bottle of crisp white wine that had been chilling on the end of a rope over the side of the boat. She was sitting in the cockpit with Damien when he picked up the sketchbook she'd been doodling in before lunch.

'You're going to make these up when you get back,' he said, but there was no inflection at the end of the sentence. It wasn't really a question. He was like that. Driven, focused, specific. Things she'd previously despised about him that now made her shiver in anticipation. There was something to be said for a man who knew how to apply that attention to detail when it came to women. Oh, yes.

Zoe shrugged and took a sip of her wine. 'Probably.'

It was difficult. Those designs had somehow become caught up in her head with the idea of having a shop, and she didn't know if she could make one real without the other. She'd have to wait, work on something else when she got back.

But Damien was learning to read her too well. 'Why not?' he asked.

Zoe gave him the kind of look that she knew used to make his red blood cells sizzle and pop, but nowadays it just caused him to do things like he did just then—carefully prise the wine glass from her fingers, place it on the bench, pull her on to his lap and kiss her.

She was so dizzy when he'd finished with her that she told him about her dream for a workshop, for getting clients who would commission one-of-a-kind pieces with her unique twist to them. A chance to really let her imagination fly.

'So...look for properties when you get back,' he said. 'Start small, build up.'

She shook her head. 'I'm not ready for that yet. I'm not at that stage. It's still early days.'

'What do you need to get it to that stage, then?'

Zoe picked up her wine glass again and pressed it to her chest, the fingers of both hands wrapped around the stem. 'I need to visit the bank manager, make some kind of projections, I suppose...' Get some guts.

Damien used a finger to tip her chin up and make her look at him.

'You can do this,' he said seriously. 'You've got spark, you've got flair. You can make this happen, even if you're not so good with the organising side of things. Doesn't matter. Get an assistant who is.'

Zoe stuttered, although she wasn't sure which word was stalling on her tongue.

'It'd be a shame to never see these designs made up,' he said. 'So do it.'

'I...I can't.'

Where had that come from? She hadn't been planning on saying that at all.

Damien, as always, zeroed in on the root of the problem,

but there was such a tenderness in his eyes that she found herself saying more things she hadn't planned.

'I'm scared.'

His thumb stroked her chin. 'Of what?'

Zoe didn't know. She was just scared. Scared of trying and failing, maybe. Of investing in something with all her heart only to see it wither and die.

She pulled her chin away from his hand and looked down. 'I wouldn't expect you to understand this, but not everybody's dreams come true. Not everyone can do what you do.'

Much to her surprise, Damien began to laugh. But the warm, rich sound she was used to was now dark and self-mocking. 'You think I get everything I want out of life?' He ran a hand through his hair and looked away momentarily. 'Believe me, I don't.'

She clutched the stem of her glass even harder. 'What dreams are still eluding you? I can't believe you've got much left on your to-do list! You're successful and confident and clever.'

His eyes flashed with sudden warmth and she knew he was grateful for the compliments, which struck her as odd because surely he knew all these things about himself.

'What am I known for, Zoe? What do people joke about me?'

Well, she knew what *she* used to say about him, but now was really not a good time to re-hash that, so she thought harder. 'That you're always the best man, I suppose. But even that's not fair. A man just looks better and better the more times he gets asked to do that. Me, I've only been a bridesmaid once and I've already got my mother telling me I'd better not make a habit of it, especially since I've got one false start under my belt.'

He squeezed her hand and his expression became more sombre. 'I understand, because I feel the same way. Don't you think I'd like to be the groom instead of the best man some day?'

Now it was Zoe's turn to laugh. 'Well, I don't think you're going to have any trouble on that score. I mean, look at you! They must be queuing up around the block.'

Damien didn't join her. There wasn't one glint of amusement in those hard blue eyes. Zoe exhaled and looked deep into her wine glass. 'If you want it so much, why haven't you got married before now?'

She felt him go still underneath her. This conversation had got too serious to be sitting on his lap, but she didn't know how to get off without making it seem like a judgement of some kind. And she of all people knew just how much it hurt to be judged when you were down.

'Haven't found the right girl?' she asked softly, trying to inject a bit of levity into this rapidly sinking conversation.

When he didn't reply she looked up at him.

'Something like that,' he said wearily.

And then a sudden knowledge hit Zoe. Where it had come from she didn't know, but she realised she and Damien had more in common than she'd thought. 'You liked someone and they didn't like you back the same way.'

Like her and Aiden. She'd worshipped him, but she suspected she'd just been an amusing diversion for him. Some mad impulse he'd thought better of eventually.

Damien's hands came around her waist and he lifted her off him and stood up. The non-slip bench was rough and cold against her legs. He sighed and walked over to the back of the boat, staring out at the water below. 'Pretty much. She was in love with someone else.'

Zoe put her wine glass down again and went to him, curled her arms around his body and pressed herself against his back.

'It'll happen for you,' she said. 'I know it.'

'How do you know?' he replied, and his tone held a tinge of bleakness.

She tugged on his T-shirt, pulled him round to face her and looked up into his face. He placed his hands on her shoulders and looked searchingly into her eyes, as if he was trying to read what she was going to say before her lips moved.

'Because you're a leading man,' she said. 'You're that type that good things happen to.'

Confusion clouded his features. 'What?'

He hadn't been expecting her to say that, had he? Now she needed to explain.

'It's like in the movies,' she began, and Damien's expression became sceptical. She slapped him on the chest. 'Hear me out, at least.'

One corner of his mouth twitched, so Zoe continued.

'I have a theory that there are two types of people in this world—the romantic leads and the backup characters. Romantic leads are the sort of people we'd all like to be, or be with, like—' she stopped herself saying *you*, thinking he'd scoff and stop listening '—like Sara.'

There was a flicker of something on his face. 'Go on.'

Zoe shrugged and smiled. 'I have to tell you that it's hard work being best friends with a girl like her. She's pretty, clever, sweet... Good things come her way naturally. She hardly has to even try. Look at her now, off in Paradise with the man of her dreams. I mean, you can't get any jammier than that, can you?'

Damien pursed his lips. He was listening to her intently now.

'And what about the other sort?'

'Oh, the sidekicks? They get their happy endings too... sometimes. It's just that it's not always as shiny and perfect. Some of them have to compromise, settle a little.'

'The two don't mix?'

She shook her head emphatically. 'Well, not long-term. The honourable best friend might date the girl for a bit, and we all think he's adorable, but you know she's going to end up with the leading man.'

Damien frowned. 'Is that what you're trying to tell me? That I need to set my sights lower?'

Zoe's mouth dropped open. He really thought that was what she meant? She gave him a shove with the flat of her hand, then, before he lost balance, she clutched on to the front of his T-shirt and pulled him down towards her for a kiss.

'No, you daft man,' she whispered. 'I'm saying you're the other sort. Look at your life, all you've accomplished. The rest will come too. Just don't lose hope.'

Damien slid his hands down to her waist and pulled her even closer, began to kiss the soft patch of skin between jaw and ear. 'So, if I'm a leading man, who are you?'

Zoe let her head drop back to give him better access. She blocked out the pang of sorrow that spiked through her at his words. Not the same, she whispered silently to herself. But she had other words to say out loud.

'I'm the girl who's making the most of having him wrapped around her, that's who.'

CHAPTER ELEVEN

DOWN a cobbled street in Falmouth was a second-hand book-shop stuffed to the brim with both yellowing volumes with a few decades' worth of dust on them and dog-eared bestsellers from last Christmas. Damien discovered it had quite a good sailing section, not surprising, he supposed, for a shop in a town like this, where white sails decorated the waterfront on almost every day of the year.

He'd moored here plenty of times before when he'd been with Luke, but he'd never been to this curious little shop, never mind this street, always in too much of a hurry to re-stock and sail on.

There'd been plenty of other places on the large and sprawl-ing estuary that he'd never visited either, but Zoe seemed to have a talent for sniffing these things out, and he was rather enjoying staying put, using Falmouth as a base and discov-ering the things that he'd never noticed before. Reaching the Scillies was now looking less and less probable, but some-how he didn't mind.

Zoe squealed. 'I don't believe it!'

She came running through labyrinthine bookshelves to-wards him, clutching a large coffee-table book, and almost sent half a display flying in her enthusiasm to reach him. He smiled. Once he'd thought her 'too much', but now he found her verve a little bewitching. Things were certainly never dull when Zoe was around.

'Look!' she said, almost yelling, and shoved the book so close to his face he couldn't focus on it.

He took hold of it and moved it to a distance where he wasn't required to go cross-eyed. 'Beautiful Beaches of Britain.'

She tugged it away from his grasp and started to leaf through it, cooing and making all sorts of exclamatory noises. That was Zoe. She couldn't just say *Oh!;* she had a whole rainbow of responses.

She had a whole rainbow of responses to him too. Sometimes she was bold and bossy, sometimes she was soft and almost shy. He never knew what he was going to get from one moment to the next. It was a bit like a roller coaster, with all of the thrills and adrenalin. Perhaps it was just as well this wasn't going to be a long-term thing. He'd like to enjoy his time with Zoe, not reach a point where he was numb and slightly nauseous and wanted nothing more than to leave it behind.

She smiled up at him. 'My aunt had this book. I used to flick through it every time we visited. I dreamed of visiting each and every one of these beaches, especially the dramatic cliff-backed ones in Devon and Cornwall. Look at that—!'

She thrust the book at him. He had to admit, it was a very fine picture of Kynace Cove, with its dramatic rocky shore and island reached by a bar of sand at low tide, not too far away from where they were now.

'So which ones do you still have to cross off your list?'

Zoe stopped smiling and her mouth hung slightly open. 'Um…'

He waited for her to remember the names, or at least point to a picture in the book. It was at least a minute before he realised that answer would never come.

'You haven't been to any of them yet, have you?'

She shook her head.

Damien chuckled in bemusement. 'Why not? You're all

grown up now. You've got a car and a free weekend every now and then. What's stopped you?'

Zoe closed the book softly and tucked it under her arm. 'Nothing, I suppose. But I...'

Damien tipped his head to one side, a lopsided smile on his face. Zoe moved the book to her front and crossed her arms over it. She looked a little confused.

'I just liked looking at the pictures...' She trailed off, obviously reliving some long-archived memory. 'These beaches seemed like dreams, not real places I could actually go to one day.' She frowned. 'That's stupid, isn't it?'

'What would be stupid would be not taking the opportunity to visit some of them when we're so close.'

The expression on Zoe's face almost made him laugh again, but he held it in. Even though they'd been sailing round the Devon and Cornwall coast for over a week now, she hadn't thought to mention this before? The possibility must have crossed her mind.

'You think we really could?' she said a little breathlessly.

Damien pulled her close, book and all, and pressed a kiss to the tip of her nose. 'We made a deal—I'm your deck hand and skipper for the next five days. I'll take you anywhere you want to go.'

Zoe's response was so enthusiastic that she dropped the book on Damien's toe.

Zoe ran up to the front of the boat as they neared Polkerris Beach. She hung on to the metal rails of the parapet and leaned forward, Titanic-style, her arms outstretched.

The photo in her aunt's book had only paid partial tribute to its beauty. Steep, rock-scarred hills rose either side of a swirl of pale yellow beach, held safe from the changeable Cornish weather by the protective arm of a curved sea wall at one end. She knew this beach had inspired a famous novelist, and Zoe had liked that book of hers when she'd read it at school, the one about the girl trying to fill another woman's shoes and not really succeeding. She'd have to read it again when she got home.

She turned to grin at Damien back in the cockpit. They'd abandoned the idea of the Scilly Isles and opted to stay in the Falmouth area, as it was the perfect base for exploring the wonderful local beaches. This was the third one she could tick off her list, the third of her childhood wishes granted. And this man had made them happen.

That night after they'd been to the bookshop he'd settled down at the navigation table on *Dream Weaver* and had got out his maps and charts. Zoe had tried to join him, but the little bench seat had clearly been made for one and she didn't have the right kind of skinny behind to slide in beside him, so she'd hugged him from behind, hanging round his neck like a college boy's sweater, until he'd shooed her away.

She hadn't even minded that he'd been completely absorbed for the next hour or so, or that she'd fallen asleep on the long cabin bench Damien used as a berth reading her book. She'd woken later in the night to find herself covered with an opened-out sleeping bag, his unconscious form across from her on the opposite bench.

Damien might have ignored her, but she hadn't cared because no one had ever done anything to make her feel so special.

Oh, she knew that had been the deal they'd made on that first morning—that he'd take her where she wanted to go. But a lot had changed since then. It wasn't because he had to any more, but because he'd wanted to.

Plans had changed. She had changed. She'd even go so far as to say that Damien had undergone a transformation, but she wasn't really sure that was true. She'd just tarred him with Aiden's brush from the beginning, not seen what was right in front of her.

He wasn't anything like Aiden. Not really.

Yes, he had the same ilk of good looks, the same kind of confidence, but Damien was kind and thoughtful where her ex had been self-important and shallow. She shuddered to think back to how much she'd adored him now, how much she'd let herself disappear and change to please him. But it had never been enough.

She should have seen the warning signs; they'd been there, after all.

She should have minded that he used to joke about their initials to friends constantly, as if he'd come up with the funniest gag in the world and couldn't resist sharing it. 'I'm the A and she's the Z,' he used to say, and Zoe had laughed along, even though, after the fourth airing, her smile had become pinched instead of open.

She turned her attention back to the sunny beach. She didn't want to think about Aiden any more. And Damien never made her feel like that—second class to his first class.

A pair of strong, warm arms closed around her. A taut, muscled body pressed against her back. Zoe stayed with her arms outstretched, eyes closed, and breathed in the moment. Pretty soon a pair of soft, firm lips began to work their way up from her collarbone to her ear. She twisted as he got there to kiss him properly, even though it made her neck ache horribly.

'I've got to drop the anchor or we'll float all the way to Portugal,' he mumbled against her lips.

Zoe sighed. 'If you have to.'

He gave her a nudge. 'You're in my way,' he whispered in her ear, his low voice tickling her skin and making her break out into goosebumps.

'Give me a minute. I just need to finish my *moment*.'

Damien just rumbled a laugh as she faced front and began to sing.

'What *are* you doing? Calling whales?'

She reached behind and slapped him wherever she could reach. 'It's the song from the film. Join in! You might as well.

We've got you, me, the front of a boat…It's the least we can do to provide the soundtrack.' And she carried on singing into the wind.

Damien just laughed harder, picked her up in his arms and threw her into the vibrant blue water. When Zoe came to the surface, spluttering a little and wiping the curls from her eyes, she yelled, 'What was that for?' But she didn't mind, not really. Damien was surprising her, doing things she'd never thought he'd do, and it was turning her carefully constructed walls into chocolate.

He was busy letting the chain out to drop the anchor. 'I fast-forwarded. That's how the film ends, after all.'

She paddled her legs to keep herself afloat. 'I think you'll find the hero ends up in a much more sorry state than you are. Still…there's time yet!'

Damien finished his job and stood smiling down at her, hands on hips, legs apart. Zoe couldn't help smiling back.

It was working. She was letting go of all that baggage she'd been dragging around with her since the night of her hen do, and it was such a relief to see it float away and disappear. She couldn't remember a time when she'd been happier.

And then there was a splash and Zoe's eyes were sprayed with salt water. She opened them again to find him swimming towards her. Her heart kicked and the resulting adrenalin spike made her want to move, to run. To fly. Since she could do neither of those things, she settled for swimming.

'Last one to the beach is a rotten egg,' she shouted, then set off to churn up the waves with her notoriously haphazard front crawl. Damien would probably catch her, but Zoe decided she didn't mind that one bit.

That night they moored where they had the first night they'd arrived in the Fal estuary: opposite the little beach with the stone cottage. But time had moved on and a few days had turned the previously absent moon into a sliver of pale shimmering white just above the horizon. When they jumped in the water the magic was gone.

It doesn't last, Zoe reminded herself. Magic like this doesn't last.

And neither would her time with Damien; she needed to remember that. Only...sometimes it was so difficult. She knew this was dangerous, knew it would be so easy to tumble head over heels for this man.

Only a few more days together. The tide on their holiday had turned and now they were heading in a different direction. Tomorrow they were setting sail back off up the coast towards the River Dart and Lower Hadwell. And then they'd go their separate ways and it would all be a beautiful memory. As long as she could last out, hold onto her heart for a few more days, she'd be okay. She could last that long, couldn't she?

Easier said than done in a setting like this, she thought, as she peeled her T-shirt off over her swimming costume. She didn't even think twice about it now, even though she got uncharacteristically shy normally when displaying her curves, but Damien seemed to like them, and suddenly it didn't seem quite as important to keep the flimsy cotton barrier on.

This time she followed Damien's lead and jumped straight in. He was right. It was easier that way, rather than prolonging the torture by climbing in slowly.

They swam to the beach and strolled along it, holding hands, stopping every now and then to wind themselves round each other and kiss. The beach was even more beautiful with a touch of moonlight to turn its sand bluish-white.

Damien stopped walking and pulled her to him, his hands exploring her bare torso, his lips working the magic that the water had forgotten.

She knew where this was leading and twin desires warred inside her—the desire to have Damien completely, to know him completely, and the desire to keep herself safe. It had taken two years to get over Aiden's betrayal and, while she knew Damien wasn't like that, it wouldn't do to fall for him. This wasn't to have and to hold, to love and to cherish; it was just for now.

Just a few more days. People did this all the time—had flings, walked away unscathed. So could she. And being with Damien would be...amazing. So what if she hadn't quite managed to sleep with anyone else since Aiden? She'd moved on. She was ready now.

He pulled away and she could tell he was looking at her intently just by the way he brushed his thumb across her cheek. 'I'd really like to take you out to dinner when we get back to London,' he said.

That was when Zoe began to wobble. Inside.

Say no.

A fling with a time limit was one thing. Something they took home, carried on back in London? That was too much like a relationship for Zoe's liking. She'd never be able to hold herself back emotionally, not if it went on for weeks or, heaven help her, months. She couldn't fall for him. Not this one. Another man who wouldn't want her for ever.

At least this one had the honesty to say that upfront, though.

She pulled away, tried to wriggle out of his grasp. 'I'll race you back to the boat,' she said brightly and stepped back.

Damien caught her hand. Gently. Far too gently. Zoe felt moisture well behind her eyes for some reason. *Please let me go*, she begged silently. *I need some distance, some kind of barrier.*

He didn't pull her back to him, but stepped towards her, keeping his grip round her wrist feather-light. She was glad it was too dark to see the look in his eyes. That might have been her undoing.

'What's wrong?' he said gently, and his free hand reached out to touch her face.

Zoe closed her eyes, partly to block him out, partly to stop the bead of moisture hanging on her lashes from falling onto his fingers and giving herself away. She shook her head, effectively dislodging his hand and refuting his words in one small motion.

He moved closer, but he didn't touch her again. He even let go of her wrist. 'I know you,' he said, his voice low and far too soft. 'Don't hide from me.'

But I need to. I really do.

It was happening already, wasn't it? She could feel herself melting under his touch, her chest squeezing painfully from his tenderness and concern for her. Even with the stupid time limit, she wasn't safe. She should have realised. She shouldn't do what she'd been planning to do with him now. It would seal her fate.

He kissed her softly, tenderly, almost drawing her secrets from her. Zoe's throat tightened even as her lips moved in tandem with his. She couldn't hold back, not any longer. So she threw away all her masks, let down every last barrier and kissed him the way she'd always wanted to, telling him what she would never say with her lips.

That was when things got really scary. And wonderful.

They were doing more than just kissing now. They were communicating. And, while their bodies were still—just about—clothed, it felt as if whoever Damien and Zoe were inside those cases of flesh and bones and nerves were totally naked. Transparent. Zoe found she couldn't breathe. She'd never realised it could be this way, but it was too... It was too much.

She pulled her lips from his, pushed her hands on his chest to help her gather just a few inches of distance before she lost herself completely.

Her voice was hoarse and thready when she spoke. 'I know we said this was a fling,' she began. 'But I don't know if I'm ready to...'

She didn't say the last bit. Coward.

Damien's warm arms closed around her shoulders, pulled her close. She laid her cheek against his chest and breathed him in.

'If there's one thing I've learned this week, it's that rushing to the destination sometimes robs the journey of its joy,' he said softly.

A wave of something washed over Zoe. She called it gratitude, but she feared it was something else.

'I know it will be amazing,' Damien said softly as his fingers ran lightly down her back, making her shiver, 'but it has to feel right for both of us.'

Zoe really wanted to tell him she wasn't sure that was such a good idea, but the soft seductive tone of his voice and the lazy circles of his fingers on the back of her hips had severed the connection between brain and tongue.

'So let's not end it now. I've spent too much of my life sticking doggedly to a self-imposed timetable. I want to do things the way you do it. I want to savour the experience, enjoy the journey, not miss the best bits because I'm rushing to the end goal.'

She shivered again, but it was nothing to do with his fingers and everything about the thought of Damien applying his new philosophy to his lovemaking. That approach could make a girl very, *very* happy.

His voice was low and coaxing in her ear. 'So, have dinner with me on Saturday night, Zoe, when we get back. Let's see where this thing can go.'

Unfortunately, while her head was firing excuse after excuse in his direction, her mouth just said, very clearly and politely, 'I'd like that.'

Oh, you stupid girl. You shouldn't have said that.

But the warm ball of hope that had ignited inside her chest at his words had completely derailed all her good intentions.

Maybe there was a chance. Maybe he really, really liked her. And, for now, *maybe* was enough because Zoe St James had not just discovered she could dream again, but she was learning how to tug their delicate strings and pull those far-off images towards reality.

They'd been lucky with the weather, they knew that, but their luck didn't hold much longer. The forecast two days later wasn't terrible; it just wasn't that good either. Damien loved it, of course. Scudding clouds and an impatient breeze behind *Dream Weaver*. Zoe, not so much, but he kept her busy on deck, where she wasn't as fond of the pitch of the boat as he was—she was still only just discovering her sea legs—but she was learning the basics well. If she ever decided to keep this up, she could be a pretty decent sailor. She had the instinct for it.

They headed for Bantham Beach anyway, but when they dropped the sail and surveyed the shore Damien held off lowering the anchor. Zoe came to join him in the cockpit and stared landward with him. 'Problem?'

Damien nodded. 'The water is shallow here quite a way out, and the surf is pounding against that shore. The flags say swimming would be dangerous, and the dinghy would probably flip over.'

'So it's no go for this one.'

'Not from a seaward approach, anyway.' He made rueful face. 'Sorry.'

Zoe frowned and stared at the beach. He waited for her to say something funny and biting to take the edge off her disappointment, but she just closed her mouth and put her hands on her hips.

She'd been in a strange mood all day yesterday: one moment enthusiastic and funny as always, the next quiet and pensive. Distant. As if she was backing away from him, which didn't make sense. He'd have thought she'd be pleased he wanted to see her again after their holiday. Maybe she didn't like him as much as he thought.

And that would be a pity. He discovered he could relax around her. Probably because, since they hadn't exactly warmed to each other on first meeting, he'd never gone into full-out *impress* mode. And it was a little late to start now. Zoe had already seen more of his bad side than most people did. However, it hadn't put her off completely, and it was kind of refreshing not to have to live up to his own reputation.

She turned away from the beach and sighed. 'It doesn't look as pretty as the picture in the book, anyway.'

He took a long, hard look at the shore, the jagged grey rocks piercing the flat and endless sand, the dunes behind them covered in fluffy grass. On a sunny summer's day this would be the perfect place for a family: rock pools aplenty to explore, a wide beach that shelved gently, leaving plenty of warm places where the sun heated shallow pools of sea water when the tide went out. But now the tide was in, angry and grey, and the breakers over the shallow sand relentless.

'A different kind of pretty, maybe. But the beach hasn't changed, has it? Just the weather. Maybe it's all in the way you look at it?'

She sat down on the cockpit bench. He sensed she couldn't quite bear to look at the source of disappointment. He could understand that, he supposed. This had been one of her favourites.

'We could always try again tomorrow,' he said.

'We've got to have this boat back on its mooring in two days, you said. I thought the schedule was pretty tight.'

It was. But he wanted to do this for her, see her happy again. 'We'll see.'

Zoe's arms dropped and hung limp by her side. 'Maybe this one wasn't supposed to come true.' And then she stood up and loped down the stairs into the cabin.

He wanted to go to her, kiss her until he saw that naughty sparkle in her eyes again, but the weather wouldn't allow it. They were too close to the shore and he couldn't let *Dream*

Weaver drift in this kind of weather. It would have to wait until they reached dry land.

For some reason, he started thinking about what she'd told him the first night they'd moored at the beach, about her fiancé. His mind had drifted in that direction quite a few times in the last few days.

What must it have been like? To have the whole of your life mapped out, a date set, a venue booked, dress chosen and fitted...for it all to come to nothing? He understood now why she had that cynical streak, why, despite her exuberant positive personality, she was reluctant to hope and plan for even little things. It wasn't a weakness of character that prevented her from pursuing her dreams, just the scars of previous failed attempts. And Damien knew himself just how hard those things could sting.

She came back out on deck an hour later, helped him as they prepared to sail into Salcombe for the night. Her smile was back on, her wit at one hundred per cent capacity. He knew it for what it was now. Emotional wallpaper. And so thin. How had he ever thought her hard and insensitive?

It made him want to turn the boat round, sail back to that beach and command the sun to come out, the waves to be still. However, despite the cracks that some of his friends made, even he didn't have the power to do those things, so he stayed silent and guided the boat up the river and towards the busy marina.

But it bothered him that he couldn't. He wanted to do something to thank her for all she'd done for him. This holiday had been just what he needed and he was ready to face life back at home now.

Then why aren't you ready to say goodbye, if you're ready to move on?

So he wasn't ready to end whatever he had with Zoe yet. That didn't mean anything. He and Zoe were combustible chemicals. Great for an instant reaction, but long-term they would be destructive. She wasn't right for his life, nor he for hers. Okay, that mental jigsaw picture of his future did not have a Zoe-shaped hole in the middle, but he was having fun. What was so wrong with that?

When they reached the marina he jumped off *Dream Weaver* to secure the bowline and as he did so he realised something.

He didn't think that hole was Sara-shaped either now. He could see someone *like* her in the picture if he tried, and that was progress, wasn't it? Zoe had distracted him enough to help him get his bearings, to at least start the process, and he was very grateful to her for that.

So why wasn't he happier? Why did he feel as if he'd been using her somehow, even if they'd both come into this with their eyes open and on equal terms?

CHAPTER TWELVE

THE last beach on the list Damien had drawn up for Zoe was Blackpool Sands, only a short distance from the Dart estuary, and they had just enough time to visit it before they left the open sea and headed upriver to Lower Hadwell for their last night aboard *Dream Weaver*.

There had been six beaches they'd wanted to visit, and they'd managed them all—bar one. Maybe one day, Zoe thought.

She knew she ought to do what Damien had suggested: make plans, book a free weekend in her calendar and drive down to add that extra tick to her list. There were still a few weeks before the weather would get colder and the leaves started to turn.

Next summer, maybe. Or the one after that.

Not yet. Because the thought of returning on her own was making her feel strangely depressed. And, really, it was time to concentrate on her career now. She didn't have the time or money to gallivant around the country if she really wanted to get a shop up and running.

She watched Damien drag the dinghy from where it had been lashed to the deck and throw it overboard, keeping hold of the painter. How different he seemed from the night of Sara and Luke's wedding. He moved easily, fluidly, the muscles across his back shifting under his T-shirt. It hardly seemed

the same body she'd done a tense rumba with almost a fortnight ago.

In fact, now that she knew him better, she realised he'd
been unusually tense that night. Hadn't he said as much when
he'd apologised for kissing her? At the time she'd thought it
was a lousy excuse, but maybe there'd been some truth to it.

The dinghy was in the water now and Damien was walking it round to the ladder at the stern, dragging it by its yellow rope.

Weddings were always stressful, she supposed. Especially
if you'd been as close to the centre of the action as she and
Damien had been.

No, that didn't sit right. The Damien she knew was contained and focused under pressure. Something had been different. He must have been *really* stressed. She knew now she'd
never have been able to push him over the edge the way she
had otherwise. If she didn't know how happy he'd been for
Luke and Sara, she'd have thought the whole idea of them
getting married bothered him somehow.

The dinghy was ready now and he grinned at her. She
smiled back.

Oh, well. Whatever it had been, he was all better now and
that was what counted, wasn't it?

While not as Mediterranean-like as the weather they'd
been blessed with the previous week, it was a passably pleasant day. The sun could occasionally be spotted between the
slow-drifting clouds and the temperature was mild. It certainly hadn't stopped the holidaymakers flocking to this popular beach, even though it was a mile or two from the nearest
town.

They left *Dream Weaver* anchored in the deeply shelving bay and took the dinghy the short distance to the shore.
Jagged pink-tinged cliffs rose either side of the beach, topped
with bright green tufty grass and populated by unimpressed
sheep. A crescent of perfect golden shingle—fine enough to

look like sand, but not fine enough to walk on without hopping now and then—arced gracefully between cliffs and road and deep blue water.

The proximity of the road meant that, unlike many of the beaches they'd visited that week, it had a car park and toilets, a café and a surf shop. After the relative seclusion of some of those other beaches, this one was all noise and colour and movement. It felt like a return to civilisation, the real world, and Zoe wasn't sure she liked that that much. The real world was close enough as it was. Let her have the last day of her fantasy holiday without being reminded it was almost over.

However, as they hopped out of the dinghy and pulled out of reach of the crashing surf, she and Damien felt like a unit of two. She hung on to that feeling.

It wouldn't be the same when they got back home, would it? Damien might change his mind about that dinner in the cold, grey light of a London morning. And maybe that would be a blessing in disguise. There would be plenty of other women around, most of them more glamorous than she was. On the boat, with just the two of them, it had been fine, but Zoe didn't do well with comparisons. She was never the first one a man's eyes went to when she went out with her single friends. Especially if that friend had been Sara.

Once the dinghy was safe they headed for the café. Zoe sat on one of the weathered picnic tables while Damien went to get ice cream. He returned with a cardboard holder containing six cones, all in different colours and flavours, and plonked them down in front of her while he started on his own plain vanilla.

Zoe laughed nervously. 'What's all this? You can't possibly want to fatten me up.'

Damien's mouth kept smiling but his eyes told her he wasn't happy with her comment. Nothing he hadn't told her in person over the last few days, nothing his obvious attraction for her hadn't chipped away at. But making a joke about her size was a hard habit to break. How else was she supposed to stop someone jumping in and doing it first? At least this way she controlled the damage, didn't look like a pity case.

She flashed a look back that communicated both exasperation and contrition. His eyes regained their sparkle.

'I got one of each flavour for you so could try them all, pick which one you like, and leave me to eat mine in peace.' And he took a huge lick of his ice cream, as if to demonstrate.

Zoe left the cones to drip while she extracted herself from her side of the picnic bench and went to sit on Damien's lap. He held his cone at arm's length, just in case, and Zoe hit him lightly on the chest. But hitting turned to touching and then she kissed him, slowly and sweetly enough not to shock any onlookers, but thoroughly enough to accomplish her goal and sweep her tongue along his lips and then inside his mouth.

She pulled back. 'Vanilla's not bad.'

Damien sat there looking a little stunned. 'If that's what buying more than one cone gets me, I'm going to do it more often,' he said gruffly.

Zoe just laughed. *More often.* He hadn't changed his mind yet, then. And she was going to make the most of that.

Right then she decided that tonight she should grab whatever bliss was on offer, make the most of a gorgeous man and a secluded boat. She'd deal with the fallout when they got back home. She knew it was reckless, but she couldn't walk away without greedily taking what she could. She wouldn't live her life wondering what it would have been like. Aiden had taught her she couldn't plan for success in matters of the heart, but that didn't mean she had to plan for failure instead, did it?

She pulled the cardboard holder over, selected the vanilla and started to lick. She didn't even slurp each of the others to see what she was missing. In fact, she donated them to a family passing by with some incredibly whiney children. The mother gave her a grateful look. Well, she did before her gaze moved to Damien and the woman almost walked into a pole.

Zoe's choice of flavour, and she was sticking to it.

Her choice.

Maybe that was where the answer lay? Instead of waiting for someone to relegate her to second choice, maybe she should be the one making the decisions for once. And the way she felt right now, with Damien's arms around her waist, the memory of warm vanilla from his lips mixing with the cold, fresh stuff from her cone, she wondered if she dared choose *this* man—the one who had pushed her over the last edge of her resistance by buying her a tray of multicoloured ice creams.

Dream Weaver rounded a bend in the river and Zoe watched the pastel coloured houses of Lower Hadwell appear with a sense of heaviness inside. Tonight they'd take the yacht back to her mooring, tidy her up and leave her ready for Luke and Sara's next visit.

After lunch tomorrow they'd both be away. Separate cars. She hoped it wouldn't be separate lives.

Was it wrong to hope for more? Because hope she did, even though she knew she wasn't Damien's usual type, knew that there would be more than a few raised eyebrows among their mutual friends when it became common knowledge that something was going on between them.

They secured *Dream Weaver* at the little marina and went below decks to start packing and tidying, after which they planned to have a leisurely dinner at The Ferryman. While she tidied, Zoe was making good use of her imagination to form *other* plans she had for Damien that night.

She had her head in the cupboard opposite the bathroom, replacing Luke's oilskin, when a muffled tinny tune chimed out from inside her cabin.

Her mobile phone!

The coverage had been so patchy for the last couple of weeks she'd almost forgotten she owned it. She quickly extricated her head and shoulders from the cupboard and launched herself into her cabin, throwing the top half of her body on to the bunk and grabbing at the little shelf on the wall where she'd left her handset.

It stopped ringing just as her fingers closed around it. She wiggled herself back off the bunk, stood up and inspected the screen.

Sara?

Why on earth was she phoning from the Caribbean? It would cost a fortune.

Zoe wandered into the main cabin, phone in hand, looking bemused. Damien looked up. 'Problem?'

She frowned. 'Don't know. I missed a call from Sara. I don't know why she—'

The phone leapt to life in her hand and she quickly pressed the button and answered. 'Hi, darling! What are you doing calling me from Paradise?'

There was a loud sniff on the other end of the line, and when Sara spoke her voice was tight and strained. 'I'm not in Paradise. I'm at Heathrow.'

Zoe dropped the phone but, luckily, she caught it with her other hand. Damien took a step closer as she pressed it back to her ear.

'You're at the airport? But you're not supposed to be back until the day after tomorrow!'

'I know,' Sara wailed. 'It's over, Zoe. The whole thing is messed up!'

Zoe's stomach went cold. 'What's over?'

'Me and Luke.'

Time stopped. Zoe's mouth refused to do anything but hang open uselessly. She swallowed and forced her vocal cords to work. 'So where's Luke?' she asked hoarsely. She was afraid she knew the answer that was coming and she didn't think she was going to like it.

Another bubbly sniff. 'Antigua, I think.'

There it was. Zoe met Damien's concerned gaze.

'You came home on your own?' she asked quietly.

Damien was closer now, his eyes fixed on her phone.

She didn't know what to do. This wasn't Sara—dramatic departures and drama queen moments. Those sorts of things were Zoe's department. Think, she told herself. What would Sara do? How would she calm you down if you were the one having the meltdown? Be like Sara—you always wanted to be and this is your chance.

Even better, she thought with a flash of inspiration, be like *Damien*. He always knew how to handle sticky situations. She'd think ahead, not just react.

'Zoe?'

'I'm here,' she said softly.

'I can't go home, Zo. Luke and I had a horrible fight. We've never had an argument like that before and I can't go back to a house full of wedding gifts waiting to be opened. I don't know what to do.'

Sara's volume was rising along with her pitch. Zoe could tell she was close to losing it completely.

'You stay right where you are,' she said. 'Book yourself into one of the airport hotels, text me the details and I'll be there as soon as I can.'

Sara sniffed. 'Okay.'

'Just don't do anything—' Zoe managed to stop herself saying *else* '—stupid, okay?'

'Okay.' She heard Sara pull in a steadying breath.

'Take a bath, order some room service and I'll see you soon.' After a few more reassuring comments Zoe rang off.

Damien's expression was taut when she looked up. He spoke quickly, words tripping over themselves to get out of his mouth. 'How is she? What happened?'

He had that look again, that look of a caged animal he'd had just before he'd given his speech at the wedding reception.

Zoe shook her head and stared back down at her phone.

'I don't know.' She met his eyes. 'They had a fight and she flew home. She's very upset.'

Damien paced down the cabin away from her and back again. Then he grabbed his jacket and started hunting for some keys. Car keys.

'What are you doing?' Zoe asked, her jaw tight.

'I was going to…' He looked up, slightly dazed, and shook his head. 'I don't know. I wanted to help.'

A hundred little details about Damien, about Luke, about Sara, came flooding into Zoe's head. First and foremost were mental snapshots of the wedding, images Zoe hadn't even realised her memory had stored: how tense Damien had seemed before the service had started, the way he'd stared at Sara when she'd walked down the aisle. The way he'd dried up just before his speech and the look on his face when he'd stared over her shoulder when they'd been dancing together.

None of those things meant anything on their own, but seen rapidly together as a montage of memories…

And then his words about the mystery girl in his past came floating back to her.

She was in love with someone else.

Zoe was sure her heart stopped beating. Dead.

No. Not like this. He wasn't doing this to her.

'*I'm* her friend,' she said sharply. 'Luke's your friend and Sara's mine, so it's not for you to go to her. That's my job.' It all came out in a rush because she was trying to drown out the little voice in her ear that was telling her things she didn't want to know.

She ran to her cabin, avoiding eye contact with Damien, and started ramming things back in her case. She paid no attention to what was going in or where it was going—much the same way she'd packed on the outbound journey, actually. She yanked her case down off the bunk and dragged it through the main cabin. Damien tried to help her but she pushed past him.

'It was her, wasn't it? The girl who didn't like you back?'

He didn't answer, and when she looked up she found him staring back at her. No words of denial left his lips.

'That's what I thought,' she said and turned to drag her case up on to the first block of the stairway. It was easily a foot and a half high and her case was probably twice the size. She didn't do very well.

Damien was standing right behind her and she let her frustration out on him. She whipped round to face him. 'How could you? He's supposed to be your best friend!'

The shame that washed over his face was all the confirmation she needed.

'It's not like that! At least, it isn't now—'

'I don't want to hear it!' she screamed at him and returned to struggling with her case. At least that way she didn't have to look at him.

It didn't matter about the timing one jot. The fact that he'd *ever* had any kind of feelings for Sara was enough.

The rush of anger produced an adrenalin surge that allowed her to heave her case on to the giant first step. Unfortunately, it didn't stick around long. Not long enough for the second step, anyway.

She felt Damien's warmth behind her, and when he gently eased the handle from her grasp and took it up into the cockpit she didn't fight him. Instead she sat down on the step and put her face in her hands.

Not again, she screamed inside her head. Not again.

And not with this one. Please.

Damien placed Zoe's hot pink case gently on the pontoon and stood beside it, looking back towards the hatch. The way Zoe had marched past him, case crashing behind her, had somehow prompted a memory of the day his father had left. Angry voices. A door slamming. A sense he'd disappointed someone.

He'd done it again. And he'd have done anything not to

see that hurt in Zoe's eyes, to know he'd made her feel that way. In fact, the strength of his own feelings on that front had surprised him. If she'd have let him, he'd have wrapped her in his arms and kissed her anger away, told her things he hadn't even realised had been in his head or heart.

And that hadn't been the only surprise.

The reaching for his car keys had been a knee-jerk reaction. But it wasn't what Zoe had thought. He always jumped in to help out friends in a crisis. It was what he was good at. And Luke and Sara's marriage was in trouble.

When he'd heard Zoe mention her name…

Sara.

For more than a year that one word had prompted a spike of adrenalin that had caused both his heart to race and his stomach to churn. But Damien had a feeling that if he took his pulse right now it would be frighteningly normal. And the only nausea he felt was at hurting Zoe.

He couldn't lie to her. He hadn't ever given her anything less than the truth and he wasn't going to stop now. And he couldn't pretend he'd hadn't felt what he'd felt. Once.

A long breath escaped his lips.

His prayers had been answered. The curse had been lifted. He didn't feel that way about Sara any more. It was such a relief. He'd hoped he'd reached that place, but his reaction to Zoe's phone call was hard evidence.

He needed to tell Zoe, to explain, make her understand. After all, he hadn't done anything wrong, even though it had felt that way sometimes.

Seconds ticked by. He kept staring at the hatch. Eventually he climbed back on board and went to look for her.

She was sitting on the bottom step, fingertips thrusting through her red curls as she buried her face in her hands. He jumped down beside her, missing most of the steps, and landed hard on the cabin floor. Then he crouched down beside her and looked into her eyes.

She sat up straight, folded her hands in her lap and stared back at him. She was angry. He understood that too.

He reached out to touch her hand and she flinched away. A flicker of something—disgust, maybe—passed across her expression and she looked away to the far end of the cabin.

'I don't think dinner tonight is such a good idea after all,' she said, her voice low and wavering. When she finished talking she risked a glance in his direction to gauge his reaction.

'Zoe, everything's changed—'

She shook her head, silencing him. 'I can't, Damien. Not now.' She looked away. 'And this never was supposed to be anything more than a holiday thing. We should stick to the plan and not make a drama out of something so insignificant.'

Damien thought he must be hearing things. Drama When Not Required was Zoe's forte. But the stare she gave him was blank, empty, and he knew better than to argue at that moment.

'Thank you for sorting out my case for me,' she said, and then she took herself and her brightly coloured handbag up on deck and off the boat.

Damien stayed where he was. He knew it was no good trying to make people stay when they got that look in their eyes. Maybe she was right. He hadn't really been thinking straight this last week. Hadn't he thought all along that they weren't the best match? Perhaps it was better to let her go now rather than discover that he couldn't be happy with her later. Better stop now, before they both got in too deep. He'd seen what that kind of rejection had done to his mother.

No.

The word entered his head and lodged there, refused to budge.

Okay, he hadn't planned on being with someone like Zoe, but he wasn't ready to give up hope yet. They'd had something. Exactly what, he wasn't sure, but he wasn't ready to give up without finding out. There was one last thing he needed to know before he let her go back to London alone.

She was almost on top of the ramp that linked the pontoon to dry land when he caught up with her.

'Zoe!' he yelled from the bottom of the slope. She turned to look at him, anger in the set of her jaw, hope in her eyes. He walked towards her, gathering both his breath and his thoughts.

'Who was the friend—the bridesmaid—the one your fiancé fell in love with?'

His heart pounded the moment the words left his lips because he feared he already knew the answer.

Zoe's eyes filled with tears. 'Sara,' she said. 'It was Sara.'

And then she turned and walked away, her suitcase whining in pain as she dragged it behind her.

CHAPTER THIRTEEN

FIVE hours later Zoe was knocking on a faceless hotel door with the sound of low-flying planes ringing in her ears. Sara opened the door. Her eyes were pink and her hair was only about one quarter in her ponytail. The rest was either falling lank or sticking up at odd angles, as if she'd been flopped on the bed sobbing for hours.

Zoe pulled Sara into a hug then guided her back into the room, an arm round her shoulders. Sara's knees buckled and she landed on the end of the bed, making it shudder. Since Zoe wanted to maintain contact, she had no choice but to go with her.

'Oh, Zo! It's such a mess!'

'What happened?'

Sara shook her head, as if she couldn't believe the images running through it. 'I don't know… It seems like it happened to someone else. It started with an argument—a really stupid one about not tying a fender on properly—but then it just got way out of control.'

'But you're going to be okay, right? You and Luke?'

Sara just pressed the heels of her hands into her eye sockets and juddered. Zoe laid her cheek on her friend's shoulder and rubbed her back until the silent tears slowed.

Sara's voice was muffled through her hands. 'You should have heard the things we said to each other! And then I…I just…snapped, I suppose. I told him if he really felt that way he'd have been better off not marrying me and then I went to the nearest telephone and booked a flight home.' Another shudder racked her body, and she looked up at Zoe with swollen eyes and sticky lashes.

'That was a bit dramatic.'

Sara's shoulders slumped further. 'I know! I've never done anything remotely like it before. It was just…just…' She suddenly sat up straighter and looked Zoe in the eye. 'What if he won't forgive me? I've been so horrible! How can I ever repair this?'

Zoe hugged Sara, a slight smile on her lips. 'Of course he'll forgive you. He loves you, remember? And you've both been under such stress getting this wedding together. I wouldn't be surprised if honeymoons weren't a bit like Christmas with the family,' she added.

Sara looked up at her, confused.

Of course she wouldn't know. The rest of her family were all as lovely as she was.

'You know… Everyone wants it to be perfect, but all those tensions that have been building all year have a habit of coming to the surface just when you don't want them to.'

That was how it was in Zoe's house, anyway. Her grandmother said they hadn't had a proper Christmas if at least one bit of crockery wasn't smashed and the front door didn't slam every half hour with the latest dramatic exit.

Sara dragged her hand across her eyes, then got up to retrieve a tissue from the box on the rather functional dressing table. 'Maybe… I did so want our honeymoon to be perfect.'

Zoe made a wry face. 'That's a lot of pressure to put on one man and a boat.'

Sara sighed and sat down on the top end of the bed, pulling her legs up and propping herself against the headboard. 'In the run-up to getting married you're supposed to be the picture of blissful happiness, aren't you? So all the little things that are irritating you, well, you stuff them away, hide them.

At least I did.' She blew out a long breath. 'I suppose there's a lot of pressure involved in being a bride, too.'

There was the way Sara had gone about it, Zoe thought. She scooted up the mattress to join Sara at the top end. 'It got to you, huh? You should have said something. I'd have understood. Been there myself, after all.'

'I didn't want to remind you.' Sara rolled her head sideways on the headboard to look at her. 'But more than that, I suppose I thought if I said it out loud at all that I'd ruin everything. I know what people think about me, what they say about me, they expect a certain standard. I felt my wedding had to live up to that.'

'Nobody's perfect,' Zoe said. And didn't she know that more than most? But it was refreshing to know that Sara felt the same pressure to perform, that Zoe wasn't the only one of the pair who could mess up badly. That realisation changed something. Suddenly Zoe felt older, stronger. More free.

'You need to tell Luke all of this,' she said to her friend. 'He's probably feeling the same way.'

'You think?'

Zoe nodded and let out a low chuckle. 'I think what you should have done is have a massive row on day three, get it all out of your system, and then have mind-blowing make-up sex.'

Sara pulled a glum face. 'But I got on a plane and came home! How are we going to get over that?'

Zoe reached over and patted Sara's leg. 'Listen, I'm the queen of impulsive bad choices and if there's one thing I've learned it's that nothing is so awful that it can't be sorted out somehow. It just takes a bit of guts, a bit of humility—and *a lot* of grovelling.'

Sara let out a watery laugh. 'Thanks, Zo. You always cheer me up, stop me taking myself too seriously. I don't know what I'd do without you. And I'm so sorry I messed up the end of your holiday too.' She gave Zoe a sideways look. The sort of look that begged information. 'How was it going?' she asked innocently.

Ah, yes. In all the drama, Zoe had forgotten about that. Time to get some answers while Sara was calmer.

'Why on earth did you set Damien and me up like that?'

Sara sighed. 'We didn't. At least not on purpose.'

Zoe crossed her arms. 'Convince me.'

'Luke and I had chatted about giving someone else the use of the boat, and I instantly assumed he meant Damien—after all, he borrows *Weaver* a couple of times a year anyway. So, when I had a chance, I talked to Damien. I had no idea Luke had mentioned it to you until the next day.'

'And when you realised you instantly rang me to let me know about the mix up?' Zoe said sarcastically.

'Luke told me about what he saw in the garden, you know...' Sara's voice was low and she nudged Zoe's leg with her foot.

Zoe stared straight ahead and kept her voice light and unconcerned. 'Oh, he did, did he?'

'So, when we realised we'd, well, double-booked the pair of you, we thought maybe it wasn't such a bad idea after all.'

In the following silence she knew Sara was waiting for her to spill her guts, as they always did about every romantic encounter, but Zoe wasn't ready to talk about Damien. Not by a long shot. And especially not with Sara.

She should have guessed, shouldn't she? Damien had plans, he always wanted the best, everything to be perfect. Why hadn't she realised that would apply to his romantic life as well as things like sailing and business? As soon as she looked at it that way, Sara became the natural choice.

And Zoe was so obviously not.

'He isn't for me,' she said eventually.

Not for you, either, she silently added. *But he's going to have to work that one out on his own.*

'Rubbish!' Sara replied, obviously distracting herself from

the mess of her own life by meddling with Zoe's. 'Damien's got a great job, he's successful, he's a fantastic friend to Luke—the sort of guy who'd never let you down—and he's... well, he's seriously hot.' She blushed a little as she said this, and Zoe felt slightly nauseous. 'He's practically perfect. What's not to like? Especially if he likes you too?'

'Nobody's perfect,' Zoe said again.

And she knew that for sure now, had discovered that elusive kryptonite that'd bring so-called Mr Perfect to his knees. She felt as if he'd lied to her, as if he'd betrayed all three of them somehow, even though she knew instinctively that he'd have never acted on whatever he felt.

Oh, why couldn't the mystery in his past, the one woman who hadn't wanted him back, been a nameless, faceless thing? Why did it have to be her best friend?

She swung her legs off the bed, fetched Sara's handbag from the desk and handed it to her. 'You need to phone your husband.'

Sara looked at her handbag as if it were about to swallow her whole. 'I'm scared,' she said in a small voice.

'I know.' Zoe sat down beside her on the edge of the bed. 'But I'm here with you.' She dropped the bag in her friend's lap. 'And you love each other. This is just the first of many bumps in the road of a long and happy marriage.'

Sara nodded. Just once. 'When did you become so wise?' she asked quietly, and then she reached into her handbag and pulled out her phone.

He'd thought she'd calm down and that he'd be able to go and see her, to explain, after a few days. Just showed how flawed *that* plan had been. In the month since they'd returned from Devon, Zoe hadn't answered one of his calls. He'd got her email address from Luke but she wouldn't answer any of those either. It was only the fact that he knew he'd have an opportunity to see her tonight that had stopped him going to her flat and banging down her front door.

Not a good idea. He knew that Zoe's response to conflict was to throw more petrol on the fire. It seemed Damien Stone was finally all out of good plans.

He stood at Luke and Sara's front door and stared at the brass knocker. He wasn't sure this was a brilliant idea, either. A thank you dinner for the best man and maid of honour. It could just turn out to be Round Two.

Luke and Sara had patched things up, but their honeymoon disaster had given them both quite a scare. When Luke had phoned him, telling him the full details of what had happened, he'd hardly been able to believe it. Not Sara. Sara didn't do that kind of thing.

Only she obviously did. Because she had.

And any remaining pieces of the idol Damien had created in her image had crumbled. She was still his friend, and she was still lovely, but he no longer elevated her to goddess status. He really had let go. Of Sara. Of even the idea of Sara. None of it had been real, anyway.

Unfortunately, he wasn't sure he could make Zoe see it that way.

He had a suspicion the newlyweds, now they were happily reunited, were trying to do a bit of matchmaking. He didn't know if Zoe had confided in Sara, but he hadn't said anything to Luke about what had gone on between them. His best friend had been putting his fledgling marriage back together—the last thing he'd needed was to get embroiled in someone else's romantic problems.

He shifted the bunch of flowers he'd brought for the hostess into the same hand that was gripping a bottle of wine and knocked on the door. It was opened moments later by a smiling Sara, wearing a floral apron, her hair caught up in a messy ponytail at the back of her head. She kissed his cheek, relieved him of flowers and wine, and led him through the house and into the kitchen.

'Luke's barbecuing,' she said, smiling as she put the wine down on the counter. 'Go and do man-stuff out there. You know, keep him company while he grunts at the fire.' She nodded in the direction of the French windows leading into the courtyard garden.

So Zoe wasn't here yet, then. Damien wasn't sure whether to be disappointed or relieved he had more time to prepare himself. His heart began to thud.

He'd missed her. Really missed her. And it was more than just being sorry about the way things had ended. Somehow his life seemed...empty. It was as if the sunshine had stayed in Devon, even though London had delivered the cloudless skies of an Indian summer well into September.

He stepped into the garden and greeted his friend with a hug. For that he was rewarded with a bottle of beer. It was only when he couldn't find a bottle opener on the garden table that he looked up and saw her, standing by the ivy-covered wall, a glass of white wine gripped between even whiter fingers.

Once again he had the sensation of being hit by a truck. But this time it didn't stop there: it ran him over, then backed up and made mincemeat of him.

Zoe was wearing that sundress she'd had on the night she'd got sunburned—a favourite of his ever since. Her untidy curls had been tamed into a twist at the back of her head, but es-capee tendrils framed her face and curled at her nape. He didn't think he'd ever seen her look more beautiful.

'Hi,' he croaked, and he didn't even notice when Sara gently prised his beer bottle from his hand, took the cap off and handed it back to him.

Zoe looked at him, head tilted down a little, with her eyes wide and her mouth thin. 'Hi.' The word shot from her mouth like a bullet.

Direct hit, Damien thought. Just hearing her voice, as cold and wary as it was, made his chest contract.

Dinner was painful. Uncomfortable. At least it was for the two unmarried guests. Luke and Sara were definitely experiencing a second wind of newly wedded bliss. Unfortunately, their loved-up state made them impervious to the awkwardness of their guests, especially when the hosts dropped hints about holiday romances and fountains in hotel gardens.

Zoe's biting wit was at its finest, and more than once he found himself as her bullseye. He took it. He'd rather see her fighting than crumbling, and in the silences in between the barbs he saw the look of raw hurt in her eyes.

Sara swallowed a mouthful of wine as they finished up their main course. 'Tell Damien about your expansion plans,' she said to Zoe.

Zoe fidgeted in her seat. She really didn't want to talk about this. Not with Damien here, because he'd been the one to start her thinking on this track, to make her realise that her business was never going to grow unless she stopped daydreaming and did something about it.

'I'm leasing one of the little shops on the fringes of Greenwich market,' she said. 'Not quite a rival to Tiffany's yet, but it's a start.'

'She's got a bank loan and everything, haven't you, Zoe?' Sara added excitedly.

Zoe rolled her eyes at her friend and nodded. When she looked back over the table at Damien, the look of pride in his eyes and the soft smile on his lips almost undid all her resolution to remain aloof and distant.

'I'm glad,' was all he said.

It was enough. Zoe didn't want to feel all warm and fuzzy at his words. She didn't want to feel anything about him at all, thank you very much.

Sara went on to talk about how much she loved Zoe's dinky new premises, how much fun they were going to have repainting the display cases of what had been an old-fashioned gentlemen's haberdashery store. Zoe didn't listen. She was watching Damien, just like she'd been watching him all evening, waiting for something—a flash in his eyes, a facial tic—when he looked at Sara that would confirm all her worst fears.

And there was one expression in particular she feared the most, and every time she felt herself weakening she made herself remember that look—the one he'd worn as he'd watched Sara walk down the aisle. It haunted her now, in painful and exquisite detail. She hadn't seen it tonight yet, but that didn't mean he wouldn't slip up one day.

Nobody could survive a relationship with that hanging over them. It would be a miserable way to live. It certainly was a miserable way to love.

Dessert was served as the sky became fully dark and Sara turned on the string of lights that decorated the little pergola in her tiny paved garden. Zoe pushed her cheesecake around her plate for a while, but decided she had to at least eat some of it. If she didn't, Sara would know that something was wrong, and she really didn't want an inquisition to start while she was sitting opposite Damien. Tonight had been hard enough as it was.

Hard, because she knew that just a slight move of her foot would have brought it into contact with his. Just a reach for the salt at the same time would have caused their fingers to brush. A million little ways she could engineer her own undoing. She wanted to touch him so badly that she was scared she'd sabotage herself and do it anyway. She needed to get out of here.

She looked up just after she'd put the first spoonful in her mouth, habitually turning it over so she could capture every speck of dessert with her tongue, and discovered Damien staring at her. The lump of cheesecake that had been dangling on the end of his fork slid on to his plate with a splat. He didn't even react.

Sara gave her husband a not-so-subtle thumbs-up sign across the table.

Zoe noticed a humming in her ears as static electricity crawled up her arms and made her body tingle. She pulled the spoon slowly out of her mouth and placed it carefully back down on her plate. Everyone watched her. Everyone was quiet.

She pushed her chair back from the table. 'Thanks for the lovely evening, you two,' she said quickly, looking down and catching nobody's eye. 'But I'm afraid I have to get going. I pick up the keys to the shop bright and early in the morning.'

The hosts were instantly on their feet. 'But we've still got cheese and biscuits to come,' Sara said mournfully. 'Stay for that, at least.' But she wasn't looking at the cheeseboard sitting in the middle of the table when she said it. She was looking at Damien.

Zoe shook her head. 'Sorry.' Her impulse had been to get out of there, and she was going with it.

Sara ran to get Zoe's cardigan. 'Well, at least let us call you a cab.'

Zoe huffed. 'I live five minutes away. Don't be ridiculous. I'll be fine walking.'

'But it's dark,' Sara added, and then she narrowed her eyes and looked from Zoe to Damien and back again. 'Luke will walk you back.'

Luke was visibly, and almost audibly, surprised by the suggestion, but one look from his wife silenced him. He shrugged and headed for the door.

Zoe started to relax slightly as she and Sara said their goodbyes by the front door, talking over the top of each other and promising to call the following day. Luke rolled his eyes and told them to get on with it, and Damien stood back and watched. She could tell his eyes didn't leave her for a second, even though she was never brave enough to meet his gaze.

A few more seconds and she'd be able to breathe again. The front door would shut behind her, blocking him from her view, and she wouldn't have to see him for another few months, hopefully, and by then she'd be better. Stronger. Over him.

But she should have accounted for Sara's more devious side, a trait that had been coming more and more to the fore in recent weeks. Just as Zoe and Luke were about to leave, Sara grabbed her husband's arm.

'Actually, even better...' she dragged him back inside '... Luke can help me clear up and Damien can walk you.'

She obviously caught the man in question by surprise too, because, despite her petite frame, she managed to shove him out of the door with no problem and she closed it swiftly behind them before Zoe could argue.

That left her and Damien standing on the front step staring at each other.

Zoe just shook her head and walked down the path. 'I don't want you to walk me home,' she said without looking at him, but knowing he would follow. 'I don't want to be near you at all.'

CHAPTER FOURTEEN

DAMIEN wasn't about to let Zoe walk away again. Or should that be *run* away? Another sleight of hand of hers, he realised. She'd flee uncomfortable situations, passing the blame to the other party, making them feel as if they'd pushed her, when really the momentum had been hers alone. And it was time to make her stop. Time for her to face what she was running from.

He caught up with her, placed his hands lightly on her shoulders. Much to his surprise, she halted instantly. But she didn't turn, just stared at the cracked paving stone illuminated by the dull orb of light from a street lamp. Rather than turning her towards him, he circled around her, maintaining contact, preventing any forward progress.

He expected to find her glaring back at him, lightning bolts flashing from her eyes ready to sizzle him to a crisp, but instead they were filled with tears. He didn't say anything, just brushed them from under her lashes with his thumbs while her bottom lip wobbled, and then he leaned in close and pressed his lips softly to hers. Just a single kiss, but he couldn't bear to break contact so he stayed there, lips touching hers. Neither of them moved. More tears slid from her closed lids and after a second he tasted their salt.

His brain had just sent a signal to pull away when Zoe stopped him before he'd even begun to move. She placed her palms on his cheeks, held him there while she returned the favour. He could feel her quivering, her hands shaking against his skin.

But finally her mouth left his and she stepped back, ran her tongue across her bottom lip and tasted the damp salt of her own tears before sweeping them away.

She blinked slowly and looked away. 'There's no point, Damien. We both know that.'

He took a step forward. 'There's every point. You don't understand—'

'I understand just fine,' she snapped. 'It was a fling. It's over. That's all.'

'What if I don't want it to be over?'

She stood tall and her chin tilted upwards. 'Then you're fooling yourself. You know I'm not the one you really want.'

That wasn't true. Not any more. But she was so blinkered, so fixed on that one point that she couldn't see anything else. Damien almost felt like laughing. How many times had people accused him of exactly the same thing? But Zoe had been the one who'd shown him a better way, made him realise how badly that approach could short-change a person, how it could rob them of things they'd never even dared to imagine could be theirs.

'I thought you were the one to follow the mad impulses, take chances.' He stepped forward until he was practically nose to nose with her, lowered his voice. 'Take a chance on *me*.'

She bit her lip and her eyes widened further.

'I want *you*, Zoe,' he said quietly, firmly.

She shook her head and took another step backwards. Then she smiled, but it wasn't a pretty smile. A millimetre less width and it would be a grimace of pain.

'I'm not right for you.' Her voice caught. 'Okay, maybe it could be more than a fling, but the fact you want more from me now doesn't change anything in the long run. Eventually you'll stop wanting me and you'll want *her*—or someone like her. They always do.'

He realised then that he wasn't going to get through to her with just talking. He also needed time to think, time to work out if his iron-clad certainty was as solid as he'd thought it was. He was very good at setting things in stone and then pursuing them blindly, wasn't he? Sometimes without asking if he was following the right path.

'Can you guarantee me you'll never look at her and wonder *what if*?' she asked, her expression hard now. 'Or that you won't regret choosing me instead?'

Two minutes ago he would have said yes in a heartbeat. But was there truth in what she'd just said? Would he, like his father, wake up one day and discover the life—the woman—he'd chosen wasn't enough? He didn't want to even consider that option, but he owed it to Zoe to be certain. He couldn't let her fall in love with him and then snatch it all away from her. She'd already had that done to her once.

He reached his hand out and let it drop down by his side again. 'No, I can't. Not yet.'

Another tear fell. She let it roll until it reached her chin and then she wiped it away with the heel of her hand. She walked around him, stepping off the kerb to give him a wide berth, and when she was back on the pavement again she turned to look at him.

'Then I can't take a chance on you, Damien. You know that. I can't be your backup plan. She will always be the one you picked first and I can't live with that.' She started walking backwards, away from him, away from the glow of the street light. 'There's nothing we can do to change that, and I'm afraid it's a deal-breaker for me.'

And then she turned and walked away. Damien waited a while then followed her, his feet heavy. There wasn't anything else he could say. Not tonight. He kept at a discreet distance, made sure she was safe until she walked up the path to her front door, where she gave him one last look as she turned her key, then went inside, shutting the glossy red door firmly behind her.

Zoe slumped against the back of her front door and let the rest of her tears fall. She pressed her hands against her face as if she could somehow stop herself from falling apart by that one simple action.

He'd broken her heart. How had he done that when she'd been so careful not to give it to him? It wasn't fair.

She had known she was right, but she hadn't wanted to be. Right about Sara, right about there being no possibility of a future for them, but it had killed her to hear him agree.

The building was little more than a shell of girders. Damien stood at the edge of the site overlooking the Thames, the sound of bulldozers droning in his ears, and stared out at the water. He was normally really excited at this stage of a project. After months of preparation, it was time to start making those plans a reality.

For days now he'd been preoccupied with trying to work out the answer to Zoe's question. For days now he'd failed miserably. How could you predict something like that? Inside his head he'd taken his mental jigsaw puzzle and arranged it a hundred different ways. He'd shuffled pieces around, trying to create a space that Zoe would fit into, so he could give her the assurances she wanted. It had been no use. It had always felt as if he was jamming that last piece unnaturally into a gap that it didn't really belong in, and that scared him.

The only option had been to pull the whole thing apart, piece by piece, and scramble it up. All the bits were sitting at the fringes of his consciousness now, out of order, and it was driving him crazy.

He had one piece left in his hands. Zoe.

The site foreman came to him with a question and Damien

reeled off an answer on autopilot. Then he called the man back and checked the details again.

'Sorry,' he said. 'Just needed to be sure.'

The man shrugged. 'No problem. It's your money we'll be pouring down the toilet if we get it wrong, and at the stage when we have to make sure the structure is right. Otherwise there's no point adding to it.'

Damien nodded and the man wandered off with his clipboard. When he was alone again he went back to his mental riddle.

Start with the thing that needs to be there to make the whole thing work. Start with the foundation.

Just like his idea of the perfect woman, his idea of the perfect future was an illusion too. He swept those pieces away.

Nothing and nobody was perfect in this world, but maybe that was okay. Maybe there was beauty and happiness to be found in it anyway. Maybe it was about appreciating what was right in front of you, instead of always wishing for something more—something his father had yet to learn to do. Something Zoe's bonehead fiancé had thankfully also done.

He took that one piece of the jigsaw he still held in his hands and put it front and centre in an empty space. Then he shooed all the other little bits away that tried to gather round and crowd it.

There was no perfect picture he could make for Zoe. But he'd been looking at it the wrong way. This was a jigsaw with only one piece. The rest would come later. He'd build it around her whichever way it fitted, be the edges messy or undefined, and he didn't care. All he knew was that he couldn't imagine his life without her in it.

Now he just had to make her believe it too.

Zoe leaned into the compact shop window that faced on to the covered hall of Greenwich market and hung a necklace on a display stand. It was her usual style: big chunky wooden beads with different colours and grains, mixed with chunky silver shapes and multi-faceted glass beads. This one was all in shades of pale beige, yellow and blue. It reminded her of the Cornish coast on a sunny day when the heat haze had risen.

Outside, the market was coming to life. Traders were filling their stalls with their wares. Today was Thursday, so it was vintage fashion and handmade toys, antiques and precious stones. Quite a few early shoppers had already drifted past and stopped at her window display. She hoped that boded well.

She'd only opened last Saturday, so it was early days yet, but she'd done okay so far. She hoped it wasn't just the novelty of a new shop and that business would continue to grow, but who knew what would happen in the future? She'd planned it out with the help of a financial adviser. The only thing to do now was hold her breath and see if she pulled it off. If she was still open this time next year she'd give herself permission to exhale.

The best way to check a window display was to see it the way the customers did—from the outside—so Zoe did just that. She stood, hands on hips, a good six feet away from her window and tipped her head to one side.

The display included colourful necklaces, bracelets and earrings. She didn't think she could fit much else in the window without overcrowding it, yet at the same time it looked empty. Something was missing. A gnawing sensation in her stomach reminded her exactly what that was.

She knew the delicate, interwoven silver designs she'd drawn on the boat would look perfect interspersed amongst the larger pieces. Pity she didn't have any to put there. Not because she'd sold them, but because they were still just doodles in her sketchpad. Imaginations.

She had the materials in her safe. She had the right tools for the job. She just lacked the guts. Partly because every time she looked at them she thought of Damien, but more because she was scared that they wouldn't turn out the way she wanted them to, that she couldn't actually pull all that intricate work off.

And now would be a really good time to pull something special out of the bag. Yesterday she'd got an email from someone wanting to commission a wedding and engagement ring set. Something unusual, the client had said. He'd given her carte blanche. And Mr Peters wanted it all kept very hush-hush because it was going to be a surprise for the lucky lady.

She had a little workbench near the till at the back of the shop and she returned to it now, pulled her leather sketchpad out from its shelf and looked at it. She left it open on the desk and went to the back room-slash-office where her safe was. She returned with a pouch containing a square-cut emerald. This stone for the engagement ring, she'd decided, although she didn't know why. It was something she'd picked up for a good price a couple of years ago, but had never really made anything it could fit into before now.

She unwrapped the stone from its little pouch as she walked back on to the tiny shop floor, eyes down. When she looked up again she almost threw both pouch and stone into the air.

A large, dark shape was filling her doorway. It was Damien, looking impossibly delicious in an immaculately cut suit.

'You did it,' was all he said, looking round and smiling.

Zoe was shaking. How was he standing there looking all normal and sounding all calm? She nodded, since her head was inclined to wobble with the rest of her.

'I knew you could,' he added. 'You just needed to believe it too.'

She nodded again, not even really sure what she was agreeing with.

'What are you doing here?' she finally said.

'Luke told me you'd opened your shop. I wanted to stop

by and wish you well.' He handed her a small gift-wrapped package. 'I thought this might come in handy.'

Zoe took it from him. It would be rude not to. And instantly recognised the contours of her favourite brand of 'emergency' chocolate through the wrapping paper.

'Setting up a business can be stressful,' he said, a slight smile tugging the corner of his mouth. 'A little red box with breakable glass and a hammer might be a good idea.'

Zoe dropped the chocolate on the counter by the till and closed her eyes. Why hadn't she leased a bigger shop? She was right at the back, and he was only a pace or so away from the door and already he was too close. She closed her eyes and her voice grew thin. 'Don't be nice to me... Just don't.'

She heard him close the distance between them and opened her eyes in panic, just as he stopped in front of her and took the emerald from her fingers. 'Lovely stone.'

She nodded again. She really must stop doing that. Otherwise she'd have to get herself a part-time job sitting on the parcel shelf of somebody's car. 'They're my favourite.'

He held it up to the light. 'I had a great-aunt who hated emeralds. She married a diamond broker, and after that she got very particular about her jewellery. She thought emeralds were second class. Something about impurities and flaws.'

'She's right. Emeralds are actually a type of beryl—which are a totally different colour—but impurities in the stone turn it green. They're notorious for their flaws, too.'

He handed it back to her and looked her in the eye. 'Doesn't stop them being beautiful.'

'No.' She gulped down a breath. Were they still talking about emeralds?

He kept looking her straight in the eye until she had to turn away. 'Why are you really here?' she asked. 'This isn't about chocolate.'

He put his hands in his pockets and frowned. 'I thought

a lot about what you said, about whether I could give you a guarantee.'

Her breathing became all light and fluttery. 'Can you?'

'No. I can't promise you a perfect future, Zoe.' He reached out and touched her face. 'But I don't think anyone can make a promise like that to someone else. Life is like sailing—you do your best to plot your course, and then you weather the conditions together, dealing with whatever is thrown at you. And I think you and I make a good team.'

She shook her hand away and stepped back. Oh, they were persuasive words, and she so wanted to believe him because she knew he meant what he was saying. But it wouldn't change anything: Aiden had worn that very same earnest look on his face the night he'd asked her to marry him.

'Maybe we do make a good team.' She shook her head, backed away a little further behind the counter. 'But I can't be your sidekick, Damien. The consolation prize who trots along beside you, while everyone else wonders why you're with her. A relationship with unequal partners just won't work.'

His jaw tensed and his eyes narrowed slightly. She was making him cross. Good. That was much better than the heartfelt looks he'd been giving her. She could handle cross.

'This sidekick thing is all rubbish,' he said in that imperious manner that used to make her want to scream.

'Oh, it is, is it? Well, I doubt you've ever been on the receiving end of that kind of treatment, so how would you know?'

He let out a dry laugh, not a pleasant sound. 'Really? Then answer me one question—and I know we've been here before—but when the joke's on me, what do they say?'

'That you're always the best man,' she said slowly, expecting this to be a trick question, which it might be.

'Exactly. Seven times now. That has to be a record. So I don't want to hear any of this sidekick versus leading man nonsense, okay?'

Zoe frowned. 'I don't see how the two are connected.'

'The best man isn't the leading man on a wedding day— the groom is—and I've never been the groom. So that would make *me* the sidekick.'

Zoe's eyes grew wide. He so clearly wasn't. 'That's impossible. You can't be.'

'No, I'm not. And neither are you, but you can't see it.' He shook his head in exasperation. 'You're right. A relationship won't work with unequal partners. But I'm not the one who believes you're second class, Zoe. It's you.'

No, that wasn't right. That couldn't be right. It was other people who labelled her, who treated like that. All she'd ever wanted was for someone to pick her first, make her their top choice. Damien had been like all the rest.

'You're dreaming,' she said, 'if you think that.'

He reached over to the small work desk and picked up the sketchbook lying there. 'I know I'm dreaming,' he said. 'But it's not wrong to hope. It's not dangerous. And some dreams are meant to come true.' He showed the sketchpad to her. 'That's what designs are, aren't they? Dreams on paper. A vision of something that hasn't become real yet.'

She frowned and took the pad from him, held it to her chest.

'I *know* we can be good together—' he tapped his finger to his temple '—I can see it. But I can't force you to take a chance on me. I can't make you believe that it's you that I want and not anyone else,' he said as he turned and walked towards the door. 'But make those, Zoe. Let yourself dream about *something*, because you're going to be miserable until you do.'

CHAPTER FIFTEEN

ZOE put the ring she was working on down and slumped back in her chair. Her secretive client wanted something unique, something one-of-a-kind and, since Zoe had been in the creative doldrums ever since she'd returned from Devon, she'd had no choice but to go back to those designs and tweak them a little. It had nothing to do with what Damien had said when he'd visited the shop the week before last, nothing at all.

It was a wedding ring, white gold. Unlike Sara's, which had been clean lines and elegant curves, this was an intricate design of interwoven strands, inspired by climbing ivy, old Art Nouveau posters and Celtic knotwork. The vision she had for the end product was stunning, but getting it right was driving her crazy. It was rough around the edges now but, if she looked carefully, she could envisage the finished version shimmering tantalisingly beneath the surface, just out of reach. She stuffed the ring into a pouch where it couldn't mock her.

She'd agreed to meet Sara for cocktails in a local wine bar and it was almost time to get going. Privately, she thought Sara was turning into a bit of a mother hen, fussing round her and asking her if she was eating properly. Seriously, when had anyone ever worried about that on Zoe's account? She was sure this was just another of Sara's mercy missions to cheer her single friend up. But maybe it was better than sitting here and getting frustrated with strips of fine metal that wouldn't consent to sit right.

The old-fashioned shop bell she'd recently fitted above the door jangled and she looked up to find Sara walking towards her. 'Normal people are shutting up shop and going home for the day,' she said. 'Ready for that Monday night cocktail?'

Zoe put the ring down and pushed her hands above her head to stretch out the kinks in her shoulders. 'Just a quick one. After that I'm going to take these home and try to finish them off. I've got to deliver them to a hotel in central London late Friday afternoon. It's all very cloak and dagger.'

'It's stunning, Zo,' Sara said, picking up the ring and examining it. 'Where's the engagement ring?'

She opened up a midnight blue velvet box sitting on the bench beside her and turned it to face her friend. Sara's mouth dropped open. 'Wow.'

Zoe smiled to herself. 'That was the effect I was hoping it would have.'

'I've never seen anything quite like it. All those twisting little strands, and that lone emerald right in the middle. It's very *you*, somehow.' She handed the box back to Zoe, then hoisted her handbag even further up on her shoulder. 'Ready?'

Zoe shook her head and began to pack away her things. 'Almost.'

She put the display pieces from the window into the safe and went round turning off lights and tidying up. With Sara's help, it was only ten minutes before she was locking the shop door behind her and pulling down the metal grille.

Even though it was still fairly early, Monday night happy hour was in full swing at the wine bar. Lots of young professionals either rounding off a good weekend or commiserating on the start of a new working week, probably. They found themselves stools near the bar and Zoe ordered herself something fun-looking and toxic, while Sara stuck to a tried-and-tested margarita. They chatted about silly, inconsequential matters as they sipped their drinks.

Things had been different between her and Sara since what they now referred to as The Honeymoon Meltdown. Zoe no longer felt like the geek who'd somehow managed to slide into the in-crowd unnoticed. She'd been guilty of believing Sara's life was perfect, when clearly she suffered from the same insecurities as everyone else. Maybe her friend would have been able to talk to her about how stressed she'd been in the run up to the wedding if Zoe hadn't also unconsciously put her on a pedestal too, adding to the pressure.

She sucked on her straw and took a sideways look at her best friend. Hmm. Putting Sara on a pedestal. Seemed she had more in common with Damien than she'd realised. And if she'd managed to change, could he?

She sighed. Damien. He hadn't contacted her in the last two weeks. So she supposed he'd finally given up, which was a shame because she'd spent a lot of time thinking about what he'd said.

He'd dared her to dream, hadn't he? And she had—by signing the lease on her little shop, by working on the designs that she knew would take her business to a new level. Now she'd stopped just reacting to the situation, to him and all the feelings his secret had churned up, she could see he'd been right. It was hard work, and it didn't always go according to plan, but the gamble was worth it. She was happier now. Professionally, at least. Personally, she was still pretty miserable.

Maybe it was time to do something about that. Maybe it was time to peel off that 'sidekick' label she'd stuck on her own forehead, because he'd been right about that too. And she had the funny feeling that sense of imbalance, of not being able to talk to her as an equal—because she wouldn't let him—might have been part of the reason Aiden had looked elsewhere. Oh, he was still a rat, she didn't doubt that, but maybe things weren't quite as black and white as she'd once thought.

Before she knew it, her glass was empty. Just as well she was getting the bus home.

Sara's eyes widened and she knocked back the rest of her cocktail to keep up. 'Another?'

Zoe shook her head. 'You run along home to your lovely new husband. Stop worrying about me.'

Sara grimaced. 'Busted,' she said.

'Besides,' Zoe added, 'I have a ring I need to finish.'

Zoe stared at the bit of paper in her hands and frowned. The address she'd been given was the name of a hotel, but this was little more than a building site. A truck drove past her, through deep brown mud, and disappeared through the gate made of dark green chipboard.

The ring box was in her jacket pocket and she absently played with its corners, finding its cuboid shape comforting. All that work. And this was…what? A hoax? One that had cost her money she couldn't afford in both time and materials.

She noticed a man in a hard hat walking towards her.

'Miss St James?'

She nodded, almost perplexed by the fact he knew her name, even though this was where she'd been told to come.

'If you'd like to come with me?'

He handed her a matching yellow hat and waited for her to jam it on top of her curls. Fabulous. It had taken hours to shop for an outfit to impress this obviously high-end client, and now this hat was going to make her look like a duck.

The man led her to one of those lifts that were really just a cage, and up they shot into the sky. Zoe hadn't realised the building was so tall. It was mostly steel girders and concrete floors. Here and there on the bottom levels things were taking more shape, but when she stepped out of the lift a minute later she could feel the early autumn breeze on her face and see the glint of the Thames way below.

Zoe held tightly on to the ring box in her pocket. This was some sort of dream, wasn't it? She was probably hallucinating. But the clang of the lift as it disappeared back down towards the ground sounded real enough. As did the gurgling of her nervous stomach.

Why had he left her alone up here?

But then she realised she wasn't alone. On the far side of a vast concrete floor a man was silhouetted against the late afternoon sun. She shielded her eyes with her hand and began to walk towards him, glad she was moving away from the edge.

'Mr Peters?'

He turned, and Zoe's quivering stomach followed the recently departed lift. He started moving towards her, crossing the rough concrete floor in long strides. Slowly, as he stepped more into the gloom of the inner building, her eyes began to adjust, make out his features...

And then it wasn't the mysterious Mr Peters walking towards her but Damien.

Why was he...? How had he...?

Oh. She got it now. One of her brothers was called Peter, so she knew it came from the Greek word for stone. Very clever. Also very devious.

But why the charade? What did it mean? She felt as if something inside her wanted to fly. She held it tight, terrified of what might happen if she let it.

Don't cry, she told herself. Don't be that pathetic. You came here to do a job, so do it. Keep it dignified.

She pulled the box from her pocket and held it out to him. He didn't smile. He didn't say anything. In fact, he had an intense, slightly pained expression on his face that she knew she'd seen before. She just couldn't remember where.

'Your rings,' she said. That was all she'd meant to say,

but then she heard herself add, 'You found a replacement for Sara pretty quick.'

Outwardly, she kept her expression neutral. Inwardly, she was kicking herself and reminding herself, not very gently, that she was supposed to be thinking before she spoke, not just firing off words in reaction to any uncomfortable emotion.

'Sorry,' she added. 'That was a stupid thing to say.'

Damien's expression was still unreadable. 'I don't want to replace Sara.'

She hadn't realised she'd let go of that fluttering thing inside her and that hope had been soaring quietly in her heart until that moment. It fell to the ground like a bird shot with an arrow.

Still stuck on Sara. Why had she expected anything else? It was the pattern of her romantic relationships up until now, after all. For the first time in her life, Zoe wondered if she'd have to cut her best friend out of her life if she was ever going to have a chance at love, something she really didn't want to do.

Damien opened the box and stared at the delicate twisting rings nestled together in their blue cushion. Although the lid obscured Zoe's view, she knew both pieces so intimately that she followed his gaze in her imagination, tracing every line and curve. He didn't speak for a long time.

'They're beautiful,' he said quietly. 'Even more than I'd imagined they would be.'

That had been Zoe's reaction when she'd finally finished them too—especially the wedding ring. She could hardly believe her hands had crafted it.

Zoe folded her arms across her front, vainly hoping it would somehow halt the rising glow of gratification his words had produced inside her.

'There's only one woman who can wear this ring,' he said as he looked up at her, and Zoe had a flash of realisation so strong she stopped breathing.

She could label that expression now. It was like the one she'd been waiting for all evening when they'd had dinner at Luke and Sara's. The one she'd seen on his face when he'd been looking past her up the aisle at Sara. Like it, but not the same. More like its big brother. More intense. More real.

That bird, the one that Zoe was sure had been shot dead, suddenly rose like a phoenix and started flapping around all over the place inside her chest. She checked over her shoulder, just to make sure no one was standing behind her, but they were all alone.

Nobody was there. Sara wasn't there.

So it must be *her* he was looking at with raw longing in his eyes.

Zoe wished that a chair would materialise from somewhere. She really needed to sit down.

'Without her my life is empty, boring—full of straight lines and tick boxes.' He looked down at the open ring box in his hand and turned it to face her. 'I want my life to be like this ring. It has form and structure, but it's also surprising and exceptional. So, no, I don't want a replacement for Sara. The woman I would like to wear this ring is one of a kind.'

Zoe's hand flew to her chest. She could feel her heart pumping a wild jig beneath her fingers. Oh, she so wanted to believe him.

'I don't know...'

Damien placed the box in her hands. The square of velvet was warm against her palm.

'I don't think we're cast at birth in certain roles—some always destined to fly, some always destined to be second in line. When it comes to love it's about finding the right person, and I've found my leading lady.' He smiled, just a little, and Zoe's eyes started to sting. 'I just made a stupid error in the casting for a while. Will you forgive me for that? We all make mistakes.'

Zoe found herself nodding as she stared at the rings. Her rings. Or were they Damien's rings? She really didn't know.

Just like that night in the hotel gardens, he pulled her close and kissed her. Zoe didn't even think about slapping him this time. This was what she'd been dreaming about, waiting for, in the long weeks since he'd come to visit her at her workshop. She curled her arms around his neck and kissed him back, gripping the ring box very tightly in one hand.

They finally drew apart and rested their foreheads against each other, their chests rising and falling in rhythm. Damien took her hand and led her towards the far edge of the concrete floor. From there she could see the Thames, grey and pink and glinting yellow in the afternoon sun, snaking its way through the city.

He leaned forward and his breath was deliciously warm in her ear. 'I've fallen in love with a real woman this time, not a perfect creature that doesn't exist.'

She jabbed him in the arm with the ring box. 'Are you saying I'm not perfect?'

He nodded and broke out one of those rare grins that lit up his face. 'Yes. But who is? Not me.'

She pulled him close, using the lapels of his suit for leverage, and kissed him again. 'I think I'm going to need that in writing,' she mumbled against his lips.

Damien laughed and kissed her back, and then he eased the box gently from her fingers, stepped back and got down on one knee. Zoe almost couldn't see him through the tears that had suddenly decided to blur her vision.

'I've never asked anyone this before,' he said, suddenly looking very young. She noticed a little nerve twitching in his left cheek. 'You're the first. The only.'

He took a deep breath and Zoe pressed her palms against her chest, one on top of the other.

'Will you marry me? Because, Zoe St James, I think you are perfect for me.'

'Yes,' she said, her voice sounding faraway and breathless in her own ears. 'Yes, I will.' And she watched in amazement as Damien eased the emerald ring from its cushion and slid it on to her finger. She didn't even notice him stand up, she was so transfixed at the sight of it there.

She laughed softly and then stood on her tiptoes and kissed him again. 'But if you think I'm spending my honeymoon cooped up together on a tiny little yacht with you, going stir-crazy...'

Damien's expression changed to that of an eleven-year-old boy who'd lost his favourite marble. She decided to put him out of his misery.

'You'd be right,' she added with a trademark saucy glimmer in her eye.

EPILOGUE

ONE year later the little church at St Just-in-Roseland was filled with flowers. No whites or creams for this bride, but a riot of exotic blooms filling the vaulted space with colour and scent.

In the creek outside, a small, recently purchased yacht rocked on the gentle waves, a large white ribbon tied to its bow. It had polished wooden decks and dubious plumbing, but her owners thought she was a dream come true. And, if the wind blew the right way and the boat swung round on her mooring, you could read the freshly painted name plate fixed to her stern—*Sidekick*.

Up in the church, the groom was standing nervously at the head of the aisle, his best friend beside him, and when the organ began to play to announce the entrance of his bride he truly thought his heart had stopped beating.

But then he turned and looked at her, and it started right back up again. Doing a rumba beat.

She was wearing a two-piece gown: a long satin skirt and a corset, the sort with laces his fingers were already twitching at the thought of undoing, and the bodice was doing something unbelievable to her cleavage.

Okay, heart was definitely working fine again, but now breathing systems were in trouble.

She winked at him as she swayed her way down the aisle. He didn't notice anyone else, not the guests, not the bridesmaid, not even the matron of honour. He felt oxygen swell in his lungs again and he smiled.

Not perfect this bride, not by a long shot. But neither was the groom. And where was the fun in that, anyway? She filled his days with colour and sunshine, and she stopped him becoming old and crusty and grumpy before his time. They fought, of course. Regularly. But making up was so much fun he hardly minded.

She reached him and he decided he couldn't wait: he had to kiss her now, even before the vows had been said and the vicar had given them permission. He leaned in close as she lifted her veil and asked her something softly, so no one else could hear.

'You're not going to slap me if I do, are you?'

She dropped her bouquet, grabbed hold of his lapels and pulled him close until they were nose to nose, lips only a breath apart. Some of the congregation cheered. The best man stuck his fingers in his mouth and whistled.

'Darling,' she said as she closed her eyes, 'I may slap you if you *don't*.'

* * * * *

WAKING UP WED

CHRISTY JEFFRIES

To Betty Lou Astleford, a consummate peacemaker who also ran off and got married despite her mother's warnings that if she married 'that man,' he would never be able to afford shoes for her children.

Your strong marriage was a priceless gift to your family and worth far more than all the shoes you bought us to prove your mother wrong. And you really taught me how to splurge on a good pair of shoes. I love you, Momoo.

Chapter One

Every morning for the first thirty years of her life, Kylie Chatterson had woken up alone.

Until today.

She'd barely rolled over on the hotel's plush mattress when her sleepy eyes did a double take at the fair-haired, angelic-looking man snuggled up beside her.

Who in the world was he—and how in the world had he gotten here?

His muscular body was chiseled like the marble statue of a Greek god, but this work of art was warmer and much more real. The brutal morning sun intruded through the wide-open curtains she'd obviously neglected to close, shedding unnecessary light on her growing sense of shame.

Kylie held her breath, commanding her body to stay still so her spinning head could add up all the facts.

Fact one. She'd flown to Reno for her friend's coed

bachelor/ette party yesterday. This was definitely the room she'd checked into because her fuchsia cheetah-print suitcase was haphazardly propped on the luggage rack at the foot of the bed. So at least she was where she was supposed to be. That was good.

Fact two. She remembered meeting up with some of the wedding party and having one or two cocktails in the casino bar. She normally didn't drink much, so it couldn't have been more than a couple. Could it? She spotted three plastic oversize souvenir cups by the TV stand. That wasn't so good, but it explained the throbbing at the base of her scalp, her queasy stomach and her lack of memory.

Don't feel, she commanded herself. *Just think and solve the problem.*

Fact three. There was a dyed-blue carnation bouquet next to an instant photo in a cheesy cardboard frame from the Silver Rush Wedding Chapel that read Hitched in Reno on the bedside table next to her. The image was too grainy—or maybe her eyes were too fuzzy to see—but she was definitely the one holding up the ugly flowers in the picture. She carefully stretched out her arm, trying to bring the photograph closer and into focus without waking the sleeping Adonis beside her. She squinted at the photo. Had they gone to some sort of Wild West–themed bar last night? Maybe that was where she'd met the guy next to her, because he was in the picture, too.

She let out a quiet breath while she carefully studied the shot for more clues. She and Mr. Adonis looked as if they were sitting in a covered pioneer wagon. Next to them sat two people wearing costumes reflecting Nevada's silver mining heritage. At least she hoped those were costumes. This was really weird, unless...

She glanced over her bare shoulder. The perfectly formed male snored softly away in her bed, and, as she let her gaze drift past the golden features of his face, she rethought her earlier angel appraisal. There was nothing cherubic about the man from the neck down. Had some of the bachelorettes ended up at an all-male revue show?

Oh, no. What if this guy next to her was a male stripper and she'd hooked up with him? Her parents would be mortified. They'd raised her to be a strong woman with an even stronger sense of self-worth—one who would never get taken advantage of by a man.

She dropped the photo and wiped her damp palm on the sheet. Kylie was a certified public accountant and she needed an explanation for this situation that would add up, one that would make sense. She had to stop jumping to conclusions and get back to her usual analytical approach to problem solving.

Besides, his body might look as though it could grace the cover of one of her historical romance novels, but his relaxed face looked too innocent to work for tips.

She rubbed her eyes before scrutinizing the picture again. Regardless of where they were or who else was in the photo with them, they'd both looked pretty darned pleased with themselves last night. Obviously, they'd had a fun time. She didn't know if that was good or not.

Fact four. She was still dressed in her matching blue lace panty and bra set—but nothing else. What did that mean? Had they or hadn't they...?

Again, she looked at her bedmate. She had no idea what he had on underneath the covers, but on top, he was wearing nothing but an impressive array of bronzed muscles and a smile. The heat of embarrassment shot up her cheeks.

Even though most people thought Kylie dressed too flashy and went out on more than her fair share of dates, the reality was that in all of her thirty years, she'd never let a man get past second base. And now she couldn't remember who the batter was or whether he'd hit a home run last night! She didn't need to be sober to come to the conclusion that winding up half naked and in bed with a stranger couldn't be good at all.

Before she could move on to fact five, the blond Adonis snuggled closer and wrapped his overdeveloped biceps around her waist. His warm strength sizzled against her taut skin, and it took every fiber of her normally calm demeanor to not leap off the bed and run away from him. She no longer had time to be analytical. If she tried to appraise the situation any more, she'd end up waking him. Maybe she could just sneak out quietly.

Wait. This was *her* room.

She might bite her tongue when some of the more gossipy women in town mocked her, but having grown up the only girl with four older brothers and an opinionated father, she was used to establishing her independence and her individuality. She was no wallflower. Kylie had learned early on that in life she needed to stand up for herself in order to stand out. She'd also learned how hold her own with men. Even gorgeous, naked ones.

She shoved at his shoulder. "Pssst."

His only response was to grip her tighter.

"Hey," she said louder as she tried gracefully to extricate herself from his embrace.

His full pink lips nuzzled against her neck, and a shocking tingle raced down her spine.

The intimate contact both aroused and startled her. She used her bare leg to shove herself away from him. Unfortunately, her heel nailed him in the shin and, just as she was pushing away, he yelped and scrambled backward. The force of his retreat timed perfectly with her launch, and she lost her momentum, collapsing to the patterned carpeted floor in a pile of long limbs and blue lace.

"What in the hell?" she cried out, trying to pull the sheet down to cover herself.

"Where am I?" he asked.

With the sheet finally wrapped around her, Kylie got to her feet so she could confront the equally confused stranger sitting up in her bed. She caught sight of her makeshift toga in the dresser mirror and lifted her chin higher. Her friends always told her that with her tall, curvaceous body, she looked just like an auburn version of Wonder Woman. Yet right now the resemblance was more similar to the superhero's secret identity, Princess Diana, who needed to defend her Amazon kingdom from unwanted males. "I'll tell you *where* you are if you tell me *who* you are."

"I'm Andrew." He rubbed at his close-cropped haircut, and she took comfort in the fact that his head must be pounding just as badly as her own.

Andrew didn't sound like a stripper name—not that she had any point of reference when it came to exotic male dancers.

"Well, Andrew, you're in my room at the Legacy Casino in Reno. Don't ask me how you got here, because I'm still pretty fuzzy on the details."

The man looked at the disheveled bedding, then back at her, his eyes traveling the length of her body before settling on her heated face. He blinked a couple of times before his hand fumbled on the nightstand and lifted a pair of wire-framed lenses to his eyes.

"You're Kylie," he said, recognition apparently dawning on him.

"Well, at least one of us knows…" She faltered as a flashback from last night triggered her own memory bank. "You know, with those glasses on, you kind of look like that military friend of Cooper's…"

His nod confirmed the sudden fear she couldn't even bear to say aloud. Oh, no. This was bad. This was very, very bad.

"Oh, my gosh." She pointed an accusatory finger at him while he looked around the room sheepishly, probably in search of his holy vestments. Or at least his pants. "You're the minister who's performing the wedding. You're Drew Gregson!"

Snippets of yesterday afternoon clicked into place, and she remembered arriving at the cocktail lounge early so she could welcome the rest of the wedding party. Drew, the groom's best friend, was already there and looking as lost and as confused as a lamb. And she'd apparently led him straight to slaughter. She sank down into the nearest chair. He hadn't stood up yet, and she wasn't about to get in bed again with a man of the cloth. "We are so going to hell."

Yesterday she'd ordered him a drink, telling him it would help him relax. Then she'd cracked a ribald joke to loosen the tension. He'd made a scandalized face before laughing, and they'd toasted the newlyweds. Everything after that was a blur. A horrible, sinful blur.

"Yes, that's me. But I'm not a minister."

She studied his face, trying to decide if he was telling the truth or just doing damage control. Maybe he was used to waking up in strange hotel rooms with women he didn't know, but he didn't seem too concerned about the fate of their eternal souls. So if he wasn't a pastor, then what was he? And why was he so unbelievably calm—and not the least bit modest?

She averted her eyes because if she had to look at his rock-hard abs any longer, she would have no hope of keeping her mind focused and figuring out how everything had gone so completely wrong last night. "Can you please put a shirt on or something?"

He pulled the comforter off the floor and dragged it around his body as he scanned the room. Any article of male clothing would do at this point, but Kylie had no idea where he'd left his. From her vantage point, she tried to look around the room, too, but her search kept returning to his bare torso and the fabric secured around his waist with his left hand. After years of being single, she resorted to her default training and zoned in on the shiny gold ring.

"What the hell is that?" She pointed to the offending object. "You're married! I just spent the night with a drunk, married man."

She pulled her white four-hundred-thread-count shroud tighter around her body, as if she could make herself vanish from the shame and his anonymous wife's impending wrath.

"What are you talking about?" Drew asked as he picked up a plain white undershirt and pulled it on over his head. "I'm not married."

"You're wearing a wedding ring."

He squinted his baby-blue eyes at his finger, looking truly puzzled by the gleaming jewelry. Then he turned his bespectacled gaze to her as if waiting for her to explain the whole situation to him.

Well, she certainly had no idea what was going on. Still, his appraising look was patient and intense, and Kylie had the feeling that Drew had probably won his fair share of staring contests. His continuing focus unnerved her, and her trembling fingers slipped on the sheet. She struggled to get her improvised garment back into position, and her breath hitched when she saw what had caught his attention.

"You have one, too." His tone was casual, lacking any judgment or accusation.

She stared at the matching band on her own ring finger.

For the first time in history, Kylie Chatterson, former

pep leader of the Boise State Cheer Team, second runner-up for Miss Idaho USA and current CPA whiz, was at a loss for words.

Her sheet slipped to the floor unnoticed as she ran into the bathroom and slammed the door.

Maybe she wasn't being very mature and rational about this situation—whatever *this* situation was—but she felt as though she couldn't breathe, and her palms were sticky with sweat.

This must be what a panic attack felt like. Or a hangover. Ugh, how much *had* she had to drink last night?

Don't freak out. Where was her inner voice of reason when she needed it most? Probably back in the hotel lounge where she must've accidentally dumped it out of her designer gold clutch, along with the rest of her morals, when she'd pulled out her credit card to pay for that first round.

She took a sip of water from the sink, then held one hand under the cool flow while she forced herself to inhale and exhale through her nose and slow her breathing. When it finally felt as if her lungs weren't going to explode, she shut off the faucet and dried her hands.

She needed to think. Why was she wearing this stupid wedding ring, and why had Drew Gregson spent the night in her room? The answer was obvious to her methodical and organized brain, even if she was completely unclear on how they'd gotten to this point.

She stared at her sloppy reflection in the mirror, as if the hot mess looking back at her could provide any explanation. Her long auburn curls were a tangled disaster and her once carefully applied makeup had probably been left behind on one of the ten pillows out there with the Angel of Lust.

Thankfully, she'd unpacked yesterday afternoon and

had left her toiletry kit on the bathroom counter. She pulled the fluffy white hotel robe off the hook and double-knotted it around her waist. After running a brush through her hair and securing it into a tight ponytail, she scrubbed her face clean. She brushed her teeth much longer than the American Dental Association recommended, knowing she was stalling for time.

Just as she rinsed out the last of the toothpaste, a knock sounded at the bathroom door. "Uh, Kylie?"

Great. He was still out there. She needed to get rid of him ASAP so she could get down to the business of figuring out just what in the world was going on around here.

"I just found some papers on the dresser," he said through the locked barrier between them. "I think we may have a little situation."

Drew's head felt as if mortar rounds were ricocheting inside his skull. The marriage license trembling in his normally steady hands looked real enough, but his hazy eyes could barely make out the words. He looked at his watch. Oh nine hundred. He needed to pick up his nephews in less than twenty-four hours. His twin brother's eight-year-olds were waiting for him at his parents' house in Boise.

At least he was now dressed and could face the unexpected crisis that had barricaded herself in the bathroom with a little decorum—unlike the behavior he must've exhibited last night. He'd found the last of his clothes strewn about as if a bomb had detonated in the hotel room. He was usually so neat and took care with his clothing. Of course, he also took care not to overindulge in alcohol or marry women after knowing them for all of five hours.

Clearly, he wasn't himself.

For the past ten minutes, he'd been trying to remain cool and controlled while simultaneously racking his foggy brain for details on how he'd ended up in bed with the beautiful woman. Thankfully, she'd run into the bathroom. He hoped she would get dressed because, even for a man who'd sworn off women, there was only so much temptation he could handle.

Yesterday afternoon, the building anxiety and uncertainty about becoming his nephews' legal guardian while his brother deployed on a top secret mission this summer had swelled to an all-time high. It didn't help that Drew was suffering from jet lag, having arrived fresh off the cargo plane from a military base in the Middle East. To top it all off, he was about to embark on a new assignment as the staff psychologist at the naval hospital near his hometown. It was a trifecta of pressure he hadn't been expecting.

He shook his head. Regardless, all the compounding mental and physical effects weren't an excuse for what he'd done—if only he knew what exactly that was. He'd counseled numerous soldiers and sailors about the healthy and effective ways of handling stress stateside after returning from war. He was pretty sure that getting drunk and marrying the first woman he met wasn't one of his usual recommendations.

Drew remembered introducing himself to Kylie at the cocktail lounge in the casino yesterday before the rest of the wedding party arrived. He'd been eager to see his buddy Matt Cooper, who was marrying Kylie's best friend, Maxine Walker. In fact, Drew had indirectly introduced the bride and groom when he'd coerced Cooper to participate in a military pen pal program with Maxine's son.

Yesterday, emotions had been running high for everyone. For Drew they'd been coupled with the unknown anxiety of what awaited him at home.

Kylie had been so friendly and so easy to talk to. As a

psychologist, Drew was accustomed to listening to other people's problems and giving guidance or counsel whenever necessary. But he'd never been the one on the couch, so to speak, and wasn't used to venting his own feelings. She'd made a joke about him needing a drink to loosen up, and he'd thought, *What could one glass hurt?*

He eyed the neon-green oversize souvenir cups shaped like slot machines and then ran a hand over his aching head. What could it hurt, indeed? Those deceiving fruity concoctions packed a punch he wouldn't soon forget.

He stared at the Hitched in Reno photo tossed on the nightstand and wondered how many souvenir cups it had taken for him to get so loopy that he'd thought saying wedding vows before God and a couple of character actors dressed in silver miners' garb was a good plan.

But he looked beyond the Boomtown theme of the photo of him in his starched jeans and Kylie in her miniskirt, noting the matching smiles on their faces. They may have been three sheets to the wind, but they looked genuinely happy. Almost blissful.

He'd attended his share of weddings and, while many were joyful events, some had been clad in scandal or anger or forced circumstances. In this picture, though, he and Kylie were looking at each other with such unadulterated elation, he went through his catalog of memories to recall if he'd ever seen a couple look as happy on their wedding day as he and Kylie had.

He'd always had an idea of marriage in the back of his mind and knew he'd tie the knot someday. His father was a minister and often preached about honoring the vows of marriage. Maybe because he was old-fashioned or maybe because of his religious upbringing, Drew knew that when he finally settled down, it would be only once. In fact, right after graduate school, he'd thought Jessica could have potentially be the one. He'd wanted to take his time, draw out their courtship, because he needed to be positive that they were perfect for each other. Turned out Jessica hadn't liked waiting for his decision.

After that, he'd vowed not to enter into any relationship—even a sexual one—with a woman without ensuring she was marriage material. He'd thought taking a break from women would be a simple test of mind over matter.

But now his self-imposed rule was being seriously tested as it never had been before. He looked down at the wedding photo and the attractive redhead in the too-tight outfit and too-high heels. Not that Drew believed in stereotypes of any kind, but Kylie didn't look anything like the spouses of some of his esteemed colleagues. He remembered thinking she was stunning when he'd met her yesterday, even if her attire was not what one would describe as conventional. Then, this morning, when she'd dropped her sheet and he'd seen her in all her womanly glory, he'd had a difficult time looking away.

Despite his promise to himself, he struggled with the same carnal feelings that most people did. But up until now, he'd been able to control his emotions. Besides, living in battle-ready military installations around the world for the past few years had limited the potential for temptation, as his social interactions with single women who weren't wearing unisex camouflage had been few and far between.

Yet Kylie's style and personality were so animated and so colorful, he couldn't help but be drawn to her.

The water in the bathroom shut off again and he braced himself for her to exit. They would have to come to terms with what they'd done.

The door opened and she held her freshly scrubbed face high, but even the oversize bathrobe couldn't do much to diminish the endowments she'd been blessed with.

She leaned against the door frame, her green, makeup-free eyes squeezed tightly closed. "Please don't tell me what I think you're going to tell me."

"If you think I'm going to tell you that this wedding picture was just a joke, then I won't tell you that."

"How do you know?" She squinted one lid open, and he handed over the very official-looking marriage license. Sign, sealed and delivered.

She was a smart woman. Drew couldn't recall how he knew this, but he remembered thinking it at some point last night. So he remained quiet and let her come to the inevitable conclusion.

"Wow." She sank down to the floor, her long, shapely legs exposed as her knees poked through the gap in the white terry cloth.

He'd learned early on that to have effective communication with people, he needed to reach them on their level. So despite the queasiness in his own stomach, he gingerly lowered himself to floor beside her.

"I'm sorry," he said, wanting to comfort her. "I don't know how it happened or why we did it, but it looks as though we're married."

She cupped her head in her hand while holding the license in the other. Her eyes traveled over the paper repeatedly, probably looking for some loophole or some hint that it wasn't legitimate. Unfortunately, Drew knew they were staring at the real deal.

"But how can we be married when it says our only witnesses were two people who signed their names as Pistole Pepe and Maddog Molly?"

Drew handed over the wedding photo. "I think that guy with the long beard and miner's hat is Pistole. This snarling woman holding the blue flowers like yours must be Molly."

"God, my maid of honor was an overweight saloon girl with a missing tooth."

"Maybe we should try to focus on the more important facts," he suggested.

"Seriously? How can you not be worried about this?" The arched red brow made him think she didn't like his suggestion. "You got totally wasted last night and forced a complete stranger to marry you. Who the hell knows what kind of fornication we committed in that bed right over there? Yet now you have the nerve to tell me that none of that is important?"

"Okay, let's recap. One, I'm a doctor. A clinical psychologist, to be exact. My job is to look at the big picture."

"But you're performing the wedding. Don't you have to be a preacher to do that?"

"Uh, no. Anyone can get certified online to do that. I owed Cooper a favor and he knows I hate public speaking."

"Well, that explains that mystery." She let out a sigh, then leaned her head back so quickly, it thunked against the wall.

"Can we get back to the current situation?" He waited for her to nod before continuing, "Two, I don't think it's in anybody's best interests to keep a running tab of potential sins. Three, I might have been somewhat intoxicated, but judging by the smile on your face in that picture, I think we can safely say that nobody forced anybody to do anything last night. Four, I'm pretty sure that whatever might or might not have happened in that bed last night wouldn't be considered fornication if we were technically married."

Drew was a patient man, but he didn't know if the woman collapsed in front of him was willing to listen to reasonable logic. How would he? He didn't know her from Adam. Or Eve. But he *did* know that if Eve had looked anything like Kylie Chatterson, Drew didn't blame Adam one bit for taking a bite of that cursed apple.

"I'll concede points one through three," she finally said. "But since you're not a minister, then you're clearly no expert on what might or might not constitute fornication."

Wait, now she was annoyed that he *wasn't* a minister? The lady needed to make up her mind, because he couldn't win this game. "Are you an attorney?"

"No, I'm a CPA. When you talk in numbers to me, things make better sense."

Drew would have to store that knowledge away for future use. "Listen, I'm just as confused and overwhelmed by this whole thing as you are. But I know that we have to keep our heads clear and our words civil if we're going to get through this."

She nodded, but her confused eyes still sought answers. "How can you be so calm? This can't be great news for you, either, but you've yet to freak out."

"Job hazard. I'm in the business of keeping calm when everything around me is blowing up. Literally."

"Well, this would certainly qualify as an explosion in my life." The back of her head thumped against the wall again as she lifted her face to the ceiling.

"There's a coffeemaker in here. Why don't I brew some and we can figure out our next course of action?"

He stood and held out his hand to her. He realized his mistake when she stared at his extended fingers before taking several breaths. He was still wearing the gold band. She probably didn't appreciate the reminder of last night, but he hadn't been able to get the thing off his oversize knuckle.

At almost six foot four and weighing close to two hundred thirty pounds, Drew was a big man. He was accustomed to things not always being available in his size.

Apparently, his selection in wedding rings was no exception.

After a few uncomfortable moments, she finally accepted his extended hand by placing her own in his. He effortlessly pulled her up and, when they were practically face-to-face, he was pleasantly surprised that she was only a few inches shorter than him.

But holding hands made it easier for her to study the his-and-hers duplicate set of jewelry. She dropped his fingers as if the rings were some sort of live grenades and then tugged on her gold band, but it wouldn't even budge.

"Ugh. It's stuck. I'm probably swollen up from all the booze."

Drew's eyes dipped from her hand to her heaving chest as she labored over the ring, and he noticed her fingers weren't the only things swollen. The way the lapel of her robe gaped open, he could see that her breasts were about to spill out of their D cups.

Heat stole up his neck, and his skin tightened all over his body. He quickly turned away to walk toward the mini-brewer tucked into a corner alcove.

With his back to her, he heard her cross behind him to the opposite side of the room. He hoped she wasn't physically distancing herself in fear that he was some sort of pervert and might attack her. She probably sensed the way his body was responding to her, and he couldn't blame her for taking precautions.

"We're supposed to meet the rest of the wedding party for brunch in less than thirty minutes," she said as he made the first cup. "Do you think they'll wonder whether something is wrong if neither one of us shows?"

"Why wouldn't we show up for bunch? I, for one, am starving. Did we even have dinner last night?"

"Don't ask me," Kylie said, then thanked him for the

mug he offered. She sat in one of the chairs, and he wondered if her legs were as shaky as his. "After we left the cocktail lounge, everything else that happened last night is pretty vague. And what do you mean 'why *wouldn't* we show up for brunch'? We can't walk in there, in front of all our friends, and act as if nothing's out of the ordinary."

"Why can't we? They obviously weren't there last night or they would've put a stop to…you know." Drew gestured toward the empty souvenir cups littering the hotel room, leaving any mention of the impromptu wedding unsaid.

"That's a good point. So you think we should just act as if nothing happened? I mean, I don't want to lie to my friends, but if we play everything off as though we had a bit too much to drink and don't remember last night clearly, that would be the truth, right?"

Drew had been raised to believe that an omission was just as serious as a lie. But it wasn't as though he needed to broadcast their mistake to the world or make it anyone's business. He didn't know what to do. Nothing about this situation was sitting well. Including the way Kylie's sweet green eyes pleaded with him.

He was a problem solver by nature and wished he could just give her some advice and then walk away. But this was one problem he didn't know how to solve.

"Can I ask you a question?" He took off his glasses and rubbed the bridge of his nose.

"Sure, but I can't guarantee I'll know the answer."

"What are your thoughts on marriage? Not this marriage, per se, but in general. I mean, you're an attractive woman. You're smart. And clearly, you know how to have fun. So is there a reason why you're not married?"

She sank her head back against the chair as if the question exhausted her. But Drew was used to waiting for people to explain things in their own ways. So he stood there, gripping his coffee mug and glasses, waiting for her answer.

"I really have no idea why I'm not married. Heaven knows I've dated enough men that you'd think I would've found Mr. Right by now." That wasn't exactly the answer Drew was hoping to hear. Sure, Kylie was pretty, and he could see why any red-blooded male would want to go out with her, but he could've done without the knowledge that had an active dating calendar.

"To me, marriage is a serious commitment," he said, trying to make a point.

"Which we entered into lightly." Kylie's posture, even when seated, was tall and impressive, and Drew doubted she could sit up any straighter.

"But still, we entered into it and everything it entails."

"Listen, I get it that not everyone believes in divorce. But I'm sure we can get an annulment or something that wouldn't taint your beliefs or your reputation."

"Some people might see that as a solution. Yet I have a feeling that we took vows before God."

Kylie looked ready to bolt and probably would've run as far from him as she could if he wasn't standing in between her and her suitcase full of clothes. "We also took vows before some guy named Pistole Pepe, which I'm sure wasn't his legal name at birth. Look, you seem like a real straitlaced guy, but there's an exception to every rule."

Maybe. Kylie looked like the kind of woman who was used to making her own rules. Yet something about her fighting spirit made him question whether he wanted an exception. "I don't know much about the legal logistics, but can we get an annulment if we consummated the marriage?"

Her charming face blushed more crimson than he would've thought possible, and he wanted to kick himself for embarrassing the poor woman. She was definitely shyer than she let on.

Despite the heat staining her cheekbones, she sat up even straighter. But her voice was a mere whisper when she finally spoke. "Did we...?"

Once again, he wanted to put her fears to rest, but he honestly had no idea. He felt like a complete idiot for not remembering. But the fact remained that they'd gotten married and they'd woken up together nearly naked. And did he mention that since he'd sworn off intimacy with women, he hadn't had sex in over a year?

"Honestly," he said, "I don't know. And if neither one of us knows the answer to that, then I'm guessing we also don't know whether or not we used...um...protection?"

Chapter Two

"Oh, my gosh. No. No. No." Kylie thought of every curse word ever uttered by her father and four athletic brothers, and then repeated one that would have shocked a war-weary sailor, let alone the confused doctor in front of her.

"Sorry," she mumbled. She hated offending Drew, who finally looked uncomfortable. It wasn't his fault she'd sacrificed her much-practiced poise for the feistiness she usually kept hidden. "I don't usually talk like that. I didn't mean to let my mouth get away from me."

He looked at her lips and she instantly regretted the words that drew his attention there. But she was too absorbed in her own panic to worry about what kind of pleasure they might or might not have partaken of last night.

"I know we wouldn't have forgotten *that*. Right?" She was too mortified to even say what *that* was.

He ran his hand through his close-cropped military-style haircut, and she wondered how she could have possibly thought this conservative, clean-cut man in the crisp jeans and J.Crew sweater was a male stripper.

"I would like to think that we both would have known better than to be so reckless." His confident tone didn't quite match his puzzled and slightly pink expression. "Yet from the looks of everything else around us, we should have known better about a lot of things."

"But you don't understand. I can't just be married. Or suddenly pregnant by someone I don't know. My father would kill me. My brothers would kill *you*. Everyone in Sugar Falls would say they knew something like this was bound to happen. I'll have to give up my accounting practice and move to Boise. Wait. Farther than that. Siberia, maybe. This is going to ruin my whole life."

"Well, at least we're equally screwed."

Wait, had he just said *screwed*? Perhaps the gravity of the situation was finally sinking in for Doctor Perfect.

"I mean, it's not as if this is going to look really great for my career or my family." He waved his arm dramatically at the room, including the empty beverage cups and her. "I'm not exactly proud of all this."

It was difficult to not take the insult personally. Why would he be ashamed of marrying her? Maybe she wasn't some stuffy Miss Priss, but she was decent in the looks department and she was financially successful. Plus, she didn't have any standout mental health concerns, addictions or genetic diseases—that she knew of. Frankly, he could do a lot worse.

Of course, so could she. And hadn't she proved just that with some of the losers she'd dated in the past? No man she'd ever been out with—and if you asked her two best friends, they'd say she'd been out with a lot—had made it past her rigid checklist of qualities for Mr. Right. Her strike-one-and-you're-out policy explained why she went through eligible men so quickly. That and her fear of taking home anyone to meet her opinionated family.

While life had taught her to be pragmatic about most things, Kylie believed in true love. She was a romantic at heart and knew that somewhere out there, her soul mate was waiting for her. Unfortunately, she doubted that her soul mate would want the pregnant ex-wife of some military shrink.

She sighed. "I'm sorry if it seems as if I'm only looking out for my best interests here. This probably wasn't exactly what you envisioned, either, when we ordered that first round last night. But at least you don't live in a small, judgmental town like Sugar Falls. You won't be carrying around a nine-month reminder of this night or have smug busybodies shake their heads at you when you pass them on the street with your love child in tow. You get to hop on the first navy plane out of here and go on about your life."

Drew knelt in front of her, his fingers cupping her chin, gently forcing her to meet his eyes. "I'm not going anywhere. Especially if you're carrying my child. You don't know me or the kind of person I am, so I'm not going to take offense at what you just said. But I'm telling you this now, completely sober and with every moral fiber in my body. We will be in this together, and any decisions that need to be made will be made by both of us."

Kylie wasn't sure if that was a threat or a vow. He seemed to have an abundance of moral fibers floating around in his perfectly formed body. Yet, behind the clear lenses, his eyes were very serious and solemn. For some reason, his words soothed her, and she no longer felt as though she was drowning alone. The fact remained, though, that she was still drowning. All she could hope was that this guy didn't sink her in his quest to save himself first.

It must've been the lingering effects of the alcohol causing her palms to sweat and her tummy to swirl. Out of all the men she'd gone out with, not once had one's nearness ever made her feel this light-headed.

Kylie needed some food to ease her roiling stomach, and they had only about ten minutes to get to brunch downstairs before their dual absence caused speculation.

"Okay," she said. "Let's agree to get through today and this upcoming week back in Sugar Falls as if nothing has happened." Hopefully, by then, she'd have some more answers—like whether she'd need to buy a pregnancy test and when he'd be on his way out of town and out of her life. "We won't make any decisions until after the wedding. *Their* wedding, that is. Maxine and Cooper's. Not yours and mine. Ugh. You know what I mean."

Great. How was she ever going to get through this brunch if she couldn't even get through a sentence?

"That sounds like a good plan." He stood back up, his hand that had gently stroked her chin now extended in a handshake. She hadn't noticed before but his right pinkie was slightly bent—an interesting flaw in an otherwise perfect specimen of man.

He had replaced an intimate gesture with a business-like stance. So she rose from the chair in order to cover up the fact that she was leaning toward him like a lost kitten seeking out a friendly pat. Had she been wearing her usual four-inch heels, she would have come close to matching his impressive height. However, in her bare feet and over-size robe, she felt more delicate and womanly than she was used to when around average-size men.

Whoa, he was well built. As his hand shook hers, she smiled, thinking that under his preppy sweater and starched jeans was a rippling specimen of a man that only she was privy to. She liked knowing that.

He still hadn't released her from his grip when two

abrupt knocks sounded at the door. Drew turned to answer it and she grabbed his forearm and pulled him back. What was he thinking?

She put a finger to her mouth and shoved him toward the bathroom. A second passed before his brows lifted in surprise. He finally figured out that she wanted to hide him from whoever was knocking. The guy was obviously not schooled in the art of clandestine operations, which was probably a point in his favor. Just not at that exact moment.

She waited until the bathroom knob clicked before opening the hotel room door.

Her best friend's former mother-in-law, Cessy Walker, and Freckles, the owner of the Cowgirl Up Café back home, brushed past her and into what Kylie was sure they would sense was her den of iniquity.

"Are we supposed to meet here for the brunch?" Cessy asked.

"Uh, no." Kylie turned quickly, hoping the women wouldn't notice the remains of last night's debauchery that still littered the nightstand and floor. "We were supposed to meet downstairs at the buffet."

Kylie's frantic search zeroed in on the wedding photo and license she'd left on the chair, and she quickly sat on top of them.

"You're not ready," Cessy said, pointing out the obvious.

"No, I'm running a little late, Mrs. Walker. Why don't you two ladies go on down and let everyone know that we're... I mean, that I'm on my way."

"Kylie." Cessy tsked, looking around the room. "You're one of the maids of honor. You're supposed to be hosting the brunch. It's in bad taste to show up late to your own event."

Hopefully, Sugar Falls's resident society matron wouldn't find out what other forms of bad taste Kylie had recently been engaged in.

"Is your shower running?" asked Freckles—who looked older than Kylie's grandmother, yet dressed as though she was a runner-up in a Dolly Parton lookalike contest.

"Oh. Uh, yeah. I was just about to hop in when you guys knocked."

"Well, we'll just wait out here for you, then. Maybe it'll speed you along."

Kylie thought about the man inside her bathroom who, right this second, was probably lathering up his well-muscled body. She couldn't go in there now or she'd see him in all his angelic glory. She would have blushed in mortification at her lustful thoughts for a stranger, but she was too busy flushing bright red at the realization that the two women looked like they were going to settle in and wait for her to do just that.

Before she could muster a protest, an undoubtedly manly shout sounded from the other side of the door. "Ow! Man, that's slippery!"

Freckles's face split into an ear-to-ear lipstick-covered grin. But her slightly younger and overcontrolling cohort looked confused.

"Who was that?" Cessy asked.

"That's what I call the evidence of a good bachelorette party." Freckles giggled, slapping her painted on jeans–clad thigh.

"Kylie Chatterson, I can't believe you brought a man back to your hotel room—and of all times. You couldn't go one weekend without one?" Cessy looked more exasperated than surprised, and Kylic's pride stung at the implication that promiscuous behavior was expected from her. Normally she would've launched a full verbal attack against any petty remarks directed at her or her loved ones. But the truth of the situation and her growing shame wouldn't allow her to defend her questionable honor.

"Stop being such a prude, Cessy," the other woman said. If Kylie hadn't been sitting across the room in the chair, refusing to budge for fear of revealing the condemning documents, the older waitress probably would've high-fived her.

Freckles was the liberal yin to Cessy's conservative and proper yang. They were a mismatched set of friends, and right about now Kylie fought back tears at their intrusive assumptions. But at this second, she couldn't argue with the evidence. So she bit her lip and tried to come up with a plan to get them out of her room.

"Well, you'd better not bring some one-night stand to my daughter-in-law's prewedding brunch. Cooper's friend, that sweetheart of a man who's performing the wedding, is going to be there. His father is a minister, and Drew himself is a well-respected and high-ranking officer. The last thing we need is for him to think the bride's best friend is hooking up with random men."

The sharp insult was a stiletto to Kylie's heart. She wanted to scream that the almighty, holier-than-thou Doctor Gregson was too busy being naked in her shower and recovering from a hangover of epic proportions to worry about anyone else's misconduct.

But she wouldn't turn this into a bigger scandal and out the poor guy like that—even if misery *did* love company.

Kylie counted to one hundred under her breath. The only thing stopping her from verbally putting Cessy Walker in her place was the fact that, in this situation, Kylie's behavior was indefensible. Even if it seemed to be what everyone anticipated. And that was what hurt the most.

Sure, Kylie wore clothes that were arguably a bit too

sexy by Sugar Falls, Idaho, standards. But underneath the beauty-queen smile, the spandex and the heels, she was a well-balanced and professional woman.

Heck, Kylie even did Cessy Walker's—as well as half the town's—income taxes. It seemed everyone trusted her sensible side when it came to important things like their finances and life savings. But nobody seemed to trust her when it came to moral values that were none of their business anyway.

She was just about to say as much when Freckles finally spoke up and pulled her friend's arm. "Cessy Walker, don't try to shame the girl for having a little fun. You were on your third marriage by the time you were Kylie's age. C'mon now, let's go meet everyone downstairs. She's a big girl and can make her own decisions. Besides, she's so smart…"

Their voices drifted down the hallway as Kylie slammed the door closed.

Just then, Drew poked his head out of the bathroom, probably making sure the coast was clear. "I, uh, don't have any of my clothes except the ones I wore yesterday. Do you think I have time to go back to my room to change?"

His slim hips were barely covered by a knotted white towel; his wide shoulders and tapering torso were too much for her overcrowded mind to take in. "Just put on the same stuff and get down there before me. Nobody will notice what you're wearing anyway."

"Listen," he started, and she could already see the pity in his face. "I couldn't help but hear Mrs. Walker's voice. I'm sorry for the way she spoke to you. I'm sure that if we put our heads together, we can figure out how to minimize the gossip."

His words stung her pride even more than she'd thought possible. She hated anyone feeling sorry for her and was mortified that he'd overheard the older woman chastising her. Her parents had raised her to be tough, and she'd been on the receiving end of worse insults than the ones he'd just overheard. What she couldn't handle was pity. His sympathy implied she had no control over her life and needed Doctor Goodbody to step in and save her.

"Don't worry about it. If there's one thing I've learned, it's that gossip in small towns is pretty standard. So just as long as nobody finds out *who* the man in my room is, I can live with one more blemish on my unearned reputation."

With that, she grabbed his discarded clothes off the bathroom counter and tossed them toward him before locking herself inside. She didn't wait to make sure he left before getting under the hot spray of the shower nozzle to scrub away her sins—along with her hurt and embarrassment. All she wanted was for him to get dressed as quickly as possible and get out of her room before she did something stupid, like let him hold her while she cried her fool eyes out.

But twenty minutes later, when she pageant-walked into the reserved dining room for the prewedding brunch as though everything in her life was as grand as could be, she realized she had seriously underestimated her friends' skills of observation.

After Drew had gone through the buffet line, loading his plate with a custom-made omelet, sausage links and four buttermilk pancakes, he'd tried to sit next to Kylie. He didn't want to seem as if he was avoiding her and, truthfully, he liked being near her. But his best friend and the groom, Matt Cooper, had steered him toward the opposite end of the table.

"You must've gotten lost last night," Cooper said right

before digging into his own breakfast. "Nobody could find you after we left the cocktail lounge."

"Hmm," Drew replied noncommittally as he forked piping-hot eggs into his mouth. He wasn't going to lie to anyone—especially not to Cooper, who was a former military police sergeant and had just been appointed as the chief of police for the town of Sugar Falls. His friend was too canny for that. And, judging from the smug grin across the guy's face, he was also too excited at the prospect of exploiting Drew's possible fall from grace.

"And it looks as though the airlines must have lost your luggage, because you're wearing the exact same clothes you had on when we saw you last."

Yep, the cop definitely knew something had happened. But as much as Drew wanted to confide in his friend, he'd promised Kylie that they wouldn't tell anybody yet. Instead, he shoved a bite of a syrup-drenched pancake into his mouth, trying to avoid answering any more questions.

Drew stole a look down the long table to see how his wife was faring.

Wife.

That sounded weird. Not horrible and scary, he thought. Just weird.

She was seated next to the bride and their friend Mia, the other maid of honor. But unlike Drew, Kylie merely pushed the food back and forth on her plate while her friends talked incessantly around her. She was several feet away from him, but he could've sworn he heard her asking the waitress if the soft-serve ice cream machine was working this early in the day.

"So are you excited about the wedding?" Drew asked Cooper, trying to change the subject. But his buddy wasn't having it.

"Kylie's being rather quiet this morning," Cooper said. "That's kind of unusual for her."

"I wouldn't know. I don't know your friends very well."

"Really? Because you two were thick as thieves last night. I got the feeling you and Kylie were getting to know each other really well."

Drew gave Cooper his listening expression but still didn't respond. He found it was the best way to get information out of people. Unfortunately, Cooper was making the same face.

"Here's the deal," Drew finally relented. "I don't remember much about last night, and I wasn't really myself. So let's just drop it, okay?"

His friend let out a guffaw before patting him on the back. "Don't worry, Saint Drew. Your secret's safe with me. Besides, you could've done a lot worse than Kylie."

"What does that mean?"

"It means that whatever is between you and my soon-to-be wife's best friend is just that—between you two. But I'm still gonna give you a hard time whenever I can."

"Yeah, you're an emotional vault, so I know I can count on you for discretion. You don't talk to anyone about anything." Sadly, Drew was serious, but he knew that since Cooper had met Maxine, his former-loner friend was starting to open up more. "But what do you mean that I could do worse than Kylie? Like I said, I really don't know anything about her."

"Kylie's a good person." Coming from Coop, who was suspicious of everyone, that was quite a compliment. "She's smart as hell and she speaks her mind. Very loyal and protective when it comes to the people she loves. So she dresses a little over-the-top and likes to go out with a new guy every week, but Maxine says she just does that because she was the only girl growing up in a male-dominated household and likes to flaunt her femininity. She's a real spitfire, but she has a heart of gold."

Drew chugged his orange juice, trying not to look at Kylie again. Cooper's assessment pretty much aligned with his own first impression of the woman. At least, what he could remember about it.

"And from the way she's sitting down there all prim and proper, trying not to stare at you just as hard as you're trying not to stare at her, I'd say something good definitely happened between you two."

"And I'd say don't make any risky bets before you leave the casino today. Gambling on the odds isn't in your best interests."

Cooper laughed again, this time drawing the looks of the other twenty or so people crowded around the table.

Drew turned the unwanted attention to his advantage and suddenly announced to the group, "I hate to eat and run, but I'm supposed to be in Boise later today to pick up my nephews. I'll see all of you in Sugar Falls in a few days for the big weekend."

He then excused himself and made his way down the table, saying his goodbyes and shaking hands before he got to the person he wanted to talk to the most.

"Ladies," Drew started, acknowledging both her and her friends, yet Kylie wouldn't look at him or meet his gaze. She kept shoveling ice cream into her mouth so quickly she would no doubt give herself brain freeze. He wanted to get her phone number or figure out a way for them to contact each other since they still had a lot to talk about.

"Drew," Maxine Walker said, looking between him and her redheaded friend. "We'll have to get together as soon as you arrive in Sugar Falls. Cooper tells me you're bringing your nephews with you and staying at the cabin for the summer."

"What?" Kylie's spoon clattered to the floor. "You're moving to Sugar Falls?"

The suspicion in her eyes made him think she was seriously opposed to the news.

"That's the plan." One he didn't intend to change just because he'd stepped out of character one night and had too much to drink.

"Drew's from Boise originally," Maxine explained, probably trying to diffuse her friend's growing tension. "He just transferred assignments and is going to be the psychologist in charge of the new PTSD unit at Shadowview Military Hospital."

"But Shadowview is closer to Boise than to Sugar Falls." What was Kylie getting at? That she would rather him live an hour away so she wouldn't have to be reminded of him or what they'd done?

"Seriously, Kylie," their friend Mia spoke up, a quiet and calm voice of reason. "The hospital is only thirty minutes from the cabin."

"What cabin?" Kylie asked.

"You know, the one off Sweetwater Bend? Where Cooper lived when he first moved to town?" Drew just stood there awkwardly, letting Cooper's fiancée explain everything he should have told Kylie last night. "It belongs to Drew's family. He's going to be living there with his nephews and taking care of them while his brother is on deployment."

"I had absolutely no idea." Kylie wouldn't make eye contact with him, and he decided to get this conversation under control before the woman he'd spent the night with made it obvious to everyone at the table that there was a reason she was acting so uncomfortable around him.

"Kylie, I wanted to talk to you about the wedding rehearsal before I left. Ladies, would you excuse us for just a moment?" He pulled her chair back before she could decline, leaving her no polite choice but to walk away from the table with him.

He hated to coerce her verbally, especially when she'd thrown herself on that little gossip grenade in front of Cessy Walker and Freckles. The only person who had ever covered for him in a potentially disastrous situation like that was his brother, Luke. But he couldn't just sit back and let her martyr herself—or her reputation—without providing his input.

She was just as haughty in her strapless floral-printed sundress as she'd been in her bedsheet this morning. But this time, when she turned to stand toe-to-toe with him, she was almost at eye level. He glanced down at her four-inch wedge-heeled sandals and decided that as regally annoyed as she looked right this second, he liked her similar height to his. As well as her long, toned legs, which made him think thoughts he had no business thinking.

"You never said anything about moving to Sugar Falls," she said accusingly, the sound of slot machines ringing in the background.

"I didn't realize I needed your permission to do so." He tried to keep his voice calm and steady. They were far away from the prying eyes and ears of their acquaintances back at the table, and nobody would be the wiser if they made a scene in the middle of the buffet area. But he knew that if he kept his cool, she would be forced to, as well.

"Of course you don't need my permission. But can't you realize how much more awkward this situation is going to be if we have to live in the same town?"

"Not if we don't *let* things get awkward."

"Maybe you have ice running through your veins, but

I can't run around pretending this—" she held up her ring finger between the two of them "—didn't happen." She must not have been able to get her band off, but she'd camouflaged it by wearing a large ruby-studded one stacked on top. He'd used so much soap in the shower, he'd almost dropped his own down the drain. He reached into his left pocket, just as he'd done several times throughout the meal, making sure it was safely tucked away.

Looking at her bare shoulders and feeling the warm metal circle under his fingers, he knew he had anything but ice coursing through him right that second. In fact, he was almost as heated as he'd been earlier this morning when she stood in front of him in the same stance, all fired up and practically heaving out of her provocative lace bra.

"I think I'm not saying this right." He slowed down his words, hoping this would slow his pulse rate, as well. "We have no idea what we're going to have to deal with in the future, and it would probably help if we could keep things friendly."

"Why are you always so rational?" She sounded as if she was accusing him of something again. Was she seriously expecting an answer? She let out a pent-up breath and then asked a more logical question. "So you're going to be living at that cabin with a couple of kids?"

"Yes."

"But it's only for the summer?"

"Correct. That should give us enough time to know what we're going to do about…uh…everything," he said as he looked pointedly at her midsection. "In the meantime, I wanted to get your number so I could—"

She interrupted him. "Why don't you give me yours instead? I never give my personal number out to strangers. Besides, I'll let you know if there's any news."

Wow. Talk about putting him in his place. Plus she apparently deemed him one who shouldn't get a say in what happened from here on out. He didn't like not being the one in control. Of course, it wasn't as though he couldn't find her if he wanted to. They had the same friends—one of them being the chief of police, who could locate anyone—and Sugar Falls was a small town.

"Okay, let me grab a piece of paper to write it down for you."

"I don't need it. I've got a head for numbers."

He rattled it off, and she repeated it back to him from memory. Impressive.

Now, if only her clever mind could tell him what they'd done last night...

Drew hadn't been able to stop thinking about Kylie the entire flight from Reno to Boise. He had taken a cab from the airport to his parents' house, planning to spend a night or two with his folks so the kids could get reacquainted with him before they left for their summer excursion.

He and Luke had been extraordinarily close growing up and had even joined the navy together when they'd turned eighteen. But their careers had taken opposite paths, and due to the transient nature of their assignments, they rarely saw each other. Which meant Drew saw his nephews even less.

Normally his mom and dad—or even their younger sister—would take the eight-year-old twins whenever Luke was sent overseas for an indefinite length of time. But Hannah was participating in a Teachers Without Borders program this summer, and his parents were getting a little too advanced in years to handle the high-energy boys. Besides, it was time Drew stepped in for some family bonding, especially when he finally had a duty station that wasn't in a war zone.

But after twenty minutes in the house with the wild and rambunctious kids, he wondered if he was equipped to handle so much rowdiness all by himself.

"Uncle Drew," Aiden called out as he stood on the armrest of the sofa. "You look just like Dad, but with hair."

"You look just like Caden, but with mustard on your face," Drew responded. "And get down from there."

"*I'm* Caden," Aiden tried to insist. But Drew was an identical twin himself and knew the old trick.

"Does the switcheroo work on your dad?" Drew doubted it did, and it was best that the boys learn right away that he was going to be just as effective at parenting as his brother. Of course, judging by the complete lack of discipline he'd witnessed so far, he didn't think the boys had been exposed to *any* effective parenting, no matter how much Luke adored his children.

"Not when he's here. But when we Skype him, we can usually fool him good. And we fool Grammie all the time."

"Well, Grammie should know better. After all, nobody's better at the twin switch than me and your old man."

At that moment, Caden ran by, shoving a brownie into his mouth as Drew's mom chased him, a rubber spatula in her hand. "Aiden Andrew Gregson, you bring that brownie back right this minute."

"Grammie, that's Caden. I'm Aiden." The boy who'd been talking to Drew giggled, still balancing on the furniture like a tightrope walker. "See? She mixes us up all the time."

"Well, it doesn't help that your names are almost identical, too. It can be confusing for anyone." Drew lifted Aiden up before planting the boy's sturdy legs on the floor. What had their parents been thinking, naming them so similarly?

But he didn't ask this out loud because he wasn't sure how the kids were reacting to their father's recent deployment. Their mother had passed away when the boys were three, and Luke had raised them mostly on his own when he wasn't playing Captain Save-the-World. Yet the past couple of years, they had bounced around so much to accommodate their dad's dangerous and unpredictable job in special ops, they hadn't had much consistency.

"Aiden, give me back that spatula," Drew's mom yelled, as she chased Caden and his chocolate-covered face back through the living room. She'd now lost her spatula and all control.

"Grammie can never catch us. We're way too fast for her," Aiden boasted.

"Caden," he called out, and the running boy suddenly halted. Drew wasn't a voice raiser and wasn't about to start now. Why yell when you could rationally explain your position? Of course, he doubted that his normal communication tools would be as effective with these two.

Plus, he was still somewhat of a novelty, so the boys were sizing him up. He motioned both of the children over to him and knelt down so he didn't tower over them. His brother had the same build, so he knew they wouldn't be intimidated by his size. But he wanted to be on eye level with them so they would be forced to look at him to hear what he had to say.

"You two are going to go wash up and get your pajamas on."

"We don't want to take no baths," Caden whined as Aiden dropped to the floor in a dramatic heap.

"Your dad and I didn't like taking baths when we were your age, either. But we weren't allowed to have brownies or play Robot Blasters unless we were clean."

"What are Robot Blasters?" Aiden hopped up to attention, his despair quickly turning to eagerness.

"It's a special game only for twins. Your dad and I made

it up a long time ago, and it's very secret and unique. I can't tell you about it until you can show that you're able to follow rules and directions."

"I call front bath." Caden ran off to be first in the bathroom, Aiden hurrying to catch up.

"I hate getting stuck in the stern," his brother complained, but he followed anyway.

Drew's mom collapsed on the sofa, clearly winded after her brownie-turned-spatula chase. "I can't keep up with them like I used to."

"Where's Dad?" Drew asked.

"He's at the health club, doing his water therapy. He's been staying away more this visit. Says his sciatica has been acting up. But I think he's just suffering from a case of naughty twinitis."

His folks had been great parents, involved in everything from the Little League to the Cub Scouts. Marty Gregson had been a youth pastor when he'd met his wife, Donna, a schoolteacher. They'd both had a natural love for children, which Drew's sister had inherited. But they were at the start of their golden years. And plainly, his unruly nephews were more than their retired lives could handle.

"I swear I love those boys to death, and so does your father. But I can't tell you how grateful we are that you're pulling a shift this summer. In fact, Dad didn't want me to tell you this, but we've already got the RV loaded up, and the minute you drive off with the kids, we're leaving for our grand tour. I thought it only fair to warn you that by the time you make it to the cabin, there won't be the opportunity for any take-backs." She must have seen his horrified expression. "I'm kidding, of course. We'll be a phone call away if you need anything. You guys will be fine."

Drew plopped down beside her, not sure if he was ready for the biggest responsibility he'd yet to face. He really needed her to tell him there would be light at the end of this tunnel. "It's only three months, right?"

"I know you can do it, honey. Sure, they're a handful, but you're a trained psychologist. You're used to dealing with behavior outside the norm, right?"

"Mom, I work with soldiers, not children."

"Drew, it's about time you settled down. You have a wonderful opportunity to spend time with your nephews and give this whole domesticity thing a try. It's time to stop analyzing everything from behind all those textbooks of yours and start actually living life. Of course, it'd probably be easier if you were married and had an extra set of hands to help you, but your brother does this on his own all the time."

Drew thought about Kylie and how, if they were married in the true sense of the word, she'd be helping him. Man, she might be helping him anyway if it turned out that she was pregnant. He didn't even know if the woman liked kids. Or wanted them.

He was pretty sure *he* did, but then he looked toward the open bathroom door and saw the soaking wet hallway carpet. Before he could ask his mom about a flooding problem or a possible burst pipe, Donna Gregson shot off the sofa, her bare feet squishing with each running step on the flooded rug.

"Boys, I told you no more playing battleship or hurricane watch in the bathtub."

A child's squeal was followed by the crashing sound of water.

"That's it. I'm going to bed." His mom retreated, completely drenched from what Drew assumed was a water attack. "You're on duty for now, Lieutenant Commander. Your father should be home in an hour if you need reinforcements." She sloshed her way down to the end of the hall, and he heard the lock on the master bedroom door click into place.

After the morning he'd had, he'd promised himself he'd never drink again. But being confronted with two unmanageable nephews—and who knew what other problems awaiting him with Kylie in Sugar Falls—it took several minutes of mindful meditation and an unearthly amount of willpower to head to the linen closet for a stack of towels instead of running directly to his parents' liquor cabinet.

Chapter Three

Kylie hadn't called him once since they'd seen each other in Reno. And this past week, Drew had been so deep in the exploits of a couple of eight-year-olds, he didn't know when he'd find a chance to seek her out now that he was officially in Sugar Falls.

Caden and Aiden had helped to take his mind off the situation, but only because they kept up a steady pace of disobedience and messes, leaving no downtime between their wrestling matches, arguments, food fights and predilections to log onto his laptop to access online video games rated for mature users.

The increasing need to keep them under constant supervision took every ounce of mental energy Drew possessed. At this rate, he didn't know how he'd make it through this weekend, let alone this summer. He enrolled the boys in a local day-camp program starting on Monday, but he feared he'd barely get to the base hospital to report for duty be-

fore getting a call advising him that the twins were being
kicked out.

He peered at his reflection in the small mirror in the
cabin's single bathroom. The man staring back at him
looked as though he'd been on a battlefield. And after
his last few deployments, he knew he wasn't exaggerat-
ing. There was a reason he specialized in PTSD and not
in child psychology.

He heard the boys getting restless in the living room
and, if he wanted them to not look like complete ruffians
before they got to the wedding rehearsal, he needed to get
out there quickly while their clothes were still somewhat
dirt- and chocolate-free.

According to his mother—who hesitated to disclose her
and his dad's travel itinerary for fear Drew would give up
too quickly and load up the boys to track them down in
their motor home—his nephews had been kicked out of
several after-school clubs, piano classes and swim lessons
and two city libraries. Their school had threatened expul-
sion last year, but Luke had stepped in and sweet-talked
the single schoolteacher into giving them another chance.

Drew wondered if his brother had ever considered sending the eight-year-olds away to military school. Or to one
of those scared-straight prison programs. As it was, the
only time Drew was able to let down his guard was when
they were both wearing their life vests and bike helmets.
At the same time.

Thank goodness he'd finally get to see Kylie tonight.
He was anxious to know how she was dealing with everything and if she'd made any decisions. He was also desperate for a little adult company and for the boys to meet
some other children their own age.

Maxine's eleven-year-old son, Hunter, would be there,
and hopefully, the older boy could take Caden and Aiden

under his wing. Or at least peer-pressure them into acting like semicivilized human beings.

Drew wrestled the kids into their seat belts and drove toward Snow Creek Lodge, where the wedding would be held tomorrow. The nonstop talking from the backseat didn't keep him from thinking of what he'd say to Kylie when he saw her. Or how she'd look.

The minute they arrived and he put his borrowed car in Park, the two chatterboxes bolted out of the backseat and ran straight for the ski lift—which, during the summer, was used to haul mountain cyclists and their bikes up to the top of the peak.

"Boys," he said when he finally caught up to them and forcibly steered them away from the moving benches. "Remember, no candy bars later if you act up while we're here." Drew hated using sweets as a bribe, but tonight was important, and he couldn't have them misbehaving.

The boys, going on their third day with no sugar since they'd yet to behave well enough to earn the coveted prize, finally fell into step—one on each side of him. The trio walked into the oversize log structure and, before he could blink, the twins took off toward a small group of boys huddled around their handheld electronic devices.

Aiden and Caden could sniff out video-game systems within a ten-mile radius. They were like arcade bloodhounds. Originally, Drew had planned to introduce them to everyone, but why ruin a good thing? They should be safe enough over there with their attention focused for a solid thirty minutes at least. And it might keep them out of trouble.

Maybe.

"There's the man in charge," Cooper, still wearing his uniform, called out as he walked toward him. Everyone else in the wedding party turned in their direction, and he found himself eagerly searching out the one woman he'd been waiting all week to see.

"Is everyone here and ready to get started?" Even as Drew asked the question, he could see that she wasn't there.

He shoved his hands into his pockets, feeling the band he'd been carrying in the left one. Was she purposely avoiding him?

"Kylie's running late," Maxine said. "But don't worry. She's been in so many weddings, she could do this in her sleep."

Or with a drunk stranger in Reno.

"Okay, well, then, let's begin." Drew directed everyone on how to walk down the aisle, where to stand and what to say. He couldn't believe this was the way Cooper was making him repay the pen pal favor and he actually had to perform this ceremony. Unlike the absent redhead, he was no wedding expert. But he was a researcher and a perfectionist and had studied enough online videos lately to get through this rehearsal blindfolded.

Maxine's son, Hunter, handed over his PlayStation to the twins so that he could walk his mother down the aisle. But the boys, both overly eager to take their turn at playing, fought over the small device, each one grappling and scratching to get control of the coveted possession.

Drew was about to head toward his nephews to break up the fight, but Kylie strode into the room at that exact moment, confident and oblivious to the childish skirmish going on nearby. When he saw her, he froze, waiting for her to see him.

She looked poised and completely unflustered—until she glanced in his direction. Her smile faltered, but otherwise, she gave no outward sign that she was uncomfortable in his presence. She also gave no sign that she was going to slow her stride long enough to talk with him.

Which was unfortunate, because if she had, the small video game console that had just been launched into the air wouldn't have hit her right in the face.

"Ouch!" she yelled, her hand flying to her right eye. "What in the hell was that?"

Caden, who wasn't used to hearing adults swear, began giggling, while Aiden made a fast getaway toward the restroom—probably to escape the pending chaos he'd helped cause.

All of the women ran toward their startled friend, asking if she was okay and trying to soothe her. The men went in the direction of the children, breaking up the video game party, while Hunter ran to his toy, which had landed with a pop and then immediately suffered the wrath of Kylie's spiked heel when she'd blindly stepped on it.

"My new game is totally broken!" Hunter cried.

Drew grabbed Caden by the shoulder and marched him toward the restroom, where he'd seen the boy's brother run for cover.

The twins had yet to see Uncle Drew at his boiling point. Really, nobody had seen the calm counselor lose his cool in quite a few years, but the two eight-year-olds were about to get a peek at what he'd successfully held under wraps for so long.

"You guys not only broke Hunter's game but also seriously hurt that poor woman out there. And all because you were fighting over whose turn it was. You've both been acting selfish and wild since I picked you up from Grammie and Pop's, and I refuse to allow things to continue like this."

Drew was livid and the boys finally looked remorseful.

"Are you gonna send us away to live with someone

else, Uncle Drew?" Aiden had fat tears trickling down his chubby cheeks.

The emotional pressure had been building all week and, with the combined stress of the Kylie situation, Drew was at his wit's end.

In the bathroom mirror, he caught sight of the vein pulsing along the right side of his neck. He took a deep breath, trying to come up with the best way to take control of this derailed mess.

"Nobody'll take us." Caden stared at his scruffy sneakers, refusing to meet his uncle's eyes. "Nobody wants us."

"Why would you think something like that?" asked Drew.

"'Cause Dad is always going off on assignments and Grammie and Pop said their new motor home isn't kid-proofed yet and wouldn't take us on vacation with them."

"Guys." Drew tried to find the ideal thing to say to ease Caden's fear, but the perfect words were escaping him. "Just because they're not here doesn't mean they don't want to be with you."

"Yeah, right," said Aiden, sniffing back a tear of his own. "Even Aunt Hannah ditched us."

What did Drew's sister have to do with this? "Aunt Hannah is doing important work teaching at an orphanage."

"So? Me and Caden are practically orphans. Why'd she have to go all the way to Africa for that unless she was trying to get away from us, too?"

The throbbing in Drew's neck lowered to his heart and became more of a dull ache. His poor nephews were dealing with something bigger than just a lack of discipline. He sighed before easing himself to the tile floor. "Listen, boys. You are not orphans. You have a big, wonderful family that cares so much about you. And nobody ditched you guys. It was my turn to get a chance finally to spend some time with you because I love you and I want you. But you guys have to love me, too. I need you to start acting as if you *want* to be with me. When you misbehave and don't follow the rules, it tells me that you don't respect me and that you're not happy being with me."

"But we *do* like to be with you." Aiden was still sniffling, but at least the tears had subsided.

"Then, you guys need to show me. I want us to have a fun summer, but we need to work together as a team, okay?"

"Okay," the boys agreed and Drew pulled them in, making it a three-way embrace.

"Good. Now you're going to go out there and apologize to the nice lady who got hit in the face. And then you're going to apologize to Hunter for breaking his video game. After that, you're going to behave for the rest of the night. Starting tomorrow, both of you will do chores around the cabin to earn enough money to pay for a new system to replace the one that broke. Got it?"

Both boys nodded, but neither one looked happy about their future plans. Frankly, thinking of the injured woman out there and her refusal to call him all week, Drew wasn't feeling too optimistic, either.

He escorted the twins back outside and, seeing that Kylie and several of the women were no longer there, he walked his nephews over to Hunter, who was still cradling the broken PlayStation in his hands.

"We're sorry for breaking your video game." Caden was the first to apologize, and Drew had to nudge the other boy to follow suit.

"Yeah. I'm sorry my brother wouldn't let me finish my turn and grabbed it out of my hands." Aiden, the one who'd been the most sorrowful looking, was now the one acting the least remorseful.

Just as the boys began to argue about who should be more sorry, Chief Cooper knelt down to talk with them. As he did, the former marine and current police chief reached into the back pouch on his utility belt and pulled out a pair of stainless-steel handcuffs. He snapped the cuffs open and closed as he spoke quietly to the boys.

As far as scare tactics went, his buddy's methods were effective. Cooper definitely had the twins' attention. And since his friend seemed to have everything under control, Drew decided to seek out the woman he'd wanted to talk to for the past five days.

She was coming out of the ladies' room, a linen napkin–covered bag of ice over her right eye. Damn—that looked bad.

"Kylie." Drew started toward her. "I'm so sorry. They were overexcited and haven't had a lot of discipline and, well, there's no excuse for what they did."

"Drew, it was an accident. It wasn't as if they threw that thing at me on purpose." As soon as the words were out of her mouth, but before he could talk to her about everything else that needed saying, the boys ran up, stumbling over their own apologies.

Drew was glad that both of them seemed sincere in their contrition. His nephews might be wild, but they weren't malicious.

"Wow, does that hurt?" Caden asked when Kylie lowered the ice pack and revealed the bruise that was already turning a deep shade of purple around her eye.

She knelt down to talk to them, and Aiden reached out his finger to touch her bruise. But Kylie's reflexes—even with only one functioning eye—were quicker. "It only hurts when something touches it."

"Well, we really are sorry," Aiden said sincerely.

"We're gonna do chores to earn money to pay for

Hunter to get a new video game," Caden added. "And Chief Cooper said he would put us to work at the police station so maybe we can make enough to pay for you to go see a doctor. Uncle Drew is a doctor and starts work at the hospital soon, so he can take you with him if you need a shot or anything."

"Thank you, boys, but I don't think I need to see a doctor or get a shot just yet. And I forgive you as long as next time you promise to try to do a better job of sharing."

"We will," they chorused.

Drew didn't realize he'd been holding his breath, waiting for her to yell at the kids. Even though they deserved a scathing reprimand, he was glad to see she was giving them grace instead.

"Now," she said, standing and tossing her ice pack on a nearby table before taking both boys by the hand. "I have a very important job for both of you." She walked with them outside and toward the grassy area where the ceremony would be held.

As Drew watched her leading his nephews around, talking to them as if she didn't think they were little monsters at all, he was overwhelmed with appreciation. She was being more than forgiving, considering the fact that by this time tomorrow, she'd be sporting a shiner of epic proportions.

If he could convince her that the twins weren't so terrible, maybe he could convince her that he wasn't the type of person who usually acted so recklessly with women. Not that he should have to prove himself, but if he was going to be living in Sugar Falls for the summer, it would be nice to know a friendly—and beautiful—face. Besides, he needed all the help he could get, and Kylie seemed to have a talent for reining in the boys. Which gave him an idea...

* * *

Kylie wasn't one for praying, but the following morning she almost dropped to her knees to give thanks—right there in a bathroom stall at the Snow Creek Lodge. Finally, ten minutes before her best friend's wedding ceremony, she got her period.

Hallelujah!

She'd thought about Drew almost every minute since he'd left Reno on Sunday, and she was desperate to talk to him. To find out how he felt about everything. To have him reassure her that their crazy night together wasn't going to ruin both of their lives.

But every time she'd dialed his number, she'd been too embarrassed to push the Send button. Normally when she was under stress, she'd immerse herself in hot-fudge sundaes and her work. She had no scientific proof, but for some reason, ice cream helped to chill out her fiery temper. And working with numbers made sense to her— they soothed her and forced her mind to think logically. She liked their dependability and the fact that she could always count on one plus one equaling two.

Yet by yesterday morning, after she'd recalculated the same column of figures three times and was too embarrassed to make a second trip into Noodie's Ice Cream Shoppe in town, she finally blew off work to go shopping. She drove straight to downtown Boise for some retail therapy in order to get her mind off the knowledge that later in the evening, she'd have to come face-to-face with Drew and what they had done.

She'd bought a new pair of designer jeans that sat low on her hips and fit perfectly. It was usually tough to find an inseam that could accommodate her extensive limbs *and* her high heels. When she'd spotted the pair at her favorite boutique, she'd taken it as a good omen and changed right there in the store.

Amazing how a new outfit could restore the confidence she'd been grasping for all week. In fact, by the time Kylie had grabbed a double-scoop cone at a nearby drugstore, hopped in her convertible Mercedes coupe and hit the country station on satellite radio, she was almost looking forward to seeing Drew again.

Well, maybe not looking forward to it, but at least she wasn't dreading the potential look of disgust—or worse, pity—on his face when he saw her.

Then she'd gotten stuck in a traffic jam coming back up the mountain and was late to the rehearsal. He might have thought she was avoiding him, and the last impression she wanted to give him was that she was hiding in humiliation or that she wasn't woman enough to handle their situation. So when she'd strutted into the Snow Creek Lodge last night, she did so in her sexy new jeans and with her head held high.

Which was probably why she hadn't been paying attention when those little towheaded mischief makers had hit her in the eye with that video game.

Kylie stood and smoothed down her bridesmaid dress— a champagne-colored sheath that Cessy referred to as "unforgiving" when the overbearing woman had seen her take an extra serving of dessert last night—and exited the restroom stall to wash up.

As she looked at her reflection in the mirror, she couldn't help the smile that tugged at the corner of her glossed lips. She was so relieved that she wasn't pregnant and couldn't wait to tell Drew the news. He was officially off the hook. He was no longer under any obligation toward her.

Of course, the makeup artist her friend Mia had hired

hadn't been able to do much with Kylie's black eye, and she wished that she could've looked her best when she finally did get her chance to talk to the guy.

"Kylie Chatterson, get the lead out," Cessy yelled through the bathroom door. "Everyone is lining up."

It was time.

Well, not *her* time. Maxine's time. But someday it would be her time. She'd been a bridesmaid for numerous cousins, sorority sisters and fellow cheerleaders. She was a pro when it came to walking down the aisle at other people's weddings.

She let out a breath, then hustled out of the restroom and took her place in line with the rest of the bridal party. When the bagpiper launched into Mendelssohn's "Wedding March," Kylie's tummy fluttered and she had to lock her elbows to keep her small bouquet from trembling.

"You okay, Kylie?" the bride asked from behind her.

"Of course I am. I'm just so excited for you." Her best friend looked so sweet in a strapless gown a few shades lighter than the bridesmaids' dresses.

"Your eye doesn't look so horrible today, Aunt Kylie," Hunter said. He was giving his mother away, and Kylie was stunned by how mature he looked.

Where was the time going? People always said that kids grew up so fast, and she felt a sting of realization that she might never have kids of her own. Or even find someone with whom she'd *want* to have kids.

Cessy cued Mia to head out, and Kylie was up next.

What was wrong with her? Two minutes ago she'd been mentally high-fiving herself in the bathroom for not being pregnant, and now she was almost despondent over the fact that she might miss her chance at marriage and motherhood.

It must be hormones putting her on edge. She'd never

been resentful of her always-a-bridesmaid-never-a-bride status, and she certainly hadn't been this anxious any other time she'd been in a bridal party. The truth was, she loved weddings.

Of course, she'd apparently loved them a little *too* much when she was drinking from tacky souvenir cups in Reno.

So if she wasn't nervous, then why was she working prime factorization problems in her mind? She only did that when she...

"And go!" Cessy pushed her through the patio doors, interrupting Kylie midthought.

Suddenly, every number she'd ever stored in her head floated away, and all she could think of was the attractive, tall blond man standing at the end of the aisle. And she didn't mean the groom.

Kylie put one strappy-heeled sandal in front of the other and made her way to him.

There was no golden aura radiating behind the guy, but seeing Drew standing up there in his full military dress uniform, there might as well have been. He was like a beacon of light. When his eyes locked on to hers, she was powerless against the reassuring smile drawing her toward him.

She'd heard of tunnel vision before but had never experienced it until now. She had no idea who was seated to her left or right, and as she walked along the white runner strewn with flower petals, she didn't care. Her nerves were drowning in a sea of emotion, and Drew was the lifeboat she needed to reach.

Why did he have to be so handsome? And so serene? And so damn tall?

For a heartbeat, she almost wished she'd married him on purpose...

Mia, the other maid of honor, had to grab Kylie's elbow

to pull her into position near the floral arch. Next, Maxine and Hunter came down the aisle toward them, but her mind didn't register anything except Drew's presence. She doubted this was how Pistole Pepe and Maddog Molly had felt when she'd walked through the doors at the Silver Rush Wedding Chapel.

She needed to get a grip. Drew was just a man. She was recovering from a stress-filled week. Numbers. Focus on numbers. *The prime factors of nine are three and three. The prime factors of ten are two and five...*

The ceremony began and she was almost to eighty-six when Drew ordered the bride and groom to face each other. Maxine thrust her bouquet at Kylie as Mia straightened the bridal train. While Cooper repeated his vows, Kylie couldn't stop herself from looking at Drew. His blue eyes were staring just as intensely at her, and heat flooded over her skin.

Had they said these same vows to each other? Had he promised to love her and cherish her? And had she promised to stand by him in sickness and in health?

Kylie had romanticized the idea of marriage since childhood. But she'd never understood the sanctity of those solemn vows until that exact moment. Loyalty had been drilled into her since childbirth. Drunk or not, how could she walk away from a promise like that?

How could he?

Drew spoke the rest of the words to formalize their friends' union, but she couldn't help noticing how many times he looked at her when he got to the important bits. Maybe it was subconscious on his part. Or maybe he was serious when he'd told her that he didn't take his promises lightly. She wondered if, once she told him he was off the hook in the daddy department, he wouldn't sweat the whole "oath before God" thing so much.

As Cooper kissed the bride, she shot another look Drew's way and could've sworn that he winked at her.

A burst of fire shot up from inside her chest and through her neck, into her cheeks.

Almost the entire town of Sugar Falls was present today, and he had the audacity to wink at her. In full view and with everyone watching. Oh, the gossip that would be fueled if the town busybodies thought she was flirting with Saint Drew. But before she could speculate about a potential Winkgate, the two little boys who'd graced her with the black eye to end all black eyes last night ran up the aisle to fulfill their job assignments.

"One, two, three, blow," they shouted in unison before releasing a steady stream of bubbles in the air. The audience soon followed suit with the small white bottles Kylie had given the twins to pass out, and the new mister and missus walked down the aisle in a cloud of bubbles.

"You are quite the enchantress," Drew whispered to her as she waited for her turn in the bridal recessional. And her face grew even hotter. "I don't know how you got them to listen to you."

Oh, he was talking about the twins. Not about her seductive appearance. Bummer.

"I had four brothers," she whispered back. "When it comes to little boys, you have to make them feel important and keep them busy. And I bought five gallons' worth of bubbles, so they should be pretty busy for at least another twenty minutes."

"Good," he said right before she departed to the sound of the bagpipes. "Because we still need to talk."

She caught his smile before she walked away, and the nerves zapping around inside her turned to butterflies. He was just as handsome as she remembered. Even more so in his formal navy uniform.

But she wasn't ready to have the overdue discussion yet. She'd been looking for the perfect man for so long, she didn't think that she could handle another failure in her ongoing quest. At least, not publicly.

Man, she needed a pint of Ben & Jerry's if she hoped to get through the upcoming reception.

Instead, she grabbed a glass of champagne from the tray of the first server passing by, wishing it was a root beer float, and tried not to guzzle it down while they posed for pictures after the ceremony.

The terraced garden of the Snow Creek Lodge wasn't that small, but Drew was never far from her sight. Or her mind.

He finally moved in next to her when the photographer took the bride and groom away for some shots by themselves. "Hey."

She'd known this moment was coming, and it was probably best if she got it over with as quickly as possible. Just like pulling off an eyebrow-waxing strip.

"Hi," she said, looking around for another server. Or her sunglasses. Anything that would keep her from meeting his incredible blue eyes.

"You've been pretty good at avoiding me all week." Wow, he wasn't even going to beat around the bush or make small talk. The man definitely said what was on his mind.

Maybe if she could flag down one of the waiters, she could ask him to bring her a milk shake. "I wasn't avoiding you so much as I was trying to figure out how I felt about everything."

"And how do you feel?"

"Confused. Upset. Cheated. Relieved. All of the above."

"Why cheated?"

"I don't know. I guess because like every other girl, I've

always dreamed of the perfect guy and having the fairy-tale wedding. Nowhere in my dreams did I envision marrying some stranger at a tacky wedding chapel in Reno."

"Why relieved?"

"Because I got my...uh...you know...this morning."

"Your what?"

The man was so straitlaced he didn't even get her polite reference. Of course, she was too embarrassed to say it, either. "I'm not pregnant," she whispered.

"Oh." Was it her imagination or did those broad shoulders of his just slump a little? He definitely wasn't smiling. This wasn't exactly the reaction she was expecting. Was he actually disappointed she wasn't having his baby? He must not have understood her.

Yet before she could tell the poor guy that he was off the hook, that they were *both* off the hook, two women approached them.

"Dr. Gregson, that was such a touching service."

Elaine Marconi and her husband owned the local gas station, making her a prime source of neighborhood gossip. The woman was known to overindulge at parties with an open bar, and judging by the flush on her cheeks, today's event was no exception.

The other woman, Marcia Duncan, owned Duncan's Market, another center for all newsworthy information about Sugar Falls.

"I hope you'll be willing to do a guest lecture at our Women in Crafting Crisis meeting while you're in town," Marcia said. "We've never had a licensed psychologist speak with our group."

"Thank you for thinking of me, but I'm a better listener than I am a speaker," the always perfect Drew answered, being perfectly polite. As usual.

Marcia's eyes widened as if her Spanx were cutting off

circulation to her brain, then blinked several times as if to regain her composure.

"But we could really use your professional help," the woman insisted. Kylie knew Marcia ran her market with a strong, meaty fist and probably wasn't used to people telling her no.

"Some more than others," Kylie muttered before looking longingly at the chocolate fountain being set up inside the ballroom.

When Drew smiled at her, acknowledging that he'd heard her impolite comment, her knees wobbled. She remembered how he'd looked in that hotel room, all bare chested and calm, and she almost wished she could be back there again.

"Let me get settled here in town first, ladies. Then we can talk more about it at a later date." Drew's words took the edge off Kylie's snide remark, which she doubted anyone else heard, judging by the way both women looked somewhat appeased.

"Good Lord, Kylie," Elaine suddenly said, as if she'd just now noticed Kylie standing right there. "What in the world happened to your eye? Was it another date gone bad?"

Her hand shot up to the bruise and she silently cursed herself for not grabbing her dark sunglasses when she had the chance. Despite the woman's implication, Kylie didn't date abusive guys.

It had been a rough week, and if Kylie wasn't such a lady, rigorously trained in poise and decorum by some of the best pageant coaches in the nation, she might have been tempted to unleash some violence of her own.

But she was stronger than that. She was better than that. She saw that sympathetic look in Drew's eye again and was briefly tempted to show him she wasn't a woman to be pitied.

"Actually," Drew spoke up, "my twin nephews did that to her. It was an accident." Was it Kylie's imagination or had Drew stepped closer to her? She must have been suffering from some sort of knight-in-shining-armor fantasy because she couldn't help but sense that he was riding to her rescue.

"Oh, I'm sure it was. Are those adorable blond cuties yours?" Marcia turned her back to Kylie, putting her greasy appetizer fingers on Drew's biceps.

"They were just so sweet, blowing all those bubbles," Elaine crooned in a voice that was one glass of chardonnay away from slurring. "You were so smart to come up with the idea for them to do that."

This was Kylie's opportunity to slip away silently, while the ladies were busy slithering up to Saint Drew. But just as she started backing up, Drew's hand shot out and snatched her elbow, pulling her to his side and back into the barracuda-infested waters with him. "Actually, that was Kylie's brilliant idea. She has a way with kids."

Although she was capable of fighting her own battles, Kylie appreciated Drew trying to defuse the situation. But she didn't know if she appreciated the strength of his iron-tight grip as he held her in place right next to him. Ugh. She knew the guy was made of solid muscle, but she wasn't used to men being strong enough to maneuver her around however they wanted.

"A way with kids?" Marcia's laugh came out as more of a snort.

"Kylie?" Elaine giggled like a teenage girl drunk on her first wine cooler. "Oh, Doctor, she may be good with numbers, but the one thing Kylie does *not* have a way with is kids."

"Or men." Marcia snorted again.

Kylie tried to pull away, but Drew's hand was like velvet-covered steel—deceptively soft on the outside but rigid in its refusal to let go. Her emotions had been on a roller coaster for the past six days, and the last thing she could stomach was standing here and letting these two offensive women insult her in front of the first man she actually liked and respected.

Oh, no. It was true. She actually liked Drew. Even though she knew nothing about him.

Except that he was standing by her side and looking at her with a growing sense of concern. "Now, ladies," he said. "I am under the impression that Kylie here can handle herself in any situation."

Perfect Drew was being his usual calm and diplomatic self. Sure, he probably thought he was protecting her, but he could protect her better by just letting her get the heck away from the reception. Why wouldn't he let go of her arm?

"Oh, we didn't mean anything negative by it." Elaine sobered up enough to stop smirking. Mostly.

"Kylie, honey," Marcia spoke up. "You know we think the world of you. We don't think less of you for dating all those guys or dressing like you do. It must be so hard to be your age and still be single."

"I'm fine," Kylie said through clenched teeth. Maybe Doctor Strong Arms thought he was helping her, but he was really just making things increasingly awkward. Even though her reputation wasn't truly earned, she hated that these harpies made her seem desperate and inadequate in front of Drew, who looked less like a saint right that second and more like a warrior. His eyes darkened to a stormy blue-black, and she could see the pulse in his neck throbbing.

Was he annoyed with Kylie? He couldn't possibly believe what these women were saying about her. Could he?

"Of course you're not fine. Your best friend just got married and you still aren't able to find a man for yourself. We should have been more sensitive."

"Don't stress so much about it, honey. The right man for you is out there somewhere if you would just stop looking so hard. Have you thought about online dating?"

The red haze blinding her eyes and the steam coming out of her ears were making it difficult to tell which woman was saying what. But then a finger brushed along her arm, and the anger broke long enough for her to glance at the man beside her.

We're in this together, Drew mouthed.

She raised her brow, not sure she understood. Her eyes went wide when he snaked his arm around her waist and pull her tighter against his side.

Apparently his annoyance wasn't directed toward her at all.

The women must have taken notice of his intimate and protective stance, because they paused midplatitude, mouths slightly ajar.

Kylie couldn't stop herself from rising to her full five feet ten inches—actually, over six feet in her gold-studded heels—and slid her free hand across Drew's chest, feeling the quickening of his heartbeat.

"Thank you for your concern, ladies, but as you can see," she said, holding out her hand, displaying the tight wedding ring she still couldn't get off and pasting on her best pageant smile, "I don't need your sympathy, because I'm already married."

Chapter Four

What had she just done?

Drew barely managed half a smile at Marcia and Elaine before rushing off behind Kylie as she walked away from the two shocked women in strong, purposeful strides, pulling Drew's hand with her.

He hadn't been expecting her announcement, and now he needed to reconfigure his next course of action.

"How fast do you think word will spread?" he tried to joke as they made their way toward the patio doors. She didn't answer because she was mumbling something about prime numbers and double scoops.

When they were safely inside the cooler air-conditioned ballroom, she finally stopped her numerical chant and let out a deep breath. Thank goodness the guests were still enjoying the cocktail hour outside so that he could be alone with her for a minute. Together, they might be able to figure out how to deal with what they'd just publically acknowledged.

"I'd wager sixty-five percent of the guests here will know by the time we sit down for dinner," she said. "The other thirty-five percent will figure it out when I'm noticeably absent from the bouquet toss. And when you take into account social media, the rest of the town and half of my Boise State graduating class will know by tomorrow morning."

She slumped into a linen-covered chair and propped her elbows on the decorated table before burying her face in her hands. Could being married to him truly cause her this much shame? He pulled his own chair in front of her and sat down facing her.

Well, he would wait her out. She couldn't hide her head forever and pretend nothing had happened. Soon she'd be forced to look at him, once she was done with her pity party, or her multiplication tables, or whatever it was she was doing. But after a few moments, she still hadn't looked up. What was she thinking?

Heck, what was *he* thinking, letting her get sucked into the nest of those two vipers? He'd known the women had been taunting Kylie, and he could tell by the way her arm had been tensing in his grip that she'd been getting frustrated. But instead of being the trained observer, watching her to see how she was going to react, he'd blindly jumped right into the snake pit.

And now the rest of the world was going to know that the naval officer they'd inadvertently designated as some sort of paragon of virtue was married to the town vixen.

At least according to Marcia and Elaine. Fortunately, Drew was a patient man and knew there were two sides to every story.

Apparently, he'd just made it clear that he was choosing her side. Like he'd told her in the hotel room back in Reno, they really were in this together. They needed to figure out a strategy to deal with this new development, stat. And it wouldn't be a bad idea to have some backup support locked into place.

"Perhaps we should go find our friends and tell them the good news before they hear it from everyone else," he suggested.

"Oh, no," she said, finally looking up at him with what could only be described as panic in her eyes. "I mean, yes. We should. And we will. But give me a second to get all my feelings in check. Ugh. I've been a shrink's wife for all of a week and already I'm blowing it. My brothers always teased me for not being able to control my emotions. What have I done?"

There went her face, back into her hands. Where was the Amazon warrior queen he'd seen back in that hotel room and then again outside a few moments ago with those busybodies when she'd flashed her ring in triumph? Kylie didn't strike him as the type to just bury her head in surrender.

"It wasn't just you. I was right there with you and didn't put a stop to it. You haven't done anything that can't be undone. So what if the town finds out about us? They don't need to know the…uh…circumstances surrounding the… uh…wedding. I'm sure we can just explain—"

She gasped. "Any moment, they're going to find out that we're married and then all hell will break loose."

It was as if she hadn't even heard him.

"Kylie, I'm sure Cooper and Maxine aren't going to make a big deal out of our wedding. When we tell them what happened, they'll probably just laugh it off."

"I'm not talking about our *friends* finding out. I'm talking about my *family* finding out. My parents are here."

"Wait. Why are your parents here?"

"Because they've known Maxine practically as long as

I have. When we cheered at Boise State together, she used to come home with me for holidays and breaks. What am I supposed to tell my mom and dad?"

Funny, this was one complication he hadn't anticipated. "Well, let's go talk to your folks and let them know what happened and that we're trying to fix—"

"There you are, Kylie!" A very loud and very large man entered the ballroom with a smaller woman trailing behind him. "What's this I'm hearing about you being married?"

Drew took in the full beard and graying red hair of the older guy and decided this was one angry papa he did not want aiming a shotgun in his direction. But he had been raised right after all, so he stood up to meet the upcoming onslaught head-on.

"Dad, this is Drew." Kylie stood up as well and grabbed his arm, pressing her body against his side and pasting a huge grin on her face. "I've been dying for you to meet him."

More like dying of shame, but Drew wasn't going to contradict her. He swallowed his shock, happy that at least she was no longer wallowing in a puddle of despair. In fact, she seemed to be putting on quite the show of happy newlywed, gushing with happiness and squeezing his biceps.

"Hello, sir. I'm Lieutenant Commander Andrew Gregson. I'm glad we got the chance to meet before the reception started." Drew stuck out his hand, hoping Kylie's dad would take the hint that other guests were now filing into the ballroom and would bear witness to any potential scenes.

"Is Captain Cracker Jack here really your husband?" Mr. Chatterson was a behemoth of a man and all kinds of fired up as he eyeballed his new son-in-law. Drew couldn't blame the man for his anger, or his confusion, but Drew's forearm would soon get sore from holding it outstretched for so long.

"Dad, please," Kylie said when it became apparent that her father wasn't going to accept Drew's handshake. "People are looking. Don't make this any more awkward than it already is."

"Oh, Jellybean, you don't even know the definition of awkward. Try finding out from some tipsy busybody that my only daughter—my precious baby girl—robbed my dear, sweet wife of the opportunity to see her walk down the aisle."

Drew lowered his hand, because obviously Mr. Chatterson wasn't quite ready for social niceties.

"Dad, I'm sorry about that. Mom, I promise I'll make it up to you."

Drew fought the urge to not do a double take at Kylie's words. How could she make it up to her parents?

"It's actually a pretty funny story," Kylie continued. "We got married on a whim because the thought of waiting for a long engagement just seemed as if it would take forever, and we're just so crazy in love that we couldn't stand not to make it official."

"How long have you two known each other?" The man was right to look skeptical. Kylie was a horrible liar, but maybe that was just because Drew knew the truth. He decided to jump in and help her out.

"Not that long, sir, but it was love at first sight." His statement might not be any more honest than hers, but they must have felt *something* at first sight back in Reno. Why else would they have done such a crazy and reckless thing? To prove his claim, either to her parents or to himself, he leaned toward Kylie and placed a light kiss on her cheek.

She smelled like the gardenias in her forgotten bouquet, and it was all Drew could do not to pull her closer. Yet despite the intimate gesture, her face remained frozen, her fake smile firmly in place. But the pink color stealing up her chest and neck gave her away.

She'd felt it, too.

Unfortunately, they weren't alone, where they could explore this possible attraction further. In fact, they were knee-deep in the most undesirable conversation ever.

Mr. Chatterson did not look even slightly appeased. At least they were of the same height, so even if Drew couldn't pacify the man with his words, he wouldn't cower from his sheer size.

"Dad, you're overreacting," Kylie said, and it dawned on him that the dramatic apple didn't fall too far from the tree.

"Bobby." The smaller woman spoke up and nudged her husband's arm, nodding toward her new son-in-law. The older man finally reached out. Drew met his crushing grip, which gave no indication of Mr. Chatterson's willingness to back down. His wife intervened again by physically separating the men's fingers.

"Well, Andrew, I'm Kylie's mom, Lacey Chatterson." Mrs. Chatterson, dressed in an expensive and conservative pantsuit, was apparently the voice of reason in this family. "Why don't we all find our seats and get to know each other better?"

Kylie's father's shoulders deflated a bit. He must have realized his wife wasn't really asking a question or even making a suggestion. She was issuing an order.

"As much as Drew and I would love that," Kylie said, "we're seated up at the head table. Maybe after dinner we can come over and talk to you guys and explain our whirlwind romance. It's really quite a humorous story."

"Well, I'm not laughing," her dad said, his eyes not leaving Drew's face, as if sizing him up for future refer-

ence. "And you'd better figure out a date during the baseball off-season that we can set for the proper wedding."

What proper wedding?

The sound of glasses clinking saved them from any
further appraisal. Kylie grabbed Drew's arm to pull him
toward the dance floor, where the DJ was introducing the
bride and groom and the rest of the wedding party. This
was the second time she'd pulled him away from an uncomfortable situation tonight, and he was actually starting
to get used to her long fingers touching him.

"It looks as if word spread pretty quickly," he whispered to her as they lined up near Mia and Alex Russell,
one of the groomsmen.

If Drew thought Mr. Chatterson's looks could kill, it
was nothing compared to the stink eye Kylie's friend Mia
was directing his way. He'd seen suicide bombers looking friendlier right before launching themselves at Marine ground forces.

And there stood Cooper, his eyes lit up and his fist
planted firmly over his smirking mouth. Drew knew their
friends all had a million questions, and he wished to God
he could have been the one to explain things to everyone.
But heck, he couldn't even explain the situation to himself.

Kylie was standing tall, but her skin was flushed so
pink, he could barely make out the few scattered freckles
along her shoulders.

"I'm sorry," she whispered back. "I didn't mean for anyone to find out, especially not my family. I panicked when
I saw my parents and didn't want them thinking I messed
up. I know I kind of went overboard with the whole crazy-
in-love bit back there, but there's no way Mia and Maxine will buy it, so we'll have to come clean with them, for
the most part. Just don't tell anyone we were drunk when
it happened. If we can ride this out for tonight, I'm sure

CHRISTY JEFFRIES 75

we can come up with a good story so that nobody is the wiser when we announce later on that we're divorcing."

Divorce? He hated the sound of that word. He didn't know why. Logically, he knew it wasn't the worst thing that could happen to him, yet he didn't like the idea that he'd made a mistake. A reckless and impulsive mistake.

Unfortunately, there was no getting around it as they clearly couldn't stay married.

But at least he could move back to Boise at the end of summer when Luke returned from deployment. Kylie's life was here in Sugar Falls, and he didn't want her disgraced while he was in town. He wasn't going to have to live or work among these people or otherwise deal with the fallout from their divorce. Or, hopefully, their annulment. So as much as it went against every controlling instinct in his body, he'd sit back and let her drive this crazy train in the way she saw fit. For now, at least.

When the DJ finished the introductions, they took their seats at the head table. The second Cooper and Maxine fixed themselves into their adjacent chairs, the bride leaned toward them and simply said, "Spill it."

And to Drew's shock, Kylie did just that. She told the small wedding party—including Mia and Alex, who came to stand behind them to hear the story better—about the night in Reno and how they'd gotten carried away and woken up with the marriage license and no memory of the night's events. Hadn't she *just* asked him not to tell anyone they'd been drinking?

Thankfully, she left out the more intimate details of how they awoke and how he'd barely been able to keep his hands or his eyes off her the following morning. Seeing her body in the clinging bridesmaid dress, he still was having a hard time not physically responding to her.

"So what are you going to do?" Mia asked, continuing

to stare at Drew as if he were an undercover spy sneaking into enemy territory.

"Well, originally we thought we'd just keep it a secret. But now we kind of pretended to everyone else that we were in love. It might've saved my reputation for the time being, but eventually we'll have to address it head-on and make it go away."

"Like get an annulment?" Maxine asked, and Kylie's telltale blush crept even farther up her cheeks.

"Or a divorce or something. We'd have to figure out what our legal options will be."

Again, the D-word hit him like a punch to the gut. Drew was trying to keep his opinions to himself, just like he usually kept his private life to himself. After all, since Kylie would be the one dealing with the social aftermath of their situation, he should probably let her take the lead on explaining things to everyone.

"I'm a dance teacher, not a lawyer," Mia started. "But I'm pretty sure you can get an annulment as long as you didn't consummate... Oh, no."

The look on Kylie's face must have given them away, because the ladies looked at their friend in shock, and Alex made a beeline straight toward the bar. But Cooper sat back in his chair and laughed until tears ran from his eyes.

"Oh, this is too good." Cooper's shoulders shook as he said the words. "Kylie and Saint Drew are married."

"You call him that, too?" Kylie asked.

"Everyone back on the base called him that. The guy doesn't get flustered. Ever. He's too calm and respectable for that. Gregson has a heart of gold, the tolerance of a martyr and the lifestyle of a monk."

"Really," Drew finally spoke up. "At a time like this, you two feel the need to compare descriptions of me?"

"No offense," Kylie said. "It's just that you're so perfect

and so nice to everyone. Even to that horrible Marcia and Elaine. Maybe if you hadn't forced me to stand there and make polite conversation with them, we wouldn't have let the cat out of the bag in the first place."

"Are you seriously blaming me for the fact that you were two seconds away from completely losing your temper and I was trying to be supportive?" The throbbing in Drew's neck was picking up speed, and he suddenly wondered if this lodge had a meditation room—or, at this point, a boxing speed bag—so he could go decompress and relieve some tension.

"How do you know I was about to lose anything? You don't even know me!"

"Uh-oh," Cooper said in a singsong voice, but not before her words hit their mark. "The newlyweds are having their first tiff."

Maxine made a shushing sound and pushed her husband's tuxedo-clad arm. The chief of police almost fell out of his chair, which would have made Drew smile if he didn't already feel as if he was three seconds away from punching his best friend himself.

"Uncle Drew!" The twins picked that moment to run over from the designated kids' table behind them. "Is it true that you married the tall lady that Aiden hit in the face?"

"*I* didn't hit her." Aiden shoved his brother. "*You* hit her. You always try to blame me for everything."

"Boys." Drew turned in his seat to break up the potential skirmish. "I thought we agreed that both of you were to blame for that incident."

He hated rehashing last night's video-game drama, but it was better than having to answer the eight-year-olds' questions about his unanticipated marriage and what it could potentially mean for them all. This past week, he'd found out that his nephews had a penchant for changing the subject on a dime and losing interest in an activity quicker than he could say "Reese's Peanut Butter Cup."

"But you *did* marry her, Uncle Drew?"

"Is she gonna be our aunt now?"

"Is she gonna come live with us at the cabin?"

"Will she bring more bubbles with her?"

The rapid-fire questions just went to show that the one time he actually wanted to divert the boys' attention, they decided to hold on tenaciously like a heat missile on target launch.

He looked at his wife, hoping she would have some answers, because he sure as heck didn't want to be blamed for saying the wrong thing.

"Hey, boys." Kylie motioned them over. "Did you see that they're going to have a chocolate fountain after they cut the cake?"

Alex Russell's father and grandfather came over to congratulate the bride and groom and temporarily distracted the rest of the wedding party. Meanwhile, Drew listened to his nephews' squeals as Kylie spoke with them about all the marshmallows and fruit and edibles that would be stacked by the fountain.

He couldn't believe the instant rapport Kylie had with the boys. Aiden and Caden were cheerfully animated as they talked to her. She listened attentively, nodding her head as if their opinion on the proper skewering order of treats was the most important discussion she would have this evening. For the first time in the past hour, he found himself grinning.

He'd probably been just as smitten with her that evening in Reno. At the time, he had blamed his reaction to her on everything from the amount of alcohol he'd drunk to the amount of time he'd gone without a date. And maybe now, with the boys being so starved for female attention that any caring woman was a novelty for them, he could argue that his tenderness toward her came from a sense of gratitude.

He was a man of science and normally didn't listen to gut instincts, but he couldn't shake the feeling that his re-action to her was caused by none of those things. It was just Kylie.

There was definitely something about her that attracted people. And there was also something about her that had his normally out-of-control nephews thinking she was next best thing to chocolate-covered marshmallows.

He couldn't help but appreciate her sweet and nurturing way with the boys. Heaven knew the twins could benefit from having someone like Kylie in their lives. And to be honest, Drew could use the help supervising them.

"Seriously, though, I gotta ask." Cooper, having fin-ished talking to the Russell men, leaned in and spoke quietly. "Kylie and Saint Drew? How did you manage to make that happen?"

"I have no idea," Drew answered honestly.

"Well, how are you going to fix it?"

Kylie stood to walk the kids back to the designated chil-dren's table, and he heard her explaining how the servers were going to be bringing them chicken strips. She told them if they promised to wash their hands afterward and wait until all the other guests got a turn at the fountain, they'd be able to dip treats to their hearts' content.

Drew shook his head.

"I have no idea," he repeated.

He watched her retreating backside clad in the form-fitting satin dress and thought he could get used to watch-ing her successfully manage his nephews. Heck, he could get used to simply watching her...

* * *

Kylie had avoided the dance floor and her parents for most of the reception. But she knew her stay of execution was temporary. She planted herself in her seat throughout dinner, the champagne toast and the cake-cutting ceremony, biding her time and trying to figure out how to deal with this stupid situation she'd gotten herself into. It was one thing to get married to a stranger, quite another to pretend she was madly in love with him.

Damn. She'd really bitten off more than she could chew this time. But she wouldn't dare allow her mom and dad to think that she didn't know what she was doing or that she couldn't handle this on her own.

When she was growing up, her parents had always told her that she let her impulsivity and her independence get the best of her. As the baby, with four protective older brothers, the family joke was that Kylie was quick to make a decision, and quicker to do things by herself, refusing to let anyone of them help her. Ever. When she was three years old, they were on a winter holiday and Kevin tried to lace up her snow boots so they could go outside sledding. She told him she could do it herself and she did. The problem was, by the time she'd finally gotten them knotted on tight enough, it was already dark and her brothers were coming inside for dinner.

She'd brought this mess on herself and, as they said in the pageant world, sometimes the best way to deal with an uncomfortable situation was to fake it until you made it.

"We have a special request for the newlyweds." The DJ made the announcement as the bars to a new song came out through the speakers. Kylie looked at the bride and groom, who had been talking to some guests across the room but were now looking at straight at her. "But not the chief and Mrs. Cooper," the DJ said into his microphone.

When the guests began to mumble to each other, she realized why everyone was turning in her direction. Oh, no. It couldn't be. Who would've requested this song? She prayed the guy wasn't going to say what she thought he was going to say.

But when the opening notes to the love ballad came on, she knew.

"So please welcome Dr. and Mrs. Gregson to the dance floor to celebrate their recent marriage." She had no idea where her new husband was or even if he wanted to be found. He must have thought she was completely nuts for wanting to pretend their marriage was real.

All the guests were looking at her and probably assuming the exact same thing: *Kylie Chatterson can't even get her own husband to dance with her.* She thought about ducking into the ladies' room, but how could she when all eyes were on her? By the time Michael Bolton began the opening lines of the song, Kylie couldn't take the stares anymore. She was about to turn and run when she felt that velvetlike steel hand on her for the second time that day.

"I guess we better give the crowd what they want," Drew said as he tugged on her elbow, forcing her to stand, and then escorted her toward the dance floor. She looked down at his hand and saw that his gold wedding band was now on his finger. Where had that come from? She could've sworn she hadn't seen it earlier, during the ceremony.

"Did you set this up?" She didn't mean to sound accusatory, but her friends wouldn't have pulled a stunt like this.

"Me?" he asked. "God, no. I hate to dance. I'm terrible at it."

And when he took her into his strong arms, she realized he wasn't lying. Drew really was a terrible dancer. The best he could manage was a reenactment of an awk-

ward junior high slow-dance version of locked arms and
feet shuffling side to side. After he'd stepped on her toes
for the third time, she finally pulled him in closer to her,
wrapping her arms around his neck. "Here, just hold me
close and sway to the beat."

She'd been a cheerleader in high school and college
and adored dancing. How could she have married someone with two left feet? Wouldn't she have at least danced
with him that night in Reno before they'd had too much to
drink and headed off to the Silver Rush Wedding Chapel?

The wool of his dress uniform was coarse under her
fingers, and she was tempted to move her hands toward
the tan smoothness of the back of his neck. To touch the
soft skin she remembered feeling in that hotel bed.

Side to side. She needed to keep swaying, to keep moving, before she did something stupid.

She'd danced with plenty of guys before, but never one
who matched her so well in size. Or who smelled so great.
Her nose was centimeters away from his upper jaw, and
she inhaled his scent of lemongrass and fresh pine. His
arms were like steel bands around her waist, and if she
closed her eyes, she could almost pretend she and Drew
were alone.

Almost.

She made the mistake of glancing around the room before looking back at Drew's face.

Kylie moved her body closer to his so he wouldn't be
able to penetrate her with that all-knowing blue gaze like
a microscope looking deep into her.

She could feel his pulse beating against the neckline of
her dress, and warmth spread through her. Maybe she'd
been too hasty, because his stare might've been the lesser
of two evils.

"I was just wondering who could've set up this little

song request." She was having difficulty drawing an even breath; her voice came out as barely a whisper.

"I have no idea," he answered, his cheek pressing against her temple as he spoke into her ear. "Besides the wedding party, I don't really know many of the guests."

"I thought your family had a cabin here. Didn't you grow up in Sugar Falls?"

"No. I'm from Boise originally. But we spent a lot of summers up here when I was a kid."

"Ah, so you're one of the bankrollers," Kylie said, referring to the wealthy tourists who provided a brisk business for many of the locals.

"Hardly. Before they retired, my dad was a minister and my mom was a teacher. Her grandparents owned the cabin, and she inherited it when they passed. So we definitely aren't part of the elite visiting class."

"Oh, wow. That really explains a lot."

"What's that supposed to mean?" She heard the offended tone in his question and cursed herself. She hadn't meant to insult his family's financial status.

"I meant about you having a preacher for a father. It must be why you're such a Goody Two-shoes." Ugh, that probably didn't sound like any less of an insult.

"Trust me. My father's profession was no guarantee for the way I turned out."

At that point, Kylie did lean back to look at his eyes. "I find that hard to believe."

"Okay, so I really wasn't all that bad. But my twin brother, Luke, was the proverbial preacher's kid. He was always in trouble. Kind of like my nephews over there." He looked toward the chocolate fountain and the kids, who were using the treat-covered skewers to do their best impression of bloodthirsty pirates. "So you'd think I'd know how to handle them better. I should probably get over there before they stab someone's eye out."

"Nah, they have marshmallows blunting the ends of their swords. The worst damage they could do is knock the fountain over. Right onto Elaine and Marcia, if we're lucky."

Drew's lips angled upward before he recovered his perfect countenance. But the small glimpse of him letting down his guard showed her he did have a sense of humor.

The song drew to a close and the booming beats for the next one started up. Several shrieking women ran toward the parquet floor. Normally, Kylie would've loved to stay put and shake her stuff with the other dancers. But after witnessing Drew's lack of rhythm to a slow song, she didn't want to be an accomplice to what he might be capable of with a fast tempo.

"Your dad is staring this way. I think he's trying to get your attention," Drew said.

She loved and respected her parents, and they deserved the truth. But not tonight. She would see them tomorrow before they left for Seattle and explain things to them then—without Drew there. Kylie saw her mother talking to the manager of the Snow Creek Lodge, her smile bright and her hands gesturing wildly toward centerpieces and the outside terrace.

Uh-oh. She knew that determined look on her mother's happy face. How had she let things get this far? Lacey Chatterson obviously had it in her head that Kylie and Drew were actually willing to go through with their wedding again, just so the mother of the bride could plan a dream reception for her daughter.

A daughter who had run off and married a stranger in secret, then stood there in front of her adoring parents and pretended to be madly in love. She gave a little finger wave toward her dad as her insides twisted up in guilt.

"Maybe we should grab something to drink and make our way over there," Drew said, reminding her they were just standing there in the center of the room.

"Oh, they're fine. I can see them tomorrow and clear everything up then."

His palm remained on the small of her back as he leaned toward her ear so she could hear him over the loud lyrics of the Commodores. "You don't have to face your parents, or the rest of the town, alone. Remember when I said we'd be in this together? I really meant it."

She'd thought he'd meant they'd be in it together only if there was a baby involved. So why was he sticking around now that he'd been cleared of official daddy status? She wouldn't blame him if he made a run for the nearest creek. But he remained right beside her, a blue-uniformed wall of muscle that, judging by the sincere look in his eyes, left no doubt that he wasn't going anywhere. For tonight, at least.

"Of course," he said as he guided her off the dance floor and toward the open bar set up in the corner, "if having me there would just make things more awkward or embarrassing for you, say the word."

She jerked her head so that she could face him. What was he saying? Would he want to explain their marriage to *his* parents without *her* there? She looked down at her cleavage and decided that with a minister for a father, he probably would. She tried not to feel insulted, but what did she expect? He was Saint Drew. And she was...

Well, she was Kylie Chatterson. She was known to be a little brassy at times and not too conservative in her fashion choices, which usually showed off her curves to great advantage. Although she was smart and successful and came from a loving family, she probably wasn't Drew's first choice of a woman to take home to meet the folks.

And if it weren't for her impulsiveness and hot temper, he probably wouldn't have had to meet hers, either. Even though neither of them knew who was to blame for their predicament in the first place, she was definitely the only one who could mitigate the current awkwardness.

"Listen, that's very thoughtful of you to offer to come with me to talk to them. I know my dad can be a lot to take, and he isn't in the warmest of moods right this second. Why don't we just drop it for tonight and try to act as normal as possible?"

"Define *normal*. Because frankly, I'm having a hard time keeping up with what's normal nowadays," he said as they approached the bar.

Was he talking about her love-at-first-sight pretense?

"Sorry for the whole lovey-dovey routine earlier. I truly don't make a habit out of lying to anyone, least of all my parents. But I was trying to avoid a big I-told-you-so moment. My dad is always telling me that I'm too impulsive. I guess I just wanted to prove that I had a good reason for what we did and that I had everything under control. I'm sure you thought I was off my rocker for implying that the marriage was anything more than a drunken mistake."

Drew cringed at her statement. What had she said wrong?

"So just so that we're on the same page," he said carefully, "you want me to go along with this charade until tomorrow, when you start announcing to the world that I was a big mistake?"

Ooh. *That* was why he had cringed. "No, *you're* not the mistake. Getting drunk and getting married was the mistake. Come on, you couldn't possibly think that any woman in her right mind wouldn't jump at the chance to be married to someone as perfect as you?"

Clearly, she was *not* in her right mind. As soon as she saw his lips curve upward, another rush of heat stole up her skin. Why in the world had she just said that out loud? She must be as red as the jar of maraschino cherries at the bar.

"A champagne for the lady, and I'll take a Coke," he said to the bartender, his warm fingers still splayed against her back. Apparently he wasn't taking any chances on drinking alcohol in her presence again. He probably figured that someone needed to be sober to make sure she didn't do or say anything else outlandish tonight.

It was just as well. The twins ran up to them as Drew handed her a crystal flute. "Uncle Drew, Aunt...uh... what's her name?" Caden stage-whispered to his brother, whose face was smeared with chocolate from ear to ear.

"It's Kyle," Aiden whispered back.

"Are we s'pose to call her Aunt Kyle?" Caden asked.

"How about you just call me Kylie?" she said, correcting their pronunciation by putting emphasis on the *e* sound at the end of her name. The boys really were too cute for words. She suspected Drew and his own brother had been just as spunky and just as mischievous as these two when they were kids.

"But Kyle is a boy's name," Caden said. "And you're not a boy."

"Kylieeeee," she repeated, then pointed at her dad. "You can talk to that big redheaded man over there at that table. He's the one who gave me such a confusing name."

The twins looked at her father, a lumberjack of a man who, at one time or another, had intimidated some of the best batters in professional baseball.

"Nah, that's okay." Aiden shook his head. "Anyway,

they're building a bonfire outside and me and Caden wanted to go out with the other kids and watch."

Drew looked at her, lifting his shoulders up as if to ask her opinion. The man gave off the most capable and competent vibe 90 percent of the time, but he really was lost when it came to his nephews.

She didn't know the boys well enough to trust them around fire without adult supervision. But then she saw Scooter and Jonesy, a couple of retired volunteer firefighters, leading a line of kids outside like the Pied Pipers of Sugar Falls, and told Drew she thought it would be a safe enough activity.

The kids scampered off, and she and her new husband wove their way through chairs and tables until they reached the empty head table—where her parents made a beeline for them.

"So let's cut to the chase," Bobby Chatterson said before pulling out the chairs reserved for the bride and groom. "Did you knock my daughter up, or what?"

"Dad," Kylie pleaded, although it wasn't until this morning that she'd been able to rule that possibility out.

"No, sir." Drew didn't bat an eye. "It really happened quite suddenly. And please believe me when I say that I would never have eloped with Kylie if I'd thought it would cause her any problems with her family."

That was mostly true. Her husband was likely well trained in phrasing things just the right way in order to calm people down. Of course, what he'd left unsaid was that he probably would never have married Kylie ever. Period.

"That's good to know," her dad said. "Because Kylie not having a proper wedding would really be a big disappointment to her mom and me. So I put a call into my buddy who runs the stadium club back home. He owes me a pretty big favor and thinks he can get your reception on the books for October."

Oh, no.

Drew, who had been taking a healthy chug of his soda, choked a bit.

Kylie sighed. "Dad, seriously. We're not going to have a wedding reception back in Seattle."

"Fine, then." Her father threw his hands up in the air. "Have it here. Your mom already spoke to the manager, and he'll give us a pretty good rate if we put down the deposit tomorrow."

Thankfully she was sitting beside Drew, because she couldn't even imagine seeing the mortified look crossing his face right that second. "Slow down, Dad. There's no need to rush into any of this."

"You're really not one to preach about rushing into anything, Jellybean."

"I have a suggestion." Drew's voice was calm and his fingers were soothing as he lightly stroked her bare shoulders. When had he put his arm around her? "Why don't we all sleep on it tonight, and then we can get together tomorrow and throw some ideas around for the big reception. Maybe come up with a game plan that everyone will be happy with."

Kylie took a drink of champagne to keep her jaw from dropping. What was he thinking?

"I like a good game plan," her dad said. "You good with that, Lace?"

Her mom stood up. "I'm good with anything that gets your mouth to stop jabbering and your feet to start moving. Get your dancing shoes on, Bobby. It's time to show these kids how to shake it."

"All right, we'll see you two tomorrow, then," her father said. "Wait, we're gonna need directions to your place."

"You don't remember how to get to my condo?" Kylie asked at the exact same time Drew responded, "The cabin's a little ways out of town, off Sweetwater Bend."

Her husband was looking at something outside on the terrace and must not have been paying attention when he'd made the slip.

"What cabin?" Her mom lifted a brown eyebrow. Her parents had seized on the discrepancy immediately. How was she going to extricate herself from this one?

"Well, it's only been a week, so we're still sorting out the…uh…living arrangements," she said.

"Hmm." Her father stroked his well-groomed beard. "It's probably better you don't live together just yet anyway. I can't really see you sharing your shoe closet with a couple of little boys. Plus, there's no way could you rough it out in some cabin in the woods."

"What do you mean, Dad? I could live in a cabin anywhere." The trapped feeling she'd been experiencing just seconds ago was now building up into defensiveness. She felt like a grenade—and her father was about to pull the pin.

"Sure you could." Her dad winked at her mom, and Kylie exploded.

"Dad, I'm thirty years old. I can live wherever I want and with whomever I want. And if I decide to move in with *my* husband and *our* nephews into *our* cabin, then that's what I'll do, because I'm an adult, and I can make my own decisions."

"Fine. I'm sure you know what's best, Jellybean. By the way, your brother Kane is still recovering from his shoulder surgery and has been eager to get out of Chicago and recuperate somewhere in private. I'll let him know he can stay at your condo since you won't be using it."

"Perfect. That settles everything," Lacey Chatterson

said, pulling her husband toward the dance floor. "We'll see you two lovebirds tomorrow at the cabin."

Ugh! She'd just done it again. Kylie'd let her temper get the best of her, and now she couldn't backpedal without making her parents suspect something was up.

And as if the hole she'd dug for herself couldn't get any bigger, Drew wouldn't—or couldn't—even look at her.

Chapter Five

Drew would've tried to stop the words before they came out of Kylie's mouth if he hadn't been staring so intently at the raging fire looming bigger and closer outside. Where were the twins—and why weren't the smoke alarms going off?

While he couldn't very well have a stranger move in with him and the boys, especially one who didn't know how to keep her hotheaded responses in check, dealing with that issue wasn't topping his list of priorities at that exact moment. He needed to get out there and make sure his nephews weren't in danger of setting the Snow Creek Lodge ablaze.

More guests were trickling outside to enjoy the brisk evening air along with the robust flames in the circular stone pit. Drew was relieved to see the fire did in fact look well contained, but he couldn't say the same about his nephews.

They were nowhere to be seen.

"What's wrong?" Kylie asked as she walked up behind him. He didn't know if she'd followed him so she could explain her outburst about moving into the cabin with him, or if she could instinctively tell that he was worried about something.

But either way, he was glad she was by his side.

"I don't see the boys." He looked back and forth, taking in every person in the dim firelight. But none of them were identical four-foot troublemakers with impish faces and springy blond curls.

"Okay. Let's think about this logically." Sure, *now* Miss Hothead could be logical. Where was her rational thinking just a few moments ago?

"It's only been fifteen minutes since they came out here," she continued. "About five minutes ago, I looked out the glass doors and saw them helping the bigger boys bring more wood over. So they couldn't have gotten far in that amount of time."

He appreciated her awareness of the twins while he'd been focused on calming her father down, but she apparently didn't realize just exactly *what* kind of chaos Caden and Aiden were capable of wreaking in that short amount of time.

He started yelling their names, but Kylie grabbed his hand and squeezed it tightly. "Let's not start a full-fledged panic. You go toward the ski lift and search for them there. I'll ask if anyone has seen them."

Drew nodded before running toward the motorized benches that hauled adventure enthusiasts up to the top of the mountain. He was really going to let the boys have it if he found them messing around on the lifts after he'd expressly told them not to get close to that area.

But the chairs were motionless, suspended in the dark

night air, and the control room with the engine and levers was tightly locked.

Where could they be?

He tried not to let the worst-case scenario sink in, but concern was wedging itself firmly in his throat. He'd promised his brother he'd look after them. What if he'd lost them out here in the forest? At least it was no longer snow season. But still, it was dark and the area was pretty remote. They could've wandered too far and gotten lost, or worse—separated.

He wondered if they were scared. One time, when he'd been five years old, he'd spotted a giant gumball machine in the Boise mall. He'd been so in awe, he'd slipped away from his mom and Luke to check it out, and before he knew it, they were nowhere to be seen. He remembered his dad had always told him that if he ever got lost, he should stay in the same place, and that was just what Drew had done. Of course, the place he'd decided to stay was wedged behind a table and a trash can in the busy food court. So nobody had been able to find him for nearly thirty minutes. It had been the scariest and longest half hour of his life. He'd cried so hard and so silently, he'd nearly made himself sick.

Two high school girls had found him and took him to their gift-wrap booth, where they were volunteering to wrap presents for their cheerleading squad's fund-raiser. One girl had held his hand while the other had flagged down a security guard to report a lost boy.

Drew's mom was there in minutes and looked just as panicked as he had felt. But worse was seeing his twin brother, Luke, who had been more upset than all of them and had also gotten sick in fear for his lost sibling. Drew tried to play off the experience as if he hadn't been frightened out of his mind and promised himself that it was better to be calm and organized in a crisis than to lose control of his emotions.

Yet here he was thirty years later, experiencing that lost, scared and helpless sensation all over again. He needed to find the boys. He needed to take control of the situation so he wouldn't feel so overwhelmed.

He ran back toward the terrace, deciding that he would enlist an entire search party if need be, but he was going to do *something*. Yet right before he got to the terrace, he caught sight of a tall redhead walking through a darkened field of overgrown grass just beyond the north end of the lodge. He probably wouldn't have seen her if it hadn't been for the way the distant glow of the fire caught the glimmering sparkle of her gold-colored bridesmaid dress.

Drew jogged past the patio and straight for her. As he got closer, he saw that she was holding the hands of two animated blond-haired eight-year-olds. One of the boys was dragging a broken tree limb behind them.

"Where were you two?" His voice cracked, the fear and anguish he'd just experienced overriding any sense of relief or gratitude for Kylie having found them.

"We were just getting more wood for the bonfire," said Aiden, or possibly Caden. It was too dark and Drew's adrenaline was pumping too fast for him to discern the difference.

"Yeah, Mr. Scooter and Mr. Jonesy said they couldn't make the fire too big without more tinder, so we went to find them some. Why are you all sweaty and breathing funny like that, Uncle Drew?"

Kylie bent down and spoke softly, calmly. "Your uncle was worried because he couldn't find you."

"But we told Hunter where we were going."

"That's who told me where to find them," Kylie said to Drew. "We already talked about it, and they both promised me that next time they decided to go off exploring, they'd tell an adult."

"Hunter's eleven. He's almost a grown-up," Caden argued.

"But Hunter's not responsible for you two. I am." He was at his wit's end, but he knew yelling at the boys wouldn't solve anything.

"Sorry, Uncle Drew. We were just trying to help make the fire grow bigger."

He let out the breath he hadn't realized he'd been holding. He'd been deployed to the front lines of enemy territory all over the world. He was trained to maintain his cool, to help other people get through their emotional issues. But this? It was too much. He'd been back in the United States for a little over a week and already he'd gotten rip-roaring drunk, married a stranger, pissed off his in-laws and practically lost his brother's children. War was easier.

His mom had been wrong. He couldn't handle the boys. He couldn't handle any of this. And he had to report to his new job assignment the day after tomorrow. How was he supposed to counsel wounded veterans and PTSD patients when he couldn't even control his own life?

His sister was volunteering at some orphanage in West Africa, his brother was on a top secret assignment and his parents were on a much-needed vacation. He had no one. For the second time in his life, Drew felt completely and utterly alone.

Where were the cheerleaders at the mall gift-wrap booth when he needed them most?

"Okay, boys." Kylie's voice broke the direction of his self-pitying thoughts. "Why don't you haul that branch over to the fire pit? But do not step off that concrete patio without talking to your uncle first."

As the boys made their way back, Kylie and Drew stayed near the stone wall separating the lodge from the overgrown trails beyond. She stood close to him as he got his breathing under control.

Her skin glowed golden in the firelight, and he knew she must be freezing cold. Even though it was June, the nights up here in the mountains still dipped into the fifties, and she was barely covered in that tight satin sheath. In fact, her shoulders shivered slightly. He took his wool uniform jacket off and put it over her shoulders. The woman might lose her temper with the gossips of Sugar Falls and her overbearing father, but she sure knew how to keep her cool around his nephews.

"Thank you," she said as she snuggled into the jacket's warmth. They were both keeping an eye on the boys, yet neither one was in too much of a hurry to gather around the fire or otherwise return to the wedding reception.

"No, I should be thanking *you*. I ran off hell-bent for leather, and you kept your wits about you and found the boys single-handedly."

"Did you just say *hell*, Saint Drew?" She looked up into his eyes, and when he saw the faint smile on her full lips, he was tempted to show her exactly how unsaintly he could be.

"Contrary to what everyone thinks about me, I'm no angel." Especially not with the way his overheated body was responding to her closeness.

She tilted her head as if considering such an absurd possibility. But then something caught her eye, and he followed her gaze to where her parents were standing just inside the ballroom, saying their goodbyes to the bride and groom.

She sighed. "I'm sorry about inviting myself to live in

your cabin with you and the boys. I promise that I never had any intention of putting you in that situation."

"So you're not really considering moving in with me?"

"As if." She tried to laugh, but the sound came out more strangled than anything else. "Can you imagine how awkward that would be?"

He didn't answer because, although he knew that it would be uncomfortable for them in some ways, it would also be a perfect solution to his biggest problem. "I don't think it would be so bad."

"Are you kidding? We barely know each other, and you've already got your hands full with the boys and your new job and everything."

"But where will you go? I mean, you could back down in front of your parents, but they did sort of call your bluff by saying your brother would be staying at your place."

"Ugh. I forgot about that. And Kane tells my dad everything. I guess I could move in with Mia or get a room here at the Lodge."

"For the entire summer?"

"Why do you sound as if you don't think the idea of me staying at your cabin is completely ridiculous?"

Was he that obvious?

"Well, sure, it might seem odd at first. But technically, we *are* married. I mean, nobody else in town would think it was unusual. And to be honest with you, I could use some help with the boys."

"But I don't know anything about kids."

"You've done a better job in the past twenty-four hours than I've done all week. Maybe it's because you're a woman and they need a mother figure, but you have a way with them. They actually listen to you and follow your directions. Look, just stay for a little while until I can learn how to do it on my own. Remember what I've been saying since the start? We're in this together."

"You know, you're way better at this whole psychology thing than I am."

"Years of training."

"Speaking of years of training, I have a full-time job. I guess I could do some work from home, but I couldn't be with the boys all the time." She was caving. He could sense it from the way she seemed to be examining it from all the angles.

"I have them enrolled in a summer day camp, but I would still need help with drop-offs and pickups and putting out any other fires—no pun intended—that might come up."

Just then, her parents walked outside. As Kylie moved in closer to him and looped her arm through his, Drew knew her dad's still suspicious expression sealed the deal for her. He was about to get a new roommate.

"Well, Jellybean, your mom and I are heading to our room upstairs for the night. We'll stop by for dinner on our way out of town tomorrow. Should we bring anything?"

"Nope," Drew said. He wasn't going to let her back out now. "We'll have everything all taken care of."

He should be wondering how he'd come up with this mad scheme, let alone gotten Kylie to agree to it. But all he could think about was how soft his new wife and roommate's skin was.

Kylie drove down the rutted dirt lane leading to the Gregson family cabin. Her Mercedes was stuffed to its closed convertible top with all the shoes, clothes and bedding that she might need for the next couple of months— or at least until her brother was no longer staying at her condo.

Of all the stupid scrapes she'd gotten herself into, putting on that newlywed act for her parents last night really took the cake. She couldn't believe she'd be stuck playing live-in nanny for some handsome stranger for the summer.

Her head was still throbbing from the two glasses of champagne she'd indulged in at the reception last night. When was she going to learn that alcohol and Andrew Gregson did not mix well for her?

She put the car in Park and eyeballed her temporary new home before getting out. The log house was small, but it seemed to be in good repair. Although the dirt driveway was going to be killer on her high heels.

She grabbed a suitcase out of the front of her two-seater coupe just as Drew came down the porch steps. "Here, let me help you with your... Hey, is all of this stuff yours?"

He squinted at the loaded trunk, and she saw his Adam's apple bob up, then down.

She had about two hours to settle in before her parents showed up for a home-cooked Sunday dinner and Act Two of her cozying up to her pretend husband.

She didn't have time to deal with Drew's analysis of her belongings. She handed him the suitcase and a tote bag stuffed with shoes before grabbing her purse, her laptop case and a paper sack full of groceries from Duncan's Market. Thankfully, Marcia Duncan hadn't been in the store when she had stopped to get supplies for tonight's meal.

Drew was dressed in jeans and a button-up plaid shirt that still had creases in it. Which only drew her gaze to his very large, very broad shoulders.

Ugh, she needed to stop looking at his body.

Instead, as they walked up to the path to the front porch, she focused on the old brown Oldsmobile sedan parked along the side of the house.

"Where's the Man Machine?" she asked.

"The what?" He looked over his shoulder at her.

"The big yellow Jeep. That's what Maxine used to call it when Cooper was staying here and driving that thing."

"It's parked near the boat shed out back. Why would she call it that?"

"Why wouldn't she? It has huge mud tires, a gun locker strapped to the rear bumper and a beer cooler as the center console. It's about as manly a vehicle as it gets."

"Hmm, well, the twins thought it was fun, but I decided my grandma's Oldsmobile would be a safer choice for a family car."

She hitched her purse higher on her shoulder as she leaned in to look inside the car more suitable for a great-grandmother than for a bachelor uncle. "It only has lap belts and no airbags. Plus six ashtrays and not a single cup holder. How kid friendly do you think that is?"

"Well, it's better than that little red matchbox you're screaming around town in."

"That's a Mercedes-Benz. It's my style—sophisticated with just a hint of pizzazz."

Were they having their first argument? If so, he needed to understand that just because he was an uptight doctor didn't mean she was going to give up her plush lifestyle to be some Suzie Homemaker wife and substitute mother.

He held the front door open for her, polite even in disagreement.

"She's here! Aunt Kylie's finally here," Caden screamed as he ran out into the living room in nothing but a pair of superhero costume leggings.

Okay, so maybe her heart melted just a tiny bit when she heard the word *aunt*. Although Hunter called her the same thing, her own brothers had yet to have any children—that she knew of—and she didn't mind the idea of these delightful cuties looking up to her.

Aiden followed, wearing only his underwear and the top half of the costume, complete with a cape around his shoulders. "Hey, Aunt Kylie, you wanna sleep in the bunk room with me and Aiden?"

"First, *you're* Aiden and that—" she pointed to the shirtless boy opening the kitchen cupboards "—is Caden. Don't try to pull that old trick on me. Second, let me get all my stuff unpacked before we figure out the sleeping arrangements."

She knew Drew wouldn't want to sleep in the same bed with her. Really, she had to agree it was for the best, no matter how good he looked when he woke up. But she really hoped she wasn't sleeping in the bunk room.

"I was thinking that I could room with the boys," Drew said as if responding to her exact thought. The guy was both moral *and* chivalrous. "There are two sets of bunk beds in there. You can take the master bedroom."

"Are you sure? How are you going to fit in a bunk bed?" Again her eyes strayed to his bulky shoulders and long, strong legs. She needed to stop looking at him if she was going to be living here. No good could come of lusting for her in-name-only husband.

"Trust me. Navy ships have much smaller and crowded quarters than these. We'll make do." He lowered his voice so the boys wouldn't hear. "Besides, I'll keep most of my stuff where it is and just sneak into one of the bunks after the kids fall asleep. I figure we should probably give off the appearance that we're sharing a room, even with the boys, so they don't slip and say something later."

"You're probably right," she said while simultaneously thinking, *How in the world are we going to fake this all summer?*

"Boys, come help get Miss, ah..." He lowered his voice again. "What do you want them to call you?"

Well, technically, she was no longer a miss. Was Drew going to expect her to take his last name while they were living here together, pretending to be the happily married couple? They had so much to figure out. What the kids called her seemed like the simplest of issues.

"Kylie is fine. Whatever they're comfortable with." Although she did like the aunt part, she didn't want to force her questionably earned title on Drew or his family.

He carried her suitcase toward the hallway. After dropping the bag of groceries on the kitchen table, she followed him for the rest of the tour.

The cabin was one large great room, consisting of an open floor plan kitchen, a comfortable living room and a dining room table separating the two. A hallway led toward what she assumed were the bedrooms and a single bathroom.

"Wow, you have a ton of books," she said when she saw the cardboard boxes lining the larger bedroom wall. "Are they all yours?"

"Yep. My mom and dad were cleaning out the garage and wanted me to take some of my stuff. I told them I'd go through the boxes over the summer and see what I can get rid of. When Luke gets back and I get a place of my own, it'll make the move easier."

Whew. It was a good reminder that Drew was in Sugar Falls for only a short time. Hopefully, come September, this whole awkward mess would be behind them.

He effortlessly tossed her oversize suitcase, which had to weigh close to seventy-five pounds, on top of the bright orange-and-turquoise-patterned quilt spread out on the bed. Realizing the strong man could probably lift her just as easily and place her on the king-size mattress, Kylie figured she needed all the reminding she could get that this arrangement was temporary.

She averted her face, which must have been an unflattering shade of crimson, and tried to concentrate on the contents of the boxes.

Psychology textbooks, philosophy books, books on world religions. He was an intellectual man.

And a seriously good-looking one.

"So I better finish unloading my car. My parents will be here in a couple of hours, and I wanted to make some dinner and at least make a pretense of being all settled in." Plus, she had a half-gallon container of Neapolitan ice cream melting in her grocery sack.

"Are they coming armed with bridal magazines?"

"I hope not. I told them that you didn't want to talk about reception plans with your nephews here because you didn't want them thinking that our marriage wasn't legitimate. So with any luck, we'll just have dinner and they'll hit the road."

"You have no idea how good a home-cooked meal sounds. The boys and I have been living off peanut-butter-and-jelly sandwiches and frozen chicken nuggets."

She looked at his flat stomach and wondered how much food it must take to keep his body looking so muscular and taut.

"I...uh...actually wasn't going to make a true home-cooked meal. I just picked up a roasted chicken from Duncan's and some stuff for a salad. I'm not really much of a chef, but I thought I could manage a box of rice pilaf. So don't get your hormones...I mean your taste buds too worked up."

Ugh. She sounded like an idiot. What kind of woman stood in man's bedroom and talked about hormones and getting worked up? He, like the rest of the town, probably thought she was beyond promiscuous, coming on to him like this.

He studied her from behind the metal-rimmed glasses, and she wished she could figure out what he was thinking whenever he looked at her. He stared at her as if she was some obscure test subject he could study and later write about in his own psychology textbook.

"Uncle Drew." An anxious voice interrupted the tension in the room. "Come quick! Aiden got his cape stuck in the post of the top bunk. And it won't come off his neck."

"Ah, jeez…" Drew said before running out of the room.

She would follow him to help. But she had to get her pulse and her mixed emotions in check before she could be of any use to anyone.

Unfortunately, her familiar litany of prime factors was short-lived. Drew yelled, "Kylie, could you come help us out?"

"What's wrong?" she asked as she entered the boys' room. But she knew the answer before Caden could control his laughter enough to tell her.

Drew was holding Aiden's suspended body, which was still clad only in the top half of the superhero costume and his underwear. But it wasn't Aiden's makeshift cape that was stuck in the bed rails. It was the little boy's curly blond head.

Bless her husband, who was trying to sound calm but looked about as frazzled as a pageant contestant who'd run out of double-sided tape. "His head is wedged in here pretty well, and I'm worried that if I let go of his body to help dislodge him, he might asphyxiate."

A good-looking and well-built man standing near her bed in a master bedroom, she could barely deal with. But this…well, *this* was a no-brainer for her. Kylie tried to keep her laughter in check as she said, "Hold him steady while I go grab something from the kitchen."

Chapter Six

An hour and two sticks of butter later, the twins were sitting on the rag rug in the living room, wearing headphones and playing a math game on Drew's tablet. Well, Drew hoped it was a math game. He'd set up parental controls the first day they got here, but these boys had proved to be tech-savvy enough to bypass those restrictions if they got an idea to. But at least they were behaving for once.

A loud knock sounded at the cabin's front door, and he said a silent prayer, hoping to get through tonight without scolding his nephews or insulting Kylie's parents. He sure hoped the Shadowview Military Hospital had a gym for employees, because Drew knew exactly where he would be spending his lunch hours this summer, working off steam.

Kylie's heels pinged along the hardwood floor as she rushed out of the kitchen and toward the door. As his wife ushered her parents into the cabin, for a second Drew wondered if they'd look down their noses at his humble family's little log house. Now that he'd seen Kylie's flashy red sports car and her mother's even flashier diamond ring, he guessed the Chatterson family was used to the finer things in life.

But the couple smiled brightly as Lacey handed over a bouquet of peonies to Kylie and Mr. Chatterson passed him a chilled bottle of chardonnay and a six-pack of locally brewed beer. Oh, how Drew was tempted to crack one of those bottles open right now.

"Hey, you're that guy from TV," Aiden said, looking up from the handheld screen. "The one on that sports channel who always yells at the baseball umpires. Coach Chatterson." And just like that, the little boy looked back down at his game, already losing interest.

"Wait, you're *Bobby Chatterson*?" Drew asked as he did a double take at the well-known scruffy red beard and the familiar emblem on his polo shirt. "As in the professional baseball player?"

Drew didn't follow major league sports too much, but even he'd heard of the Hall of Fame pitcher. He could've sworn that Kylie had mentioned her father's name when she'd introduced him, but for some reason—maybe because of his stretched-to-the-breaking-point nerves—Drew's mind hadn't connected those dots.

"You're not a real fast learner, are you, Captain?" Bobby said before giving a knowing side look to Lacey and planting his large frame on the living room couch.

"Dad, Drew's a well-educated psychologist. And he's a lieutenant commander, not a captain," Kylie said. Drew followed her into the kitchen to uncork the wine and help get the meal on the table faster, leaving his guests to linger in the living room.

She looked back to her parents, who were now watching the boys play on the electronic device. "Okay, everyone, dinner is ready. Mom, I know you don't believe in kids not sitting at the table, but Drew and I figured we'd just have the boys eat at the coffee table in the living room so we could talk about, uh—" Kylie coughed as if the words were strangling her "—our marriage."

"Your house, Jellybean, your rules," Bobby said. Drew didn't argue that, technically, it had been Kylie's house for only a couple of hours.

"Maybe next time they can sit with us," Lacey suggested. Drew took the twins' plates to the living room, hoping that there wouldn't be a next time.

"So, Drew, you're a military psychologist?" Mr. Chatterson walked over to the table and sat down before grabbing a large knife.

Kylie had set the chicken out, and looking at the way the large man was already carving off half the bird for himself, Drew's stomach growled painfully at the thought of making do with just salad and rice.

"That's right, sir," Drew said as he took a seat. "I've just been assigned to the Shadowview Military Hospital."

"You must've gone to school a long time for that," Mrs. Chatterson said as she took a sip from her wineglass.

"Well, I joined the navy as a reservist right out of high school. After I finished undergrad, they sent me to the Uniformed Services University of the Health Sciences for my doctorate. I did an internship at Walter Reed before they sent me out with ground forces."

"So what does a military psychologist do?" Bobby asked. "Study psychological warfare and whatnot? Figure out how to play head games with the enemy, that kind of thing?"

"Actually, I specialize in post-traumatic stress disorder. As in how to treat it and how to train other soldiers in recognizing it in themselves and others."

"Huh. Well, I guess they need people for that, too. Personally, I think psychological warfare would be more interesting."

"Really, Dad?" Kylie said. "What do you know about it?"

"Jellybean, I wrote the book on psychological warfare. That's what pitchers do. They sit up on that mound making the batter wonder, 'Is this guy gonna throw a curve ball or is he gonna purposely aim to the left and bean me with a ninety-five-mile-per-hour rocket?'"

Wow, his father-in-law was a world-famous athlete *and* an author. Funny, out of all those books boxed up in the master bedroom, Drew didn't recall seeing any written by major-league relief pitcher Bobby Chatterson.

But Drew tamped down his inner sarcasm and held his tongue throughout the rest of the meal, allowing Kylie's dad to expound on the limitless ways he exercised mind control over his opponents.

Which made Drew wonder if his new in-laws were even the least bit fooled by this whole farce.

Kylie loved her parents to death, but it wasn't until they left that she felt as if she could truly breathe. She finished off the ice cream in her bowl as Drew wiped down the kitchen counters. The boys were watching an animated movie about outer space on television, and Kylie longed to take a hot bath and climb into bed.

In fact, she longed to escape from this total wreck she'd made of her life.

She looked at the rustic simplicity of the cabin and the two pajama-clad children sprawled out on the living room rug. For the next few months, this was her world—a cabin in the woods, a lack of skills in the kitchen and a set of eight-year-old twins who needed some understanding and some structure. She might live in a remote small mountain town in Idaho and she might have been raised with a lovable but overbearing father and four brothers, but she was still a girlie girl.

She didn't do wilderness or cooking.

She liked pedicures and shopping trips and running water, which, thank goodness, she'd found when she spotted the old claw-foot tub in the cabin's single bathroom. So maybe she'd have to move the Lego sailboat and the *Star Wars* figurines out of the way while she relaxed in the bubble bath. She was going to have to get used to moving around a lot of things in her life now.

As Drew finished up in the kitchen, Kylie sneaked away to her room to grab her toiletries and something to sleep in. She locked the bathroom door and ran the water, climbing into the tub before it'd even had a chance to fill up. She dozed off in the water and woke only when she heard a light knock on the door.

"Kylie," Drew whispered. "Is everything okay in there?"

After what he'd witnessed in Reno, he probably thought she was prone to running off and hiding in bathrooms whenever the mood struck her. And maybe she was. "Yes, I'm okay."

"Well, the kids have fallen asleep, and I was going to hit the sack myself. I just wanted to see if you needed anything."

Yeah, she needed a plan. A schedule. If she was going to embark on this crazy pretend lifestyle with Drew and his nephews, she at least needed some sense of organization.

"Hold on." She stood up from the lukewarm water and grabbed the blue towel, since it looked the least used. Step one in her plan was to find out if Drew had a washing machine and start a load of laundry.

Step two. Establish a schedule.

Step three. Find someone to teach her to cook. Kylie'd felt horrible when she realized that a single rotisserie chicken would barely feed her dad, let alone Drew and two growing boys. She should've known better—or at least have paid better attention to how her mom handled cooking for a house full of men. She couldn't do takeout every night and, as cute as the boys were, she wasn't convinced their manners were quite restaurant-worthy yet.

She slipped on a pink tank top and ruffled pajama shorts and exited her temporary sanctuary. Drew was folding blankets in the living room in his own set of pajama bottoms and a snug, faded blue shirt that read Go Navy.

Wait, step one should be to set up some ground rules for how they were supposed to deal with each other and her growing attraction to the man.

"Hey," she said, holding her arms crossed under her chest and then moved them to her hips before returning them to their original position.

Ugh. Why was she so awkward around him? She'd never been so physically attracted to a man. Andrew Gregson made her question every rational thought in her head.

He met her gaze before glancing down her body. She felt her body heat up as though his large, tanned hands were touching her. She cleared her throat and he dragged his gaze back toward hers.

"So, uh, tomorrow," he said. That was all he had to say? Was he going somewhere with this?

"Yep. That's the day after today. What about it?"

He coughed. "Tomorrow I have to report for duty at the hospital, and the boys start their summer day camp."

"Which day camp are they going to?"

"The Junior Crafters. It's the one through the community center."

"Don't you think that one might be a little too juvenile for them?"

"Well, they are juveniles."

"No kidding. What I'm saying is that maybe they need to be in a program that will stimulate them a little more so they'll find less of a need to seek out inappropriate activities."

He tilted his head, and she wondered if she'd already overstepped her role as temporary aunt. "What would you recommend?"

"Alex Russell does a white-water rafting day program for older kids. Maxine's son is enrolled, and the boys seem to look up to Hunter. I think the twins might have more fun there."

"That sounds a little dangerous."

"It's all supervised. And better for them to be rafting, hiking and doing wilderness activities with a professional than to sneak out of the kindergarten-level art class at the community center to see if their basket-weaving projects can float down the river."

"You might have a good point."

"Besides, Alex is good with young boys and runs a tight ship. I have a feeling the teenagers working at the community center won't be able to keep up with Aiden and Caden."

"But is it too late for me to enroll them?"

She tapped her lip, thinking. "I'll tell you what. I'll take them over to Russell Sports in the morning and enroll them. I can also pick them up when I get done with my last client."

"Are you sure?"

"No problem. I might even be able to swing by the market, too. Listen, I'm sorry about not having enough for dinner tonight. I should've been used to how much my dad eats, but for the past few years, I mostly only prepare food for one or else eat out. So this is my late disclaimer that I can help out with the boys and I can help clean, but I'm not much use in the kitchen."

Drew smiled. "I've had roommates who've been less capable."

Did he just call her a roommate?

Of course, that was all she was to him. That and some free babysitting. But it wasn't as if he'd *asked* her to move in. She'd been the one to put them both in this awkward position. And they *still* hadn't clarified things with her parents.

"So if we're all set for tomorrow, I'm going to turn in." She nodded her head toward the bedroom. "Are you sure you don't mind me taking the big bed?"

"Not at all. Sleep well. Let me know if you need anything."

Kylie made her way into the bedroom. She was used to sleeping alone, to living alone. So then why, in this house full of people, did she feel so lonely?

A shrill beeping shook Kylie out of her dream, causing her to roll over and send the biography of Sigmund Freud toppling to the floor. She pushed the screen of her phone, effectively silencing the alarm, and then looked at the fallen book she'd dug out of the boxes to help lure her to sleep last night. It certainly had done the trick.

She listened to the silence as she stretched under the bright homemade quilt. Maybe she should sneak out of her room before anyone else awoke and grab a cup of coffee to help get her through the morning. If today was anything like last night, heaven knew she was going to need it.

She didn't bother getting dressed, figuring she could set up the pod machine she'd brought over from her place and get started on some hazelnut-laced caffeine before hitting the shower.

As she made her way into the kitchen, she saw Drew sitting at the table, an open box of Honey Smacks and a quart of milk beside him.

Maybe she should've put on her robe.

But it wasn't as if he hadn't already seen her in her pajamas last night—or a lot less the morning in Reno. Besides, he must've had the same idea to sneak into the kitchen for a quick breakfast before the chaos of the day began.

"Morning," she said, looking at his faded T-shirt, which stretched across his muscular chest. Seeing his short, spiky hair caused her fingers to twitch. The only things proper looking about Saint Drew at this exact moment were his wire-rimmed glasses. He looked so warm and so masculine and so...

Coffee. She needed coffee, not lustful thoughts about cozying up with her handsome quasi-husband under that king-size quilt.

"Hey," he said simply.

Maybe he wasn't much of a morning person.

But as she plugged in her top-of-the-line brewer and filled it with water, she felt him watching her. A couple of times, while rooting around in the cupboards for where she might've stored her K-Cups, she noticed the tilt in his head as he stared at her. Well, she wasn't much of a morning person, either, and enough was enough.

"Why do you keep looking at me like that?"

"Like what?" he asked, not even straightening up.

"Like you're trying to figure me out."

"Sorry, I can't help it. I slept wrong last night and somehow tweaked my neck."

"Oh, no. I knew that bunk bed was going to be too

small for you. From now on, you're sleeping in the master bedroom."

"Then, where will you sleep?" Her mind flashed to them curled up together on that big bed. "It's not like you're that much shorter than me," he added, and she realized that she'd stepped closer to him, and his head was angled so that he was staring at her long, bare legs.

"Oh, I can sleep anywhere." She walked behind his chair, mostly to put herself out of his line of vision, then felt silly for standing there uselessly. She put her hands to his bare neck and began to massage. "I could sleep on the sofa."

He groaned and leaned toward the table, offering her better access. "I can't very well make a lady sleep on a couch while I'm all cozy in a king-size bed. Besides, what if the twins woke up and found you sleeping in the living room?"

"Then, I'd tell them their uncle is a terrible snorer."

"I'm not, though."

"How do you know you're not?"

"Because nobody that's ever shared a bed with me has complained."

Her hands froze. Whoa. Were they still talking about snoring? Kylie sure hoped so, because the thought of Drew doing anything *but* sleeping in a bed with someone else had her feeling like an upside-down can of whipped cream, ready to discharge.

Speaking of which, an ice cream sundae would really help her cool down right now.

Ugh, she was being ridiculous. Of course he'd slept with other women before. He might've even lived with another woman before.

She forced her fingers to keep moving along the warm

skin of his neck, and before she could change her mind, she asked, "Have you ever been married?"

"What?" He tried to crane his head around to look at her but groaned in pain. "Of course not."

"Ever come close?" Boy, she was really on a roll now.

"You mean, was I ever engaged?"

"Or, you know, living together with a long-term girl-friend? Anything like that?" It was as if she couldn't stop with the personal questions. Thank goodness he couldn't see her face right then.

"I was in a long-term relationship a few years ago, but I don't know how serious it was. I mean, for me at least. She wanted to get married, but I didn't, so we went our separate ways. What about you? Any past boyfriends I need to worry about upsetting because you're suddenly off the market?"

Was she off the market? Obviously she couldn't really date anyone until they got this whole marriage thing re-solved. But it was kind of weird to realize just now that her love life was going to be on a temporary hiatus.

"I don't think we'll have any major issues on that front," she said as her hands dipped below the collar of his shirt. She heard him suck in a breath, and thinking he might still be in pain, she wanted to put his mind at ease. "For the next couple of months, I'm all yours."

His shoulders stiffened and he jumped up from his chair, shaking the table and sending cereal and milk slosh-ing out of his bowl.

"It's fine. I'm fine. My neck's better." His voice was huskier than before, but the angle of his head indicated that she still hadn't worked out the cramp. Had she said something to make him uncomfortable? "I'd better go get dressed before it gets crazy. In here. With the kids wak-ing up and stuff."

Drew jogged toward the bathroom, and it wasn't until she heard the water running that Kylie began to wonder whether it was her personal questions or her intimate touch that had caused such a weird response from the normally cool and reserved psychologist.

It *couldn't* be her touching him. Could it?

Before she could bask in the possibility of her womanly charms, the twins sprinted out of their room and straight for the unattended box of Honey Smacks left behind on the table.

Drew was right. It truly was about to get crazy in here.

After his shower, Drew quickly donned his uniform and left Kylie to deal with the mayhem of getting the kids fed and dressed. Sure, it was the coward's way out, but his hormones were already raging to new heights. It wasn't until he was away from the cabin and driving down the mountain that he allowed himself to revisit that awkward scene in the kitchen this morning.

When he'd seen her long, toned legs in those ridiculously short pajama bottoms, he'd been immediately aroused. Then, as she had begun rubbing his aching neck and making her way to his shoulders, he'd known he was on the edge of losing control. Not to mention, their conversation had taken a sudden intimate turn, and all he could think about was how fabulous her hands were making him feel.

But hearing her say that she was all his was his complete undoing.

How could any male on the planet withstand that kind of temptation? He might've looked like a complete bumbling idiot when he'd knocked over his cereal and raced into the bathroom. But better to be an unsocial fool than

to risk pulling her onto his lap and kissing her until neither of them could think straight.

If he wasn't a more disciplined man, he would've done
exactly that. And possibly more. But he'd had years of
practicing self-control, so he'd gotten the heck out of there.

Last night, they'd decided that Kylie was going to drive
Nana's Oldsmobile, since she was dropping off the kids
and her Mercedes didn't have enough seat belts, let alone
seats, for two extra passengers. The old Jeep his family
kept parked at the cabin didn't have an adapter for his
iPod so, during his commute, Drew had to listen to the
radio. When one of his favorite gym songs came on, he
thought about hitting his punching bag later that day, if
there was time.

He looked at his crooked pinkie, a reminder of a punch
gone astray. He'd taken up boxing when he'd first joined
the navy, but by the time he was in graduate school, he'd
decided a peaceful and genteel physical outlet would be
more suitable. So now Drew's workouts of choice were a
combination of yoga and strength training. Controlling
his mind and body at the same time usually helped to redirect any of his stress and negative energy.

But today he realized that blasting loud music and boxing might be the only thing that pushed his mind and
body to their absolute limits, which wouldn't necessarily
soothe him but would allow him to temporarily block out
everything else.

He pulled the Jeep into the staff parking lot and turned
off the Metallica song before taking a few deep, cleansing
breaths and heading into work.

He spent the morning meeting his commanding officer
and the hospital chief of staff before being shown into his
new office, a beige room near the orthopedic outpatient
wing. Some might have thought the psychology depart-

ment should have been housed in or near the psychiatry unit, but he liked to plan for his team and his patients to be near the physical-therapy rooms. Sure, the issues he dealt with were mental in nature, but he wanted the soldiers who came to him for help to know that their battlefield scars shouldn't be treated any differently or with any more stigma than a physical injury.

If the proximity of his office allowed him better access to the exercise facilities, then that was a bonus. And after seeing Kylie in her skimpy tank top, her pebbled nipples pressing through the thin pink cotton, then feeling her warm, long fingers rubbing along his neck, he needed more than some planking and pikes to get his mind back where it needed to be.

He was organizing his desk when his cell phone vibrated. Drew read the incoming text from Kylie, hoping that getting the kids out the door hadn't proved too much for her.

It took some finagling but I made a deal with Alex Russell to enroll the boys in the adventure camp.

What kind of finagling? And what kind of deal had she promised the owner of the sporting-goods store in order to get special treatment?

Wait. Why did he suddenly care who Kylie was talking to or bartering with? He'd never been jealous in his life. Not even when he'd dated his ex-girlfriend, which probably should've been an early indication that he hadn't been as serious about that relationship as Jessica. He still couldn't believe he'd told Kylie about that this morning. But her question had been simple enough, and really, Drew was pretty curious about Kylie's past, as well.

I'm all yours, she'd said this morning. Even though it

would be unreasonable for him to expect her to give up her dating life temporarily, he didn't like the idea of her ditching him with the twins to go out with another man.

He checked his racing thoughts before he wrote back, Great. How did you swing that?

I told him he could store his camp gear underneath your old boat shed. I also promised to do his quarterly taxes for the next fiscal year.

He let out a breath. Of course she hadn't promised Alex any sexual favors. He wanted to think that Kylie wasn't the type of woman to do something like that. Though honestly, he didn't know what kind of woman she was.

But he didn't like that brief rush of envy that had made its way through his coiled muscles and up into his brain.

Clearly he wasn't thinking straight. Drew rolled his neck, grimacing over the stiff pain still lingering there, then arched his back, stretching out his shoulders. He was hungry. And stressed. Possibly a little tired from trying to sleep all night in a kid-size bed, knowing a sexy and scantily clad redhead, who also happened to be his lawfully wedded wife, was sleeping just a bedroom away from him.

But mostly, he was hungry. Dinner last night had barely filled him up, and this morning's cereal had been left half eaten when he'd made a mad rush for the bathroom to cover up the fact that below the waistband of his pajama pants, his body was reacting way too strongly to Kylie's proximity and touch.

He planned to meet with his new staff at the hospital cafeteria for lunch, but maybe he should tour the building first. Refocus his thoughts. He grabbed the cell phone off his desk, hoping no emergencies would come up for the rest of the day.

At three o'clock, Kylie texted him again, letting him know that she'd picked up the boys from camp and asking him if he needed anything from the grocery store. He remembered her overdone mushy rice and thought about offering to do the cooking tonight, but he was supposed to sit in on a group session that started a few minutes ago and figured he could just call her on the way home.

When he left work for the day, he'd barely gotten his Bluetooth set up when his phone rang. He saw Kylie's name on the display and couldn't answer quickly enough.

"We have a change of plans for dinner tonight," she said by way of greeting. "The microwave caught on fire, and we had a little incident with the fire extinguisher."

He should count his blessings that he'd almost made it a full day without a phone call like this or a trip to the emergency room. "Is everyone okay?"

"Yes, we're fine. The kitchen's a mess and we're trying to air out the cabin since it smells like a chemical explosion at a fishing village."

"How on earth did they set the microwave on fire?"

"Well…uh…it wasn't the boys. It was kinda my fault."

Drew let out his breath, but the sudden thought occurred that Kylie might be covering for his nephews. He gripped the wheel tightly as he wound his way up the mountain and back toward Sugar Falls.

"You see, I was going to try to make a tuna casserole for dinner because Aiden said that was his favorite meal. So we went to the store and got some groceries and I tried to follow a recipe I found online. Then, right when I was about to pull it out of the oven, I realized I forgot to add the tuna."

"Okay," he said when it seemed as if she was waiting for a response. But he still didn't understand exactly what had happened.

"So I figured that I could just heat the tuna up separately and layer it on the top." *Tuna* and *layer* were two words Drew doubted the chefs on the gourmet cooking website used together too often. "Anyway, I threw it in the microwave and then I got busy showing the boys how to separate their laundry and load the washing machine when, *boom*, the whole package burst into flames and smoke started pouring out everywhere."

"Wait. You put an aluminum can in the microwave?"

"Of course not, Drew. I'm not an idiot. It was one of those little pouches that are supposed to be better for the environment, and, well, apparently that has aluminum in it, too. They really should label that kind of thing on their packaging. Anyway, I'm terribly sorry, and I'll buy you a new microwave tomorrow."

He should have taken the time to send her the text offering to cook. "It's fine. Don't worry about it. We can just have plain noodle casserole for dinner."

"Actually, we can't. That's where the fire extinguisher part of the story comes into play."

"What happened to the fire extinguisher?"

"Nothing happened to it. We used it."

"We?"

"Well, not me so much as the boys. I was calling the volunteer fire department, but the twins were smart enough to remember that you kept the extinguisher on the back porch. So they ran and got it and there was a little issue getting it to shoot but... Hey, you know what? We just pulled up, so I'll tell you all about it when you meet us."

"Where are you?"

"Drew, focus." He heard her sigh. "The kitchen is a mess and the casserole was ruined from all the spray. So I brought the kids to Patrelli's for pizza. I'll see you there soon."

She disconnected the call, and Drew didn't know whether to laugh, cry or drive straight to the hardware store for a backup fire extinguisher. Yet one more instance when his perfectly planned life went perfectly wrong. He took a few deep breaths and cranked up the radio. AC/DC was almost done playing by the time he parked the Jeep in front of the Italian restaurant on Snowflake Boulevard.

Chapter Seven

Sugar Falls hadn't changed much since Drew used to come here with his family as a kid. Downtown consisted of a main street lined with old Victorian buildings. Most of the eating establishments and business were on the first floor, with office buildings or private living quarters upstairs. The Sugar Falls Cookie Company was the biggest business in town. Maxine Cooper owned the famous bakery, which was one of the top tourist hot spots on the weekends. She, Cooper and Hunter lived in the renovated apartment above it.

City hall, along with the newly formed police department, was just a couple of blocks down—near Freckles's Cowgirl Up Café. The small town catered to the tourists but during the week, it was mostly just locals hanging out on Snowflake Boulevard. As he walked toward the large oak door under the Patrelli's sign, Drew remembered eating here occasionally when his parents would bring them for the summers. They'd had the best pizza and the newest arcade games.

He stepped into the dimly lit restaurant, and the scent of garlic and yeasty dough told him they probably still had the best pizza. A look toward the arcade in the back told him the games, on the other hand, weren't as new. But the red vinyl booths were full, and the excited kids gathered around the pinball machine and the Pole Position game suggested the patrons came there for the same reasons after all these years.

He spotted his wife immediately and made his way toward her. An older woman wearing an Idaho Steelheads cap stood near the table, looking at the wedding ring on Kylie's finger. Drew's steps slowed, his own left thumb fingering the back of the ring he'd slipped on after Kylie had made that unexpected announcement at the wedding. He wondered if his wife was ashamed of the plain gold bands they'd bought who knew where. Did she wish she had something bigger to show off?

"Drew, this is Mae Johnston." Kylie made the introduction when he arrived. "She's Mayor Johnston's wife. I was just telling her about our...whirlwind courtship."

"It was quite a whirlwind, all right." He smiled and slid into the empty side of the booth, taking Kylie's outstretched hand. Apparently, the pretense was still alive and well.

"I'm glad I'm finally getting the chance to meet you, Doctor. I just think you two are so dang cute together. When you were dancing together at the wedding, I told Cliff you guys looked as in love on that dance floor as we felt on our own honeymoon back in the day."

"How long have you and the mayor been married?" Drew asked, wanting to turn the attention away from his sham of a marriage and that awkward first dance.

"We were only married for a few months that first time. But then we met up again last year at our fiftieth high school reunion, and neither one of us had anything else going on, so we thought, meh, why not?"

"How, uh…romantic?"

"Not really. Now, me and Don—that was my in-between husband—we had us one of those big loves. You know, the kind you read about in stories? But I lost him back in oh-eight. He also had a big romance with bourbon, you know." Mae extended her pinkie out and tipped her thumb toward her lips as though she was drinking out of a bottle. "His ol' liver couldn't take it no more. But me and Cliff make do. Anyway, it was nice getting a chance to meet up with you two. Congratulations."

Mrs. Johnston gave a little wave, then moved on to the next table to make conversation and schmooze. He guessed being married to the mayor, twice, came with certain social duties and civic obligations.

"The boys are in the game room with a stack of quarters, and I ordered you the large meatball sub," Kylie said as she slid a red plastic cup full of soda toward him. "I figured if that wasn't enough, you could share some pizza with us."

"Sounds great," he said and took a big swallow to help appease his stomach, which had begun growling the moment he walked in the door.

"I'm sorry again about dinner. And about your microwave."

A waitress brought out their food, and looking at everything covered in freshly made tomato sauce and piping hot cheese, Drew wrestled with the urge to confess to Kylie that he would have preferred this dinner over tuna noodle casserole any day. It was actually a win-win. "Don't worry about it. You're a whiz with the kids, and you managed to keep them all in one piece today."

"I also negotiated a pretty sweet deal with Alex for their summer camp." Kylie gestured for him to start eating. "Go ahead. The kids will be in there awhile."

"How did their first day go, by the way?" Biting into his toasted sandwich, he let his taste buds get acclimated to what real food was supposed to taste like. A burned-up and oversprayed kitchen was well worth it to savor this kind of heavenly, meaty goodness.

"Actually, Alex said they did pretty well. I guess about halfway through the day, he split them up and assigned them to different wilderness teams, which helped keep them out of trouble."

"Ah, divide and conquer. Why haven't I tried that approach?"

She smiled, and he tried to ignore how natural it felt to talk to her about every day family life.

"My guess is it's easier when there are other kids around to distract them. Plus, it sounds as though they stayed so busy, they didn't have time to get into any scrapes."

"You have no idea how relieved I am that they haven't been kicked out yet."

"Drew, they're sweet boys. Sure, they're a little rambunctious, but they just need some guidance and an outlet for all their energy. Plus, Alex knows he's getting a good deal and will put up with just about anything to get free accounting services from me."

"Kids really aren't my forte," Drew admitted. He also wasn't well trained in having other men indebted to his wife.

"Well, cooking isn't mine. We can't all be perfect, Saint Drew."

"I'll make you a deal. You keep doing what you're doing with the twins, and I'll do all the cooking."

She raised her arms above the red vinyl booth in a sign of victory. "It's a deal. I've waited two hours for you to say those exact words to me. You really know the way to a girl's heart."

Drew motioned toward the mayor, who had just walked up to his wife and greeted her with a playful swat on Mrs. Johnston's rump. "Well, with an example like those two, how can I not try my best to charm you?"

Kylie nodded as she put slices of pepperoni pizza onto plates for the kids. "Just think. If our marriage only lasts a few months this time around, we can always try it again when we turn seventy."

Why in the world had she made that stupid joke about getting married again when they were older? Kylie had been kicking herself all week for saying it. Sure, Drew had chuckled at the time, and luckily the kids had run out of quarters and returned to the table, saving them from any further conversation on the subject.

But a couple of days later, as she sat at her desk, she still wished she could take the words back.

They had settled into a nice routine at the cabin off Sweetwater Bend. Drew usually left for work right about the time the boys woke up. She fed the twins but didn't even have to drive them to Russell's Sports since the day campers now met at the boat shed on the Gregson property, where Alex Russell was storing rafts and kayaks and other river gear. Then Kylie would go to work at her office, a small space she rented above the antiques store on Snowflake Boulevard.

By the time her husband came home in the evenings, the twins were so exhausted from all the hiking, paddling and swimming they'd done during the day, they barely kept their eyes open for dinner—which Drew wasn't much better at cooking than Kylie. Once they got the boys bathed and in bed, he would take off for a couple of hours to do who knew what. She didn't ask him where he was going, but last night she'd sneaked outside and saw that he hadn't actually driven anywhere, which made her realize the light inside the boat shed was on and loud music was coming from the old wooden structure. She wasn't sure what he was doing in there, but at least she was less suspicious that he was off seeing another woman.

Of course, Drew didn't strike her as the kind of man who would cheat on his wife—even a wife in name only. Which made her all the more curious as to what had happened between him and the ex-girlfriend he'd mentioned. He'd said something about the woman being more serious about the relationship than he was, and Kylie had come to the conclusion that Drew didn't like his women getting too clingy.

So she allowed him his space in the evenings and would either read a novel in her room or catch up on all the emails she hadn't gotten to at work. Man, she didn't know how working moms did this kind of thing every day. The twins were fun, but they were a full-time job. Thank goodness it wasn't tax season or there would be no way she could keep this up.

Her phone pinged and she knew it was three o'clock—time to meet the kids. She'd had to set the alarm on Tuesday when she'd gotten so caught up in researching tax code that Alex called her to ask why she hadn't picked Aiden and Caden up from camp yet. Out of four days, she'd forgotten them only once. Not too bad for a new aunt turned surrogate mom overnight.

But tonight was Thursday—her official girls' night out

with her best friends. They'd been meeting every week for the past few years, and she wasn't about to go AWOL now. Although she was settling into her new environment well enough, she would eventually be returning to her real life and needed to try to keep things as normal as possible.

She grabbed her purse and the leather shoulder bag containing her laptop before locking the office door on her way out. As she navigated her way down the steps to the alley behind the antiques store, she fired off a quick text to Drew to let him know about her plans tonight.

She dropped her satchel on the pavement as she fumbled in her designer handbag for the keys to Nana's Oldsmobile. Even though she didn't need the big four-door sedan for kid-hauling purposes since camp drop-off and pickup was now right outside their back door, the rutted driveway to the cabin had seen better days, and she'd gotten her Mercedes stuck in one of the potholes yesterday. So she was back to driving a car that looked like something out of an old episode of *The Brady Bunch*.

She tried to stick the key in the door lock when her purse tipped and half its contents fell on the ground.

"Oh, come on. Would it be too hard to ask for a car with a remote or keyless entry?" she yelled to the empty alley. She decided Drew needed either to pave the road to the cabin or to find her a more updated mode of transportation.

An appreciative whistle came from a passing truck as she bent over to retrieve her belongings. She stood up quickly to yank her skirt down. Maybe it *was* a little too short, now that she was somewhat of a mother figure. While she was used to being on the receiving end of unsolicited pickup lines, she would have been mortified if someone actually hit on her when the twins were with her.

She sat in the Nanamobile, rethinking her entire wardrobe and feeling a decade older already. She envisioned herself dressing like Mrs. Johnston in head-to-toe velour tracksuits, with an old ball cap covering her plain gray hair. If she didn't hit the town tonight with Maxine and Mia, she might as well kiss her thirties goodbye.

Her phone lit up right as she started the engine and she glanced at the screen, but she didn't have time to read Drew's text. Alex told her he was going to charge extra if she came late to pick up the boys again.

When she pulled up beside the cabin, she waved at Alex, who was directing several kids trying to carry man-size kayaks. She reached for her phone and read Drew's message.

I should be home by five ;)

She was frozen in the driver's seat, the engine shut off and a handful of preadolescent boys looking at her as she tried to make heads or tails of the message. Was he flirting with her? Or had he meant to type a smiley face with a wink?

She jumped out of the car, muttered a few words to Alex, waved the kids inside to get them snacks, then got showered and changed.

Drew arrived right on time, but Kylie tried to keep her conversation with him to a minimum—partly because she was still flustered over the text wink and didn't want to read too much into it, which was probably where Drew's ex-girlfriend had gone wrong.

"Are you going to be out late?" He looked pointedly at her jeans and high-heeled boots.

"Not too late, I don't think. It's not as if there's too much nightlife in Sugar Falls."

"Dressed like that, you could generate enough action on your own to last a lifetime."

Before she could ask whether he'd meant his comment as a compliment or a commentary on her fashion sense, the boys ran into the room and launched themselves at her.

"Goodbye hugs!" They both latched on to her, and she squeezed each one three times.

"Is this a new thing?" Drew asked, but he smiled as though he approved of the affection she was showing his nephews.

"Kind of. When I leave for work, it's a little ritual we do." Kylie had started the routine when she realized the boys were clinging a little closer than normal to her on the first day of camp. Surely, with Drew being a psychologist, he could appreciate that the twins might have some issues with separation, especially considering their family history.

"Yeah, Uncle Drew," Aiden said. "You gotta give Aunt Kylie your three biggest hugs so she can think of you at least three times while she's gone."

"Go on, Uncle Drew," Caden added. "Hug her three times."

Drew adjusted his glasses as he looked helplessly at his nephews. Well, it wasn't as if they hadn't touched each other before. And he'd been the one to insist that they keep up appearances even in front of the children.

So she raised her arms and walked toward him. He shrugged before putting his hands lightly on her back and patting her a couple of times.

"No, Uncle Drew. You gotta make them *big* hugs."

"Yeah, like your tightest and best hugs ever."

Drew pulled back and looked down at her. "Three of them, huh?"

She couldn't have been any more embarrassed, so she barely managed a nod. He wrapped his arms tighter, his warm bands of muscles squeezing her until her Italian leather boots were lifted off the floor.

Kylie had no choice but to cling to his shoulders, which reminded her of the last time she'd touched him there. She hoped Drew couldn't tell how damp her palms were.

"One. Two. Three," he counted as he lessened his grip only slightly between each number. "And an extra one for the road so she thinks about me four times tonight."

The boys dissolved into giggles and Drew slowly released her, keeping her body against his until her stiletto heels touched the hardwood floor. It took her a few moments to feel steady enough to stand on her own, let alone walk to the car.

"Okay. Well, goodbye, then." She made the mistake of looking back at him as she wobbled away, and would've traded her favorite pair of designer jeans to know what that parting smile of his meant. She had a feeling she was going to be thinking about Drew way more than four times tonight.

Normally on Thursday nights, she and her girlfriends did an exercise class at Mia's dance studio and then had dinner at a local restaurant. But tonight she really needed to let off steam, so they were bypassing yoga and going directly to the privacy and comfort of Mia's kitchen. Shortly after Cooper had moved into Maxine's apartment over the bakery, he'd begun hosting poker night with some of his new friends, so the women couldn't go there. Thank goodness Mia knew how to cook, because if Kylie had to eat mac and cheese one more time this week, she was going to scream.

Plus, after the massage and the goodbye hug, the physical tension between her and her husband was now reaching an unprecedented level, and she didn't know how to handle it.

Maxine handed her a margarita and a bowl of guacamole as soon as Kylie walked in the door. "We want details," her friend said, foregoing any formal greeting.

She'd given both women brief overviews on Sunday morning as she was packing to move into the cabin, but the updates this week had been vague and via text. "What do you want to know?"

"Like, what were you thinking?" Mia asked first as Kylie plopped onto the kitchen counter stool.

"What's it like living with Doctor Handsome?"

"How's it going being an instant family?"

"How did your dad take the news?"

"Who's doing the cooking?"

The questions came at her rapid-fire, and she couldn't blame her friends their inquisitiveness. If their positions were reversed, she'd be asking the same things. But that last question from Mia brought a halt to the interrogation.

"Really, guys? My whole life is completely upside down and that's what you're worried about? The cooking?"

"Well, it's just that kitchen duty isn't one of your stronger domestic talents," Maxine pointed out. It was a well-known fact.

"But you're great at laundry," Mia said, ever the peacemaker.

"Some claim to fame—I wash a mean load of whites. Which is actually a blessing because living with three extra people, the old washing machine on the back porch never stops running. It's as if my entire day just got three times more stressful. Maxine, I have no idea how you did it as a single mom."

"It was tough, and I only had one little boy. How are you doing with two?"

Kylie sighed. "Actually, not as bad as people might think."

"Who might think that?" Mia turned away from the skillet sizzling on the stove, her face suggesting outrage for anyone who said otherwise. See, this was why Kylie loved her friends. They looked past her outer appearance to the person she really was.

"Come on, you guys know what the town thinks of me. Outrageous and wild Kylie. Great with accounting, horrible with men. Marcia Duncan and Elaine Marconi made it pretty clear at the wedding that they questioned my ability with children."

"But you're great with kids. You do all those pageants with young girls, and your family is huge. Hunter adores you, and you're one of the favorite guest teachers at the Snowflake Dance Academy."

"Hmm." Kylie took a sip of her drink, then pushed it aside in favor of the tortilla chips. "I will say that Aiden and Caden are pretty awesome. They're a little wild, but they are really cute. And funny. It's kind of sad, because they miss their dad and I don't think they really remember their mom. They just need a little structure and some routine, which they got once I enrolled them in Alex Russell's wilderness and adventure camp. And they come home every afternoon exhausted, which is a plus. The kids aren't really the issue here."

Maxine reached toward the chip bowl and pulled it closer to her. "Is the cabin an issue? I know it's pretty remote, but when Cooper lived there for a while, it seemed comfortable and pretty well equipped."

"No, the cabin is fine. I mean, it's a little different than what I'm used to, but you guys know I'm not a snob. Except I will admit that I am absolutely done with that stupid car I got stuck driving. I don't know if I can make it the whole summer motoring around town in the Nanamobile."

"Is that what I saw you driving the other day down Snowflake Boulevard?" Mia asked as she spooned their chicken fajitas onto red pottery-style plates. "I had to take a second look because I thought it was Mae Johnston at first. She has almost the exact same car."

Kylie flinched. Just one week of married life and she was being mistaken for a seventy-year-old woman. And by her best friends, no less.

"So the car situation can be fixed. Just go rent a different one. It's not as if you can't afford it." Maxine's observation was true and not intended as a reference to her family's known wealth. Kylie rarely spoke to anyone about her personal finances, but her friends knew she believed in living strictly off her own income as a CPA—which was fairly substantial considering most of the businesses in town paid her a pretty hefty fee for her services.

Mia put their plates on the small kitchen table. "So if it's not the twins or the cabin, and the car situation can be fixed, it must be Doctor Handsome."

"Stop calling him that," Kylie said as she joined her friends to eat.

"No," Maxine replied as she reached for a warm flour tortilla. "I don't think we will stop. Remember how you used to call Cooper Gunny Heartthrob all the time? Consider this payback."

"But you and Cooper were perfect for each other. And you're the one who said the guy made your heart literally throb when you first met him."

"So you don't think Drew is perfect for you?" Mia asked.

"I don't know if anyone is perfect for me. And trust me,

I've looked far and wide for someone to fit that bill. But more important, I know that *I'm* not perfect for *Drew*."

"Stop it," Mia said at the same time Maxine argued, "Don't be crazy."

"Ladies, we're talking about Saint Drew here. He looks at me as if I'm a test subject in a psychology experiment."

"No way. I saw the way he was dancing with you at our wedding, and I guarantee you he looked at you as though he wanted to devour you."

"No offense, Max, but you're so crazy in love, all you see are roses and rainbows. Forgive me for thinking your opinion is a little skewed right now."

"Well, I'm not all doped up on pheromones and love," Mia said, referring to her general disillusionment toward most men. "Yet I get the impression that the guy is really into you. How can he not be, Kylie? You're an amazing woman. You're smart, funny, loyal…"

Bless her friends for trying to cheer her up, but they were obviously biased.

"Okay, let's say that Drew possibly *is* physically attracted to me." Which might not be too much of a stretch, considering how she did catch him staring at her sometimes. Or the way he'd hugged her an hour ago. "He's made it clear that this marriage thing is just temporary for the summer. The guy's too straitlaced to want someone like me on a long-term basis. And he's way too proper and polite to act on his attraction."

"So you guys haven't…you know…done anything since that night in Reno?" Mia asked. Her friends knew that Kylie had maintained a tight resolve on her decision to not sleep with a man until she was sure he was The One.

"Ugh. Neither one of us knows if we even did anything back then. I mean, I'm sure we did, because every time I'm in the same room with Drew, my insides get all liquidy and my skin gets tight. I may not know much about sexual attraction, but I'm smart enough to recognize that I can't really control my body when I'm around him. But the not knowing really sucks." Kylie dropped her fork and put her forehead in her hands.

"Oh, honey," Maxine said, and patted her back. "My first time was after the Boise State homecoming game in Bo's dorm room. He hung a sock on the door so none of his fraternity brothers would bother us. It really was the most unromantic night of my life, but every girl deserves to have at least a memory of it. I hate it that you can't recall yours."

"Why don't you pretend Reno didn't happen and have another first time with him?" Mia asked. "One that you *can* remember."

"Yeah, right." Kylie lifted her head only to find Maxine nodding along. "No. Really, you guys, I can't just rewrite history."

"Mia's right. If a column of numbers doesn't add up, you simply erase the answer and start over again. Besides, if you're going to have a do-over, at least you already know that Doctor Handsome is physically compatible with you."

"*Compatible* is a bit of a leap. I said that I was attracted to him. But he's never given me any indication that he wants something more than a roommate."

"Then, why don't you convince him that he does?" Maxine asked.

"How? By seducing him? I can't do that."

"Sure you can."

"Seriously? If I actually made an attempt at it, I'd look stupid, and he'd see right through me. He's trained to read people. Do you have any idea what it's like to live with somebody so calm and in control all the time? Not to mention, I have zero experience in that department, and I'd be a nervous wreck and wind up turning him off completely."

"So you *do* want him," Maxine said triumphantly.

"I never said that." Kylie took a bite out of her fajita, only to have all the seasoned chicken and vegetables fall out the bottom. Ugh.

"You didn't have to say anything. It's written all over your face. You're actually giving this whole seduction idea some thought."

"See? If I'm that obvious to you two, a clinical psychologist is going to figure it out like that." She would have snapped her fingers, but she needed both hands to put her meal back together.

"Let me ask you this." Mia passed her the salsa. "Are you attracted to the man?"

"Obviously. But does that mean I want to have a first-time redo with him? I don't know. We're still strangers. I mean, sure, we're living together, but we really haven't spent that much time together. As soon as he gets home from work, he cooks dinner, we eat and then I get the kids to bed. After that, he takes off for a couple of hours and I crash from exhaustion."

"Wait, did you just say *he* cooks?"

"That may be an overstatement. Maybe I should've said he prepares dinner. Like, he grills the hot dogs or mixes the boxed ingredients together for the macaroni and cheese. There's really little cooking skill involved."

"Still, he's willing to step foot in the kitchen, which shows potential. I say we come up with a plan for you to get him from the kitchen into your bedroom."

Kylie rolled her eyes in frustration. "You think I should sleep with a guy because he knows how to boil noodles?"

"No, we think you should sleep with the man because

you're obviously attracted to him and could use a little spark in your life." Maxine winked at her.

"You guys know good and well that I have no business seducing anyone. Especially when I have no idea what his feelings are on the issue."

"Have you thought about asking him?" Mia asked.

"Of course I have. But we're never alone together."

"Good point," Maxine said. "It's not as if you can ask him in front of the twins. Okay, forget the whole seduction thing. But you definitely need to get him alone so you guys can hash everything out. Here's what I'm thinking…"

Drew got the okay from Cooper to bring the boys to hang out with Hunter at poker night while Kylie was out with her friends. Besides Monday's dinner at Patrelli's, he'd just eaten the best meal he'd had all week. Who knew such a tough and quiet Marine turned police chief could be such an amazing cook? He'd need to get his friend's recipe for chicken-fried steak and show Kylie that he could bring a little more to the table. Literally.

She was doing so much around the house with the boys, and all he seemed capable of was going to work and making dinner. But even his meal efforts left much to be desired. Maybe that was why she'd been in such a hurry to get out for the night. But did she have to dress as if she was on her way to a modeling shoot? He hadn't been able to stop looking at her long legs in those jeans…

He'd felt like such a dope after that goodbye-hug stunt. He'd done it because his nephews were watching and seemed to expect it. Plus, he'd known how important it was for children to have a sense of routine, and he should've expected the boys to have some separation-anxiety issues.

But he didn't know how much more of this fake physical affection he could take. When he'd felt Kylie fully pressed up against him, he hadn't wanted to let her go. She must think he was the world's biggest walking hormone, because she'd practically flown out the door the second he'd released her.

"So how's married life treating you?" Thankfully, Cooper had waited until after the boys went back to Hunter's room to play video games to ask the question.

Alex was shuffling the cards, and Drew thought the man seemed overly eager to hear his response. It wasn't the first time he'd wondered if the outdoorsman was interested in his wife.

See, there he went again, thinking of Kylie as his real wife. But it was just so easy to do. They'd fallen into a comfortable domestic pattern, and she was amazing with his nephews. Heck, she was amazing in general. But it wasn't as if what they had would last much longer than this summer. In fact, after the way she'd nearly torn the transmission out of her sports car as she'd hauled down the bumpy driveway in an effort to leave tonight, he wondered if they'd even last another week.

"It's going all right," Drew said, not wanting to give up much information, but knowing the cop was going to keep asking until he got the answers he wanted. "It's only been a few days, so we're still establishing a routine."

"Are you guys getting to know each other pretty well?" Cooper didn't have to remind anyone that Drew had met his wife less than two weeks ago.

"It's a process." Okay, maybe that was a stretch. He hadn't been able to stay in a room alone with her long enough to learn much. He could tell she had a great heart, she adored the kids and she took her job seriously. But everything he'd assessed came from analysis at a distance. It wasn't as if they were at the stage where they could ask each other personal questions. Or have meaningful conversations about what they wanted out of life. Probably because every time he looked at her, he envisioned her in her skimpy pajamas—or worse, nothing at all—and his head would cloud up with lust to the point that he had to do something to burn up the sexual energy building inside him.

When he folded for the fourth time that night, his two buddies exchanged a look.

"How's that punching bag I set up in the boat shed working for you?" Alex asked.

"It's pretty good. I've tried a few yoga classes at the hospital during lunch, but I've been going out to the shed and doing some hitting for a couple of hours every night after the kids go to bed."

"A couple of *hours*?" Alex asked, incredulous.

"Every *night*?" Cooper followed.

"Yep. It helps me unwind." The two men exchanged another look. "What?"

"Well, if I had a woman who looked like Kylie in my bed," Alex said, "I could think of a lot more enjoyable ways to unwind than punching some bag in an old, drafty boat shed."

"Well, you don't have *my wife* in your bed, and I'd appreciate it if you would refrain from speculating what it would be like if you did."

"Whoa, Saint Drew. Is this jealousy I'm sensing?" Cooper was doing that blasted smirking thing again. "That's not very Zen of you. Maybe you need to stop boxing and focus more on your yoga classes."

"I'm not jealous." But even Drew knew the statement was a lie.

"Listen, man, I meant no offense." Poor Alex. He really hadn't said anything that most red-blooded males wouldn't have been thinking. Drew did have a beautiful woman sleeping in the room next to him, and perhaps he was on edge because there wasn't a thing he could do about it.

"I'm sorry, guys. It's just been really stressful with the new job, and I'm still not used to taking care of the twins. Then this whole business with Kylie is somewhat unexpected territory."

"Hey," Alex said. "Don't worry about it. When Cooper was falling love with Maxine, he was an absolute bear to those poor boys on our Little League team. He would make them run bases just for looking at him sideways."

"I'm hardly falling in love with Kylie." Drew tried to laugh but threw down his cards instead. Man, he sucked at poker.

"Yeah, that's what Cooper thought when it happened to him." Alex drew two more cards.

"If you want some advice," Cooper said, matching the four cookies already in the pile on the center of the table, "things will probably go easier for you if you just let go of all that stupid control you're used to and enjoy getting to know her."

"I'm a licensed psychologist, you know. I don't think I need marriage counseling from a guy who is using his new wife's bakery inventory as poker chips."

"Hey, we all win when Maxine's cookies are used for bartering. And right now, I'm ahead three chocolate chips and four maple pecans."

Alex was eating his winnings, so there was no way to know for sure who was really ahead.

"Are you guys going to the Marconis' costume party this weekend?" Cooper changed the subject.

"We'll see. We haven't made many social appearances together yet, so I'll have to ask her."

Social appearances meant pretend displays of affection. And when it came to Kylie, it was becoming more difficult for Drew to just pretend.

Chapter Eight

Drew couldn't believe it was already Saturday night—the one-week anniversary of the unexpected announcement of their marriage. And they were once again venturing out into public. He looked in the bathroom mirror at his makeshift costume. He was an educated man, but he had absolutely no idea what a bedroom sheet had to do with a grown man's birthday party.

"Hey, Kylie," he called out to the woman with whom he now shared a house and kid-raising responsibilities, but absolutely nothing else. "Why do I have to wear this thing again?"

She squeezed into the small bathroom and stood behind him. Through the reflection in the mirror, he took in her oversize hot pink fluffy bathrobe as she repleated the bed linen over his shoulder. She was always doing little stuff like this for the boys and around the house, making things in their lives better, smoother.

A guy could get used to that kind of treatment...

"I told you," she said as though patiently explaining herself to a child. "The Marconis have a big celebration every year for Chuck's birthday. A few years ago, people started wearing themed costumes to the party. Well, Sugar Falls residents do not like to miss an opportunity to dress up—you should see the town on Halloween."

But it wasn't Halloween and Drew wasn't one to play make-believe. He tried not to tense as her long fingers grazed his skin under the white fabric of his homemade gladiator costume.

Her hand stilled on his shoulder, and he caught her expression in the mirror. She was looking toward his lower back, and he remembered the last time they had been in the same room wearing nothing but the linens from the hotel room bed and her lacy underwear...

"Maybe I should put a shirt or something underneath this." He wasn't feeling particularly cold. In fact, the temperature in here seemed to be rising. And a small part of him wanted her to comment on his appearance.

"Maybe," she replied, her voice sounding huskier than normal.

He turned toward her, but her gaze remained below his shoulders. He tipped her head up, and his breath caught when he saw the heat in her eyes. His finger stroked her chin, and she leaned her face closer to his.

But before he could claim her full lips, the bathroom door slammed into him. "Aunt Kylie, are you *sure* that no other boys are going to be dressed as a two-headed Jabba the Hutt?" Caden asked, his brother squirming beside him under mounds of green fabric.

The woman Drew had been about to kiss jumped back and gave her full attention to his nephews, breaking the intimate spell.

"Well, if there are, they won't be as big as you two."
Kylie caught Drew's eyes in the mirror. He had to give her
credit for the brilliant idea of pairing the boys up in a joint
costume that would keep them attached to each other and
easier to locate in a crowd.

"Okay, but can we have light sabers, too?" Aiden asked
as she escorted the twins out of the bathroom.

Drew braced one hand on the counter, steadying his body
and then steadying his breathing. That had been close. He
took off his glasses and splashed some cold water on his
face. If it hadn't been for him leaving the cabin every night
to work off some tension, this week would've been filled
with a whole lot more dangerous moments like that one.

And that would've been so unfair to both of them. Not
only because of the commitment he'd made to himself
not to get involved with another woman until he was sure
that she was The One, but also because Kylie was such a
kindhearted person, she deserved to have that knight in
shining armor she'd admitted to dreaming about. This charade was meant to last only the summer, but if they took
things to a physical level, he didn't know if he would be
capable of letting go.

It was like Icarus flying too close to the sun. He was
dying to touch the warm and vibrant woman who was
his wife but was too afraid that once he did, his defenses
would melt and he would spiral out of control.

"C'mon, Uncle Drew," a voice called out from the living room. "We're gonna be late."

He took one last look in the mirror, then followed his
temporary family out to the car. Kylie didn't make eye
contact with him the entire drive over to the Marconis'.
Drew wondered if she was tense about seeing Elaine since
the woman had insulted her last week, or if she was thinking about what had almost happened between them just

now. Luckily, the boys chattered nonstop in the backseat, oblivious to the silent adults in front of them.

Apparently Kylie had been right about this party. It was one of the more popular events of the year. So popular, in fact, they had to park a few blocks away. The partygoers walking toward the Marconis' restored Victorian home off Snowflake Boulevard were dressed in similar attire.

"There are Hunter and Cooper," Aiden shouted, pointing at what appeared to be Gandalf and Frodo. At least Drew wasn't the only grown man here not wearing pants. The boys jumped out of the car the second Drew put it in Park and ran toward their new friend and his stepdad.

Kylie was still sitting in the front seat, messing with her pink robe, so he exited and called out to the police chief, who waved and pointed two fingers to his eyes, acknowledging that Cooper would watch the twins. Drew straightened his costume as he walked over to her side of the vehicle.

When she finally emerged, his chest almost exploded from his sudden intake of air.

She was dressed in a short, white, gauzy skirt that barely covered her perfectly curvaceous rear end. A snug corset trimmed in gold pushed against her full breasts. Her legs were bare except for the straps of her sandals, which wrapped all the way up to her knees.

"What are you wearing?" He tried to keep the shock from his voice, but his heart rate was wreaking havoc on his brain function.

She looked down at her figure, then tilted her head. "A costume?"

"That is *not* a costume. I've seen bathing suits with more material."

"Well, technically, I'm supposed to be Diana, goddess of the hunt."

The only thing she could possibly be hunting for in that getup was men. A green haze clouded over his eyes, and he tried to dismiss the alien emotion he'd been experiencing all week.

"You should probably put that robe back on." He reached past her to open the car door and grab something, anything, with which to cover her up.

"Why? It's not going to be cold once we get inside, and I don't want to leave it behind accidentally. It's my favorite robe."

If it was truly her favorite, then why hadn't he seen her wear it since she'd moved into the cabin? Instead, she'd paraded around the place in those skimpy pajamas that had him racing out to the boat shed to exercise and clear his mind.

"But your outfit is a bit too…" How did he put this delicately without revealing his jealousy? Or sounding like a complete prude?

"A bit what?" Uh-oh. She was standing up straighter, and he'd seen that defiant look in her eye before. She was like that Amazon queen back in their hotel room, ready to do battle.

"What I'm trying to say is that your outfit might draw too much attention."

"I'm used to being stared at. Don't worry. It doesn't bother me."

"I'm not worried about it bothering *you*. I don't like the way it's bothering *me*!"

"I thought nothing rattled you, Saint Drew."

He planted his hands on his hips so he wouldn't be tempted to show her just how completely rattled he actually was. He would've shoved them into his pockets if he'd had any. "Well, right now that skimpy costume is doing a pretty good job of it."

"How can my outfit possibly affect you?"

Oh, there were plenty of ways it was affecting him right this second. But he wouldn't admit that. Instead, he said, "I'm more concerned about the way it's going to affect the other men at the party." Well, that was partially honest.

She looked genuinely confused, almost as though she didn't realize how powerful her appearance was. "Drew, I like how I look and I like what I wear. I dress for myself. Not for you, not for the uptight busybodies in this town and definitely not for the men."

He couldn't believe she didn't understand what he was trying to tell her. "But the men will still be looking at you."

"Why can't they look at me?"

"Because you're *my* wife."

And as if to sear his brand on her, he snaked his arm around her waist and pulled her toward him, dipping his head to press his lips to hers. She startled in surprise, and he took advantage of the opportunity by brushing his tongue along her slightly opened mouth. Fire shot through him the moment her tongue tentatively met his, and he pulled her tighter against his body.

The satin-covered wires of her corset dug into the side of his chest that had been left bare, and it was all he could do to not tear the ridiculous garment off her and feel her soft skin against his.

She wrapped her arms around his neck and leaned in closer, her desire matching his own.

His body had wanted this from the moment he'd seen her standing in the hotel room in Reno. And finally, he was giving in to what his brain and his conscience had been denying him. He let his hands wander down past her waist and over the curve of her bottom. He pulled her hips closer to him. Just for a second, he thought. Just long enough to ease the aching arousal beneath his gladiator costume.

She was so tall that even standing up, she nestled against him perfectly, and he knew that the mere pressure would never be enough.

He wanted her.

He needed her.

And if he wasn't careful, he'd have her—right here against the door of Nana's Oldsmobile.

The thought should have sobered him, but her moan only incited his passion, and he was immune to any rational thought. He'd been right. One touch, one taste of Kylie would never be enough.

It wasn't until she pulled back and urgently spoke his name that Drew realized they weren't alone. He'd been so caught up in their kiss, in her, that his senses had tuned out the rest of the world.

"Are you two going to come inside and join the party?" Cessy Walker asked when Drew regained enough control to release his wife and what was barely covered by her minuscule skirt.

"From the looks of things, I'd say you lovebirds were creating your own party out here." Freckles's laugh threatened to pop a few sequins off her wicked-witch ensemble.

"You ladies go on ahead. We'll be right behind you," Kylie said, her voice not quite as shaky as Drew's would have been—had he been able to find it.

"Sure you will." Cessy, dressed in Glinda's pink ball gown and tall crown, shot them a disapproving look as Freckles sang the chorus from "When a Man Loves a Woman." The women walked on, their costumes a direct contrast to their personalities.

Drew clenched his jaw. He was ashamed. And speechless.

This wasn't him. This wasn't how he acted. His parents had raised him better than this. Yet he was behaving like a sex-starved maniac, treating Kylie as though she was some cheap hussy in a back alley. This was why he didn't let himself lose control—why he'd spent years studying the mind and its cognitive functions. This was why he'd had to redirect and distract himself physically every night this past week by working out.

He didn't look at Kylie. He couldn't bear to see her embarrassment—or worse, her disgust—at finding out she was married to an absolute ogre who couldn't even put a lid on his lustful urges when they were out in public.

"We should probably make our way to the party," she said.

He should have been relieved she wasn't asking him to drive her home. Of course, after the behavior he'd just exhibited, it was wise of her to not get into a car alone with him. She probably wanted to be as close to other witnesses as possible.

He chanced a peek at her and saw her adjusting her corset and using the side mirror to fix her smeared lip gloss. "I'm so very sorry." It was the first response that came to him.

"There's nothing to be sorry about," she said, starting to walk down the street.

He caught up to her. "I know you probably would prefer to forget what just happened. But I just wanted to make it clear that I know it was wrong and I promise nothing like that will ever happen again."

Her steps quickened, but otherwise, Kylie gave no indication that she'd heard him, let alone believed him.

"It was bad enough your former mother-in-law caught us making out like a couple of teenagers," Kylie whispered to Maxine in a corner of the Marconis' lit garden. The party had spilled from the hosts' elegantly restored

Victorian mansion and into their yard, but she was too twisted up inside to enjoy the twinkling lights or the professional catering. "But then he told me that kissing each other was wrong. I told you this plan would never work."

"Kylie," Mia said, joining them. "I just saw your husband pacing over by the buffet table like a lion trapped in a cage. Every time someone comes up to him to congratulate him on his marriage, he goes straight for the bacon-wrapped scallops and crab cakes. I know the cooking situation at home isn't ideal, but if he keeps downing the seafood appetizers like that, he'll wind up with a stomachache and tonight will be ruined."

"Stop worrying, you two," Maxine said. "Mia, the plan is actually going better than we expected. Doctor Handsome got all worked up when he first saw Kylie in her costume outside, and they got busted getting all hot and heavy against the Nanamobile."

"Eww!" The dance instructor scrunched her nose.

"Don't worry. He only kissed me to prove a point. Then he apologized and promised it would never happen again."

"But how was the kiss?"

"It was fine." She tried to focus on the other guests and feign an interest in the party. But she knew her friends weren't buying it. "Okay, so it was wonderful. Beyond wonderful. I've never been kissed like that before, and if Cessy and Freckles hadn't walked by when they did, I doubt we would ever have made it inside."

"You guys got busted by Mrs. Walker? Double eww."

"Thanks." Kylie crossed her arms in front of her, wanting to duck farther into the corner. "That makes me feel way less mortified about the situation."

"Sorry," Mia said, putting her arm around Kylie. "Maybe we need to restrategize."

"I don't think so." Maxine nodded toward Drew. "See

how he's staring at Chuck Marconi and the rest of the good ol' boys club holding court over by the open bar?"

"Hmm." Kylie glanced at her husband, who didn't look at all like his normally poised self. "I wonder what they did to get him all bent out of shape."

"Kylie, he's giving them the evil eye because those men are all gawking at you and your costume."

"First of all, my costume is not that bad. There are other women here with outfits similar to mine."

"Yeah, but those women are working with a lot smaller curves than you."

She rolled her eyes. It wasn't as if she could help the way her body was shaped. "Second of all, if you think he's upset because they're looking at me, you're seriously…"

She lost all sense of what she was about to say because the subject of their conversation was striding toward her, looking more like a Special Forces sniper than a scholarly navy psychologist. She swallowed and glanced at her friends, hoping for some sort of support. But they were just standing there with silly grins on their faces.

"Drew, how are you?" Maxine said when he arrived, seemingly ready to pounce. "We were just talking about Kylie's costume and how beautiful she looks in it."

"*Beautiful* is one way to describe it." He glanced over his shoulder at the men by the bar, then stood closer to Kylie, as if he was trying to block her from their view.

What had gotten into him? When she'd chosen her outfit, she'd had no intention of trying to make him jealous. She'd simply wanted him to see her in a sexier light. Or at least draw his physical interest. "Seriously, you guys. Stop giving me a hard time. I'm supposed to be Diana. You know, the Greek goddess of the hunt?"

"Wasn't Diana also the goddess of fertility?" Mia

murmured before Maxine nudged her in the ribs. Kylie frowned at her friends.

"Anyway, Drew," Maxine said, "did Kylie tell you that Hunter invited the twins to come stay the night at our place tonight?"

"Ah, no. I'm pretty sure that never came up," he said, finally dragging his attention away from the group at the bar. "I don't think the boys are ready to handle a sleepover just yet. They're still getting used to being with me and, even though they're settling into a routine, I don't know if I trust them not to be a handful for you."

He was putting the brakes on this whole time-alone thing, and Kylie couldn't help but suspect he was doing so wittingly. He didn't want to be alone with her tonight and knew that if he allowed the twins to stay with Maxine and Cooper, he'd lose his towheaded buffers.

"Of course they won't be a handful. And we'd love to have them. I can understand you worrying about them spending the night somewhere new. I was the same way with Hunter the first time he went to a sleepover. But I promise that Cooper and I will take good care of them, and we'll even make extra pecan waffles in the morning for you when you come pick them up."

"Are you sure?" he asked, and Kylie's pulse took a little leap. She didn't want to think that the only reason he was relenting was the promise of another home-cooked meal. But when he looked at her, one eyebrow raised as if to ask her opinion, she couldn't help but hope he was silently asking her if she was comfortable with the arrangement.

She honestly didn't know if she was. But she *did* know they couldn't continue living together and pretending the kiss of the century hadn't just happened. She gave a tentative nod, hoping they could use the kid-free opportunity to have a good, long talk and sort out their feelings—or at least set some ground rules for the rest of the summer.

After several rather transparent reassurances from Maxine, Drew went to speak to the boys, and she could hear the children's squeals from across the yard. Part of her wanted to squeal as well, but the other part of her wanted to run straight to the Nanamobile and drive directly to Noodie's. She'd never needed some serious ice cream therapy more than she did at this exact moment.

Saying their goodbyes and doing their three hugs—with two excited kids in one oversize costume—created enough of a scene without her having to wonder if every townsperson home was snickering about why the newlyweds were leaving early.

Her husband was perfectly polite—as usual—but did not touch her as they walked back to the car. He opened the door for her and she thanked him, but otherwise they didn't speak. She was too afraid he might suggest dropping her off at her condo—with her brother, who'd been as surly as a grizzly bear when she'd talked to him a few days ago.

Instead, she repeated prime factors in her mind until he turned onto Sweetwater Bend. Apparently, he was taking her back to the cabin. She didn't know whether to exhale the breath she'd been holding or to start sucking in more air to prevent her from hyperventilating.

"I always forget how beautiful the stars are up on this mountain," he said, finally breaking their uncomfortable silence.

She craned her head, leaning forward to see out the windshield. "I think it's because the air is so pure up here."

See, they were making small talk. She could do this.

"My brother, Luke, the twins' dad, used to say that the

sky was better in Sugar Falls than anywhere else in the world because it was so close to heaven."

"Do you miss your brother?" There, that was a neutral enough subject.

"I do. We're twins, so we have this connection—I don't know how to explain it. Sometimes, when we're not together, I feel things as though I'm experiencing them with him."

"Is he anything like you?"

Drew chuckled. "Hardly. My mom would say we're exactly alike when it comes to certain things, but mostly, we're complete opposites. Luke is way more intense and impulsive. He knows what he wants and he goes after it. I'm more of a thinker, a planner. I manage my emotions better than he does, which is why we went into such different fields."

Kylie didn't want to point out that just a couple of hours ago, Drew certainly hadn't managed his emotions all that well. And she'd been enjoying it.

"He was the fun twin growing up," he continued. "The wild one. I was the dependable son. I always went out of my way to follow the rules, as though my perfect behavior would offset his recklessness. When he married the twins' mom, he became a little more like me—methodical, but still passionate about life. I know it sounds weird, but back then a part of me thought that if matrimony made him more like me, then maybe finding a wife of my own would make me more exciting like him."

"So then why didn't you marry your last girlfriend?" This was the kind of conversation they should be having on date number two, not on the second week of marriage. He'd touched on his prior relationship before, but now Kylie was wondering exactly what Drew was looking for in a wife.

He turned onto the private dirt road toward the cabin, and she wanted to tell him to keep driving. To keep talking.

"I don't know. I dated Jessica for a few years, but it just never felt right."

Wait. Did he say a few *years*?

He parked the car and shut off the engine. Kylie wanted to ask him if this moment together felt right. If *she* felt right. But the man had just admitted that it had taken him a hell of a lot longer than two weeks to decide if a woman was the one. Besides, on this night of all nights, she didn't want him comparing her to his ex. Or to any other women.

She needed him to realize that she was special. That she was unique and that she'd already given him something sacred that she'd never given another man. Even if neither one of them could remember it. Tonight's conversation had to be about just the two of them, because she didn't know how long she'd have him in her life, and she wanted to know that what they had—even if it was only temporary—was meaningful.

He rested his arm along the back of her seat and turned to look at her. Maybe it took Drew years to figure out his feelings, but apparently Kylie was making quick work of hers. No doubt that if he looked at her this way two weeks ago, even without the cocktails in souvenir cups, she would've had a hard time staying away from him.

"Listen," he said, keeping his hand nearby but not touching her. "I just wanted to apologize again for my behavior earlier."

Whoa. There he went with his stupid regrets again. "I told you that you had nothing to be sorry for."

She shoved open her door and then slammed it closed behind her—no small feat considering it had to be two hundred pounds of solid steel. She was stomping up the steps to the back porch when he called after her.

"If I shouldn't be apologizing, then why are you so clearly upset?"

"I'm not upset." Disappointed? Yes. Humiliated? Totally. She stormed into the cabin with him close on her sandaled heels.

"Really? Because I'm pretty sure I'm the expert on recognizing people's emotions."

"Well, Doctor Perfect, you certainly aren't the expert on me." She threw her small gold clutch on the table and turned to face him, ready for the showdown. How dare he presume to know how it felt to have the sainted Andrew Gregson regret their kiss? To have him vow not to make the same mistake with her twice?

"Kylie, I think we need to address this. I don't want you to feel uncomfortable or worry that I can't control myself around you."

"Drew, has it ever dawned on your expert mind that I don't *want* you to control yourself around me?"

She could hear the air hiss between his clenched teeth.

"Then, you'd better be really sure about what you *do* want, Kylie, because as you saw before we went inside the party, once I get close to you, I don't know if I'll be able to stop."

It took every bit of courage she possessed to put one foot in front of the other and walk toward him. This was it. There'd be no going back now. "I don't want you to stop."

Chapter Nine

Before Kylie could take that final step, Drew came toward her, placing one hand on her cheek a split second before molding his lips against hers. She knew the kiss they'd shared a couple of hours ago had shaken her senseless, but she'd never imagined a man could make her feel like *this*.

As though she was melting, yet she couldn't get warm enough.

For a guy who always practiced such an unusual amount of caution, he was certainly leaving her no opportunity for second-guessing and no time for doubt. And she didn't mind one bit, because she'd never been more certain of anything in her life. His mouth delved farther into her own as he drew her body closer. His fingers tangled into her long auburn hair, keeping her head exactly where he wanted it.

His chest was chiseled, hard as rock, and she ran her hands along its ridges, amazed that something so firm could also be so hot. The upper section of his homemade costume had come unpinned, and she felt even more heat as his exposed skin pressed against the flesh rising above her corset. He must have felt the same heat, because his fingers were immediately at her back, working the small stays that barely managed to hold her top closed.

Drew didn't show the slightest hint of slowing down, and Kylie worried that she'd soon be topless in the living room. This might not be her first time with him, but it was the first time she would be able to remember the experience, and she didn't want it occurring out in the open.

"Should we go into the bedroom?" she murmured against his lips. His response was to move his hands to cup her bottom and then lift her up, forcing her to wrap her long legs around his waist.

She was pretty sure that he carried her to the king-size bed. But by the time he laid her down, she didn't care how she'd gotten there, only that she didn't want him to let her go.

His mouth never left hers as he tore what remained of her corset and flung it to the ground. His large hands covered her breasts and she arched into him, unfamiliar with the sensation, yet craving more.

She had never been ashamed of her body, but suddenly she was hyperaware of everything he was doing to it and wondering if her response was normal. How could she experience this sense of floating above the bed when his tall, golden body was planted so firmly above her?

He balanced himself on one arm, kissing a trail down to her tightened nipples, as he used his other hand to slide her skirt and panties past her hips. When he brought his fingers back up, he did so along her inner thigh. The metal of his wedding band was cool against the delicate skin near her core, and she couldn't help but think, *This man is my husband. I'm finally giving myself to my husband.*

He was passionate and he was perfect and he was hers, just as much as she was now his.

She reached for his head and pulled his lips back to hers, wanting to seal her realization with a kiss. The movement caused his body to wedge itself between her open legs and, without hesitation, he drove into her. Her muscles clenched and she stilled, the small burst of pain already ebbing away.

He pulled back and looked at her face. "You're a... You've never... We've never?" There was no accusation in his blue eyes, only tenderness.

"I guess that answers the question of whether or not we already did this in Reno," she said, not sure of what she should do now. All she knew was that she didn't want to ruin this beautiful moment with any recriminations. She shifted her hips and his shaft slid deeper inside her.

He buried his face against her neck and said, "Forgive me, honey, but I can't stop."

"I don't want you to."

He groaned before slowing his pace long enough for her to meet his rhythm. She moaned as the pressure built inside her. When she wrapped her legs around him to draw him in even farther, the dark room went brighter. Then the light exploded into a thousand tiny fragments right as he called out her name.

Drew held Kylie close to him even as he cursed himself. He was an animal. A monster. He'd taken his wife's virginity and hadn't been able to control himself long enough to ensure she wasn't hurt.

"I'm sorry for not being more gentle," he said, while hoping she wasn't too sore. He didn't want to cause her pain, but she felt so perfect in his arms, he didn't think he could wait to have her again.

"I thought you weren't supposed to apologize anymore."

"That was before I knew you were a… That you'd never done this before."

"It was perfect. I wouldn't have wanted you to change a single thing." She snuggled in closer to him, and he felt her breath warm against his neck.

The woman was incredible.

When their breathing had slowed to a normal pace, she stretched, then sat up on the bed, pulling the quilt in front of her and up under her arms.

He reached for his glasses on the nightstand but couldn't find them. "Where are you going?"

"To get my robe."

"Like that? I think it's still out in the car." He stroked his hand down her bare back. He knew she'd said otherwise, but he worried her newfound modesty was due to the way he'd just ravished her. When she turned her head toward him, her long auburn curls fell around her creamy shoulders, and she smiled at him. His stomach flipped over.

At least he thought it was a smile. He couldn't be sure without his glasses.

"I guess I'll have to stay like this until morning."

"I don't mind if you don't," Drew said as he tugged on the quilt, using it to pull her back into his arms.

She came willingly and he tried to command himself to go slow, to be gentle. But any thoughts of her still being tender were a distant memory as his passion once again took over his brain. They made love a second time and then collapsed in each other's arms. The quilt was nowhere to be found and the sheets were in a tangled heap at the foot of the bed.

But Drew didn't care. His body was still burning and he didn't need anything but Kylie to keep him warm.

He awoke to the sun streaming through the bedroom window and the smell of Kylie's shampoo tickling his nose. Using his free arm, he tried not to wake her as he reached for his glasses, this time determined to see his wife in all her splendid glory.

But he couldn't find the wire frames, or even feel the sturdy oak table that was usually pushed up against the bed. He squinted at the room, and his blurry eyes landed on the nightstand, which had somehow toppled over onto its side, several feet away.

How in the world had that happened?

He ran his fingers through his hair, careful not to disturb Kylie, who was sleeping soundly, pressed up against his side. He hadn't been with a woman since Jessica, and during that time, he'd never experienced the uninhibited reckless abandon he'd felt last night. Honestly, he'd never experienced anything like that before with anyone.

His cell phone chimed, the low decibels indicating it was coming from the other room. He thought about the possibility of an emergency and gently disengaged his arm from under her shoulders. He almost stepped on his discarded glasses before picking them up off the floor and walking naked into the living room.

"Hello?" he whispered into the phone, only to realize Kylie'd followed him out. And apparently she'd found the bed cover, because she was wrapped up in it.

"Hey, Uncle Drew," one of his nephews responded. "Chief Cooper is making waffles and wants to know if you and Aunt Kylie are coming for breakfast."

"I…uh…don't know."

"Is everything okay with the boys?" she asked.

He put his hand over the mouthpiece. "They want to know if we're coming over for waffles."

"Are they making the pecan ones where he uses the maple-cream-cheese glaze?"

He relayed her question to his nephew and waited for the response. But seeing her in the living room, barely covered, her hair all wild and tousled from their love-making, Drew suddenly didn't feel so hungry—at least not for breakfast.

The little voice came back on the line. "He said yes, although me and Aiden don't want no nuts, so he's gonna make ours plain. But he's also making bacon and scrambled eggs."

Drew's stomach growled and he nodded at Kylie, conveying the information.

"Tell them we'll be there in twenty minutes," she said.

He disconnected the phone, calculating how far downtown was from the cabin. She certainly hadn't left them very much time. He walked toward her, and it wasn't until she looked down and then up again that he remembered he was completely nude.

She bit her lower lip and he asked, "Are you sure you're in such a hurry to leave?"

"Well, he *did* say bacon and..."

He interrupted her by kissing the column of her neck. Man, she had smooth skin. He traced a finger along her shoulder, then toward the edge of the quilt, right where her breasts were rising above the fabric.

"Are you terribly hungry?" he asked.

"Starving." She dropped the bedding to the floor before rising up on her tiptoes to meet his lips.

Thirty minutes later, they were still naked and still in the living room, stretched out on the discarded blanket and once again trying to catch their breath.

"We should probably act like responsible adults and go pick up the children." She spoke first. She was smiling, but Drew hated the reminder that he had again lost all control and rational sense.

"You're right." He should apologize, but he wasn't feeling very sorry. In fact, he was feeling quite the opposite. He was glad they'd made love and he was looking forward to doing so again.

"I wonder if they'll have any food left by the time we get there." She walked toward the bathroom, twisting her hair up into a bun on top of her head, and he was tempted to follow her into the shower.

But she closed the door behind her and he thought she was already transitioning into modesty mode. Perhaps she already regretted what they'd done. He walked to the bedroom, stripping off the sheets and then remaking the bed with fresh ones. He moved the nightstand back where it belonged and picked up the disheveled linens, including his discarded costume. He found her corset hanging off the dresser and looked at the torn edges. He remembered getting impatient with the tiny hooks last night, but had he really ripped her top off her?

He shoved the ruined garment in with the rest of the dirty laundry and walked out onto the back porch to start a load of wash quickly, before she saw the evidence of what he'd done last night.

When she emerged from the bathroom, the towel wrapped around her torso barely covering her damp, warm skin, he tried to avert his eyes. Somehow, the act of getting ready together seemed way more intimate than anything they had already done last night and, until she told him otherwise, he wanted to respect her privacy.

He took a cold shower, then put on a fresh pair of jeans and a clean T-shirt. When he came out to meet her, she was in the living room, folding up the quilt, a slight blush tinting her cheeks.

"Are you ready to go?" he asked.

She took a look around the room—probably to ensure they'd left no other trace of their passionate night—and said, "All set."

He opened the passenger door of Nana's Oldsmobile, and she slid inside. "Listen…" he started, but she held up her hand.

"You're not going to apologize again, are you?"

"Actually, I wasn't. I just wanted to say thank you. For last night and, well, for everything."

She tilted her head and smiled at him. "Do you think they'll notice anything is different about us?"

"Who? Our friends or the kids?" He walked to the other side of the car and got in.

"Ugh, I hope the kids don't notice." She slid on her sunglasses, and he could no longer read her expression. "I meant Maxine and Cooper."

Instead of answering, he made a big pretense of trying to drive in Reverse and avoiding the potholes as he backed down the driveway. Why didn't she want the people closest to them to know that things had now changed between them? Drew thought they had changed for the better, but maybe she didn't feel the same way.

The plan had been for her to move out at the end of summer, and he'd been fine with that before last night. But now, the thought of her departure left an ache the size of a small hole in his heart.

Just then, the other growing hole inside his body rumbled again, and she laughed. "Sorry, my stomach is pretty much running on empty."

"Drew, I think your stomach is *always* running on empty."

He smiled. He could manage small banter. But it wasn't like him to avoid an important issue. Hadn't he been the one last night who insisted on her talking about what had happened between them? He usually liked to address things right off the bat, but now he couldn't change the subject quickly enough.

"I'm a growing boy," he said. "I need my food."

"You know, speaking of food, I was doing some research on PTSD."

"Really? Why were you doing that?"

"Because I wanted to learn more about what you do." Apparently she had taken a definite interest in his job, and maybe, in turn, in him. That hole in his heart began to close up. "Anyway, I came across this article about soldiers taking culinary classes as a sort of therapy, and was curious whether your team offered anything like that at Shadowview Hospital."

"Yep, I've heard about that. There are so many helpful types of therapy out there. We already have a yoga class, a canine companion group and a creative-art group." He made a left onto Snowflake Boulevard. "But with so many patients and so many personalities, we were looking into expanding some of the treatment options we provide."

"Oh, good. Because I was talking to Freckles the other day when I was having lunch at the Cowgirl Up Café, and she said she'd be more than happy to volunteer to teach you—I mean, your patients—some basics in cooking. If, you know, you'd be interested in offering something like that."

"That would be great, actually. Captain Donahue is really into baking and recipes and stuff. I bet she'd like to spearhead a project like that."

"Um, Drew, I was thinking that maybe you could lead the group. Or at least take part in it."

"Are you saying you don't like my cooking?" What else didn't she like about him? He parked the car behind the Sugar Falls Cookie Company and unbuckled his seat belt before he looked at her.

"Of course not," she said a little too quickly and then put her hand on his arm, as if to pat him. "You're a great cook."

"Really?" he asked, knowing she was full of it, but wanting her to keep consoling him with her touch.

"No. Not really. But you're better than me." She smiled, and he couldn't help but lean toward her for another kiss. She met him across the armrest, and he decided that as long as she kept touching him like this, kissing him like this, he'd volunteer to lead any kind of therapy class she wanted.

He had practically pulled her onto his lap when an eight-year-old hand knocked on the window. "Hey, you guys better hurry. They're all out of the plain waffles, but Mrs. Maxine says they still have the ones with the nuts."

Kylie blushed and scrambled to open her door. She was probably embarrassed that the kids had seen them together. Drew adjusted his jeans, then got out and followed her up the stairs to Cooper and Maxine's apartment, a little confused by her reaction.

In fact, weren't they *supposed* to be acting all in love, like their marriage was real? In his opinion, making love last night just made their roles that much more believable.

"Drew, my mom just called," Kylie said to her husband as he helped the boys finish stacking their Jenga pieces into a tower. It had been only three weeks since they'd started sleeping together, and already she was getting used to thinking of him that way. "She said my dad is on his way to Boise State this evening to scout one of their pitch-

ers, and he plans on stopping by my condo to check in on
Kane and then swinging by here to say hi."

"Just to say hi?" Drew lifted a brow at her but continued to stack wooden blocks, his crooked right pinkie at
risk of knocking down the tower.

He was so cute when he played with the boys, and
even cuter after they put the twins to bed. Without either
of them saying a word, he had easily transitioned into the
master bedroom with her and, although they'd stuck to
the same daily routine with the kids, their evenings alone
had become much more entertaining.

"Well, she *says* that, but I think we all know he's dropping in to size up the situation and see if everything's
going well. He's always checking in on me unannounced
like this. But at least my brother is getting one this time,
too. Surprise inspections, Dad calls them."

"I thought your dad was drafted into the major leagues
straight out of college. Was he actually ever in the military?"

How sweet that Drew had taken the time to do research
on her family. Maybe he wanted to investigate how deep
the craziness ran before he got himself in too deep with
her. It probably hadn't taken him much work to figure it
out, though. Her family might be a little quirky, but she
loved them to pieces. Especially her dad. "Nope. He just
likes to remind his kids that he runs the ship."

"So," he said, standing up and walking toward her. He
pulled her into his arms and kissed her neck. She commanded herself to breathe and wondered if she would ever
get used to the feeling of his large hands splayed around
her waist. Or his lips on her sensitive flesh. "Have any of
your previous boyfriends failed a surprise inspection?"

"Are you kidding? As if I wasn't smart enough to keep
my dates as far away from my father as possible. Not that

I really kept men around long enough to get to the meet-my-parents stage." She blushed, still apprehensive about the fact that Drew was the first man she'd slept with and her lack of sexual experience.

"Your mom's personality is way lower key. They have an interesting dynamic."

"Oh, trust me, my mom just allows my dad to *think* he's running the show."

Drew started pulling items out of the fridge. Thank goodness he hadn't taken offense at her therapy-cooking suggestion. Things had definitely improved in the bedroom *and* in the kitchen. Kylie dreaded the day it would all end.

"He's not one of those antifeminists, is he?"

"Actually, he's the opposite. He always told me that if his sons could do something, his daughter could do it ten times better. But he doesn't get all the fuss with women's fashion or what he calls 'female flash and glitz.' He couldn't understand why I would want to go out for the cheerleading squad when there was a perfectly good softball team at my high school. In fact, he raised a big fuss with the league about trying to get me on the boys' baseball team. When I told him I didn't want to play, he asked me why I would want to cheer for a team when I could *be* a star player. I'm the only girl, yet he's always acted as though he wants me to be one of the guys."

"Well, there is definitely nothing masculine about you."

"Pshh. I think I overdid it on my rebellion because I went completely opposite. It doesn't get much more girlie than me."

"I like all your girlie parts," he said with a wink. The Jenga tower collapsed with a deafening bang and they were reminded the boys were nearby. "So what time will he be here?"

"Less than an hour."

"Wow. That definitely is a surprise inspection."

"I think my mom felt sorry for us and decided to blow his cover at the last minute. Like I said, she's the one who really runs things. Can I help you with dinner?" She picked up a box of pasta and he practically tore it out of her hands. Was he that afraid of her cooking?

"How about you make the salad?" He pointed to the head of romaine sitting on the counter.

Hmm. Salad duty.

Lately, she'd been hoping things would keep progressing between them. She didn't know if she was ready for anything permanent, but she felt a sudden need to prove to Drew that she was capable of so much more than assisting him around the house and with the kids and the groceries.

"Well, Doc, if that psychology career doesn't work out for you, I'm sure they could find a place for you in the mess hall," Bobby Chatterson said after finishing his second helping of chicken cacciatore.

Drew was impressed with how easy it was to follow some of the recipes Freckles had been writing down for the PTSD cooking group. But thank goodness he'd gone to Duncan's Market yesterday and stocked their pantry. His new father-in-law could eat like a bear.

He'd also witnessed a softer side to the man, who, during the meal took the time to explain patiently to Aiden and Caden why it was important for them to go to college first instead of trying to get drafted into the major leagues straight out of high school. By the time he'd finished, he had the boys convinced they would have no problem becoming both Harvard scholars and professional athletes. The man had high expectations not just of his daughter but of everyone.

"So, Jellybean, does this husband of yours know his way around a dishwasher, too?"

"Dad, knock it off. I'm more than capable of cleaning up a kitchen. Maybe you should go check out Drew's workout equipment in the boat shed. Did you know he's a great boxer?"

Other than the punching bag he'd been using with less frequency lately, Drew wasn't exactly sure how Kylie knew about his boxing ability. But judging by the defensive way she'd just squared her shoulders, his wife was apparently trying to prove his masculinity to her father.

"Well, I'll believe that when I see it." Mr. Chatterson winked at him before getting up from the table. He held the back door open, and Drew followed him out of the cabin, feeling like a lamb being led to slaughter.

They hadn't gone more than a few yards when his father-in-law leaned in and whispered, "Did you see what I did there, son?"

Drew looked back to the cabin. "What you did where?"

"Oh, boy. I can see they didn't teach you much in all those fancy doctor classes. Back there? In the kitchen? That's called reverse psychology."

He wouldn't define it as a textbook example, but Drew was curious to see where the man was going with this.

"My baby girl is as smart as all get-out, but she falls for it every dang time. Try to suggest she can't do something and she bends over backward to prove you wrong. And now that she's taken you under her wing, she's gonna get her dander up and protect you."

Apparently, the ability to manipulate his daughter didn't work all the time, because Coach Chatterson hadn't convinced her to dress more conservatively or quit the cheer team. "So you're saying you were trying to get her to do the dishes on purpose?"

"Yep. I haven't had a chance to get to know my son-in-law yet, and I figured we were about due for a man-to-man talk." *Oh, great.* As much of an expert as the man might be in "psychological warfare" on the pitching mound, Drew wasn't about to be intimidated. "Anyway, I know my Jellybean better than anyone else does, and I figured you might need some advice on how to handle her."

Did her father think Drew was doing a poor job of it so far? He opened the boat shed and gestured for Bobby to go inside. With the awkward direction this conversation was taking, he wanted to make sure they were well out of his wife's earshot. "Sir, Kylie's a strong woman, and I don't think she'd appreciate anyone handling her, let alone me."

"See, I knew you were the one. Looks as if you're starting to get it."

"To get what?"

"Reverse psychology. You gotta let her think things are her idea. She has a fiery temper, that one. Gets it from her mom." Somehow, Drew sincerely doubted that. But he let the man ramble on.

"I'm not saying you should play games with her or mess with her head or any bull like that. I'm just saying that my Kylie is special, but she's strong-minded. Now, I don't believe that just because she's my baby girl and I'm crazy proud of her. I believe that because I'm an excellent judge of character, and that one back there—" he jerked his thumb toward the cabin "—has character to spare. She knows what she wants, and she is more than capable of making sure she gets it."

A lot of what he was saying was true, yet with his questionable approaches, Drew had to wonder if his father-in-law actually knew what he was talking about. "Then, why the need for reverse psychology?"

"Well, now, sometimes she can be just a touch stubborn. Gets that from her mom, as well. And I don't like to see her miss out on something good for her or wind up regretting doing X when she should've done Y. It might sound as if I'm being a little controlling, but when you two have kids, you'll see. You just want what's best for them."

The thought of having children, especially with Kylie, brought a little tingle to the back of Drew's neck. But a good kind of tingle, like how he always felt when he was a kid waking up on Christmas morning. "So how often does this trick actually work?"

Bobby sighed. "It was easier when she was younger."

"That's interesting. According to Kylie, she rebelled and went in the complete opposite direction of what you wanted."

"That's how good I am at it, son." Bobby Chatterson smiled, his straight white teeth proudly displayed beneath his long beard.

"Wait. You're trying to tell me that when she was growing up, you tried to talk her into playing baseball because you actually *wanted* her to join the cheerleading team?"

"See, all my life I wanted a daughter. Every time Lacey got pregnant, I prayed for a little girl. Don't get me wrong. I love my boys and I'm damn proud of them. But when I finally got my little princess, I was in heaven. I'd spent half my career in a locker room and men like me and you, well, we need to be exposed to that softer, feminine side of life."

Drew was trying to keep his expression as neutral as possible. As much as he was coming to like and appreciate Kylie's father, he couldn't for the life of him see the similarity. "You think we're a lot alike, do you?"

"Of course we are. That's why I trust you enough to have this conversation in the first place. I wouldn't be giving this advice to just anyone. Let me tell you, Kylie has dated some real boneheads in the past, and if I wasn't one hundred percent certain you two were completely perfect for each other, I'd reverse-psychologize her to dump your sorry butt."

Drew almost laughed at the coined term, but just then a sharp pain exploded under his rib cage.

He winced before coming down hard into a sitting position on the wood floor.

"You okay, son?" Bobby Chatterson knelt in front of him.

The pain was already fading, but Drew gingerly felt along the side of his torso. There was no specific reason why he should've felt as if his skin was being ripped open.

Unless somewhere out there, his brother, Luke, had just felt the same thing.

Chapter Ten

Drew's head began spinning, thinking of the potential danger his twin could be in right this second. He tried not to panic. After all, if he could feel Luke's pain, wouldn't he then be able to feel if something worse had happened to his brother? Wouldn't he know if his twin had…died?

He took a deep breath and exhaled slowly, then repeated it. The ache was definitely easing, and he was able to get his thoughts a little more under control.

Either way, sitting in a boat shed with baseball legend Bobby Chatterson wasn't going to solve this mystery for him. And he certainly didn't want to explain to his father-in-law the idea of twin telepathy. "It's just a muscle cramp. I think it's going away, though. I'll be fine."

"I've had more than my fair share of those." Bobby Chatterson moved Drew's hand away. "You probably should get inside and rub some Icy Hot on it. Besides, I still need to stop by and see Kane tonight. Now that I've got you and Kylie all squared away, I need to go talk some sense into that boy."

Drew was relieved to find that standing up didn't re-trigger the soreness. He locked the door to the shed, and they made their way back to the cabin.

"So, a few minutes ago, you said you thought I was perfect for your daughter. Why?" Drew not only wanted to get the man's attention off his odd injury but also was curious to hear an outsider's opinion about the potential for their relationship.

"Knew it from the moment I asked that DJ to play that song for you two at the reception and she went all swoony."

Drew stopped in his tracks. "That was *you*?"

"You bet. I knew no matter how stubborn she was being about downplaying you guys running off and getting married, she wouldn't be able to resist a classic love ballad like that. You get that girl on a dance floor and she becomes an open book."

"Let me guess. She gets that from her mom, too?"

"Hell no. She gets her lack of cooking skills from her mom. Her ability to dance and her great taste in music are courtesy of yours truly."

Drew would have laughed if the effort wouldn't have further aggravated his side.

Although the suspicious pain had gone away hours ago, Drew had been restless most of the night. Luke was on a classified assignment and Drew was anxious to get to his office, which had a secure phone line, and pull some rank to find out where his brother was and whether something had happened to him.

He hadn't told Kylie about his conversation with her father the night before or about the possibility of his brother being injured. By the time he'd gotten the twins to bed after Mr. Chatterson had left, he'd walked into the bathroom to find Kylie soaking in a tub of steamy bubbles. He'd locked the door, and neither one of them had done much talking after that.

That morning, he kissed her goodbye and drove the Jeep entirely too fast down the mountain in his rush to get to work. After almost flipping it at the turnoff onto the state highway, Drew reminded himself that he was trying to avoid arriving in an ambulance, although working at a military hospital did have its perks.

It took several calls and a lot of red tape before he finally found out that Luke was just coming out of surgery aboard one of the navy's hospital ships somewhere in the Indian Ocean.

It took another two hours to be connected with him via satellite phone.

"Luke, what happened?" Drew practically shouted into the receiver when he heard his brother's slightly raspy voice.

"Well, our op ended prematurely."

"No, I meant what happened to *you*?"

"I'm surprised you found out so soon." Drew didn't tell him the reason he knew. And if Luke felt the same connection, Drew didn't need to tell him. "It was just a little cut. Had to have a few stitches."

"Sounds like more than just a cut to me. You had to be airlifted to a ship on a humanitarian-aid mission, brother. I've been in war zones, too, you know. Stop trying to minimize what happened as if you're talking to Mom."

"You haven't told her yet? Or my boys?"

"Nope. I just found out myself. But if you don't tell me how bad it is, I'm going to speak to your commanding officer and request that he give her a call and fill her in."

"Okay, okay. Jeez, Saint Drew, it's not like you to fight

so dirty. It's really not that big of a deal. I fractured a couple of ribs and had to have surgery to get everything back in place. I guess I'm just having a hard time wrapping my head around it all."

"You mean you finally realized that you weren't invincible?"

"Something like that. I've never worried too much about death before."

"Is that why you've been hell-bent on taking so many chances with your life?"

Luke was silent for a moment. "I guess that when Samantha died, a part of me wanted to die, too."

Drew shook his head. All along, he'd known the reason for his brother's attitude, but it'd been painful to watch things escalate to this level. "I love you, Luke, and I don't regret the fact that we all walked on eggshells after your wife passed away. But it's been a few years, and it's time someone told you that you need to face your reality. People lose their loved ones and it sucks. I can't even begin to imagine the hell you went through. But you aren't doing your sons any favors by running off to play Captain Save the World every time you need to escape what happened."

"Dammit, Drew. You don't think I worry about those boys every single minute I'm away from them? Have you ever stopped to think that maybe Aiden and Caden are better off with someone more stable in their lives?"

"No. That asinine thought hasn't crossed my mind once. You're their father. They love you. They need you. They miss you like crazy. And there isn't anyone more capable of loving them and providing for them than you. So if you think they need someone more stable in their lives, then you need to man up and figure out how to be that someone."

He could hear his brother's sigh on the other end of the

line. It was hard to be so brutally honest, but they both knew Luke needed to hear it.

"I know. You're right. The past twenty-four hours have been a complete game changer for me, and I've had nothing but downtime to sit here and make some tough decisions."

Drew's stomach dropped, and the pain in his side lit up again. His twin brother had never been the best at thinking things through. He usually acted first and improvised as he went along. Which was why Drew no longer went to professional sporting events with the guy. Drew looked at the crooked pinkie finger on his right hand that served as a reminder. "What kind of decisions?"

"Like whether or not I want to stay on the team and keep putting my kids in jeopardy of becoming orphans."

"And what conclusion have you reached?" Drew knew he could browbeat his brother to death, but Luke needed to come to this realization on his own.

"That maybe I should talk to my commander about a reassignment."

"To where?" Drew rubbed his ribs. No matter how much he believed Aiden and Caden needed their father, the thought of Luke moving the boys away just now when Drew was beginning to build a relationship with them was a real blow.

"Well, all of my stuff is currently in a storage facility near the base in San Diego. But my life, my family, is in Idaho. I can't keep uprooting the boys and taking them away from the people who love them every time a new mission comes up."

"So what are you saying?" *Please don't let it be that he's going to move the boys back to California.*

"I'm thinking the navy needs recruiters, and there's a reserve unit in Boise, so I'll speak to the CO about working on a transfer there. I haven't talked to Mom and Dad about it yet, but I figure I'll need to lie low for a couple of weeks anyway to recuperate."

"Wow. It sounds as if that might actually work out pretty well." The doctors must have had him on some serious medication, because usually Luke never was good at planning.

"Okay, enough about me. Tell me how my sons are doing."

"They're great," Drew said, actually excited to be able to give his brother a good report. "Kylie got them enrolled in this wilderness-adventure camp, and they're having a blast. She has them on a routine, and the boys are absolutely crazy about her. She's even got me doing a cooking therapy class and learning how to make us fresh, home-cooked meals. Overall, it's been a fantastic summer so far."

"Who's Kylie?"

Drew's smile fell, and he took off his glasses to clean the lenses. By checking in with periodical emails, he'd been able to avoid telling anyone in his family about his wife because he didn't know how long things between them would last. But Luke was the twins' father and deserved to know who was helping care for his children. "Listen, there's something I need to talk to you about. I kind of got married."

"I knew it!" Luke's triumphant laugh made its way through the wonky satellite connection, and Drew could imagine him pumping his fist in the air.

That was his brother's response? Not doubt? Not worry for his brother's unorthodox mental state? Not even recriminations for having a wedding without him?

"What do you mean, you knew it?" They had never talked about their bond or how they sensed things in each other. But acquiring a wife wasn't like a physical ailment or a career-ending injury to the rib cage that the other twin could simply...feel.

"I just did. It was the strangest thing. There I was, flying over the middle of the... Well, that's classified. Anyway, I was about to do a low aerial jump out of a C-130 and normally, I'd be the first person to pack my chute and launch out of the plane. But something made me pause. I hesitated and radioed in to double-check our target's coordinates. I told myself I was overthinking the mission. I was smack dab in the middle of a hot combat zone, and I was acting like Saint Drew, the great analyst. But just then, a projectile grazed the wing of the plane and the sudden force threw me across the deck of the interior cabin and halfway out the open cargo hold. We were suddenly under serious fire by some low-grade surface-to-air guns our intelligence had completely missed. And there I was, hanging out of the plane like a rag doll. One of their shots grazed me, tearing through my vest just as my team was pulling me back into the cabin."

Drew squeezed his eyes tightly closed, unable to get the image of his brother practically being shot down out of his head.

"I can sense your brain working, Drew, and there's no rhyme or reason to any of it, so don't start that what-if business. You got married and I'm going to be fine."

"Wait. Explain to me how my marriage, which you didn't know about, was somehow responsible for practically getting you killed?"

"Don't you see? My hesitation was completely out of character, but it actually saved the whole unit. There were tanks and ground units carrying antiaircraft artillery that our radar hadn't picked up swarming the jump perimeter. I knew something was off, and if I hadn't taken the time to call in the coordinates, or if I'd just done my usual balls-to-the-wall routine, we'd either be dead or the United States government would be getting a ransom call from a remote cave in... Well, again, that's classified information. Anyway, I can't wait to meet the woman who married my brother and saved my entire team."

Drew took a few moments to digest the information that his brother was alive and well. And that he'd be coming home for good. "Do you know when that meeting will be taking place? When will you be coming home?"

"I don't know. I'll keep you posted."

They disconnected the call, and Drew leaned back in his desk chair.

He was relieved and more than thrilled to know he'd be seeing his brother again soon.

But his stomach dropped at the thought of telling Kylie. They'd just started getting to know each other. If she thought the kids didn't need her, she would be out the door like a cork popped out of an expensive bottle of champagne. Yet he also knew he shouldn't keep her in the dark about Luke coming back into the picture. But he needed time. After they'd made love initially, he thought he'd have the whole summer to convince her that they should stay married. But his brother's reassignment changed everything.

He needed to figure out a way to keep their marriage together before Luke came home and turned their fragile world upside down.

Kylie had sensed a tension in Drew last night after he and her father had returned from their manly talk in the boat shed. And while she'd been dying to ask Drew what they'd said, she never really got the chance once he'd locked himself in the bathroom with her.

Then, the following evening, her husband was back

to his usual sweet but practical self—up until they were alone, at which point he seemed to lose all control and Kylie threw common sense out the bedroom window.

She must've misinterpreted his earlier mood, because things only got better as the week went on. It was probably impossible for him to become any more perfect, but seemingly he had. And if his passion grew any hotter, she would need to start wearing a flame-resistant suit to bed. Or at least not expensive lingerie. He'd now ripped several pairs of her underwear and two of her favorite bras. Not that she was complaining.

Since he had the weekend off, they'd taken the boys out and about to explore Sugar Falls. They went hiking up to the waterfall and Drew carried a picnic lunch he'd packed for them before they hit Noodie's Ice Cream Shoppe after dinner on Saturday night. On Sunday, they rented mountain bikes from Russell's Sports and hauled them up to the lifts at Snow Creek Lodge so they could teach the twins how to navigate down the kid-friendly bike paths.

It was almost as if they were the perfect little family.

"Why are you smiling like that?" Aiden asked, bringing her back to the task she was supposed to be performing—which was opening up a new box of Honey Smacks. These kids had their uncle's appetite.

"Like what?"

"Like Jake Marconi's little sister smiles at Caden right before she paddles after him in her little pink canoe."

Caden shoved his brother. "She doesn't chase me as much as she chases *you*."

"She does not."

"Does so."

Kylie sighed. "Okay, boys. Eat your cereal. We have some important stuff to do today."

Cessy Walker had talked to her ex-husband, who owned

a luxury car dealership in Boise, and arranged for Kylie to get a great deal on a slightly used SUV. She wasn't quite ready to trade in her convertible yet, but after the way her relationship with Drew was progressing, she was feeling confident that a more modern-looking family vehicle was in keeping with the direction her life was heading.

Summer camp was closed for the week before its up-coming Fourth of July camping trip, and Kylie had to take the boys with her to the dealership. They were bundles of energy when they arrived. As she spoke with the dealer, she told the twins they could look at some of the new models on display. Unfortunately, when she wasn't paying attention, they sneaked into the service department and tried to do a tire rotation on another customer's car. She couldn't fault them for being such bright and inquisitive children—especially when their abundance of curiosity led to the salesman's exasperation and acceptance of her lowball offer just to get her out the door and the eight-year-olds off the property.

After lunch, she knew they needed a physical outlet since they'd been cooped up in the car and doing errands with her most of the day. She thought about taking them swimming at the rec center, then remembered Mia was doing a free cheer clinic for children at the Snowflake Dance Academy this week.

She didn't want to ask Drew's permission, because she didn't know how he would feel about his nephews engaging in a female-dominated sport. But Hunter had gone once and, although he'd complained the entire time, Kylie thought it was good for children to experience all types of activities in order to make an educated decision about which extracurriculars were the best fit.

After all, where would she be if her own dad hadn't begrudgingly allowed her to go to the cheerleading rehearsal tryouts in high school when he clearly would've preferred to see her spending her afternoons at the batting cages with her brothers?

She parked along Snowflake Boulevard, careful not to pull too close to Scooter and Jonesy, the volunteer firefighters, who were dismounting near the hitching post in front of the Cowgirl Up Café.

"Hey Mr. Scooter and Jonesy," Caden yelled out the window. "Check out my Aunt Kylie's new car."

Her heart flipped. She definitely wasn't getting tired of being called *aunt*. Just then, she saw Kane coming out of the hardware store a few doors down, his right arm still in a sling.

She waved at her brother, and he walked over to them. He'd met Drew and the twins a handful of times, but he'd been trying to keep a low profile since arriving in town, hoping not to draw too much attention to the recent scandal that sidelined his baseball career. He smiled at the boys as they pet the nearby horses. "Your face looks kinda funny, Uncle Kane."

"Oh, my gosh." Kylie pulled off her sunglasses. "You shaved off your beard!" She had never gotten used to the extreme facial hair he'd grown when he started his major-league career. She would always see him as her baby-faced brother.

"Yep. Figured it was time for a change." Kane pulled his hat lower on his head as a car drove down the street. Kylie understood her brother's need to hide his identity.

"How's the shoulder?"

"Team doctor says I'm out for the season, and possibly the next one, as well. Dad wanted me to see a specialist, but I have a feeling they're gonna tell me I've done way too much damage over the years."

"So what are you going to do?"

"Stick around Sugar Falls, I guess. Most of the towns-people leave me alone, and I can avoid the tourists when I need to. Since I have some downtime, I figure I might try my hand at building renovation. I picked up that old property out by Sprinkle Creek pretty cheap and plan to move out there to fix the old barn up."

"Hey, Uncle Kane, you wanna go camping with us this weekend?" The boys finally came over to join them. It touched Kylie that Drew's nephews had latched on to her own family, as well.

The twins talked about the big wilderness camping trip as Kylie reached for her purse and the gym bag on the pas-senger side floor. The two-day trip was an opportunity for Alex Russell and his staff to reinforce all the wilderness skills the kids had learned.

She worried for Aiden's and Caden's safety, and for the leaders' ability to keep a close eye on the mischievous boys. But she was also looking forward to a whole week-end alone with Drew.

"I might come out if you promise to bait my fishing hooks for me, seeing as how I'm one-handed right now."

"Deal!" Both boys jumped up and down, and Kylie shook her head. Now she had to add the possibility of the twins getting hooks through their eye to her ever-growing list of camping-trip worries. Sometimes she didn't know what she would do with all these maternal feelings mani-festing inside her once Drew said goodbye at the end of summer and she was no longer their aunt.

Other times, she refused to let the idea cross her mind.

The sound of hip-hop music blasted out of Mia's dance studio across the street. "All right, boys, we'd better get to class before we're late."

She hugged her brother, then took one of the boys'

hands in each of her own as they made their way across the crosswalk.

Normally, when the class started, Kylie would've allowed herself to forget about the outside world and just get lost in the music. But today, she had promised to assist Mia, which was really better than being forced to sit on the sidelines and make small talk to the stage parents who thought their kids were going to be the next big stars.

It wasn't until the last routine of the day that Kylie was finally able to get her mind back onto a more positive train of thought. She'd been wrong about Drew being tense the Sunday before last. Things were going so well between them. She just needed to bite the bullet and have a real conversation with him about where they stood.

When the twins went on their camping trip, it would be the perfect opportunity—as long as she and Drew could keep their clothes on long enough to actually talk.

When Kylie and the boys pulled up to the cabin, Drew was sitting on the porch. Wait, that wasn't Drew. She was so crazy about the guy and so anxious to see him, she was now imagining him—like a mirage. She turned off the engine, trying to figure out who the strange man was before letting the boys out. The man stood up, and Kylie realized his resemblance to her husband was uncanny.

That was weird. Drew only had one brother and he was away...

"Daddy!" both of the boys screamed before flinging open the doors of her new SUV.

It couldn't be. What was Luke Gregson doing back so soon?

This wasn't how she'd expected to meet her new in-laws. She took a deep breath and got out of the car. She could do this.

Her legs were a little shaky as she made her way across the driveway, and she doubted it was due to the intense class she'd just taught.

"This is Aunt Kylie," Caden said, and Kylie sent up a silent thanks that the boys were there to help neutralize this awkward moment. "She was a cheerleader and we got to go to dance class with her and Miss Mia and even boys are allowed to be on cheer teams if we want to."

Maybe she needed to rethink her thankfulness.

"So Drew's wife is a cheerleader." Luke smiled and held out his hand to shake hers. "I should've seen that one coming. My brother has had a thing for girls with pom-poms ever since a squad of them rescued him one time in the mall."

Well, there was a fun fact she'd have to ask her husband about later. But right now, she was dying to know how Luke knew about her in the first place. And why Drew hadn't told her that he'd been in contact with his brother or that they should be expecting him sooner.

"Was. I *was* a cheerleader." He glanced down at her bright orange Cheer 4 BSU tank top, and she wished she had packed something else in her gym bag. Something that didn't make her appear as if she was trying desperately to cling to the glory days like a fifty-year-old former high school quarterback. "It's nice to meet you, but forgive me for not being more prepared. I thought you weren't coming until the end of summer."

"Yeah, Dad, I thought you were on another top secret mission," Aiden said as he and Caden cuddled side by side with their father.

"Didn't Uncle Drew tell you?" Luke kept one arm around both his sons but was hugging the other close to his side, as though he were protecting something. And that was when Kylie noticed the outline of a large bandage under her brother-in-law's shirt. "My unit had to cut the operation short, and I've been reassigned to a new unit closer to town. Closer to my boys."

"Does that mean you're gonna live with us all the time now?" Caden's face showed nothing but excitement and wonder.

"That's exactly what I mean. We're going to be a real family. And this time, I'm going to be a better dad than ever before."

The boys whooped it up, and Kylie tried to paste her best pageant smile on her face. But she wanted to shout that no, Uncle Drew hadn't told any of them a damn thing. But she couldn't begrudge the kids their excitement or enthusiasm.

"Did you bring us any surprises?" one of the boys asked as they ran for the large canvas duffel bag propped up against the door.

She swiped at a small tear as it threatened to overflow from her eye. Her heart was tied in knots and her emotions were bouncing out of control. She was excited for the twins, who were ecstatic that their dad was home. Although she'd never met him before, she could only imagine what Luke must be feeling, getting to see his children again.

But at the same time, she couldn't help the growing premonition that Luke's arrival was going to change everything.

"Let's get settled, and I'll see if I can find something in this ol' bag that might interest you two." He rubbed the boys' curls as they walked inside.

Wait—was he staying here at the cabin with them? That earlier premonition grew to a dark cloud that threatened to rain on the brief happiness she'd so recently found with

Drew. Aiden and Caden deserved to have their family back together again.

Even if it meant she was going to lose her temporary one. Because if Luke was home for good, then Drew no longer had to take care of the twins. And if he didn't need her to help out with his nephews...

Then he wouldn't need her at all.

Chapter Eleven

Drew pulled up to the cabin after work and didn't see Kylie's new SUV. That was weird. She should've been home by now. He got out of the Jeep and heard squeals of laughter coming from inside the cabin.

Something was off. If the kids were here, where was his wife? He took the steps two at a time and then felt that weird tingle along his rib cage again.

Luke.

He knew his brother was there before he even saw the military-issue rucksack lying open on the living room floor. He made his way to the boys' bedroom and found all three of them wrestling on the floor.

"Have you been cleared for active duty?" Drew asked his impulsive brother, who should have known better than to roll around on the floor with a couple of eight-year-olds jumping on top of him. He was just a little over a week out of surgery.

"Saint Drew, I'm under fire down here, waiting for re-inforcements, and you want to stand there and give me a medical evaluation?"

"I'd prefer to give you a psych exam, but I fear I already know what the results would be. Where's Kylie?"

"She said she was going to Patrelli's to pick up some dinner for us. Should be back any minute. Now, are you gonna stand there worrying about that pretty cheerleader of yours or are you gonna rescue your twin brother from enemy attack?"

Drew smiled, relieved. She hadn't left him. At least, not yet. He took his glasses off and set them on the top bunk before making the sound of the cavalry charge and jumping into the fray.

It was only a few minutes later when he saw her standing in the doorway of the bunk room, holding a pizza box in one hand and her chest in the other. "Jeez, you guys scared the heck out of me. I heard all the screaming from outside and thought someone had the children tied up, torturing them."

She looked beautiful, but wary.

"More like the other way around," Luke said, slowly rising to his feet and rubbing his side. "When did you two kiddos get so tough?"

Drew followed suit, straightening his uniform. He should've known better than to encourage this kind of behavior. His brother had probably torn his stitches and could've done even more long-term damage.

"Here, can I help you with that?" he asked, walking toward her to take the pizza.

"Nope, I've got it."

She was doing that thing where she acted all poised and in control, but he could tell by her false smile that some-thing was definitely off.

"Okay, boys, let's go wash up for dinner," Drew said, then caught himself as he looked at his brother.

"You guys heard your uncle," Luke said, giving no indication that Drew had overstepped any boundaries.

The twins' real father was home now. Drew was no longer their parental figure. Nor was he the one cooking the meal. It didn't escape his notice that, as glad as he was to see Luke home safely, everything was slowly shifting. This must be what the Jenga tower sensed when it was just a couple wooden blocks shy of a possible collapse.

Everyone sat down at the table with its matching place settings, and the boys were quick to put their linen napkins in their laps.

They'd been married less than a month and already Kylie'd left her mark on the cabin, as well as on him and his nephews.

There was so much to say and yet, Drew and Kylie remained absurdly quiet.

Finally, Luke started off the dinner conversation. "Did your Uncle Drew tell you about the one time I had to save him?"

Drew flinched before looking at Kylie. The last thing he needed her thinking was that he was a hotheaded young punk who hadn't spent years in graduate school and countless hours practicing yoga to get his temper under lock and key. "Please don't tell this story right now."

"We want to hear!" the boys yelled at the same time.

He shot his brother a look, but Luke kept right on talking. "So I had just married your mom and you two were still in her tummy. Drew was on a ship that was temporarily docked in Ventura and he had a forty-eight hour leave. We decided to go to a Lakers game and had those great floor seats. Remember that, Drew? Anyway, there were a couple of young dudes sitting next to us, and they'd had way too much to drink. Drew was getting pretty annoyed with them—"

"Wait," Drew interrupted. "That's not exactly how I remember it. I believe you were the one getting annoyed with them, and I was being the calm voice of reason."

"Maybe. Anyway, they started making comments about Drew's uniform and how he looked like the Good Humor Man and trying to order a couple of cones from him." When Luke got to the part about ice cream, Kylie sat up straighter in her chair. "We were ignoring them for the most part, until they started doing the kissing cam up on the Jumbotron—you know, where they put the camera on couples and everyone cheers them on while they kiss?

"Well, the drunk guy grabbed one of the team dancers— see, I told you my brother likes pom-poms—and Drew didn't take too kindly to someone putting his hands on a female like that."

"So I stepped in and got him to release the lady. End of story." Drew passed out plates.

"Wait. Then how did Dad save you?"

"Your uncle neglected to mention that the way he got the guy to let go of the cheerleader was that he punched the guy so hard Drew broke his pinkie finger."

Kylie looked at him, and Drew couldn't tell if it was in surprise or disgust.

"So you fixed his finger?" Aiden asked.

"No. Uncle Drew's finger actually never healed right after that. The part where I came in to save the day was when they actually showed the fight on the Jumbotron. Drew was worried that his superior officers would find out and throw him the brig. So I called his commander and told him it was me on the Jumbotron."

Oh, of course when Drew looked like a raging maniac

during the story, his brother was completely fine with looking like the hero riding in to save the day.

"So, boys," Drew said, "the moral of the story is, don't lose your temper and get in a fight with someone, or it might get broadcast on ESPN later, and your brother could get in big trouble with his boss."

"But you were saving the cheerleader," Caden said.

All these years, Drew had seen the moment as him losing his cool and acting without thinking. Afterward, he'd immediately given up boxing, worried he was fostering a penchant toward fighting, and had taken up yoga as an alternate way to redirect his stress. Funny, but hearing an eight-year-old sum it up as an honorable act put things into a different perspective.

As they ate their pizza, Luke and the boys were laughing and telling stories, oblivious to Kylie's discomfort, or the fact that she'd barely touched her own food. Drew glanced from his brother to his wife and then back to his brother. He hadn't expected everything to change so soon, and he felt like a jerk for not having taken the time to explain everything to her. She was probably calculating the exact moment she could leave.

The second the boys pushed their plates away, full of pizza, she immediately stood up and started clearing the dishes.

"Here." Drew jumped up so quickly, he almost knocked the whole table over. "Let me get that. You don't need to wait on us."

"Oh." For a split second, she looked hurt. Or annoyed. But before he could get a good grasp on her expression, she pasted on a perfect fake pageant smile. "Well, in that case, I better be on my way."

"On your way where?" he asked, his voice sounding

a bit too edgy. He returned her phony smile, not wanting her to think he was being too clingy. Or worse, desperate.

"Um, back to my condo. I figure you guys all probably need some time to catch up and do more male bonding."

"What about Kane?"

"His doctor told him he's going to be out at least another season, and he's decided to stay in Sugar Falls a bit longer. He closed escrow on that old property out by Freckles's house and moved in there last week."

Why hadn't Kylie told him this before? Had she secretly been planning to move home all along?

"Hey, Dad," Caden said, completely unaware that his uncle's life was unraveling right before their eyes. "There's supposed to be a UFC match on TV tonight. We should watch it so you and Drew can learn some tips to take on me and Aiden."

Luke grabbed one kid under each arm to carry them over to the couch and turn on the television.

This was Drew's opportunity to stop Kylie, to talk her out of leaving. But it wasn't as if they could have a marital heart-to-heart conversation here in the testosterone-filled living room. And after that little dinnertime story, he figured she thought all the Gregson men were a bunch of fighting heathens. He took off his glasses and wiped them on the edge of his T-shirt.

"Maybe we should step outside so we can talk about things more," he suggested, but he didn't want to push her. He'd taken her dad's warning seriously and had seen firsthand how she reacted when someone tried to force her to do something she didn't want to do.

"What's there to talk about?" She was standing very stiff and tall, as if she was already prepared to do battle. Maybe he should just let her go home and call her in the morning. He was often telling his patients that they didn't have to make any big decisions overnight.

"I don't know. About us? About how—" he glanced over the trio gathered around the television "—things might be a little different now?"

"It's not as though anything has changed. I mean, we were all expecting this at some point, right? I guess we're all just off the hook sooner than expected." Then, still wearing that fake pageant smile, she turned and walked out the door without giving the boys their normal three-hug goodbye.

He longed to beg her to stop—but Drew had a feeling Kylie had already made her decision.

"I could tell he wanted to get me outside so he could give me my walking papers in private," Kylie told her friends, who had driven straight over to her lakefront condo when she'd called them, crying. "He was probably worried that the boys were already too attached to me and didn't want them to see me leaving. One minute he was rolling on the floor with his brother, playing like a couple of overgrown golden retrievers, and the next, he kept insisting he could do the dishes and I no longer had to wait on them. It was pretty clear the whole situation had changed and he didn't want me around. He might as well have been wearing a shirt that said Pseudo-Wives No Longer Needed."

"Don't you think you're being a little dramatic?" Maxine asked, opening a bag of potato chips and handing them to her. Normally Maxine was the one who needed the chips during times of stress. Right now, Kylie only wanted a gallon of ice cream.

"No, I think I'm being pragmatic," she said as she got off her Italian-leather sofa and went to her rarely used stainless steel Sub-Zero refrigerator to look inside the freezer. Empty. Kane must've taken her stash with him when he moved out this afternoon. "I'm looking at the facts and they all add up."

"What facts?" Mia reached into a brown paper bag and pulled out two cartons of macadamia-nut brittle. "Noodie's was closed so I picked up your favorite Häagen-Dazs on my way over. Anyway, it seems to me as if you've got no concrete proof. Just mere speculation."

"Fact one," Kylie said before prying the lid off with her teeth as she grabbed a spoon out of her utensil drawer. "He asked me to move in with him to help with the kids. Not because he wanted to give our marriage a shot. Fact two. We've been physically intimate for the past few weeks, yet he's never once told me that he wanted anything more out of our relationship."

"But you've been acting so much happier ever since Chuck Marconi's birthday party. I thought the plan worked."

She licked her spoon clean, then reached for the bag of chips. Maybe she needed both. "Well, not exactly. I mean, there were some things we resolved, but we never talked about the specifics or came to any kind of understanding."

"Then, what kind of understanding did you come to?" Mia asked.

"I bet I know exactly what kind." Maxine snickered, and Kylie threw a chip at her giggling friend. "Seriously, though, you thought you could just spend the whole summer with the guy, living together as man and wife, but having no real conversation about what either of you expected out of the relationship?"

"Not the whole summer. Actually, the boys had that camping trip this weekend, and I was kind of thinking that it would be a good opportunity for us to talk things out since we would finally have some time alone."

"Sounds as though you guys were using your alone time for other purposes. Hey, stop throwing those at me. You're wasting perfectly good chips."

"We've only had quick moments when we're able to get away and, well, we don't do so much talking when we're locked in the boat shed or the bedroom or the Nanamobile."

"Eww!" Mia covered her ears. "Not the Nanamobile!"

"Fact three," Kylie said louder as if that would get her brain, and her friends, back on track. "He never even told me that Luke was coming home early. Apparently he knew about it and didn't give me the slightest bit of warning."

"So you think he was purposely deceiving you?" Mia leaned forward, her antennae suddenly up.

"I don't know if *deceiving* is the right word. But he didn't tell me, which means he didn't want me to know. My guess is he sensed how attached I was getting to him and he wanted time to break the news to me gently. He was totally nervous when he asked me to step outside so we could talk about how 'things might be a little different now.'"

"I don't think you should've left," Maxine said.

Kylie finished the last spoonful of her pint of ice cream and moved on to the next container. "Fact four. He was in a long-term relationship with a woman and broke up with her when she started getting too serious about marriage."

"Did he say he wanted to break up?"

"Not in so many words. But he's too polite, and I've got too much pride to stick around and wait to be humiliated like that."

"Remember when we had to have that intervention with Maxine when she was all gaga over Cooper but wouldn't make a move? Kylie, I think it's time you started following your own advice."

"I did my best, you guys. That night, after the party, I threw caution to the wind and took a huge leap of faith." She pointed her spoon at them. "And look where that got me—all kinds of crazy in love with my husband, the man who is probably writing his own psych textbook about the calmest way to dump an unexpected wife. So you guys can give me all the suggestions in the world, but deep down, I'm a numbers person. Things need to add up for me. And right now nothing does—except all these calories and fat grams I'm inhaling."

"He's a man, Kylie, not a number. Sometimes, two plus two ends up equaling five."

"Well, now that Luke's home, it's definitely five of us. So it looks as if I'm the odd man out." She stood up and threw away both empty cartons. She looked in the brown grocery bag on the counter, but there was only a container of peanut butter and a package of graham crackers left in it. Apparently her friends didn't realize she was dealing with a gallon-size heartbreak.

She broke the seal on the peanut butter and opened up another bag of chips, then dipped them into the creamy spread.

"Uh-oh, this is way more serious than we thought," Mia said, reaching for her precious jar.

"Listen, Kylie," Maxine said as she confiscated the chips. "We love you and we support you. But you're jumping to conclusions. It's late, and you aren't going to fix this by hiding out in your condo and feeling sorry for yourself."

"Who says I'm feeling sorry for myself?"

"Now, that sounds more like our girl." Mia smiled. Her friends were right. She wasn't the type of woman to indulge in these kinds of pity parties. At least, not for more than one night.

She said goodbye to her friends, then drew herself a bubble bath as hot as she could stand it. It really was nice to be back in her oversize whirlpool tub, but she kind of missed the smell of green-apple kid shampoo and the eighteen army action figures the boys left lined up along the rim.

It had been only a couple of hours and already she was missing them something fierce. She sank deeper into the water until the foam reached under her chin, and tried to count the teeny-tiny bubbles, wishing she could be counting their hugs instead.

She should've stuck with the numbers all along. She'd known things with Drew weren't meant to last. She could blame the night in Reno on the booze, but she now needed to shoulder some responsibility for allowing herself to become too vulnerable. Although she'd dated plenty of men in the past, she'd never let any of them get close enough to break her heart.

Her dad had once told her that she'd never be able to settle down because she loved the thrill of the chase too much. But when she'd been with Drew this past month, she hadn't missed dating the least bit. In fact, she was suddenly determined not to go on another date until she was thirty-five. Love was too hard.

If she stayed single forever, then so be it. She had a goofy but loving family, supportive friends and a job she adored. She didn't need a man, and she certainly didn't need Andrew Gregson.

The problem was, no matter how many times her sensible brain said it, the fact remained that her heart wasn't listening.

* * *

When Drew woke up the following morning, he didn't even have to reach for Kylie's side of the bed to know she wasn't there. He'd had a hard enough time falling asleep last night. He'd kept picking up his cell phone to send her a text message. But what would he say?

"Please come back"?

He remembered when Jessica had told him it was over. He'd asked her to stay, to give him a few more months, promising he would know by then whether or not he would be ready to get married. She'd told him it wasn't fair for her to have to sit and wait for him to make up his mind. If he didn't know after five years of being together, then several weeks wasn't going to sway him. She'd also said it had been unfair of him to keep her waiting, wasting so much of her time just so he could get everything squared away in his calm and calculated mind.

It was then that he'd sworn not to get involved with a woman until he knew for sure she was perfect for him. And he definitely wasn't going to suggest Kylie stay in a relationship in which she wasn't mutually satisfied.

His alarm pinged, and he looked at his phone again. No missed calls or texts. He got dressed and headed out to the kitchen, meeting his brother along the way.

"I forgot how small those bunk beds were," Luke said, rubbing his bandaged side.

"Sorry. Considering you're still recovering, I should've offered you the master bedroom last night." He made a cup of coffee using Kylie's fancy high-tech brewer and wondered when she'd be coming to pick up this and the rest of her belongings.

"Nah, I wouldn't have accepted. I missed the kids and wanted to sleep in there with them. Besides, when your new wife comes home, I'm sure she's not gonna want to share the bunk room."

"That's the thing. I don't think she's coming home. Well, at least not to my home. I think she went back to her own life."

"And she gave up all this?" Luke gestured around the cabin, where several blankets and ropes were strung up across the living room as a makeshift wrestling ring. "Is it because I'm here?"

"No. Well, not entirely." Drew told his brother about the deal they'd struck and how Kylie had moved in here only to help with the boys and to get her parents and the local gossips off her back. "So my guess is that you coming home early let her off the hook, and now she's free to go back to her world."

"Your *guess*? She's a woman, Dr. Gregson, not a hypothesis. When are you going to stop scrutinizing every tiny facet of your life and start living it?"

His mother had said the same thing before he'd come to Sugar Falls. "Lately it seemed as if I was doing just that."

"So then do it again."

"It's not that simple."

"Crap, Drew. *You're* not that simple. Stop overthinking everything. It doesn't take a doctorate in psychology to see that you're crazy for her."

"Of course I'm crazy for her."

Which was true. Unlike in his last relationship, it had taken him no time at all to know for sure that Kylie was the woman he wanted to be with. Yet his stupid perfectionist mind made him wait too long in order to strategize the best way to tell her how he felt.

"Well, brother, you're the one who's supposed to know all the right words for sticky situations like these."

That was his problem. When it came to his wife, he never seemed to know the right thing to say.

Kylie looked at her partially empty closet and decided she needed to retrieve her belongings from the cabin. The best time would be when Drew was at work and the boys were off in the wilderness. But the boys didn't leave for their camping trip until tomorrow. She didn't want them to see her moving out, or to ask her any questions she didn't know how to answer.

Maybe she should wait and get her stuff this weekend, while they were gone. She had plenty of clothes and shoes to last her until then, but she didn't have any groceries. She didn't need to meet with any clients today, so she pulled out the first thing she found in her dresser drawer and threw it on before heading out to the Cowgirl Up Café for breakfast.

"Oh, no," Mia said as she sat down next to Kylie at the café's long counter. "It's worse than I thought."

"What's worse?" she replied as Freckles set a piece of huckleberry pie à la mode in front of her.

"Honey, it's a workday, and you're wearing loose-fitting jeans and ballet flats. And is that your dad's Hawaiian-print shirt?"

"So?" Kylie spooned the ice cream into her mouth, not really interested in the other part of the dessert, which she'd ordered only because it was too early in the day to ask for a hot-fudge sundae. At least this gave the appearance of eating a morning pastry.

Mia took away the plate of ice cream and asked Freckles to bring them each a veggie omelet and wheat toast. "So you're clearly not acting...or dressing like yourself."

"Fine." She took the two loose ends of the shirt and secured them into a tight knot, baring her midriff, which was currently in danger of poufing out from too much ice cream.

"Better," her friend said after rolling up the cuffs of her jeans for her. "If people think you don't care about your appearance, they'll know something is wrong between you and Drew."

"Everyone is going to find out anyway when they see that my husband kicked me out."

Freckles put their omelets on the counter. "Darlin', if I was your hunky husband, I'd kick you out, too, for dressing all dowdy like that."

"This isn't dowdy." Kylie started to defend herself, then looked at Freckles's teased hair and low V-neck shirt. Compared to the waitress, everyone dressed a bit more muted. "And I would appreciate it if you didn't announce to the rest of the restaurant that Drew and I are...ah...on sabbatical from each other."

"Hmm. Sabbatical, huh?" Freckles tapped a long fingernail on her chin. "I ain't never heard that one. Anyway, people will figure it out soon enough if you go around town dressed like a bowling team reject and eating up all my ice cream. By the way, your daddy would have himself a conniption fit if he saw you in that getup."

"Are you kidding? Dad has been begging me to dress like this my entire life. Maybe I should've played baseball and listened to him all along. Clearly he was right, and I'm not cut out for married life."

Freckles almost dropped her orange juice carafe, she was laughing so hard. The sudden attention and unwelcome stares caused Mia to squirm in her seat, and Kylie reached across the table to tug on the waitress's leopard-print apron.

"Hey, keep it down. And what's so funny anyway?"

"You are, thinking that your dad would want you any

less feminine than you've always been. Now, I've only met the man a handful of times, but I've seen most of his games. The guy is a world-class dominator on that pitching mound. You don't get that good by not being able to size up your opponents and forcing them to swing for the fences when they should be bunting the dang ball. The few times I've seen you with your old man, it was pretty clear what he was doing."

"What are you saying?"

Mia held her fork in the air, looking sideways at Kylie. "You mean, you never realized it?"

Suddenly, scenes from her childhood began clicking into place, and she was swiftly seeing things in a different light. No wonder her dad always gave in to her demands so easily. They were his ideas in the first place. If she hadn't loved the man so stinking much, she would have been fuming.

"Darlin', seeing as how you're married to a professional head doctor, I would've thought you understood all about reverse psychology."

"Did you catch on to it, too?" Kylie asked her friend.

Mia nodded. "I had my suspicions way back in college. We were all staying at your house for Christmas break once, and you lost your temper with him when he told you he thought you should be an airline pilot or an oil-rig engineer so you could live life in the fast lane and see the world. You know I love you, but sometimes you can get all fired up when people try to tell you what you should and shouldn't do. When you came back downstairs and announced you were going to become an accountant, he waited until you walked out of the room before smiling that big grin of his and telling your mom that at least you would have a career that settles you down and keeps you grounded."

"Of all the manipulative, underhanded, conniving…"

Freckles interrupted her tirade. "Can you blame the man for wanting what he thought was best for his only daughter? He loves you. And when he requested that song for you and Dr. Gregson at Maxine and Cooper's reception, I've never seen a father more content."

"That was *him*?"

Just then, the minihorseshoe wind chimes dinged above the café door, and her husband's twin walked in with his sons.

"Aunt Kylie," the boys yelled in unison before running toward her.

"Are we going to another costume party?" Aiden asked. "Is that why you're wearing that ugly outfit?"

Okay, really, it was not that bad. She thought people would have preferred her dressing like this.

She greeted Luke, then introduced him.

"I haven't had biscuits and gravy in longer than I can remember." He smiled his most charming smile at Freckles. "So I thought I'd bring the boys out for breakfast."

"Well, if your brother thought he could send you in here to smooth talk me out of my secret recipe, he's got another think coming. Tell him he'll have to keep bringing me back to teach at those therapy sessions if he wants to learn how to make my gravy."

Luke laughed, but as much as he resembled his twin, Kylie's heart didn't do cartwheels like it did when Drew smiled. "Kids, go find us a good table and look at the menu. I want to talk to your aunt for a sec."

"Well, I'm late for dance class." Mia stood abruptly and was out the door before Kylie could yell *traitor*.

Freckles picked up a coffeepot and moved on to another table, also abandoning her. Kylie squared her shoulders, waiting for the other cleat, or in this case, combat

boot, to drop. She'd already found out that her dad had
been bamboozling her this whole time. What else was she
about to learn?

"You took off so quickly last night, I never did get a
chance to thank you for stepping up to the plate and helping out with my children this summer."

Oh, was that all this was about? She leaned back on
her counter stool. "Please. No thanks are necessary. The
boys are adorable, and I loved spending time with them."

"What about their uncle?"

"What about him?"

"Do you think he's adorable? Did you enjoy spending
time with him, too?"

She bit her lip, wondering what his purpose was in asking her such an intimate question.

"Because I'm hoping you did. I don't know if you've
noticed, but Drew can be a little straitlaced."

She took a sip of her juice. "Yeah, I kind of *did* notice that."

"He's a great listener, but he's never been the type to
open up about his feelings. He doesn't usually get emotionally invested in people until he has mentally examined
the relationship from all angles."

"So what does this have to do with me?"

"Because with you, he's not really himself. Which isn't
necessarily a bad thing. I was hoping that maybe you could
be a voice of reason for him, because I don't want to see
him lose a good thing."

Was this guy talking in code to her? "A voice of reason? About what?"

"Jeez, infiltrating an enemy camp under heavy fire is
easier than communicating with either of you two. Look,
you're an accountant, right?"

"Yes."

"Then, let me break it down for you like this." He motioned to Freckles to bring him a pen, and then wrote an equation down on her paper napkin. "KYLIE + DREW = A GOOD THING."

She read the words, and her heart did another cartwheel. But how could her brother-in-law be so sure? "Did he tell you that?"

"He didn't have to."

"But you said he's doesn't open up about his feelings. If he's that hard to read, then how do you know?"

"Oh, he's not that hard for *me* to read. I'm his twin, remember? Anyway, I just wanted to let you know that I'm going to go on that camping trip with the boys tomorrow, and Drew is going to be home at the cabin, stewing in his own misery. Alone."

He picked up a slice of her wheat toast before standing up and giving her one last piece of advice. "But when you stop by to talk some sense into him, maybe don't wear that outfit."

Chapter Twelve

There was no point in Kylie staring at her home computer screen any longer. She hadn't been able to concentrate on any figures this morning. She was tempted to drive into town for another pint of ice cream, but she'd had enough wallowing in misery. Plus, yesterday, the staff at Noodie's asked her if they could take her picture for their Customer Wall of Fame.

She needed to fix this Drew situation, but she couldn't let her impulsiveness get her in trouble again.

Kylie waited until she was positive the wilderness-adventure crew had departed before she even let herself think of going to the cabin uninvited.

But it wasn't as though she needed an invitation. After all, half of the contents of her closet were still there—along with her heart.

She hated variables and uncertainties.

Wait. Why was she hanging back, doing all the wondering? It wasn't like her to sit by meekly and allow someone else to decide her fate. If he wasn't at the cabin when she showed up, then she would sit in her car and wait until he got home and confront him. She wanted some definite answers, even if she didn't like what he had to tell her, and she wasn't going to let her temper or her pride get in the way of finding out for certain.

She wouldn't file a tax report without having all the necessary receipts and documentation. So why wouldn't she run an emotional expense report on her marriage before making a determination of its net worth?

She was going to lay her heart out and demand he do the same. And if their feelings didn't add up, then she could go her own way knowing that she'd solved the problem to the best of her ability and hadn't made any incorrect assumptions or jumped to any wrong conclusions.

She pulled out her highest heels and her reddest dress from her walk-in closet, arming herself to conduct the most serious audit of her life. Thank goodness her father had tricked her into becoming a girlie accountant.

Drew had just dropped Luke and the boys off for their camping trip, but within five minutes of entering the too-quiet cabin, he couldn't take the solitude.

He was dying to see Kylie and was damn tired of being the patient and rational one. He needed to tell her how he felt. If she laughed in his face or gave him the brush-off, then so be it. At least he could say he'd tried. He'd already put her in enough compromising positions that one more wasn't going to hurt.

He was halfway out the front door when she pulled up in her new SUV, the one she'd bought to make all of their lives easier.

How could he not love a woman who would make those

kinds of sacrifices for children who weren't her own? His surprise at seeing her caused him to freeze in the doorway. He should've expected her to beat him to the punch, but maybe she was here for another reason—like to pick up her skimpy pajama bottoms and her gardenia body lotion. Well, if that was the case, she was about to get a lot more than that. No more analyzing. He was going to tell her every single thing he'd been thinking since he met her that night in Reno.

"You're beautiful," he said the moment she stepped out of her vehicle, holding herself like the Amazon queen he admired. She really did look gorgeous, but then again, she always did, since the first moment he'd seen her.

She looked startled. "What?"

"I said you're beautiful. I've been meaning to tell you that for a long time, but every time I got the chance, I ended up blowing things by rushing you into bed."

She approached him a bit unsteadily. Maybe it was the heels. "You didn't rush me…"

"No, wait," he interrupted, not wanting to revert to his usual role of listener. "Let me say what I've been bottling up this whole time. I love you, Kylie, and I don't want you to move out just because Luke is back. The boys still need you. More important, I still need you. I think my subconscious has known it since that night we got married. When you're around, I'm not my usual boring uptight self. I feel passion and excitement—as if nothing else matters but us being together. When you left the other night, I wanted to beg you not to go."

Her steps slowed, as if he'd thrown her off stride. "Then, why didn't you?"

He stepped off the front porch, finally moving closer to her. "I wanted you to make that decision on your own. I know what it feels like to be unsure about a relationship and have someone try to pin you down and force you to make a choice. I knew that if I tried to make you do something you didn't want to do, it'd blow up in my face."

Her shoulders relaxed slightly. Hey, maybe this saying-whatever-was-on-his-mind thing was actually working. "Why didn't you tell me your brother was coming home?"

"Because I didn't realize it would be so soon. I promise I wasn't trying to hide anything from you. I just needed—wanted—more time to figure out a way to convince you to stay."

"And you didn't think about simply asking me?"

"I thought of a hundred different ways to ask you. But every time I had a chance, something else would come up. Even right this second, it's taking every fragment of self-control I can muster not to take you in my arms and show you exactly what you mean to me."

She smiled, and it nearly undid him.

"So let me make sure I've got all of this straight," she said. "You love me?"

"Yes."

"And you want to stay married to me, even though you no longer have to take care of the kids."

"Yes. However, we would still need to watch the twins for Luke when he goes out of town for training or recruiting assignments."

"So we would still live here, all together in the cabin?"

He could see her mathematical mind running the details, making sure everything added up. So far, she hadn't said no. Why hadn't he just told her all of this in the beginning? He closed the distance between them. "What are you thinking?"

"Fact one. I love you, too," she said. He closed his eyes, letting her sweet words sink in. "Fact two. The thought of no longer being married to you breaks my heart so badly,

Noodie's Ice Cream Shoppe would have to open a second location to handle my orders alone. Fact three. I'm kind of getting used to this aunt gig and wouldn't mind spending more time with your family. And taking care of the twins any chance we get."

What? No. She couldn't actually mean she wanted to live permanently with his brother and nephews. He stroked her cheek, letting his other hand graze her waist. The nearer he got to her, the more his rational thought process diminished. Which was the only explanation he could muster for why he was about to resort to unconventional tactics.

"Hmm. I was thinking living here would probably be easiest for you. I mean, you wouldn't want me moving into your private lakefront condo. It would be too peaceful, too romantic."

"Saint Drew, are you trying to use reverse psychology on me?"

"Well, your dad told me it would work."

Kylie rolled her eyes. "Don't even get me started on that man. I've got years of grief to get back at him for."

Drew laughed and gave in to his urge to pull her into his arms. "Let me know if you need any help planning your psychological warfare. Remember, we're in this together."

She wrapped her arms around his neck and he pressed his lips to hers, finally sealing their words with a kiss.

* * * * *

ONE NIGHT WITH
THE BEST MAN

AMANDA BERRY

To my husband and children,
Thank you for helping me follow my dream.

Chapter One

"How's the bride?" Penny Montgomery stepped into the church dressing room, where her best friend since childhood, Maggie Brown, was getting ready to walk down the aisle. This church, one of five in the small town of Tawnee Valley, was the one Maggie's mother had dragged Maggie and Penny to when they were growing up.

"Nervous. Excited. Trying to remember to breathe." Maggie hadn't stopped smiling. Her gown was lovely and simple. Classically A-lined styled with no train. Her light hair was pulled up in a loose knot with tendrils left to play around her neck. She looked stunning and had the truest heart of anyone Penny had ever known.

"You look beautiful," Penny said. "Your mother would have loved to see you like this."

Maggie nodded. Tears sparkled in her eyes but they didn't fall. For years, Penny and Maggie had been each other's rock. Now Maggie had found her dream man and was forming a family. Penny had Maggie and that was enough family for her.

"Mom would be happy."

A lump formed in Penny's throat and she coughed to clear it. "Brady wanted me to give you this."

She held out the little gift-wrapped box.

"Thank you, Penny." Maggie held on to Penny's hand. "I mean it. For everything. For being with me when everything was so hard and for nudging me in the right direction when I needed a shove."

"What are best friends for?" Careful of her long slip dress, Penny stepped back and sat on the antique couch. The pale gold silk gown slid against her skin.

She ran a finger over the worn velvet of the couch. If it were refinished it might fetch a nice price in What Goes Around Comes Around, her antiques store, but it suited the old chapel the way it was. Years of wear from weddings to funerals to christenings had made this couch unique. The story behind antiques always made them more valuable in Penny's eyes.

"Well," Penny prompted, needing to lighten the mood. "Open the gift. I bet it's a ring. Probably the kind that vibrates. You know, the kind that goes on his—"

"Penny!" Maggie was too serious for her own good sometimes. Penny just smiled and shrugged. She hoped that she helped to corrupt her friend just a little.

"Just because that would be something *you'd* like for a gift…" Maggie took off the ribbon and opened the box. She drew out two diamond drop earrings. "Oh, my."

"Looks like someone is making up for lost time." Penny smiled, kicked off her heels and drew her already-aching feet under her. The devil himself had made those heels, but she wouldn't tell Maggie that.

"Brady being here now is all that matters." The light caught in the facets of the diamonds and burst into tiny dancing lights around the room. "They are so lovely."

"I'm so happy for you." And Penny meant it. If anyone deserved a happy ending, it was Maggie.

Penny wasn't made for marriage. Whenever she wanted a man, all she had to do was go out and find one. The clubs were only an hour away in Springfield. And if she just wanted to stay warm at night, Flicker, her new shaggy puppy, could help her out.

Maggie put the earrings on and turned to face Penny. "How do I look?"

"Like you are in love. Glowing. When Brady sees you, he's going to be the happiest man in the world." Maggie's bliss was contagious. It radiated from her like the brightest star. Maggie had made it through all the suffering and losing her mom.

After a moment, Maggie gave Penny a worried-momma look. "Luke made it in last night."

"Great." Penny gave Maggie a grin, even though her heart beat a little heavier. "It would look a little weird if I didn't have a best man to walk me down the aisle. Plus he's going to be part of your family soon."

"Are you sure you are okay with this?"

Penny took a deep breath and gave Maggie a reassuring look. "It was nine years ago, Maggie. Teenage puppy love. I'm sure he's over it by now. I am."

"So no drama?" Maggie raised her eyebrow.

"If there's drama, I won't be the cause of it." Penny uncurled from the couch and stood, shaking any wrinkles out of the floor-length gown. The energy levels in her body had suddenly surged and she couldn't sit anymore. Suppressing a whimper, she shoved her feet back in her shoes. She nervously checked the mirror. Her makeup hadn't smeared. Her red hair had been pulled into a tight bun, and at least one can of hair spray had plastered it into place. With the extra few inches the heels provided, she'd at least be able to look Luke Ward in the chin after all these years.

The noise level in the hallway picked up. Someone knocked on the door.

"Five minutes, ladies." The door muffled an older woman's voice beyond recognition.

"He's not seeing anyone," Maggie continued. She picked up her veil and worked the comb into her hair.

"Too bad for him, I guess." Penny held the end of the veil and straightened it to keep busy. "Seriously, Maggie, I'll be okay. Luke is here for one weekend. The worst thing that could happen is that I'll step on his foot during the bridal party dance with these fabulous heels and he'll have to bandage himself up."

"If you're sure…" Maggie didn't sound as if she believed Penny.

"I'm sure that if we don't get out there soon, the groom will think you ran away." Penny picked up the bridal bouquet and handed it to Maggie. "You worry about walking down that aisle and not about me."

Penny gave Maggie a once-over before picking up her own flowers. The last thing her friend should be worried about today was what would happen when Luke and Penny were in the same room for the first time since she had driven him away.

It was not as if they had the type of love that would last forever. Teenage love never did. First loves never did.

Luke had been heading off to college, and she'd barely earned the grades to graduate high school. If it weren't for What Goes Around Comes Around, the only work Penny would be qualified for was as either a gas station attendant or a fast-food worker. When she had inherited the quaint store along Main Street from her grandmother, it had been bleeding money, but the shop meant too much to Penny to let it fail. After her grandmother died, she had no family left to rely on. Her father had been a no-show since she was born, and her mother had ditched her years ago to continue boozing without a child in tow. But Penny was an adult now. She had managed to turn the shop around and make it a tourist attraction in their little one-stoplight town.

Through it all, she'd always had Maggie's support. Maggie and her daughter, Amber, were her family, and she wouldn't dream of making a fuss on one of the happiest days of Maggie's life. Even if that meant putting up with Brady Ward's younger brother.

The moment she stepped into the hallway, she saw him.

Luke stood about a dozen feet in front of her. The air around her crackled with energy. Dark hair, blue eyes, towering height, these were all features shared by the Ward brothers. Luke wasn't as tall as Sam, the oldest brother, but he still towered over her even in her three-inch heels. The lankiness of high school was gone, replaced by a filled-out but trim figure his tuxedo suited just fine. His dark hair curled slightly at the ends, where it touched his collar. If this were any other man, Penny would be placing bets that she would have him in her bed before the night was over.

But this was her Luke. At least he had been hers. Behind the bleachers, in the backseat of her car, in the field on a blanket looking up into a night sky that seemed to go on forever. They'd made promises neither of them were old enough to keep. Things had seemed so clear to her then. He loved her. He'd promised forever, but she knew forever was just a word. Love didn't matter. Back then it had been only a matter of time. And when—not if—he had left her, she would have been the one picking up the pieces. She straightened her shoulders and loosened the death grip on her flowers.

Plastering a smile on her face, she stepped forward.

"Penny!" Amber's voice burst out from behind Luke and the speeding golden bullet of eight-year-old energy raced toward her. "Penny! Penny! You have to meet my uncle Luke. I have two uncles now. And he's a doctor."

Penny was powerless as Amber grabbed her hand and dragged her toward Luke. Not exactly the image she'd wanted to project, but Amber didn't wait for graceful entrances.

"Amber, I've met your uncle Luke. We went to school together." Penny managed to not fall off her heels as Amber stopped in front of Luke.

"She's got quite the grip, doesn't she?" Luke smiled down at Amber as Penny tried to compose herself.

Amber spotted Maggie and took off in the direction of her mother.

"You should see her with my puppy, Flicker." Penny held her breath as Luke's gaze floated over her dress up to her face. She wasn't eighteen anymore. What if he didn't like what he saw?

Nonsense. She never let a man make her feel insecure.

Luke finally met her eyes. "I'm supposed to walk you down the aisle."

Her world was lost in a sea of blue, so rich and inviting that if she could, she would strip naked and dive into their warm depths. Warmth soaked through her body and her knees felt loose in their sockets.

She shook herself out of his spell and managed a smile that didn't feel entirely plastic. "Yes, you are."

"Or from the looks of those heels, keep you from falling on your ass?" That mischievous twinkle she'd always loved lit in his eyes.

"Oh, these little things?" Penny lifted her shoe to contemplate it.

Apparently the past was where it belonged: in the past. She smiled easier. Luke hadn't changed much since high school, but his shoulders seemed less tight. Maybe he'd finally learned to let things go. When she'd first noticed him as more than just another classmate, he'd been filled with anger and grief after the death of his parents. She knew what it was like to be left by the ones you loved. And even though his parents hadn't meant to leave, the pain he'd felt had seemed close to her own.

"Looks like we'll be spending most of the evening together," Luke said.

Penny blinked up at him as her stomach gave a little flip of joy at the remembrance of nights spent in his arms. Hot nights in the back of her beat-up Chevy. They'd laughed and forgotten about the rest of Tawnee Valley while they lost themselves in exploring each other. Fogged windows. Naked skin to naked skin. His hands and mouth had made her forget how to breathe.

"I'm the best man," he said, slowly. "And you're the maid of honor…."

"Of course." She tried to laugh it off, but it came out stilted as she tried to control the heat bubbling within her. "I'd hate to keep you from your date, though."

"I didn't bring one."

"She couldn't make it?" Penny fished just a little, knowing that if there was a *she,* Penny needed to shut down this attraction. She didn't mess with taken men.

"There isn't a she." He looked over her shoulder briefly before returning his gaze to her eyes. "What about your date? Won't it make him jealous that I'll have you in my arms most of the night?"

"If he existed, it probably would." The men she hooked up with were always free agents and never more than that. "I guess that means I'm yours tonight."

His dark eyebrow lifted as if his train of thought had just arrived at the same station. A spark of awareness raced down her spine.

"If everyone could line up," Beatrice Miller called out in her singsong voice. The kindergarten teacher helped out at the church for the wedding coordinator. She treated every wedding party like a group of five-year-olds who needed to get in line and wait patiently for their turn. Many of them had had her as a teacher, so it wasn't hard for her to rein them in.

Luke held out his elbow, and Penny hesitated for only a moment before slipping her hand over his jacketed arm. They were to be the first down the aisle.

"Mom and Dad should be here," Luke said so softly that she almost missed it.

Her fingers squeezed his arm and she leaned against him. "Yes."

As they stood by the door waiting for the procession music to begin, the crisp, clean scent of Luke wafted over her. He pulled her in tightly to his side. His warmth penetrated her silk dress. He was as solid next to her as he'd always been. Almost as much a safe haven to her as her grandmother's antiques store had been when she was young. Had he stayed in Tawnee Valley, would things have been different for them?

The doors to the chapel opened, and Penny straightened and put on her smile. This was Maggie's day. The past was gone. Only right now mattered. The entire town had turned out for the wedding. And they were all looking at her walking arm in arm with Luke Ward.

She could almost see the matchmaking gears in ole Bitsy Clemons's head turning on overload. Bitsy had brought every eligible man in Tawnee Valley to Penny's store. As if Penny would die if she didn't marry soon.

It was bad enough to be walking down the aisle with an ex, but to do so in front of everyone who had known how hot and heavy they had been...

They made it to the preacher and split ways. As Luke went to the other side of Brady, she turned and their eyes met. She saw a hint of humor and speculation in those eyes. She could definitely lose herself in him for a night or two. After all, he could only improve with age.

Amber started down the aisle and tossed wildflowers on the path before her. When she reached the front, she turned and sat in the pew next to Sam Ward.

The music changed and the doors reopened to reveal the bride. The congregation stood as she walked slowly down the aisle with a smile filled with such love that Penny couldn't stop the tears that sprang to her eyes.

As she reached the wedding party, Maggie passed her bouquet to Penny to hold and took Brady's hands.

Brady looked as if he'd just been handed the most precious gift in the world. It hit something inside of Penny, and she had to look away. Luke came into sharp focus.

Years ago, she'd thrown away what they had together, but she'd never forgotten. Every man she had been with, she compared to him, never truly letting him go. Once tomorrow came, she'd have to let him go again, but to-night was filled with potential.

Chapter Two

"Thought you were going to miss it," Sam said.

Luke raised an eyebrow but continued to stare out the truck window. "I was called to scrub in on a last-minute surgery."

Sam grunted. "Family's not that important."

If the reception had been any closer to the chapel, Luke would have walked rather than get in the truck with his oldest brother. Sam had helped raise him after their father died when Luke was fourteen. Two years later, their mother had succumbed to cancer and Brady had gone off to college, leaving only Luke and Sam.

"Of course family is important." Luke flicked a piece of lint from his tux sleeve. "Which is why I'm here today. When it matters."

Sam gave a noncommittal sound as he pulled into the parking lot of the Knights of Columbus. The hall was a standard block construction on the outside. It might not be big-city classy, but Tawnee Valley didn't offer much else in the way of reception halls.

The parking lot was already filled with trucks and cars. As soon as Luke stepped out of the truck, he could hear the music floating out of the double doors that were outlined with a pretty trellis of flowers.

"I don't know why Brady didn't just have the wedding in New York," Luke mumbled.

"Because the people in this town are as much his family as we are." Sam walked past and into the banquet room.

Luke followed him in and actually did a double take. If he hadn't just driven up to the concrete building, he would believe that he'd been dropped into a grand ballroom inside a five-star hotel. The stage had had a face-lift since the last time Luke had been here, which had to have been almost five years ago. One of his high school friends had his wedding reception here, but it had been a potluck with lots of balloons, not an elegant buffet with waiters bringing guests drinks and appetizers. The room was decorated to rival the most elegant of ballrooms, down to the artful arrangements of wildflowers on every table.

"Kind of blows your mind, doesn't it?" Penny appeared at his side.

"Definitely." Just as she did. His pulse quickened. Penny hadn't been at that wedding years ago, and they'd managed to avoid each other the few times he'd been back since their breakup. This was the first time they'd seen each other in nine years.

"Brady arranged most of it, but Maggie had the final say." Penny was every bit as attractive as he remembered, from her coppery-red hair to her brown eyes to a body with curves in all the right places to her full lips that begged for his kiss. "Come on. I'll show you the table and give you a quick walk-through of what you missed last night."

Her fingers threaded through his as she pulled him forward into the crowd. The heat of her worked its way from their entwined fingers to the center of him. Her gold dress seemed like more of a long negligee made of slightly thicker material. His fingers itched to run over her silk-covered flesh.

"The DJ is one of the best in the industry."

Luke followed her gaze to the DJ table. "Wyatt Graham?" Wyatt had graduated high school a few years after them.

Penny smiled and winked. "The local industry isn't that diverse. He'll be playing a mix of modern and oldies. We'll be required to dance together at the end of the bridal dance and for the next few dances after that."

As Luke glanced around, he noticed more familiar faces—from the waitstaff to the cooks in the opening to the kitchen. All local people, from either Tawnee Valley or the neighboring city of Owen.

"Brady could have flown the whole town to New York for what this cost."

"That wasn't the point." Penny pulled him behind a large curtain thing that gave the room its illusion of class, and leaned against the old paneled walls of the hall. The scent of musty wood overwhelmed the small space. The lighting barely filtered through the curtain. It even deadened the low roar of the crowd and the soft music playing in the background. Everyone disappeared. It was just the two of them. His imagination went wild with possibilities, but he reined them all in.

He opened his mouth.

Penny put her fingers over his lips. "Just because

you are a hotshot doc from the city doesn't mean that everything should happen in the city. Brady wanted to give the people around here a chance to be part of the wedding. It was important to both of them, so not another word about anywhere else but here."

The dim light caught and danced devilishly in her brown eyes. Her fingers were warm against his lips. They stood close together. It would take only a second to pull her into his arms and claim a kiss. He let out a breath across her fingers. Her breathing hitched, but she didn't pull away.

"Now." She sounded breathless, and his body reacted. "Do I have your promise to behave?"

The wicked glint in her eyes made her request comical.

"Do you want me to behave?" His words caressed her fingers.

He felt the tremor ripple through her. Her lips curled up in an invitation.

The music in the room suddenly changed and Penny's eyes widened. "Oh, crap, it's the entrance music."

She grabbed his hand once again and pulled him out into the open. It had been so easy to forget about the whole wedding reception happening beyond the curtain. He was half tempted to pull her back and forget about the party altogether.

Maggie and Brady walked into the hall and the crowd burst into applause.

"Brady looks happy." Luke couldn't contain that little bit of skepticism from his voice. Luke's memories of Brady were tainted with the death of his parents and the iron rule of his brother. Brady had been one of the reasons he'd finally calmed down enough to graduate high school. Penny had been the other reason.

"He should be." She leaned against his arm. "She's happy."

A wistfulness he could have imagined had entered her voice.

Luke became aware that Penny was still holding his hand while they stood watching the couple work their way through the crowd. "Are you happy?"

She gave him a mischievous smile and squeezed his hand. "I could be happier."

The suggestion was far from discreet. If it were any other time and any other woman, he might have walked away from her right then. He didn't play games. His career was his primary focus and it didn't leave time for anything else.

But tonight was his brother's wedding in his hometown, and he was standing next to the girl who had rocked his world as a teenager before she ripped his heart out and threw it back in his face. Tomorrow he'd be on a flight to St. Louis to continue his residency and Penny would return to his past, where she belonged.

"I could always tell when you were overthinking something." Penny's finger reached up and traced a line between his eyebrows. "You know that's going to form a wrinkle if you keep doing it, right?"

"So you're saying I shouldn't think?" Luke tried to read her facial expressions, but Penny had always been careful to mask what she was really feeling. He'd thought he had been behind her wall once, but he knew better now.

"Thinking is highly overrated." Penny winked at him. "We need to go to the table now. Do you think you can turn off that mega-powered brain of yours for the evening and just enjoy?"

Did she mean that he should enjoy her again? Or

was it just wishful thinking on his part? One thing was certain—he wouldn't make himself a fool for Penny this time. "I'll try."

Penny sat between Maggie and Amber, and Luke sat on the other side of Brady next to Sam at the hour-long gourmet dinner. Penny wanted to continue flirting with Luke during the meal, but it was fun talking with Amber and teasing Maggie. Her wineglass never seemed to empty and she lost track of how much she'd actually had. She felt a bit tipsy but not drunk. With her family history, she tried to be careful with alcohol.

When Maggie, Amber and Brady got up to go visit guests at their tables, Penny scooted over into Maggie's chair and leaned across Brady's.

"Having fun yet?" She batted her eyelashes at Luke in mock flirtation.

"I can say the view definitely just got better." Luke's gaze rested on her cleavage and her gaping neckline.

She didn't make any move to cover herself or even to sit up straight. "Do you have your toast ready?"

He patted his jacket. "Color-coded index cards and all."

"You really know how to get a girl's motor going." She purred and moved back to her seat. She straightened the top of her dress and winked at the elderly man sitting at the table in front of the head table. He blushed and turned away.

Penny and the town of Tawnee Valley hadn't always been on the best terms. As one of the juvenile delinquents most likely to be pregnant at sixteen and most likely to have an arrest record by the age of twenty, she'd surprised them all with the success of her store.

But that didn't mean she didn't enjoy poking at the town's notions of propriety now and then.

The wedding coordinator, Rebecca, directed Maggie and Brady over to the cake. Rebecca had performed miracles to turn this old men's club into a ballroom worthy of Maggie. Given it was the woman's first time coordinating an effort this big, she had done an amazing job. Penny was impressed with the transformation of the hall, and even the chapel had been given an overhaul.

Everyone watched Brady and Maggie cut the cake while the photographer took at least a dozen photos. When they gave each other bites, they were respectful of each other and didn't goof around as Penny would have.

The couple returned to their seats as the waitstaff brought everyone a piece of cake and poured champagne into their flutes. Down the table, Luke picked up his spoon and clinked it against his glass as he rose to standing.

"I'd like to say a few words." Luke reached into his pocket and pulled out a stack of index cards. He glanced her way slyly as he fanned through the colored cards.

Penny stifled a laugh. She'd thought he'd been joking.

"I could tell you lewd jokes or make fun of my brother for the way he used to run around the farm in his underwear and a cape when he was seven, but I won't. I could talk about the fights we three used to get into and the trouble we helped each other out of, but I won't. I could tell you about Brady's adventures overseas or his high life in New York City, but I won't." Luke set the cards on the table and his gaze went over the crowded room.

Penny found herself leaning forward to listen to

whatever he was going to say next. When Luke spoke, even back in grade school, he commanded his audience's attention. He made sure to meet everyone's eyes in the audience to make them feel included. His even tone and that deep voice kept her mesmerized. His raw emotion and honesty bonded him with the audience.

His gaze briefly met hers before settling on Brady and Maggie.

"Everyone in this room is aware of the struggles our family has had to endure. We didn't always make the right decisions, but in the end, it looks like Brady found the one thing that matters most. Someone who loves him and wants to share a life with him. A hidden treasure waiting for him to come home."

Penny could feel a thickening in her throat and blinked to hold the tears back.

"We brothers have lost so much, but Brady has finally found his family. Here's to many years of shared joy and love. To Maggie and Brady."

The crowd repeated, "To Maggie and Brady."

A pause lingered while everyone took a drink. Penny met Luke's eyes over the rim of her glass. As the crowd applauded the speech, Penny smiled at Luke before standing.

She waited for the noise to die down and then cleared her throat. "I may not be as eloquent as our doctor, but I'll give it my best shot."

She turned to Maggie. "When I was a little girl, there was one place I always knew I'd be welcome. Maggie has been my best friend, my confidante, my family for as long as I can remember. She's always been there for me and I've always tried to be there for her."

Maggie reached out, took Penny's hand and gave it a

gentle squeeze. They both had the battle scars on their hearts to prove their long-standing friendship.

"If anyone is capable of loving forever, it's Maggie, and I know I'm not the only one in the room thinking that Brady is the luckiest man alive." Still holding Maggie's hand, Penny looked at Brady. "There aren't many people I would trust with my best friend's heart, but I trust you to keep it safe and to love her until you are old and gray and need to yell at each other to be heard. I love you both and wish you happiness."

Clearing her throat, Penny blinked back the tears that had snuck up on her again. She turned to Amber. "Amber made me promise to wish you one more thing." She held up her glass and gave a grin to the rest of the hall. "To a wonderful family, and may they be blessed with a little brother or sister for Amber."

The crowd chuckled as they clinked glasses once more. Penny sank into her seat and took a drink. The DJ put on some background music and the low din of conversations grew again. Maggie and Brady were lost in their own little world. Amber had wandered off to the kids' table to be with her friends.

Suddenly Penny felt isolated. Maggie had always been the person she talked to at these types of things. Not that she needed constant attention. Lord knew she spent more than her fair share of evenings at home with no one to talk to but the dog.

She used to see Maggie everyday. But now... Brady, Maggie and Amber would be leaving to go on their two-week vacation slash honeymoon at Disney World in a few days. It would be only a few weeks, but Maggie had been preoccupied with the wedding and Brady for months now, giving Penny a lot more alone time than usual. Penny was happy for her friend, but it didn't make her miss Maggie any less.

"I think this empty chair is a better conversationalist than Sam." Luke sat in Amber's seat. His smile warmed her down to her toes.

Her heart pounded a little harder. The champagne must be going to her head because all she could do was smile at him.

"The chair has definitely improved since you arrived," she said. She could spend hours just listening to the sound of his voice. Her whole body flushed with heat and tingled in anticipation of just the slightest touch.

It was crazy. For years, she'd avoided the emotional and clung to the physical. But with Luke, it had been different. Still, that was a long time ago. They were adults now. She was more than happy to bask in the warmth of his smile for the hours they had together.

Chapter Three

"Presenting Mr. and Mrs. Ward for their first dance," the DJ announced.

Luke stood next to the dance floor with his hands in his pockets as the strains of some slow song pounded out of the speaker behind him. This was how Penny and he had started. A school dance. It had been the social hour after a football game. The student DJ was set up in the cafeteria. No fancy lights had lit the floor then. In fact, most of the lights had been turned off, making the small space feel even tighter. He'd been standing on the side with the other football players, and Penny had appeared out of nowhere in a pair of cutoffs that would have gotten her sent home from school and a T-shirt that hugged her young body.

He knew Penny Montgomery. They'd shared classes since fifth grade. In high school, she'd transformed into the kind of girl who was hard for a teenage boy to ignore. From her red hair to her smoking body to her devil-may-care attitude, she was a high school boy's fantasy.

"Dance with me." She'd smiled with her red lips and pulled him onto the dance floor before he could say anything. The music had heavy bass and a bump-and-grind rhythm.

"I don't dance," he'd managed to protest once they were in the middle of the floor.

She gave him a pout and the wicked glint in her eyes had made his pants tighten. "Don't worry. I'll show you what to do."

A touch on his shoulder brought him back to the present. Penny stood there with a smile on her lips. Her makeup was softer now, but she was just as beautiful. The slow song was about halfway through.

"Would the rest of the wedding party join in?" the DJ said over the speaker.

Luke shook off the past and held out his hand to Penny. She slipped her hand in his and followed his lead out to the dance floor. She moved into his arms like a missing puzzle piece.

Sam and Amber followed them onto the dance floor, drawing everyone's attention. Amber put her feet on top of Sam's and he held her hands. It was strange watching Sam with a child. As Luke's pseudo-parent, Sam had been distant but controlling. Now he seemed perfectly at ease talking with his niece, even if he didn't smile.

Luke's attention returned to the woman he held in his arms for the first time in almost a decade.

"Looks like someone's been practicing," she said. That flirtatious tilt was back in Penny's smile.

"I try to maintain appearances."

"I'm sure you have your admirers." A teasing glint

in her eyes and a soft smile on her lips betrayed nothing of what she really felt, but that was Penny.

"I do love compliments." He led them toward a darker area of the dance floor as other couples joined in.

"I bet you do."

Years ago, that first night, when the music had slowed down she'd moved into his arms and her breasts had pressed against his chest, her body close to his. Hormones had flooded him, making it hard to think… Why was he getting wrapped up in the past?

His fingers tightened into the softness of Penny's waist.

She closed the slight gap between them and whispered, "Stop thinking, Luke."

"Why aren't you with someone, Penny?"

"I'm with you right now." Her eyes may never reveal her inner thoughts, but he noticed a slight hesitance in her words. Her body pressed slightly closer until there was no more than a whisper between them.

"You know what I mean." Luke tried to hold on to the thoughts in his head as his body tried to make them all vanish. Her light perfume smelled like spring flowers, the scent's innocence at odds with the seductive woman. It surrounded him, begging him to bend down and breathe in. To touch the warmth of her neck with his lips.

"Who should I be with? The town drunk, the divorcé with the ex from hell—"

"Sam."

She stopped dancing and her lips drew tight. "Sam?"

Penny was in his arms and he wasn't about to back off. Not when her soft curves filled in his rough patches. This was important. He didn't want to step in between his brother and anyone, even if that anyone had been the only girl Luke had ever given his heart to.

"You two were pretty tight last time I saw you." The last time he'd seen Penny, at his graduation party, she'd been kissing Sam.

She pushed against his chest, but he didn't budge. Her eyes flashed up at him. Was that hurt? It had been there for a moment, but it was gone so fast he must have imagined it. It felt as if she was going to push again, but instead she softened. The walls closed in her eyes.

"Sam never meant anything to me." She placed her hands back on his shoulders. "We never had more than a kiss. I'm surprised he didn't tell you."

"Why would he?" Some of the tension released from his grip. Luke's brain was quickly losing the battle with his body's needs. It shouldn't matter why she kissed Sam or even that she did. It had been years ago. It had stopped him from making a major mistake.

Sure it had hurt then, but he'd brought it up now to draw out the woman he'd known from this seductress before him.

She shrugged. "You don't really want to talk about Sam, do you, Luke?"

He didn't know what he was trying to prove. He looked around the dance floor. Now wasn't the time to rehash the past. No time would be the right time. "No."

"How about a drink?" she said. Her gaze flicked over his face.

"A couple of glasses of wine between old friends? Why not. Wait here."

Penny's heart pounded as she sank into a chair and watched Luke walk away. Her knees had barely held her up. Without Luke's arms around her, she would have been down on the ground. She watched him move through the crowd.

Sam had been a means to an end. She'd hated herself for using him, but it had done exactly what she needed it to. Luke had to leave for college without her.

As the DJ cued up some fast dance music, Penny took a deep breath. Tonight had turned out perfectly for Brady and Maggie. They were dancing with Amber in the circle of people on the dance floor.

If her knees recovered, she might go join them. A glass of wine appeared over her shoulder and Luke's breath teased the hairs on the back of her neck. "I had to turn down a lot of eligible ladies to get back here."

Glancing over at the bar, she took the wineglass and felt him sit in the chair behind hers. All of her cells were attuned to whatever frequency Luke gave off. At the bar stood a gathering of white-haired women all giving Luke come-hither looks and finger waves.

Penny choked back a laugh. She tried her hardest to look serious when she turned to Luke. "I hope you let them down easy. It's just as hard to find a man at their age as mine."

Leaning in so he could speak in her ear and be heard over the music, Luke's cheek rubbed against hers, sending a wave of heat through her. "I always try to be gentle."

"I'm sure you do." She could feel his cheek lift in a grin. A shiver rippled down her back.

He moved back until they were eye to eye. "They were actually encouraging me to hit on the wedding coordinator."

Penny glanced over at Rebecca in her peach suit. She was a few years younger than Penny and looked as if the pressure of this wedding was about to make her explode.

"I suppose you could go for Rebecca…." Penny put on a pretend thoughtful look.

The music changed to a slow song again. "Come on. You can tell me all about what that look means on the dance floor."

Luke pulled her out of the chair and guided her into his arms. She'd given up on love songs when Luke left, preferring the rawness of modern rock. Slow songs messed with her brain and made her think about things she couldn't have.

"So are we for or against chatting up the wedding coordinator?" Luke raised his eyebrow as he looked down at Penny.

"I think she'd have an aneurysm if 'we' approached her." Penny mocked Luke's look.

Luke laughed. "Fair enough. Besides, I'm only here until tomorrow. Wouldn't be fair to get anyone's hopes up."

"No, you wouldn't want to do that."

He pressed his hand into the small of her back and she allowed herself to move closer to him. To breathe in his scent. To feel the heat of his body against hers. The song didn't matter as long as it didn't stop.

"Besides—" he leaned down as if he had a secret to whisper in her ear "—I always heard that the best man was supposed to hook up with the maid of honor."

Penny's breathing hitched as she met his eyes. "I think it's actually a written law somewhere that if both parties are single, it's required."

"So we'd be in a lot of trouble if we didn't at least attempt to…" He wiggled his eyebrows.

"Heaps of trouble." Her heart beat hard against her chest as she tried to keep a teasing tone.

"We wouldn't want that." Luke gave her a cocky

smile. "But then you were never the type to follow rules."

"I'll have you know I'm one of the upstanding citizens in Tawnee Valley now."

"Really?" His sarcastic tone made her laugh.

"I'm a valued member of the Chamber of Commerce. My shop brings in tons of tourists."

"I guess that nails it, then." He made a serious face even though his eyes were twinkling. Still dancing, he led her to the side of the dance floor. "Rules are rules, after all."

She swallowed as liquid heat flooded her system. Her fingers locked around the back of his neck. "I suppose after the reception..."

The heat in his blue eyes made her breath catch. He didn't have to say he wanted her. It was there and it scorched her through to her soul. She didn't want to wait. It had been too long since she'd held him, since her skin had brushed against his.

His smile grew cocky. "Why wait?"

Penny glanced around them. The music had shifted to a fast song again. Most everyone was on the dance floor. Amber was dancing with her parents. Sam was brooding in a corner with a glass of liquor. The older folks were on the other side of the dance floor gathered around a few tables. It looked as if they were shouting to talk above the music.

His hand closed firmly around hers and she met his eyes. Apparently they'd reached the same conclusion. No one would miss them if they ducked out at this moment. She doubted anyone would even think anything of it if they did disappear.

Luke started backing up, pulling her with him. Giddiness welled inside her, the same feeling she used to get in high school when Luke would pick her up for a date. Anticipation mixed with the knowledge that no one would know what they were doing. Something hidden that was hers alone.

"You know, I'm not this type of guy." He stopped and pulled her hard until she stumbled into his chest. His teasing smile made her heart skip a beat. "I usually require dinner and wine first."

She smiled up at him. "Good thing we came to a wedding, then. Dinner, check. Wine, check."

"I wouldn't want you to think less of me." He was joking around, but her heart wouldn't let her say something flippant. It demanded she let him know this much.

"Nothing would make me think less of you."

He glanced over her shoulder toward the rest of the party as they approached the exit. "Where should we go?"

When he turned back to her, she forgot to breathe, let alone think. She knew that in Luke's eyes, they were equals, but she'd always known she wasn't as good as he was. During sex was the only time she felt like his match.

"Follow me." She led him past the curtain and into the darkness behind it. The closet door opened easily and she slid in with Luke behind her.

"Classy," Luke muttered. The door closed and the small space seemed to close in on them. Even the music was muffled beyond recognition. The smell of lemon cleaner tinged the air.

"If you'd rather go out in the parking lot and risk causing Bitsy heart palpitations when she sees me straddling you in your brother's truck—"

"Stop thinking, Penny." In the darkness, he moved closer until she felt his whole body pressed against hers.

Her breath quickened as she waited. For his next move. For his touch. For his kiss.

She felt the brush of his arm next to her and caught her breath. The click of the lock could barely be heard over the sound of their breaths. The warm, clean scent of Luke filled her.

"You don't have to do this." Luke's whispered words caressed her earlobe. "Just because we're here at a wedding doesn't mean we have to have sex."

"Are you trying to give *me* an out, Luke Ward?" She laughed, releasing some of the tension that had been welling within her. "I must be pretty darned good if you think this is all your idea."

He chuckled and his knuckles brushed over her jaw, ending her own laughter. "I don't want you to think I only want sex."

"What else would you want?" She didn't bother trying to hide the breathiness of her voice.

His forehead pressed against hers and his hands ran up and down her arms. "I don't know."

Her heart beat with his quickened breath. Once, twice, three times.

She slid off her heels and lifted onto her toes. Pressing a kiss to his jaw, she could feel his heart beat in time with hers against her palm. "I want you."

His lips closed over hers. Sparks rippled through her as he pulled her in close. Relief spiraled out of her heart even as her pulse quickened. Her memories of his kisses collapsed under the weight of this one. It wasn't the technique that had her clutching at his dress shirt—though the technique was definitely good. It was the man.

In an instant, she knew if it were ten years from now,

even a hundred, and Luke kissed her, it would still feel like this. Explosive, powerful, soul shattering.

Desire pulsed within her, and that little piece of her that would always belong to Luke throbbed with satisfaction. He was kissing her as if they had only moments to live. Maybe they did. Maybe she felt alive only when Luke was here. Kissing her.

His hands clutched at the fabric around her hips, slowly easing the silky material up her calves and over her thighs. It was as if the silk were his fingers trailing ever higher, stealing her breath.

She unclenched her fingers and started undoing the buttons of his shirt. The need to feel his skin against hers was overwhelming. His warmth beckoned beneath the fabric. The cool air caressed her legs as her dress slipped up over her hips. The crisp fabric of his tux pants brushed against her skin.

Pulling his shirt free of his pants, she opened it. His fingers brushed under the edge of her panties at her hips. She leaned back against the door as his lips left her mouth and trailed kisses along her jaw.

The warmth of his chest beckoned. She ran her fingers over the muscles, making a mental picture in the dark. Memorizing the contours. As her hand slid down his abs, he sucked in his breath and nipped at her neck.

Power coursed through her veins as she eased down his zipper and brushed the hardness underneath. He grabbed her hands and pushed them against the door, reclaiming her mouth.

The silk dress rushed down her thighs, but caught as his knee moved between her legs. The door and Luke had her captured, unable to escape. Not that she wanted freedom. If she could, she would spend eternity in this little closet with Luke.

This wasn't like a one-night stand or even a booty call. Luke wouldn't fill just her need for an orgasm. She craved relief, but she didn't want this to end.

She'd made a mistake.

Having Luke one more time wouldn't fulfill some need for closure. The sound of his pants dropping filled the space between them.

Even knowing this was a mistake, she wanted him. Even though it would only widen the hole he'd left behind. Even as her body hummed from his touch, she wanted to cry.

She'd take what she could from him and he'd leave. That would be the end of it. She'd survived before and she'd survive this time.

"Are you okay?" He kissed her next to her ear as his fingers teased the edge of her underwear.

She sucked in a breath as his hand slipped under the fabric and touched her skin. Wrapping her hands behind his head, she pulled his mouth to hers. She was beyond being okay. She needed to shut down her brain and feel. Brand him the way he branded her.

He slid off her underwear. Her dress remained bunched up around her waist. His bare skin brushed against hers. Rough against soft. She heard him open a condom packet.

After a moment, his hands returned to her hips and his mouth returned to hers. He lifted her against the door and she wrapped her legs around his waist. In the darkness all she could do was feel. The real world was far away. The fact that they were in a closet at a wedding didn't matter. All that mattered was that he was with her now.

"Say my name," he whispered against her ear. The darkness engulfed them. They could only feel and hear.

But she knew it meant more to him. It was his way of claiming her, of making sure she knew it was him and not any number of guys.

She wanted to please him, needed him to know that it was only him. That it had always been only him.

"Luke." Her world came unhinged as he entered her slowly. His hands held her hips. The tears she'd been holding back pressed forward. She repeated his name and muttered words she couldn't be held accountable for as he moved within her, the only thing she could allow herself from him.

The tears edged over her eyes and trailed down her cheeks as her body rejoiced. It felt like coming home and like nothing she'd ever felt before. Dangerous and tempting. Something she never should have messed with. He lifted her higher and higher until she fell over the edge into bliss. He joined her with her name on his lips.

She choked back a sob and held him tighter, never wanting to let go.

Chapter Four

Luke fought to steady his breathing in the dark room. Penny fit against his body perfectly. He wanted to continue to hold her, but the noise of the party beyond the door told him that they needed to get back. Her breath shuddered in and out. Lowering her gently to the floor, he stepped back. In the dark he couldn't see her, but it sounded as if she was crying. "Did I hurt you?"

"No."

Suddenly the dark that had wrapped them in an intimate fog pissed him off. He could tell she was lying but couldn't prove it.

"Something's wrong." Luke felt the wall next to the door for a light switch.

"Nothing's wrong." She reached past him and the light blinked on. For a moment he was blind as his eyes adjusted to the brightness.

Penny had bent down and retrieved her underwear. "We need to get back out there."

"Nothing's wrong, my ass." Luke pulled up his boxers and pants.

"What do you want me to say?" She turned her back to him as she fixed her clothing. "It was fantastic, wonderful, the best thing ever."

"What's gotten into you?" The lightness in his chest grew heavy. Trying to recapture the mood, he dropped a kiss on the nape of her neck.

Her shoulders tensed but then relaxed. When she turned around, the plastic smile was in place. He closed his eyes for a moment and took a deep breath. Whatever had made her upset, she wasn't going to tell him.

"I'm fine. Really. We just need to get back." Her flirtatious smile returned. "I had a really good time."

She moved to open the door, but he grabbed the knob to hold it closed.

"Fine? You are far from fine. You can act all you want for the revolving door of men you have, but I know you." The anger raging within was tempered by the orgasm he'd just had. After he'd left all those years ago, he'd heard about her escapades from classmates and folks around town. They had acted as if he should step in and do something. He didn't tell them that he'd heard the rumors of her with other guys the entire time they'd dated.

She didn't even bristle. She reached up to fix his collar as if they were discussing the weather. "Is that what you are worried about? That I'm comparing you to other lovers?"

"What I'm worried about is the fact that you don't seem to feel anything anymore." Luke brushed her hair away from her face. "Does anything matter to you?"

Her smile didn't show even a hint of anger, which just made him more determined to break through that wall. To what end? He didn't know.

"You're leaving tomorrow?" Her brown eyes lifted to his.

He nodded, not really wanting to be reminded of that at this moment.

"Let's go out to the party and afterward…" She held on to his shoulders as she slipped her feet into her shoes.

His imagination could do a lot of things with *afterward*.

She kissed his jaw. "Afterward."

The background noise changed. It had been so subtle he hadn't even noticed the music and laughing beyond the door, but the sudden lack of it gained his attention. He thought he heard someone call his name.

"Something's happening." Luke opened the door and found his way out from behind the curtain. The overhead lights were on and everyone was hovering near the dance floor.

Luke's heart pounded against his chest as he saw someone lying on the floor beyond the crowd. His training kicked in as he rushed forward.

Breaking through the crowd, he froze when he saw Sam unconscious on the ground, his face ashen. Luke's world lurched. "What happened?"

"He just fell over," an old man who looked familiar said.

"Everyone back up and give him some space," Luke ordered. "Has anyone called 911?"

"Yes. The ambulance is on the way."

Luke checked Sam's pulse. He was still breathing, but his pulse was faint. "Bring over a chair."

Luke pulled Sam's bow tie off and unbuttoned his

collar. When Amber dragged over a chair, Luke lifted Sam's feet up onto the seat.

"Where are Brady and Maggie?" Luke asked the nearest woman.

"They just left."

"Is he going to be okay?" Tears ran freely down Amber's cheeks. Penny kneeled next to Amber and held out her arms. Amber collapsed against her but kept her big blue eyes on Luke and Sam.

"We need to get him checked at the hospital." Luke met Penny's eyes and saw the worry there.

He tried not to think about it as he worked on evaluating Sam's condition.

"The ambulance is here," someone said.

The paramedics came in and Luke gave them a rundown of what he knew, which wasn't much. Sam had fainted and hadn't regained consciousness.

"Should I call Brady and Maggie?" Penny asked as Luke stepped out of the way to let the paramedics work.

"Not yet." Luke ran a hand over his face. "They just left for their wedding night, and we have nothing to tell them. They'd just worry or, worse, spend their wedding night in the hospital waiting room."

She nodded, still holding on to Amber. "Maybe I should take Amber home."

"No." Amber shook her head. "I'm going with Uncle Sam."

"It's late. We can go wait at my house with Flicker, and your uncle Luke will call with any news." Penny's gaze met Luke's, looking for his support.

He nodded, but that wasn't enough for Amber.

"I'm supposed to stay with Uncle Sam tonight," Amber said. If Luke knew anything about his family, it was that stubbornness definitely ran in it. But he had only just met his niece.

"What if—" Penny looked up at Luke "—we go to the hospital and see that Uncle Sam is taken care of, then you and I will go get Flicker and drive out to check on the farm?"

Luke nodded in agreement. What else could he do until he knew what was going on with Sam?

"I wanna ride in the ambulance." Amber turned her stubborn little chin up at Luke.

"No," Penny said, her voice more firm than he'd ever heard it before. "You ride with me or the deal is off, kiddo."

"Okay." Amber pouted but went to grab her flowers and sweater from their table.

"Did you want to ride with us or with the ambulance?" Penny's presence actually calmed his racing heart for a moment.

"I'll drive Sam's truck and meet you there." Luke watched as the paramedics wheeled Sam out the door. He felt lost, as if he could have prevented whatever was happening.

Penny wrapped her arms around him in a hug that had nothing to do with sex. "He'll be all right."

He returned her hug and breathed in her floral scent. The knot in his stomach loosened slightly.

She released him before he wanted to let go, but things had to get done. "We'll be there in a few minutes. I'm going to talk to the wedding coordinator and make sure everything is taken care of before we head to the hospital."

Amber came back over with tears in her big blue eyes. "Can I ride with Uncle Luke? Please?"

Penny gave him a questioning look, leaving it up to

him. He looked around at the people waiting and the chaos beyond. It might take Penny a half hour or more to finish up here and Amber would be left sitting alone. He remembered how that felt when his father had been rushed to the hospital. No one had taken the time to tell him what was happening. He was just left waiting.

Luke held out his hand to Amber. "Sure. Let's go."

An hour later, Luke sat in the waiting room of the hospital in Owen with his niece fast asleep against his side. Sam had woken during the ambulance ride and had been cranky as ever. When he arrived at the hospital, the doctor ordered several tests to make sure he hadn't had a heart attack or wasn't on the verge of having one. The doctor had insisted Luke go to the waiting area since Sam didn't look to be in any eminent danger.

A flicker of gold caught Luke's attention. He lifted his head in the direction of the hallway. Penny sauntered toward him with her heels in one hand and a soft smile on her lips. It had been only an hour or so since he'd held her in his arms, but it felt as if an eternity had passed.

Careful not to wake Amber, she sat gently on his other side and whispered, "How's Sam?"

Luke took a deep breath and released it. "No word yet. Apparently a few months ago, he had an X-ray that showed an enlarged heart, but he skipped his follow-up with the cardiologist. The fainting could mean a number of things, from cardiomyopathy to hypothyroidism to hemo—"

Penny took his hand between hers. "Lots of doctor mumbo jumbo. Is he going to be okay?"

"I hope so." He ran his other hand through his hair. Their family history of heart disease was the reason Luke had gone to med school and why he'd specialized in cardiology. If Luke had known at fourteen what he knew now, maybe he could have prevented the heart attack that killed his father. The warning signs had all been there. No one had pushed Dad to get checked out. Not that his father could have been pushed. A trait Sam inherited.

"I guess I should take Amber home and get her into bed." Penny didn't move and he felt her eyes on him. "Unless you want me to stay."

Luke didn't know what he wanted. Earlier it had been easy to just pull Penny into his arms and forget the past and future. He would definitely prefer to argue more with Penny instead of sitting in a waiting room with months-old magazines and a news channel on a muted TV. If his niece weren't here, he might even flirt, if only for the distraction.

As if sensing his hesitation, Penny leaned forward to look around him at Amber. "If I wake Amber now, she'll be a bear to get back to sleep. Why don't I just keep you company while we wait to hear about Sam?"

"Why are you being like this?" Luke stared at the television in the corner. There was no reason for Penny to be here for him now. Not even after what happened in the closet. They weren't anything more than exes thrown together at a wedding. She didn't have to be nice to him.

She settled next to him, pulling her feet up under her and leaning her head against his shoulder. "Being like what?"

He looked down at the top of her auburn head. "It doesn't matter."

She shrugged. "When should we call Maggie and Brady?" A yawn followed as she squirmed herself into a more comfortable spot.

"It's late. We'll wait until morning and give them a call. No reason to disrupt their wedding night. As long as Sam remains stable, there's nothing they could do but worry anyway." Sam was only thirty and relatively healthy, but fainting was serious…especially with an unknown heart condition. Luke needed to get up and do something, but he couldn't without disturbing Amber. His leg started to bounce.

Penny kept hold of his hand in her lap. He should ask to look over Sam's chart and figure out if they were doing all the necessary testing. EKG, echocardiogram, CBC. Maybe he should talk to the doctor about a transfer to the nearest medical school hospital. He wondered if they could Life Flight him to his hospital in St. Louis.

"I hear you got into one of the better programs for med school," Penny said.

"What?" He pulled his gaze from the doors the doctor had vanished behind recently.

"Med school. Good program?" Penny repeated and looked up at him.

"Yeah. It took a lot of cramming, but I got the grades to get in." If he could figure out a way to slide out from under Amber without waking her, he would go through those doors that said "Authorized Personnel Only." Surely they missed something on the chart. Most hospitals generally had rules against working on family. But they probably didn't have a cardiologist on staff.

"I was glad to graduate high school with a C average," Penny scoffed. "You always were the smarter of the two of us."

"That's not true. You were just a misguided youth." He smiled at the memory.

"Remember when we were studying for my final

in Geometry? If it hadn't been for you, I wouldn't still have the useless phrase SOH CAH TOA in my head."

Luke chuckled. "Do you even remember what it means?"

Penny screwed up her nose. "Of course not. If it had been useful, then I definitely would have remembered it. I bet I haven't used half of what they forced us to learn in high school."

"You probably use more than you think." Luke sank farther into his chair. His legs relaxed out in front of him. "If we'd been together longer, I bet you would have received straight As."

"You definitely made studying fun." She rubbed her thumb across the back of his hand. "Do you remember that one night we walked all the way to Owen to The Morning Rooster to have breakfast at 2:00 a.m.?"

"I remember heading back and having to carry you piggyback half the way."

"I didn't know we were going to walk eight miles each way when I decided on my shoe choice for the evening. Most nights I didn't even need my shoes."

"I remember talking about everything that night. Philosophy, love, family, sex, shoes." He squeezed her hand. "We were quite the rebels."

"More like trendsetters. Apparently it's a new dare among the kids in Tawnee Valley. How far are you willing to walk to breakfast?"

Luke laughed. "Not like there was much else to do on Saturday nights. Especially when Sam would take away my car privileges."

"And my car was in the shop. You know, I kept that old beater until it finally coughed its final gas fumes into the air about five years ago."

"I'm surprised it made it that long." This was the part

of Penny he'd missed the most. The quiet times when it was just the two of them talking. That piece of her that only he got to see.

The doors swung open. Dr. Sanchez came into the waiting area and walked their way. "Don't get up."

Luke had automatically started to rise without thinking about Amber and Penny leaning on him. She smiled down at the three of them. Penny released his hand and he missed her warmth.

"So far the test results have been promising. It doesn't look like he suffered from cardiac arrest, but we can't rule out a future one. We'd like to keep him overnight for observation."

Luke breathed out as if he'd been holding his breath for days. No cardiac arrest was good, but Sam wasn't out of the woods yet. "What's the plan once he's released?"

"Until we have a few more test results, we won't know for sure the type and extent of damage. I can't give you any more information until tomorrow."

"But he's going to be okay?" Penny asked, straightening in the chair.

"We'll know more tomorrow." Dr. Sanchez smiled that doctor smile Luke was all too familiar with. The one that said we don't know all that much and all we can do is hope for the best. "For tonight, I suggest you go home and get a good night's sleep. We've already given Mr. Ward something to help him sleep."

"Thank you," Luke said. Because of privacy laws, the doctor wouldn't tell Luke much more, so he didn't push. Besides, until the tests were completed, the doctor wouldn't know any more than he did.

Dr. Sanchez disappeared behind the doors again.

"Why don't I drive us all out to the farm?" Penny

stretched like a cat. "It's closer to the hospital and Amber won't pitch a fit if she wakes up there. I asked Bitsy to look in on my dog when she left the reception."

Luke hesitated. It felt odd to invite Penny back to Sam's house. "It's not that I don't appreciate the offer—"

"I wasn't doing it just for you." She stood and looked down her nose at him. "Maggie is family to me. That makes Brady family and Sam by extension. I need to take care of Amber and make sure things go smoothly so those two can take their daughter to Disney World on their honeymoon and make me more babies to take care of. I'm tired and I just want to crash and be there when Amber and Maggie need me in the morning."

Luke stood and picked up Amber. Thinking of Penny with babies did something strange to his heart. "I just didn't want you to think that I needed you—"

"Trust me. I know you don't need me." He saw a flash of hurt in Penny's eyes. "Maggie and Amber need me."

"I'm sorry, Penny. I didn't mean…" Oh, hell, what did he mean? If it meant avoiding a fight and not disappointing Amber, who was he to care whether they stayed here or went to the farm? They could work out the details when they arrived. Right now, he just wanted to look at something besides these four walls. "Look, we're both tired. Why don't *I* drive us out to the farm and we'll work on it from there? It doesn't look like I'll be flying out tomorrow."

"If you are talking about staying for Sam, maybe I can help."

Help? She was the reason he hadn't been out there to help Sam in the first place. His brother might have been showing signs that he could have picked up on if he hadn't been too busy making eyes at the pretty woman in front of him. "He's my family. For now, let's go home."

"He'll be okay." Penny rested her hand above his heart.

Penny's touch comforted him in a way he'd almost forgotten. For a long moment, he searched her eyes. With Sam's condition unknown, Luke couldn't just leave. Depending on what was wrong, he might need surgery or just bed rest. His mind shuffled through all the possible diagnoses, but he didn't have the chart to see what they'd uncovered when they'd examined him today. He trusted the doctor to make the right call regarding Sam's treatment.

Regardless, his brother might be here longer than a night. What happened after tonight with Penny? They hadn't promised more than tonight because that wasn't an option. Maybe it still wasn't an option. He didn't know Penny that well anymore, but from what he heard she rarely made a habit of any man.

He needed to get out of his head. There was plenty to worry about tomorrow. First he had to get through tonight. "Let's go."

Chapter Five

Penny shut the door of the bedroom. Amber had taken very little coaxing to fall back to sleep in Brady's old bedroom. Reassuring her that Sam would be okay and they'd see him in the morning was all it had taken. The old wooden stairs creaked under her feet as she returned to the first floor. It was past two in the morning, the lights were all still on and she didn't feel tired at all.

The sound of a chair scraping across the linoleum in the kitchen drew her that way. She stopped in the doorway and leaned against the doorjamb. Luke sat at the kitchen table, his head in his hands. If she had stayed with him after high school, would things have turned out differently? Would he have made it through med school with her dragging him down? Where would she have been when he left her? Stuck in some city where she wouldn't know a soul and Maggie would have been here all alone dealing with her mother's illness and raising Amber.

She could play the what-if game, but she had decided a long time ago to live in the present. And presently, the weight of the world was on Luke's shoulders. He'd always taken on too much. All she'd ever wanted to do was take some of that weight off him. In high school, it had been easy. Nothing takes a man's mind off his problems like sex. Now they were adults with a complicated history. She had no idea of the problems he was facing in his day-to-day life, but Sam's collapse was one more thing to deal with.

Even though it had been years since they'd been together as a couple, she'd known at the hospital that he needed her to be there with him. To keep him out of his head.

"Hey," she said and shoved off the wall to join him in the kitchen.

He lifted his head and gave her a weary smile. "Hey."

"Not exactly how I thought this night would end." She flashed him a smile and leaned against the counter, putting one bare foot on top of the other. She'd ditched her killer high heels next to the door as soon as they'd walked in. They looked a little obscene next to the work boots and sneakers stacked there.

Her feet felt only half as weary as Luke looked. She wanted to go over and pull him into her arms and just hold him, but she needed to let him dictate what he needed. Whether it was just to talk or…

He rubbed his hand over his hair. "You want some coffee?"

"Nah, I should sleep at some point tonight, so I can wake up when Amber gets up." A knot formed in her stomach. He probably thought she was pushing for him to invite her to sleep with him. For once she felt awkward. This was one of those situations she avoided for just this reason. She didn't sleep over and she didn't let anyone near her bed. She was all for sex, but cuddling wasn't her style.

He started to rise from his chair. "I can set up the guest bed—"

"Is that really necessary?" She put on her best brazen-it-out smile. Typically she didn't "sleep" with anyone except her puppy, but the last thing Luke needed to do tonight was worry about making her comfortable in his family home. She'd be fine whether he wanted her in his bed or on the couch. "I can crash wherever."

When she shrugged so that he would know it wasn't a big deal, the strap from her gown slid down her arm, drawing Luke's gaze. She felt it like a physical caress. The air in the room was suddenly charged.

"You always liked to finish what you started." His gaze met hers and his eyes flamed with desire.

Her body responded with all the repressed heat she'd sidelined since their closet interlude. Her body always would react to his. But she didn't want to push him, not with everything else weighing on his mind. "You know me. I'm always game. But I leave the decision up to you. I know you have a lot on your mind right now—"

"I'd rather not think at all." Luke crossed the kitchen floor and pulled her into his arms. Her toes brushed against the warm, soft fabric of his socks. "I'd rather forget everything outside of these walls for the rest of the night. Stop my mind from circling around what I'll need to do to be able to stay here with Sam. Stop from worrying that he might not be getting sufficient care. Stop trying to figure out—"

"Just stop," she whispered and drew his head down to hers. "I won't ask you for anything."

"I know," he said before claiming her mouth.

The creak of the bed woke Luke from a deep sleep. He automatically reached for his phone on the night-stand but hit only air where his nightstand should be. He blinked into the darkness and squinted at the dim light coming through the window. Instead of city lights, he saw the moon lighting up the fields rolling into the distance. The crops swayed slightly in the breeze.

The night came rushing back to him. The wedding. Sam's collapse. Inviting Penny into his bed. A shadow moved in front of the window.

"What are you doing?" Luke sat up and rubbed his face.

She flinched and turned around to face him. He couldn't see her features, but his eyes were quickly adjusting to the darkness. Her light skin glowed in the moonlight that managed to sneak through the curtains. Standing only in her underwear, she held the rest of her dress at her waist like a shield in front of her. "I was… going to get a drink of water. Do you want some?"

"No, I don't want some water."

"More for me, then." She started to move away.

"Enough bull. What is really going on, Penny?"

She glanced at the door to the hallway and then back to the side of the bed that was still warm from her body. "I just thought…" She shrugged.

"That there isn't enough room? I snore too loudly?" He shifted off the bed and flicked on the lamp, casting the room in soft light.

She blinked but didn't move to cover herself. "What does it matter?"

"Just get back into bed, Penny. I swear we'll only sleep."

"Isn't it the woman's job to be needy and clingy?"

"Far be it from me to stop you." He stepped away from the bed and held his hand out. "I just thought you might want to be comfortable for the night. The last thing I'd want to do is make you feel needed."

Penny's shoulders pushed back and her chin tipped up. "Contrary to popular belief, a woman does not need a man to need her to feel complete."

Though her words and actions were angry, saying them nearly naked was having the opposite effect on his body. "I made you feel complete at least three times if my count is correct."

She threw her dress at him. He caught it and dropped it to the floor.

He strode across the room and grabbed her elbows, pulling her flush against his chest. "Unless you plan to traipse around the farmhouse in your underwear." At the devilish glint in her eyes, he added, "Remembering that my niece could wake up at any moment, I suggest you come back to bed."

Her body was tense against his and fire crackled in her eyes. "Maybe I don't want to sleep with you."

His hands rubbed her back. "If you don't want to sleep with me, I'm sure I could be convinced to stay awake."

Apparently he was starting to speak her language because she softened. Her curves molded into his and the heat that had pooled in his stomach flooded his system. "I've never been good at sleepovers."

"I doubt there are many people who would accuse you of being good at all." He lifted her into his arms. Penny was a puzzle. One he would be better off not trying to solve. One he should be pushing away instead of carrying back to his bed.

He lowered her onto the mattress, never releasing his hold on her body.

"Good is overrated." Penny pulled him down to her. "When has being good ever gotten you what you wanted?"

At one point, the thing he'd wanted most had been her. He'd been willing to do anything to keep her, except share her with anyone else. He lowered his head to hers. "Being good has gotten me nothing."

Chapter Six

Waiting rooms weren't nearly as bad as sitting in a patient's room, especially when the patient was Sam. Luke had taken the recliner, whereas Amber had chosen to sit at the end of Sam's bed. Apparently Sam was confident that he wasn't staying there because he'd been dressed in his tux, minus the jacket and tie, and ready to go as soon as they'd come in. When Luke had given Sam a bag with some of his clothes from home, he'd grunted a thank-you and immediately changed.

"I made sure to give the baby calves their bottles." Amber had been listing all the chores she'd insisted on helping with this morning. "I'll walk the fences this afternoon to make sure there aren't any breaks."

"I knew I could count on you." Sam smiled at his niece, if you could call the slight curve to his lips a smile.

Luke still couldn't understand Amber's loyal devotion to hardheaded Sam. This morning at the breakfast table, she'd run off a list of all the chores that she did when she stayed at the farm. While Luke had been amused with the list, he'd barely been able to keep his eyes from the woman who had kept him up all night.

Penny had moved around the kitchen with ease, as if she made breakfast there frequently. For all he knew she did. She had said she and Sam had had nothing more than that kiss years ago, but how could he believe a word that slipped past those wicked lips?

Wearing one of his T-shirts and not a whole lot more, she'd slipped out of his room. He'd assumed she'd join him after using the bathroom, but when he woke a few hours later from little feet creaking down the stairs, Penny was not in his bed.

He'd found her on the couch with an afghan pulled over her, fast asleep.

"Can I name the new piglets? Please?" Amber brought his attention back to the present. They were waiting for the doctor to talk to them and discharge Sam. Penny had excused herself as soon as they got to the hospital to go check on her puppy and to change out of Luke's oversize T-shirt and sweats.

"We can just call them Pork Chop, Ham and Bacon." Sam rested against the elevated back of the hospital bed. Luke couldn't remember the last time he'd heard Sam tease someone. Maybe when Luke had been Amber's age. Before Dad... Before Mom...

"That's not very nice, Uncle Sam." Amber gave him a look that reminded Luke of their mother when she'd scolded them even though she wanted to laugh at their antics. Sam just chuckled lightly, drawing Luke's questioning gaze to him. Sam shrugged.

"When am I getting out of this place?" Sam looked

toward the door as if willing the doctor to appear with his release instructions.

"I'm sure the staff is just as anxious for you to go," Luke said before standing. "I'm going to go find a cup of coffee. Do you want anything?" He looked at Amber.

She turned her bright blue eyes up to him and shook her head no. "I'm going to take care of Uncle Sam."

He believed her. He didn't know why she was so attached, but somehow Sam had become her hero. Or maybe Amber would be his savior. Either way, Sam must have done at least one good deed in his life to deserve her devotion.

The hallway was bustling with energy. Nurses darted in and out of rooms. The high-school-aged candy stripers were unloading the breakfast trays. The various beeping and swishing sounds of equipment blended into a discordant symphony. The smell of antiseptics filled his nose. It invigorated him. Hospitals had been his home for the past few years.

He wasn't used to being a visitor, though. Instead of part of the natural flow, he felt as if he was in the way as he walked to the coffee machine in the waiting area. As his coffee finished brewing, he caught Penny's voice behind him.

His pulse surged like a teenager in heat. Last night had to be the end of it. She laughed deep and throaty, and he twitched. Grabbing his cup of coffee, he turned, ready to do battle, and found her walking with Maggie and Brady.

"How's Sam?" Brady searched Luke's eyes.

"We're waiting for the doctor to come in and let us know the test results." Luke glanced at Penny. She stood there as if nothing had happened between them.

Nothing had changed. That was how he had wanted it, after all.

"Amber's with him?" Maggie shook her head and smiled. "That girl... I'm amazed you were able to tear her away from his side last night. Penny said it was a good thing you were there for Sam."

"I'm glad I was there, too." Luke felt the collar on his black T-shirt tighten around his throat. "Sam never told me he was having heart problems or I would have been more diligent." And not been having sex in the closet.

"You know Sam," Penny said. "The strong, silent types rarely give you a clue into their hearts."

He narrowed his eyes on her. This wasn't the first time she'd referenced Sam as if she knew him better than just another person in the small town where they grew up. Everyone he kept in touch with had alluded to the fact that Penny got around. Hopping from one bed to another. Was Sam's one of those beds?

It wasn't inconceivable. The number of eligible men in Tawnee Valley, and even in Owen, dropped off after high school. Although the farmhouse looked as if a monk lived there, Sam might have had a booty call or two.

"Which room is he in?" Brady drew Luke's attention away from Penny, who had started to give him a strange look.

"I was just heading back there." Luke turned and walked with Brady down the hallway. Penny and Maggie chatted lightly behind them.

"You could have called me last night," Brady said.

"Ha! And interrupted your wedding night? No way." Luke took in a breath. "There wasn't much you could have done. Sam wasn't in immediate danger. They just wanted to monitor him overnight and run tests in the morning. Besides, they won't tell us anything unless Sam lets them."

"I'm glad you were here to take care of things." Brady stopped him. "What do you know about his heart?"

"He said you knew about the X-ray." At Brady's nod, Luke continued, "Glad to be in the loop. His problems could be caused by a number of possibilities. Until the test results are back, they won't be able to determine a course of treatment."

"How bad could it be?" Brady glanced back at Maggie and Penny, who had stopped discreetly a little farther down the hall.

The fainting had him most alarmed. Heart failure. Structural issues. But it could be just dehydration.

Luke took in a deep breath and released it. "Honestly, it could be as simple as monitoring and as complicated as a heart transplant."

"Damn."

"We won't know anything until the doctor comes in."

"Right." Brady ran a hand over his dark hair. "Right. Let's go, then."

When Luke glanced at her, Penny's insides turned molten. Luke had definitely improved with age and had gone about proving that to her with a fierce determination that had kept her up all night. If it weren't for his glances that seemed to be trying to dissect her, she would be afraid of falling for him again and begging him not to leave her. As if that would happen.

"Earth to Penny." Maggie waved a hand in front of Penny's eyes, breaking her view of Luke's butt in denim.

"Sorry. Did I miss something?" Penny blinked and tried to maintain an air of innocence.

"You aren't fooling me for one minute, Penny Montgomery." Maggie took her arm as the men started to move again. "I've known you practically all my life and I know when you've done the naughty."

"The naughty?" Penny laughed. "Good lord, woman, just call it what it is. Sex. S-e-x. Sex. Down-and-dirty, in-and-out sex. Which you should know because everyone is assuming you had sex last night, too."

"Shh. We're in a hospital, for goodness' sake." Maggie looked around as if a group of avenging nuns would descend on them.

"Yes, and it was good." Penny smirked. Damn good, if truth be told. She'd known that Luke had ruined her from falling in love ever again, but she'd hate it if he ruined her for sex, too.

"Hey." Maggie pulled her to a stop. Her hazel eyes searched Penny's. "He's not seeing anyone...."

Penny laughed. "You sound like Bitsy. You do know that I have a shop to run and he has a medical thingy hundreds of miles away, right? How's that supposed to work without the capability of time travel?"

"If you are in love, there are ways."

"Spoken like a true romantic." Penny tugged Maggie forward. "I'll just have to reserve myself for my weekly Winchester brothers viewing and let you stay the hopeless romantic."

"You know *Supernatural* won't be on the air forever." Maggie turned into the room.

"That's why I own the DVDs." She wiggled her eyebrows. "More Sam and Dean all to myself."

Penny couldn't make Maggie believe that she was determined to stay alone for the rest of her life. Okay,

maybe not alone. She had Maggie and Amber, and she
had Brady by marriage and any little ones that would
come along. She'd be happy with that as long as they
stayed right around the block.

Her heart pinched. Brady could have to move with
his job. Even though he claimed he wanted to settle
down in Tawnee Valley, how long would he be happy
with small-town life? If Maggie left, where would
Penny be?

God, she never got this emotional, even with lack of
sleep. She'd deal with them moving if it happened. She
turned the corner into the almost-full hospital room.
Sam and Amber sat on the bed, and Luke and Brady
stood beside Dr. Sanchez. Maggie joined Brady, who
wrapped his arm around her.

There was no place for her. She glanced once at
Luke, who had his head down over the chart the doctor had given him. She didn't belong with him. Taking a deep breath and ignoring the choking tears in the
back of her throat, she left the room and the only family she had.

Dr. Sanchez was good at her job.

Luke didn't question that, even as he reviewed all
her notes and the test results and cardiologist reports
from St. Mercy in Springfield from last night and this
morning. He wasn't looking for errors, just making sure
that what she was saying was correct. Maggie had taken
Amber to find some ice cream for Uncle Sam, while
Brady and Luke stayed to listen to the doctor.

Luke checked the picture from the echocardiogram
they had performed this morning. The still images had
the measurements marked, showing the aortic valve.
This wasn't what Luke had been expecting. His hand

quaked as he turned to the next page. "Why didn't you mention the murmur last night?"

"Dr. Ward, you are well aware of HIPAA." Dr. Sanchez waited for his acknowledging nod before continuing. She couldn't release any information without Sam's consent, which he obviously hadn't given. "Everything points to severe aortic stenosis. We'd like to get Sam on the schedule in the next few days for surgery at St. Mercy Hospital in Springfield."

"Is this because of the enlargement of his heart?" Brady leaned against the windowsill with his arms crossed. His brow furrowed as he assessed the situation.

"Most likely the doctor who examined the X-ray couldn't tell that only the left side was enlarged from too much blood." Dr. Sanchez started writing on her chart. "That's why they strongly suggested that Sam go to a cardiologist, but I'm sure they told him not to worry. Some athletic men have slightly larger hearts, and for them it's nothing to worry about."

Sam had remained silent while the doctor spoke in her no-nonsense manner. Luke wanted to berate Sam for not following up, for not calling him to talk about his medical problems. Luke was training to be a cardiologist. The one person Luke had never understood—besides Penny—was Sam. Hell, maybe Sam and Penny were meant for each other. They both drove him nuts.

"I guess we'll cancel the trip." Brady looked at his phone. "I've already got the time off work, so I should be able to help out around the farm while Sam's recovering."

Before Luke could speak up, Sam said, "Who says I'm having the surgery?"

Dr. Sanchez held the chart to her chest and stared at Sam with dark, serious eyes. "If you were asymptomatic, we might be able to treat with drugs or even wait awhile, but your heart valve has already started to calcify. The fainting was only the beginning of your problems. If you don't have the surgery, you could go into heart failure."

Sam kept his lips together tightly. Not a single word. Just as he'd done all those times the principal had called him to the school for Luke's misconduct. Just as he had when he'd had to come to the police station to pick up Luke after a fight off campus. It was as if Sam just stopped caring at some point.

"I'm staying here." Luke stared into Sam's eyes, daring him to contradict him. Wanting him to. "I'll take family emergency leave to help out at the farm and help Sam out after his surgery."

"You need to get back to being a fancy doctor." Sam pushed up out of the chair.

"Brady deserves to go on his honeymoon and you need surgery."

"I'm fine. I don't even need to be here now."

"Bull." Luke saw red. "Of all the stupid, arrogant things you could do…. Do you think you are invincible? That you won't die if you don't have this surgery?"

Sam went lockjaw again. His face was stone.

"I'll let you discuss this in private." Dr. Sanchez backed out of the conversation. "I'll have the nurse call St. Mercy's to set up the necessary procedures."

The door shut behind her, leaving the cold silence. Luke didn't drop his gaze from Sam's eyes. If Sam could be stubborn, so could Luke. Sam was the tallest of the three, but he didn't have much height over Luke. They were practically eye to eye. Backing down wasn't an option. He wasn't a child who Sam could order around anymore.

Brady sighed and sank into the chair. "Are you guys going to stare at each other all day? Because I'd like to go have lunch with my wife and daughter."

"I'd be happy to leave now—" Luke brushed his hand over his hair "—but I'm not going to let another stubborn Ward die because he didn't listen to what the doctor was saying. I know the statistics. I know the symptoms. The doctor wasn't being completely honest."

Sam narrowed his eyes. The muscle in his jaw twitched.

"You will die if you don't have the surgery." Luke kept his expression flat and emotionless. "Within a year or two. Maybe sooner. This isn't something you can brush off…unless you have a death wish."

"What do you know about running a farm?" Sam said quietly. "The time and effort? The brute strength required? The long hours—"

"I'm a freaking doctor, Sam. I've spent twenty hours on shift before, followed by being on call. I know all about long hours and sacrifice." Cold seeped through him, taking the heat out of his words. Luke sat on the edge of the bed and rubbed his hand over his chin. He was not giving up, but he needed another tactic. "You need the surgery, Sam. I'm not ready to dig any more six-feet-deep holes."

Sam turned to Brady, who dropped his gaze to his hands. "Luke's right, Sam. I'm not ready to bury any more family. If it will save your life, I don't know why we are even having this discussion."

"They want to cut into my body and mess with my heart." Sam's face screwed up as if he'd eaten something bad. "While they are in there, they are going to take out part of my heart and replace it with a fake valve."

"And you'll feel better and live longer," Luke said. "I don't see what the problem is."

Sam shook his head and leaned against the end table. His gaze fell to the floor. "What if I don't make it?"

Luke took in a deep breath. He'd gone through this with patients before. The fear of the unknown. He hadn't expected Sam to be afraid. Not the Sam who had taken on Brady and him as a young man. Who'd stood at their mother's and father's gravesites without tears in his eyes.

In Luke's world growing up, Sam was brave and uncompromising. He was stern and unyielding. But he was never afraid.

"This surgery is less invasive than open-heart surgery." Luke stopped acting like a younger brother and became the doctor. "Every surgery has risks, but the benefits of this surgery far outweigh them. You'll be down for a few weeks and then able to do some light work. Before you know it, you'll be full Sam again. Except you'll feel better."

Sam grunted. "I have been feeling a little sick lately."

Luke wanted to exclaim disbelief but he held it back. Most likely Sam had felt like hell for weeks before this collapse. But pushing Sam would get him nowhere. Luke always got so frustrated with Sam that he forgot and blew up, even now as an adult.

Luke placed his hand on Sam's shoulder. "We'll get through this, Sam. Together."

Chapter Seven

"Hey, there you are."

Penny turned toward Maggie's voice. She'd found a magazine in the waiting room with a semi-interesting article on Chris Hemsworth and had decided to read instead of mope. She didn't need to mope. No one to love meant no one to leave you when you least expected it, when you really needed them, when you were starting to trust them again.

"I looked all over for you." Maggie sat down next to Penny and glanced at the article and the picture of Chris without his shirt on. "Nice." She smiled. "They are finishing up Sam's paperwork now, so we should be out of here soon. Then we're going to stop and grab some lunch before heading to the farm."

"What's the verdict?" Penny's stomach clenched. If Sam was okay, Luke would go back to his life in St. Louis.

If Sam wasn't, then Luke would hang around for a while. She wasn't sure which she wanted.

"Sam needs heart valve surgery." Maggie took in a deep breath. "Luke is insisting on staying and handling everything and that Brady and I go on our vacation after the surgery, while Sam is recovering. But I don't know. Sam and Brady were just starting to get to know each other again and if something happens to Sam…"

Penny took Maggie's hand. "We've gotten through worse before."

Maggie nodded and looked up at the ceiling as if to stop tears from forming. "But Sam's young and strong and we didn't even know he was sick."

"Sometimes it's like that." Penny could see her mother's drawn face twisted and ravaged from the years of abuse. For all she knew, her mother was dead. She shook off the image. "He's otherwise healthy. He'll get through this."

"Brady and Luke are talking the logistics." Maggie brushed her hair behind her ear. "I don't know what's going to happen, but would you be willing to help out while we are out of town? I can't imagine Luke being able to do everything by himself."

"He's perfectly capable." Penny shifted in her seat. "But I'll do what I can."

Maggie stared out the window into the blue sky. Some thought must have made her happy because she smiled softly. "It wouldn't be so bad."

"What's that?"

"Getting back together with Luke."

Penny laughed sharply as her heart ached. "I don't do relationships. I keep my options open. You never know when a hottie like Thor here will roll up into town. It'd be a shame to have to waste the eye candy because I'm *with* someone."

"You don't fool me for a minute, Penny." Maggie glanced down the hallway before returning her hazel gaze to Penny. "You talk a good game, but I know you. I know how much you loved Luke in high school. I don't know all of what happened between you two, but it couldn't have been too bad if he was willing to sleep with you last night."

"We didn't sleep." Penny winked, trying to throw off Maggie's speech. She was hitting a little too close to Penny's heart.

"You know what I mean." Maggie tightened her hold on Penny's hand. "I know you aren't happy with the way things are. You may enjoy other men, but I've never seen you light up the way you do when Luke is nearby. I know you've been hurt, but maybe it's time to heal a little. Maybe this is the second chance you need."

"Second chances like that are pretty rare." Penny looked out the window as a small brown bird flew by. If she let Luke in, he'd hurt her because she actually could love him. "And you got the only second chance we're going to see. Don't worry about me. I've got all the men I need in my life right now."

Maggie looked skeptical and opened her mouth.

"I swear, Maggie. I'm happy the way things are. I don't need anything more."

"Weren't you the one who said it wasn't about need?"

"That was to get you laid." Penny stood and brushed the wrinkles out of her slacks. "I'm doing just fine on that part."

Maggie stood. "This discussion isn't over."

"Yeah, it is. I don't need Luke and he doesn't need

me. We had a good time together. It's all good. Now, what's the plan? Is there food to be had?"

Maggie shook her head. "Come on."

When they got to the room, Penny's gaze met Luke's. He gave a hint of a smile, but the wrinkles on his forehead betrayed his worry. She hoped that Sam pulled through. Losing both his parents had devastated Luke. He couldn't lose Sam, too.

"I take it you guys have this all sorted?" Maggie asked as she touched Amber's dark hair.

Amber pouted. "We're going to Disney."

"You were excited for this trip, Squirt," Penny said.

"But who's going to take care of Uncle Sam after his surgery?" Amber turned to Penny. "You'll take care of him, won't you, Penny?"

Penny glanced around the room. Sam didn't make eye contact. Luke was intensely watching for her answer. Brady and Maggie just smiled indulgently.

"You always take real good care of me when I'm sick." Amber reached out and took both of Penny's hands. "If I know you'll be there, I might be able to have fun while I'm gone."

Amber's face was hopeful. Penny knew that no matter what she said Amber would have fun at Disney, but if it helped to get her on the plane without causing Maggie too much grief…

"You know I'll do whatever I can." Penny squeezed Amber's hands. "But you have to promise to have fun."

"Only if you call every night with an update."

"You drive a hard bargain." Penny bit out a laugh. Amber narrowed her eyes as if Penny weren't taking her seriously. "Sure. I'll check in with Luke every day and then call you."

"Check on Uncle Sam," Amber clarified.

Penny glanced over to Luke. "Your uncle Luke will be there—"

"I want you to."

"That's enough, young lady," Brady finally spoke up. "Penny has promised. Now let's go get something to eat and then get Sam set up at home. We have a lot to do to prepare for Sam's surgery and while we're on our trip."

Luke's eyes never left Penny's. Her pulse throbbed. She didn't know what he was searching for, but she didn't have anything left to hide. She wasn't Luke's girl anymore. He was just another notch on her lipstick case. Even though she'd have to talk to him and maybe even see him, nothing else was going to happen. A few weeks and he'd be gone and out of her life again.

Maybe she was the one with a heart condition. She rubbed the ache in her chest.

The surgery was set for Wednesday. Frankly it couldn't come soon enough. Keeping Sam indoors was proving to be a feat even for both Brady and Luke combined.

"You need to stay off your feet and rest." Brady shoved Sam toward the living room. "Play Xbox or watch a movie."

"I'm not an infant. I can do more than sit on my butt."

Brady headed back to the kitchen to talk to Maggie.

"Not if you want to live." Luke stood in the doorway. "We all grew up on this farm and each of us has done these chores a million times. I'm not sure why you think we're going to mess something up."

Sam grumbled something under his breath as he plopped in the worn-out recliner and grabbed the remote. Hopefully killing zombies on the Xbox would make Sam content to stay inside. He could pretend they were Brady and Luke if he really wanted to take out his anger. Lord knew that Luke had pretended they were Sam when he was younger. Luke turned and nearly ran over Penny.

"Sorry," he said. His breath caught in his throat as she looked up at him, startled.

"It was my fault," she muttered.

They'd barely spoken since the morning at the hospital. Apparently where Maggie and Amber went, Penny wasn't far behind. The three ladies worked on scrubbing the house, while he and Brady worked on straightening up the outside. Mom would have been thrilled that her house was being put back in order. They needed to get ahead on the farm chores for the days that Sam would be in the hospital for his surgery and recovery.

The unfortunate side effect was that Luke kept running into Penny, both figuratively and literally. Every touch caused his pulse to kick into overdrive. The house wasn't that big, which meant everyone was in everyone's way. It also meant that he hadn't been alone with Penny since the night of the wedding.

Penny still stood in front of him, looking at him with her brown eyes that always carried a hint of a devilish glint in them.

They weren't going to have sex again, he reminded himself for the tenth time that day. The night of the wedding was a one-time deal, but his body clearly had misread the memo.

"Did you need something?" Penny asked. A hint of a smile tugged at her lips.

Did he need something? How 'bout a convenient closet or bed for an hour or two? "No, I'm just heading out to work on the fence."

"Sounds exciting." She stretched her arms over her

head, which pushed her breasts against her tight black T-shirt.

His pants tightened and he had to restrain from adjusting himself.

"I get to clean the living room," she said in a fake excited voice. "Maybe afterward we can go beat laundry down on the rocks in the creek? Won't that be fun?"

Luke chuckled. "Better than gathering up the pigs for market."

"At least when Maggie and Brady leave, we can slack off once in a while." She leaned in conspiratorially. "I hid a package of ice cream bars in the back of the freezer behind a bag of frozen broccoli."

"Always thinking ahead—that's what I like about you, Montgomery." Luke relaxed.

"Someone has to." Penny took a deep breath and looked around. "Back to dusting. Yay?"

As she passed by him, he grabbed her hand. She looked at him with a question in her eyes.

"Thanks." Luke released her hand and flexed his still tingling fingers.

Penny winked. "Anytime."

Things with Penny were less complicated right now than his relationship with Sam. He really did appreciate that she got it. He knew, even though she didn't say it, that she did.

Penny's relationship with her grandma had always been similarly tense. They'd called her Grandma Tilly the Battle Ax.

She'd been old and alone when Penny's mother had dropped Penny off at her doorstep. Penny was more rambunctious than most kids and everyone knew that Tilly wasn't happy about having to raise her granddaughter. The stricter Tilly got, the wilder Penny got.

They were opposites in everything. Luke remembered the endless nights on a blanket staring up at the stars with Penny lying beside him. They'd talk about her grandma and Sam—the people who had gotten stuck with caring for Penny and Luke. They vowed that they'd never make anyone feel the way their caregivers made them feel. Like inconveniences instead of kids hurting from the loss of their parents.

He shook his head. Such thoughts didn't help anyone. He needed to focus on the farm and on getting Sam better. Not on Penny.

Chapter Eight

The days passed quickly, and before Luke knew it, it was Wednesday. Luke had driven Sam and Brady the hour to the hospital in Springfield. Everything ran smoothly. Checking Sam in. The staff preparing him for surgery. Watching them take him away.

Luke found himself once more in the hospital waiting room, this time with Brady. They talked for a little bit, but there wasn't much new to say because they'd spent the past few days working together.

Luke missed Penny's presence. She'd wished them the best last night before leaving and said she'd check in. He wished she were here now. She could always distract him, whether it was through flirting, having sex or just sitting and talking.

Now all he could do was run through the surgery in his mind's eye. Noting all the things that needed to happen. Everything that could go wrong. The steps to fix the mistakes. When he'd run through the procedures three times, he rubbed his face and turned to look to see what Brady was doing.

Brady had his laptop out and was working on some spreadsheet with numbers and formulas that Luke would need a business degree to understand. Luke pulled out his iPhone and scrolled through the emails he'd missed over the past few days. The signal out at the farm was questionable. Sometimes he received his emails, and other times, the battery drained from trying to connect to the server.

"Dr. Ward?"

Luke looked up at the nurse in scrubs. "Yes?"

"Sam is in recovery. The doctor would like to talk to you and your brother."

Luke glanced over to where Brady had been. His laptop was back in its case, but Brady wasn't there.

"Sorry, had to use the bathroom." Brady came down the hall toward them. "Everything okay?"

"Sam's out and in recovery." Luke took a deep breath. A lot of things still could go wrong, but the worst part was over.

After another hour, Luke had all the post-op information and had talked to Sam briefly. On the way home, he and Brady talked about the surgery and what they needed to do to prepare for Sam's homecoming in a few days.

When Luke pulled the car up to Maggie and Brady's house, Brady turned to him.

"Do you want to come in for a little bit? Maybe for some dinner? Maggie's a great cook."

Luke looked past Brady to the lights in the old Victorian's windows. He could see Maggie and Amber heading to the door to greet Brady. "Nah, you go ahead.

It's been a long day. You'll need to start packing for your trip."

"You sure?" Brady wasn't just being nice. He was sincere, but Luke wasn't in the mood for company.

"Yeah, we'll see each other tomorrow."

"'Night." Brady got out and without a backward glance walked into his family's arms.

Luke remembered what that felt like. To hug someone who cared more about what you were feeling than their own agenda.

It had been a long time since he'd felt that way. Dating in med school had been hard. He'd dated other med students mostly and everyone was mainly concerned about their grades and their shifts. No one really worried about anyone except themselves.

He didn't have what Brady had. Someone who would welcome him with open arms. His gaze went to the direction of Penny's house. It was only a block away.

Penny stared at the inventory screen of the online auction. It had a few good pieces that would look wonderful in What Goes Around Comes Around. A pair of gilded-and-silvered metal vases from nineteenth-century France and a seventeenth-century Italian writing desk had captured her attention. Although they were a bit ornate for her local customers, the tourists loved finding these types of treasures in her little shop.

Most of her inventory consisted of American furniture, artwork and tableware. But she loved to have a few older pieces from across the ocean for interest. People would come in to look at the vases and notice a set of silver or glassware that their grandma had and buy that instead.

She put in her bids and stretched. Flicker perked up

at her feet and looked at her hopefully with his giant brown eyes.

"No, I'm not taking you for a walk, you overgrown mop."

Flicker wagged his tail, knocking it against the table leg.

"If I'd known you were going to weigh almost as much as me, I would have let Brady take you back to the farm." When Brady had shown up with a surprise dog for Amber, Maggie had blown a gasket. Penny had stepped in and offered to keep the puppy. At the time, it had seemed easy and Amber loved the dog. Having never had a puppy before, Penny had been in for a treat.

The dog looked up at her with utter devotion. Penny couldn't resist an answering smile.

"Go back to sleep and maybe later we'll get a quick walk."

Flicker jumped up and headed to the door.

"Not now." Why did she say the word *walk?* "Flicker."

The dog growled and then barked.

"What's—"

Someone knocked on the door. Most likely Amber or Maggie. They'd spent the afternoon together working on a new scrapbook for Amber. Penny shut her laptop.

When she opened the door, she didn't see anyone for a moment.

"Hey."

She jumped and looked to her right. Luke stood in the shadows. "You startled me."

"Sorry about that."

Flicker rushed out the door and sniffed at Luke. Luke rubbed the dog's head, and the poor thing turned to putty in his hand. Penny was way too intimately familiar with the feeling.

"This must be the legendary Flicker." Luke didn't look up at her as Flicker put his front paws on Luke's chest in an effort to lick his face. His jeans, slung low on his hips, drew her attention. He filled them out nicely. She forced her gaze up to his button-down white shirt.

She ran her suddenly damp palms over her pink cotton shorts. Expecting to be alone this evening, she'd already changed into her pajamas. She hadn't thought to grab her sweater before answering the door since it was probably Maggie or Amber, and her comfy pink cotton tank didn't help against the cool evening air.

"Did you want to come in?" Penny grabbed Flicker's collar and tugged him off Luke. "It's a bit chilly out here."

Luke's eyes caught on her breasts before lifting to meet her eyes. "Sure."

He followed her into the house.

"Have a seat. I'll put Flicker out in the backyard." She motioned to the living room and hauled the dog out through the kitchen door. When she got back, Luke was staring at the pictures on the wall.

Her heart stopped. Most of the pictures were of Maggie, Amber and her, but the one he was focused on was the one of Luke and her. The night hadn't mattered and hadn't been anything special. It could have been any night or every night, but that picture showed how much in love they had been.

"Can I get you something to drink?" She wanted to ask why he was here. What had happened with Sam? Did he feel this intense, almost-drunk feeling when she was near, as she did? It made her feel comfortable and on edge in the same moment. "I have a beer or I could make some tea."

"No." He reached out and stroked a finger down the picture.

She shuddered as if he'd touched her. Goose bumps rose on her arms. It wasn't the chill in the air affecting her. It was the electric current running between them that had her body humming like a live wire.

He turned toward her. His blue eyes glowed in the dim light the lamp offered. "Are you expecting someone?"

"No. I was just working some before going to bed." She didn't normally have anyone over during the week. Before last weekend, it had been quite a while since she'd hooked up with someone. She was busy with work and helping with Maggie's wedding. It definitely didn't have anything to do with the fact that Luke would be coming home.

He glanced over her shoulder, down the hallway. A thrill shot through her. He knew exactly where her bedroom was. They hadn't had the chance to use it very often as teenagers, but he'd snuck in a few times. He was the only guy who had made it to her bedroom.

Suddenly she felt vulnerable and naked.

It had nothing to do with her state of dress. She wouldn't care if she were literally naked in front of Luke, but he'd been inside her head and heart as a teenager. Maggie knew her, but not as Luke did…or, rather, had.

"Sorry I interrupted you." Luke sank into the worn recliner.

"I had just finished up when you knocked." She hesitated in the doorway for a moment before she shook herself. She wasn't shy when it came to men, but something about Luke threw her off her game. She walked into the room and sat across from Luke with her legs tucked up under her. "What's up?"

"Sam's surgery went well." He combed his hand through his hair.

"It must have been a long day for you." Her heart beat mercilessly against her rib cage. Why was he here? To talk? To vent? To have sex?

"I just dropped off Brady."

To not be alone? She'd been there many times.

His fingers stroked sensually down the ruby-red glass of the Egermann Bohemian perfume bottle on the end table next to him. It didn't take much for her to remember those fingers tracing the vein in her neck.

"And since you were in the neighborhood, you thought you'd pass along the news of Sam?" Not bloody likely. This whole week had been an exercise in chastity. Something she wasn't entirely comfortable or familiar with. They'd never had a moment alone, which was probably good. If they had, she would have dragged him somewhere and to hell with her promises to her heart to keep him at arm's length for the duration of his stay. Besides, all promises were meant to be broken.

"Something like that." He seemed way too fascinated with the glass. It was as if he was trying to put her on edge. Draw her attention to the fingers that had provided her with hours of pleasure.

Keeping up this conversation was pointless. If he were here to drive her mad with desire, it was working. And since he hadn't touched her, she'd be on her own tonight. He'd hardly acknowledged the fact that she was barely dressed. If they weren't going to get busy, she would have to work through her desires by herself. She started to stand up.

"Wait." He held up his hand, still looking at the bottle.

She returned to her seat, not because he'd ordered her to, but because she was curious.

"Tell me about this." His words were so quiet and his voice so deep she almost didn't hear him.

"It's a ruby perfume bottle made by Egermann after 1860 in Bohemia."

Luke lifted his gaze to hers. "Penny?"

"Yes?"

"Give me its story."

She drew in a deep breath. When she was younger, she'd been fascinated with the antiques in her grandma's store. She'd spent countless hours there, wondering where everything came from, making up their stories to make them so much more than they were: things left behind by people who were either gone or no longer wanted them. "The real one?"

"Give me your story."

She hadn't thought up stories in years. Something in his lost look made her want to draw him into her embrace and just hold him for hours until whatever haunted him went away. He hadn't asked for that, but she could give him a story. "The year was 1867. There was a man who desired a woman very much."

He watched her with an intensity that took her breath away. "Go on."

She licked her lips and continued, "She was everything to him, but she didn't see him. Not as a man. Not as a person. One day he saw her standing in a store. In her hands she held that very perfume bottle. She stroked it with longing and smelled deeply of the perfume, which had the rich scent of jasmine in it. He could tell she wanted it very much."

Luke stood and crossed the room. He hunkered down

in front of her. His knuckles brushed her bare leg. "Tell me more."

She swallowed. "The woman put it back because she didn't have enough money for it. After she left the store, he went to the bottle and spent every last coin he had in his pocket on it, confident that with it, he would finally have her love. That night he went to her house and presented her with the bottle."

"What did she do?" He brushed her hair behind her ear and cradled her head in his hand.

Her breath whispered past her lips. "She invited him inside."

"Will you?" He pulled her head down toward his. She didn't resist.

"Will I what?"

He stopped before their lips touched. "Let me in."

Penny closed the distance between their mouths, answering him the only way she knew how. Their lips met and clung together. Sparks flew behind her eyes. Her skin tingled with the longing to be touched. Liquid heat flowed through her and pooled in the center of her.

Without breaking the kiss, he rose and took her into his arms. This was crazy. Foolish. The future was an unknown. The past was gone. This was perhaps the worst mistake she could make. But right now, Luke was the only thing that mattered to her. This connection. His mouth, his body, his essence…the fuel for this raging passion within her.

Chapter Nine

Luke hadn't known what to expect when he knocked on Penny's door. He wouldn't fool himself into believing his intentions had been any less than kissing Penny until he managed to release the devil that had been riding him since their night together.

He pulled away from the kiss. Her body was flush against his, her chest rising and falling with every breath. He ran a finger under the strap of her tank top.

"I never figured you for a pink-cotton girl." He rested his forehead against hers.

"My black and red lace teddies are all in the wash." Her fingers tangled in his hair.

"Liar." He pulled her from her chair and sat back on the floor with her on his lap.

"You've discovered my secret." She ran her fingers along the neckline of his shirt until she reached the top button. With a flick of her finger, she released it. "I have an all-encompassing passion for cotton pajamas. Shorts, pants, T-shirts, tank tops. I can't get enough of them."

He ran his hands up her bare legs until he brushed the cotton of her shorts.

"I can't let you leave here," she said. Her expression was serious, but the glint in her eyes ruined the effect.

He cupped her bottom and pulled her tight against his hardness. "Why is that?"

"Because you know at least one of my secrets." She dipped her head to kiss his neck. A pulse of pure heat went straight through his body. She pushed him back until he lay flat on the carpet. "I have to find out what else you know."

Her fingers wove with his and pressed his hands into the floor. He could easily overpower her if he wanted to. She took his mouth with hers. Her tongue danced with his. His blood ran hot through his veins and his brain began to short-circuit. His fingers twitched with the desire to explore her lush body. She released his mouth and stared down into his eyes.

"What if I'm not willing to talk?" Luke leaned up and nipped her chin.

She smiled wickedly. "We'll see about that."

Penny took her time removing his clothes, button by button, kissing every inch of skin she uncovered until Luke couldn't think straight. By the time she had him fully naked, he was sensitive everywhere. The slightest breeze from the open window made him stiffen with desire. He allowed her to do what she wanted, enjoying her attentions more than he probably should.

When he couldn't take any more, he lifted her top over her head and helped her out of her shorts and underwear. Having her naked skin against his was the most enticing feeling in the world. She was intoxicating. So sure and aware of herself as a sexual creature.

He wanted too much from her. He knew that. He wanted everything, every piece of her down to her very soul. But it was impossible. He'd learned that lesson years ago as a boy. As a man, he would take what she offered and enjoy her without reading too much into her moans of delight and her desire to please him.

After covering him with a condom, she hovered above him. Aphrodite herself. Her flesh pressed intimately with his. He had so many things he wanted to say, needed to tell her. Things she should know. She was one of a kind. In nine years, he hadn't been able to replace her in his mind or in his heart. No one compared to her.

"So beautiful." He reached up and stroked the side of her face.

Her passion-glazed eyes met his. She took his hand, pressed her lips against his fingertips. "I want to come apart with you."

She came down on him. They both gasped in air as if they were starving for it. She set a slow rhythm, but he couldn't take it. He grabbed her hips and set a new pace. He watched her every expression until she tightened all around him, taking him over the edge with her.

She collapsed on his chest. Both of them worked to catch their breaths.

A laugh escaped Penny.

"Not something a guy likes to hear after sex," he grumbled and kissed the top of her hair.

She rested her chin on her hands on his chest to look at him. Her brown eyes sparkled. "Trust me when I say that laugh *wasn't* about your performance. And may I say, 'bravo'?"

"You can applaud if you like." He smiled and pushed her hair from her face. "But I think you did most of the work."

"I wouldn't call it work." She squirmed against him and raised an eyebrow. "But you know, if you have some pent-up energy you need to expend—"

She squealed as he flipped her onto her back.

He leaned over her, his hand tracing along the side of her breast. "Since you seem in the mood to laugh, let's see if I can remember where your tickle spots are."

Penny hummed as she dusted the shelves of her shop the next morning. She still wasn't entirely sure why Luke had come over last night, but she definitely wasn't complaining after the christening of her living room rug.

"Penny dear, did you get bit by a mosquito?" Bitsy Clemons was making her morning rounds. With only a few shops on Main Street, Bitsy could spend a lot of time in each and still make it home for lunch.

Penny reached up and touched her neck. "Uh, yeah, nasty little buggers."

"We need to spray for them before they get bad this summer." Bitsy wandered down the aisle to the jewelry trays.

Penny glanced in one of the antique mirrors on the wall. Sure enough, she had a huge hickey from Luke as a greeting card this morning. Damn.

Luke had left sometime during the night and she'd crawled into bed exhausted. This morning, she'd overslept and managed to roll into the shower and pull on some clothes just in time to get to the shop for opening. She'd forgotten to look for collateral damage.

The bell above the door rang—hopefully announcing Bitsy's departure.

Some damage Penny had noticed—thankfully. The rug burns on her knees were discreetly hidden by her slacks. Bitsy would have a heart attack if she'd seen exactly how Penny had gotten those puppies. She chuckled.

"Someone's in a happy mood," Luke's voice slipped over her like a satin nightie, causing her knees to turn to gelatin.

She grabbed a shelf to hold herself steady before turning to face him. "Well, I did get lucky last night."

He moved in, drawing her closer with the crisp scent of his cologne. "Maybe you are on a winning streak."

"God, I hope so." She smiled up at him.

He leaned toward her as if to kiss her. The tinkling of jewelry being sorted alerted him that they weren't alone. He stiffened and took a step back. "Maggie, Brady and Amber went next door to grab something for their trip. They should be here in a minute. I'm driving them to the airport and they insisted on saying goodbye. Afterward I'm heading to the hospital to sit with Sam for a while."

"Cool." What power did Luke have that he always made her feel awkward when he was near? She didn't know what to do with her hands or how to stand. Which was ridiculous because this was Luke. He'd seen and touched every inch of her body.

"Is that Luke Ward?" Bitsy came hurrying down the aisle as if Luke might take off at the sight of her. Her blue floral skirt billowed out behind her like a cape.

Luke gave Penny a help-me look.

Penny just smiled and returned to dusting.

"My goodness, you've grown into quite the man. I remember when you were knee high to a grasshopper."

Bitsy eyed Luke as if he was the prize pig at the county fair. If he weren't careful, she might start poking and testing his muscles. Penny covered a laugh with a cough. "And a doctor, too."

"It's a pleasure to see you again, Mrs. Clemons."

"Oh, stop." Bitsy blushed to the roots of her silver hair and waved her hand. "We're all adults here. You can call me Bitsy."

Luke smiled. "What are you looking for today, Bitsy?"

"I just come to browse and help Penny in her quest for true love." Bitsy placed her hand on Luke's arm. "I know you two were involved once upon a time, but really she needs to settle down with someone before she's too old to have children."

Penny stopped her dusting. "True love? Kids? And here I thought you were just setting me up with men for the fun of it."

"What's wrong with kids?" Luke had a mischievous look in his eyes, as if he was enjoying her torture.

"Nothing's *wrong* with kids as long as they are someone else's." Penny raised her eyebrow, daring him to contradict her.

"Now, now, Penny. Take it from an old lady who never had kids of her own. One day you'll want kids and it will be too late." Bitsy nodded her head sagely. She'd married late in life and never had any children. She'd been friends with Penny's grandma and had always slipped Penny sweets when she came by to talk with Grandma Tilly.

"Don't worry, Bitsy. I have a few good years left if I want to push out a brat or two."

"Ticktock," Bitsy scolded. She glanced to the clock on the wall. "Oh, time to go see Mr. Martin. It was good seeing you, Luke, and if you have any single doctor friends, make sure to send them Penny's way."

They watched her scurry out of the store. Alone once again with Luke, Penny's heart fluttered. Talking about kids and men in front of Luke had been extremely awkward. But now that they were alone, they didn't have to talk at all.

He closed in on her, forcing her to look up to meet his eyes or stare at his chest. Hmm, decisions, decisions. It was such a fine chest. She sighed and met his eyes.

"Ticktock." He grinned down at her.

"Not you, too." She took a deep breath and her breasts grazed his chest. "I've got years before I even need to worry about that damned clock."

His fingers stroked a strand of hair that had escaped her messy bun. "Do you want children?"

"You offering?" She intended to throw him off. With him standing so near, her insides were pooling into liquid warmth that flowed through her whole body.

"Stop trying to distract me, Penny." He dipped his head slightly and she swore he was going to kiss her. Talk about distracting. "What are your future plans? What happens after right now?"

"I get lucky?" She flashed him a grin. She certainly hoped she would.

"What do you want?" he whispered close to her ear, stealing any breath she had left. His voice was rich and soothing. She swore she could listen to him read a dictionary and be turned on.

He pulled back. His blue eyes were dark pools, begging her to strip naked and dive in. He was close enough that his heat made her want to sway forward and rub against his warmth. She wanted him. 24/7.

"Do you want kids?" he asked.

Kids? A baby? With Luke's blue eyes and her red hair? Someone she could love and who would love her in return. Who would rely on her for everything. Who she would disappoint.

A shard of cold went through her.

"I—" She swallowed and stepped back against the shelf. Straightening, she slid away from him down the aisle. She didn't want these thoughts. She knew what she could and couldn't have, and a child was a *couldn't*. "I need to get back to work."

"I want children," Luke said as if she hadn't walked away from the conversation. "I want a wife and home and children. Someday."

Her chest ached. She didn't look back at him. Thinking of Luke with his future wife and their perfect house and perfect children was enough to make her want to lose her breakfast.

"That's great," Penny choked out and blinked back the burning tears in her eyes. "You'll make a great dad."

His hands rested on her shoulders. His touch brought on another surge of tears. "Penny—"

The bell on the door jingled and Brady's, Maggie's and Amber's voices broke their solitude. She heard his sigh before his hands slipped away. She rushed to the back into the storeroom and shut the door behind her. She took a great shuddering breath in and scolded herself.

Luke wasn't hers. In no universe would he be hers. She'd made sure of that years ago. So why did the thought of him with someone else burn through her stomach like a branding iron? She set down the duster and grabbed a tissue. After a few deep breaths, she pulled herself together.

Just because they were having some fun didn't give

her any hold over Luke. Just because she'd loved him
once didn't mean she was in danger of being in love
with him again. Just because the thought of a child, his
child, made her clench up inside with longing didn't
mean she wanted one.

She picked up the present she'd wrapped for Amber
and opened the storeroom door, prepared to do battle.

Chapter Ten

Luke stepped out from behind the shelving and into the open part of the store, where the front desk and cash register were.

"Where's Penny?" Amber asked.

"She went into the back for something." Most likely to get away from him. She was upset and she had every reason to be. He didn't know why he'd pushed so hard. Maybe it was because Bitsy hadn't thought he'd be the right guy for Penny. If he had any single friends... Not in this lifetime. "I'm sure she'll be right out."

"Everything okay?" Maggie asked.

"Yeah." No, it wasn't. "Did you guys get what you needed?"

"We're all set," Brady said as he picked up a little blue bottle, which looked as if it might have once had medicine in it, off a shelf.

"I hear someone is going to Disney World." Penny

appeared. It was as if nothing strange had passed between them. She smiled at Amber and held out a little box, gift-wrapped and tied with a bow.

"For me?" Amber took the box and opened it very carefully.

Penny glanced up at him before returning her gaze to Amber. He saw how much she loved being around Amber. Why wouldn't she want that for herself? His heart beat a little harder with the thought of Penny with a baby in her arms. Would they already have a few kids if she'd come with him to university? He could imagine lying in bed with her on a Sunday morning with kids climbing onto the bed with them. One happy family.

He startled. He could have been happy with her, but not if he couldn't even be sure if the kids were his. What was so fundamentally broken with her that she couldn't be with just him? Hadn't he been enough? Lord knew he couldn't get enough of her. Even now.

"O.M.G. It's a Mickey necklace. Mom, it's a Mickey necklace." Amber brought him back to the here and now.

"I see that," Maggie said.

"Oh, thank you, thank you, thank you. I've always wanted one." Amber threw her arms around Penny and Penny squeezed her tight.

As soon as Amber released her to go show Brady, Penny looked at Luke. It was there in her eyes, that longing for something she couldn't have. Whether she told him she wanted children or not, that look told him everything. She wanted a child, but she was content holding her best friend's daughter as her own.

He kept his gaze on Penny as they all said their goodbyes. Brady's family would be gone for ten days and then they'd be back to help out again. After that, Luke could leave at that time if he wanted to. As they exited the shop, Penny met his gaze. He knew the only thing he wanted right now was her. And although she seemed to want him now, who's to say that tomorrow, she wouldn't want someone else?

"'Bout time you showed up." Sam lay in his hospital bed in a robe and hospital gown, looking distinctly uncomfortable. "When do I get out of this place?"

"You only had surgery two days ago," Luke sat in the chair next to the bed. "They want you to stay one more night."

"How am I supposed to get better with all these tubes in me?" Sam held up his IV with disdain. "This sucks."

"I'm sure it does." Luke looked out the window. Springfield wasn't nearly as big as St. Louis, but it was a decent size for the middle-of-nowhere Illinois. The surrounding buildings seemed dreary and worn-out.

"How's the farm?" Sam picked up the remote and flipped the channel on the TV. A news channel played in the background with the sound on mute.

"The animals are tended. The Baxter boys have been by to help with the fields."

John Baxter was a neighboring farmer who helped Sam out in the spring and fall during seeding and harvesting. His two sons went to the local community college and helped out year-round. Sam returned the favor by giving them bales of hay at baling time.

"That's good." Sam rubbed at the stubble on his chin. After a few minutes, he said, "I made an appointment with the cardiologist. His office is around the corner from the hospital."

"There isn't anyone closer?" An hour's drive both ways every day to the hospital to check up on Sam was annoying, especially because Luke kept going to Penny's before going home. Last night they'd barely spoken when he'd shown up at her door. He hadn't said a word, just took her in his arms. She'd pulled him into her dining room, where they'd made good use of the table and chairs. He had yet to see the inside of her bedroom. He barely managed any sleep before waking for the morning chores. "What about Dr. Patterson?"

"He retired. Tawnee Valley hasn't had a doctor in years, and Owen only has a handful of specialists. No cardiologists." Sam fluffed a pillow and shoved it behind his head.

Luke leaned forward, thinking of the ramifications of sick people having to go an hour just to get to their doctor. Most people would either just not go to the doctor at all or go to the emergency room rather than make the trip. Filling up the emergency room with people best seen in an office made it hard for the true emergencies to get in. The hospital in Owen must be a nightmare of never-ending patients.

"You get the tractor running?" Sam asked, interrupting Luke's thoughts.

"What? Yeah, it only needed a new fuse."

Sam nodded and continued to watch the TV.

Luke returned to his thoughts. It was bad enough that a lot of patients came from miles away to see specialists in the hospital he worked at in St. Louis, but those patients usually had a doctor close by who they could follow up with.

The population of Tawnee Valley and even Owen was skewed to an older than average age. Those people shouldn't have to sit in a car for an hour just to get some medical advice. Especially just for checkups to make sure nothing has changed or whether a new medicine was working or not.

"Anything new?" Sam said.

"What?" Luke turned to look at Sam.

Sam rarely spoke outside of direct questions and answers. He looked highly uncomfortable. "I'm stuck in a hospital bed watching bad TV. I'm bored."

Luke smiled. "You want me to bring you my laptop next time? It has solitaire on it."

"I better be going home tomorrow. If you won't take me, I'll hitch a ride." Sam shoved the remote away. "Or maybe Penny would come get me."

If Luke were a rooster, his feathers would be rustled. "Why would Penny do that?"

"She and I are a lot alike. Both alone." Sam closed his eyes and put his arm behind his head.

The idea of Sam and Penny together burned Luke deeper than thinking of her with any other man. Sam was his brother, his guardian. He was supposed to watch out for Luke, not steal his girl. Even if his girl had been a willing participant. "You won't have to call Penny because I'll be here."

"Good."

Luke sat for an hour more with Sam, answering his random questions and silently fuming. He couldn't get the image of Sam kissing Penny out of his head. The night of his graduation, he'd been outside with his friends when he went back into the house to get a drink. Through the kitchen door, he could see Penny with her hands around Sam's neck, her body tight against his. Her lips pressed against Sam's. Sam's hands had been on her hips.

He hadn't needed to see more. All that locker room talk. All the times Penny had talked him down from kicking some guy's ass for saying he was nailing her. It had all been true. What he had thought was love had been a lie.

All those hours they'd spent, dreaming and planning, had been for nothing. He was just another one of her guys. He just hadn't realized it.

The drive home didn't help his dark mood. If Sam and Penny did end up together, she'd be his sister-in-law. He'd have to see her with him at every family get-together. Participate in her and Sam's wedding as if he were happy to be there.

By the time he drove into Tawnee Valley, it was late. He could have gone straight to the farm and just skipped seeing Penny tonight, but that wasn't going to happen.

He parked his car in front of her house and stared at the dark street ahead of him. It was all in the past. He'd moved on. She'd moved on. What they were doing now…that was just for fun. Something to keep the boredom away.

It had taken him a year to get over the betrayal. But he'd never truly let it go. Maybe that was because he'd been so sure that they had been in love. He slammed his hand against the steering wheel. This was stupid.

The past shouldn't matter. Penny wasn't the same girl. She had solid roots in the community. A sensitive side that she rarely showed. So she enjoyed sex. Since when had that been a crime?

If she and Sam were involved, they didn't act like it. Even if they were just having sex, it would be a while before Sam was up to anything. This was ridiculous. Luke was here for only another week or so. He didn't have any hold over Penny or control over who she spent her time with.

But he'd make damned sure who she would spend her time with tonight.

Penny was just about to give up on Luke coming over when she heard a knock on the door. The fluttering in her stomach made her want to not answer. He was getting to her, and that could be very bad.

Sex didn't equal love in her world. But Luke…Luke was an intensity she couldn't deny.

She crossed the room to the door and pulled it open. Their eyes met. No matter if it was the first time or the thousandth time, when Luke came near her she melted.

She moved out of the doorway to let him in, as if she had a choice. In her heart she knew that anytime Luke wanted her, she would let him in. Into her home. Into her body. Into her heart.

He moved past her into the living room.

"Who are you sleeping with?" Luke asked as he sat on her couch. His long legs spread out before him.

His question took her aback, but she wasn't intimidated by it. It didn't prevent the pain that gouged her heart at his question. She remembered how easy it was for him to believe the worst in her. Did he worry that she was sleeping with someone else now? Was he afraid she couldn't juggle the workload? She curled up in the corner of the couch next to, but not touching, him. She let him stew a few minutes before meeting his gaze.

"Honey, I'm not sleeping with anyone." It was the God's honest truth. They hadn't slept together. They had mind-blowing sex and then he left to go out to the farm so he could rise with the roosters.

"You know what I mean."

"Someone's a little testy this evening." She stretched back and put her legs across his lap.

He met her eyes and held them. Every bit as serious as he sounded. "Are you having sex?"

"With you? Not yet." She gave him a wink. What was he after? If she played this game long enough, he'd get to his point sooner or later or give up entirely and get to the good part of the evening.

"I'm serious."

"I know you are." Penny sighed and put her arms behind her head. "What do you want from me, Luke? An oath of fidelity? My declaration of love?"

His eyes narrowed, but then he took in a deep breath and pulled her by her legs toward him. She went willingly. When he had her straddling his lap, he took both her hands and placed them on his shoulders. "This isn't normal for me."

"This position or this situation?" She cocked a grin at him. Her core pulsed.

"I'm supposed to be working right now."

"I know and I wish you'd get on with it already." She ran her hands down his T-shirt, feeling the hard muscles twitch beneath it.

"Penny, stop."

"Killjoy."

"I want to have a conversation with you."

"Why?" Penny traced the bottom edge of his shirt with her fingernail. "Why do we have to talk at all? What is there to say that would make any difference?"

"How about 'I care about you'?"

She held her breath, waiting for the *but*.

"I want to know that you take care of yourself. It seems like we skipped some of the important conversations to have before having sex." Luke placed his hands on her hips lightly.

"What kind of conversations?" she asked suspiciously.

"How many people have you been with?"

Her heart hitched. This seemed like a huge trap. "I don't want to play this game."

She moved to get off him, but his hands held her tightly.

"Okay, no numbers," he said. He clearly wasn't happy about it, though.

She stopped trying to move off him. The real number probably wasn't as high as he imagined it was. She had no reason to be ashamed of the amount of men she'd been with, but this was Luke. Her first and her latest.

"Have you always been safe?" His eyes delved into hers.

"Is this the doctor asking?" she teased, trying to ease the tension growing inside her.

"No, it's the man who's having sex with you and plans on doing it again. I know we are using condoms, but have you always?"

"Yes, always." She met his gaze head-on. If he wanted to know the details, why the hell not? "You?"

He nodded and his fingers relaxed their grip of her hips. "Do you get tested?"

She nodded and raised her eyebrow at him as if to say, *Do you?*

"Of course." He shifted slightly beneath her. "When was the last time you had sex?"

"You should know. You were there. Was I that forgettable?" She fake pouted and then winked, not able to resist trying to lighten this conversation. Why was he suddenly being so serious?

He pulled her in tightly against him. He was solid everywhere and it made her want him more. "With someone else."

She threaded her fingers through his hair. "Well, Doctor, let's see.... It was before the wedding, before planning the wedding, before Maggie and Brady got back together.... Was it spring last year or winter? Damn, it's been a while. Good thing you're here."

Leaning into him, she placed a kiss on his lips. His arms wrapped around her, holding her, and he opened his mouth beneath hers. Pleasure raced down her spine as his tongue brushed against hers. It was as if he were rewarding her for her answer. If those were the types of rewards he was doling out, he could ask away. He pulled back and she whimpered. His satisfied smile made her want to key him up and then leave him hanging as he was doing to her. The most sensual torture.

"I'm not done asking questions," he said.

"What if I'm done answering questions?"

"Fine. Ask me a question, then."

She sat back and thought for a moment. "When was your last serious relationship?"

For a moment, hurt flashed in his eyes. Was he remembering them? His smile didn't reach his eyes. "I haven't had time for serious."

That one hurt. This great guy hadn't had anyone in his life. What was the point of breaking it off if he didn't find that special someone who would be the woman he needed? She asked, "Semi-serious?"

He shook his head. This crazy feeling started in her chest, like a boa constrictor releasing its prey. She shouldn't feel this way about Luke. It was dangerous to even consider anything past tonight. She'd just end up more ruined.

"You?" he asked.

"Not even kind of serious." She met his eyes and could see the relief in them, but there was still some reserve. Something he was holding back.

"Have you loved anyone?" he asked.

Since you? She couldn't make her voice work, so she shook her head.

"Me neither." He relaxed against the couch and pulled her hips forward. "Do you think we are broken?"

"How do you mean?"

"Like the reason we can't love someone is because of the stuff we went through as kids?" Luke leaned his head back and looked up at the ceiling. "I was a mess after Mom and Dad died."

"You weren't that bad," she said softly and cradled his face in her hand.

"I was a walking disaster. I almost had to repeat a year in high school because my grades were so low. I picked fights with anyone who looked at me the wrong way—"

"You were hurt. You were lashing out."

He'd been a wounded animal. She'd recognized him as a kindred spirit right away.

"You were, too." He brushed her hair off her cheek and cradled the back of her head. "We should have self-destructed. Instead we came together."

"You needed someone. I needed someone." She shrugged. "We made sense."

"What about now?" He pulled her in close but held back from kissing her. His breath was warm against her lips. Tantalizing, teasing. "Do we make sense now, Penny?"

Heaven help her. Her eyes fluttered closed, waiting for him to take her. "Didn't we self-destruct back then?"

"I want you." He brushed his lips across hers. "I can't get you out of my head. When I'm sitting alone, I wish you were there to talk to. When I'm working on the farm, I want you there beside me."

"So you can push me in the mud?" She tried to inch forward, but he held her back.

"Can't you be serious for one minute?" He tsked and leaned down to nip at her neck.

She released a low moan as he hit a spot that made her whole body quake with desire. "I want you, Luke. Any way you want me. Anytime. I want you now. I'll want you tomorrow and the next day. I crave your touch and covet your time."

He pulled back and rested his forehead against hers. Their eyes locked. "What's happening?"

"Do we have to pick it apart?" she whispered. The ache in her core was driving her insane. "Do we have to analyze this? Can't it just be what it is?"

"But what is it?" Luke brushed his thumb over her bottom lip. "Is this just a sex thing? Or is more going on?"

Her hands started to shake, and deep in her chest that boa wrapped tightly around her heart again. She wanted to scream that she was unlovable. That even if he thought he was in love with her, it wouldn't last.

"Are you willing to admit that we have more than sex between us?" Luke brushed his lips against hers again.

"Do you want me to admit that I need you? Because that's not going to happen. I don't need anyone. I have my house, my business, my dog—"

"I'm not asking you to need me, Penny." Luke lifted her to her feet and stood before her.

"Then what do you want?"

"A chance. A date. To get to know the woman you

are and not the girl I knew." He stroked his knuckles down the side of her face. "I don't know where any of this is going. Or what's going to happen in a week. But I know I want to spend time with you."

"So you want to hang out without having sex?" She looked up at him through her eyelashes.

"Yes."

She smiled and raised her eyebrow. "No sex?"

"I'm sorry, but sex is definitely on the table...or the floor, if you prefer." Luke grabbed her hips and pulled her close. "Or even a bed. You do own one, right?"

"Of course I have a bed."

He wiggled his eyebrows wickedly. "Point the way."

She put her hand to his chest to stop him. "My bedroom is off-limits."

Wrinkles formed on his forehead. "You do live alone, right?"

"Yes, I live alone. My rules." She didn't want to tell him that it was her personal space and that to invite someone in was too scary.

"I'll go out with you and have sex with you, but not in my bedroom."

Luke held her hand against his heart. "Someday you'll have to let someone in."

She smiled sadly. Not today. Never again.

"Can I offer you a drink?" She took his hand in hers and led him through the dining room. With her other hand, she started unbuttoning her blouse. "There's a lovely view out of the kitchen."

"I don't think the view could get much lovelier."

"Keep up lines like that and I might let you take me to dinner."

"I can keep it up all night if you like."

Chapter Eleven

"I can walk myself." Sam shoved Luke away for the third time.

Luke ran his hand through his hair. "I'm not trying to hold your hand, you ninny. The gravel drive isn't a stable surface and you have steps up the porch."

"That I've been climbing since I was one." Sam gave him a menacing look when Luke stepped closer. "I'll be fine, but *you* won't if you keep trying to touch me."

"Fine." Luke held his hands up. "Just don't take one step past the downstairs bedroom."

Sam made a rude gesture and continued to plod his way to the house.

The screen door opened and Penny came out. Her ginger hair shone in the sunlight. She wore a pink tank top and a pair of cutoff jeans with sandals. Even though the days were warming up, the nights were still cool.

"I just finished putting away the groceries," she said as Sam shuffled past without even a look.

Clearly, Luke had misread the few times either of them had brought up the other. Seeing that kiss had colored his view. They barely acknowledged each other even when they were in the same room.

"Thanks, Penny." Luke leaned over and kissed her before going into the house. His chest felt warm; being able to claim her in public put him in a great mood. Before he'd left to pick up Sam, they'd had breakfast at The Rooster Café in Tawnee Valley. She'd even held his hand across the table. It was ridiculous how good that made him feel when hours before he'd been in heaven in her arms.

"I'll get dinner ready, but then I need to go into town." Penny shut the screen door and moved to the stove.

"You aren't going to eat with us?" Luke set down Sam's hospital bag and came up behind Penny. He pulled her back against him while she lit the stove under a pot with water and potatoes in it.

"I have to get some work done and put Flicker out."

He bit down lightly on the place where her shoulder and neck met. "What about later?"

"Sam's here. You are going to have your hands full. I've got a big day tomorrow at the store." She turned in his arms to face him. Her smile didn't quite reach her eyes. "We can see each other the following day."

Sam's here. Did that have anything to do with her not wanting to be with him? God, he *was* clingy.

"That's fine." He returned to Sam's bag and lifted it. "I'm going to make sure Sam is settled in."

"Yup." She turned back to the potatoes.

Something was up, but after pushing her so hard last

night, he didn't know if pushing her today would be a good idea. Penny had always bottled her emotions. It'd been difficult for her to be honest about her feelings. He wanted to respect that, but at times it drove him crazy.

"Your room is all set up and you can easily get to the family room from here." Luke paused in the doorway. Sam sat on the bed, holding his side. His face was crumpled in pain.

"What happened?" Luke dropped the bag and moved forward. He automatically reached for Sam's pulse.

"I just got winded." Sam took a shaky breath in. "You don't think they gave me a bum heart valve, do you?"

His pulse was fine. A little higher than Luke would like, but not in a danger zone. "You need to lie down for a bit and rest."

Luke kneeled and undid Sam's sneakers.

"I'm not a baby." Sam coughed and groaned.

"No, but you just had surgery, so lay off." Tossing the sneakers to the side, Luke helped lift Sam's legs onto the bed. "You have water on your nightstand and also a bell."

"A bell?" Sam looked over as if Luke had said a snake was over there.

"To ring when you need something."

"I can take care of myself."

"No. You can't. When you ring the bell, I'll come help you. Trust me, it's only temporary. Don't get used to it." Luke stood and put the curtains down to block some of the sunlight. "Rest."

"Whatever." Sam punched the pillow. He laid back and closed his eyes.

Luke started out of the room.

"Luke?"

"Do you need something?"

Sam didn't open his eyes. "Thanks."

Luke didn't hide his shock. "You're welcome."

Sam grunted and rolled to face away from the door.

Luke stared at his back. How long had it been since he'd had a conversation with Sam that wasn't just a status update? How long since they'd been honest with each other? Luke had never brought up Sam's betrayal, but it had eaten away at what had been left of their relationship.

Shaking his head, Luke left the door open a crack before returning to the kitchen. Perfectly at home, Penny moved around the kitchen to make dinner for him and Sam.

"Are you sure you won't eat with us?"

Penny stopped midreach for the salt in the cupboard. Her mouth opened as if she was going to say something, but then she closed it as if she'd changed her mind. She shook her head instead and grabbed the salt.

"No salt for Sam." Luke leaned on the counter next to the stove.

"Oh, right." She set the salt on the counter and stirred the pot. "That's about as spicy as I get with cooking, I'm afraid."

Luke crossed to the cabinet and pulled down a few dried herbs, which had probably been in there since his mother died. "Try these."

"Thank you."

He wanted to say more. He wanted to talk about Sam, but she seemed so distant. Was she already starting to push him away? Why, after letting him closer last night? It was a vicious cycle with Penny. Even in high school, one day she'd be warm and caring. The next she'd be cold and distant. He'd thought it was the birth control she'd been on, but maybe it'd been more her than he'd wanted to believe.

"Are you going to stare at me while I cook? Aren't there chores or something to be done?" Penny glanced over and flashed him a wicked smile. "Don't make me get inventive with this wooden spoon."

His chest loosened and he held up his hands in surrender. "I don't know what you have in mind, but something tells me I wouldn't like it. I'll go see if the pigs could use some cuddling."

Penny hadn't exactly lied about having work to do this morning, but she could have stayed longer last night if she wanted to. The problem was every time she was near Sam she felt sick to her stomach. She may not be overly discriminating with whom she went out with these days, but back then...

She picked up the small tea sets and placed them on her cart. Once a month she did a full cleaning of the store. Everything came off the shelf. She cleaned each and every piece and did an inventory. It took her about a week to get through the entire store, but it made the store smell less like old stuff and more clean and fresh, with just a hint of old-stuff smell for atmosphere.

The door jangled as someone entered. She set down her rag and wiped her hands on the towel.

"Hello?" she called out as she walked to the front of the store.

"Hello?" returned a male voice that seemed familiar.

"Can I help you?" She stopped when she saw him. Jasper Ballard stood at her door. All six-foot, well-built, hunky goodness of him. Dark hair and brown eyes and a dimple on his right cheek.

"Hey, I was passing through town..." He smiled that

lopsided smile of his that had always gotten her motor revving. But not this time.

She shook herself out of her shocked stillness and headed for the cash register and the desk that would separate her from him. "How long are you in town?"

Her actions seemed to confuse him. She was usually overly friendly when he made his jaunts through Tawnee Valley. The local eligible male population was sadly lacking and most of them didn't hold a candle to Jasper. Jasper wasn't exactly a migrant worker, but he went from place to place looking for farming work. She rarely saw him in the winter, but when he was in town, he definitely liked to hook up. Normally she was all for it, but this time, it was complicated.

"For a few weeks. Looking for some easy money." He leaned his hands against her desk.

"Easy? Right. Because working on a farm is a piece of cake."

"For me it is." He flexed his arms, showing her their strength. If possible he'd developed more muscle since the last time he'd been in town. "Can I see you while I'm in town?"

"Uh…" Penny didn't want to burn this particular bridge. He was easy on the eyes and good in bed. But right now, she didn't want anyone but Luke. But Luke wouldn't be around forever, and eventually she'd have an itch.

The bell above the door saved her from having to come up with some excuse without blowing him off entirely.

Her eyes went to the door. Her heart froze in her chest. Luke.

His gaze took in Jasper's form and his casual stance.

Then those blue eyes flowed over her. He noticed every detail, making her want to squirm under his scrutiny.

"Penny." He closed the distance between them and the air around her grew heavy. Luke stuck out his hand to Jasper. "Luke Ward, and you are?"

"Jasper Ballard." Jasper's gaze flicked to hers for a moment before returning to Luke. "You part of the Ward farm?"

"Yeah, my brother owns it."

"I was heading out there this afternoon." Jasper stood with his feet apart and his arms crossed. "Sam usually has some odds and ends this time of year that he uses my help on."

"Sam's sick," Penny interjected, though neither man looked her way.

"I'd be willing to come out and help. My next job is in a week or so, but I work hard and don't mess around," Jasper said. "You can ask Sam about me if you want his approval. Here's my card."

Luke took the card and flipped it over in his hand. "I'll have to check with Sam about the finances, but we could use some more manpower."

"Great. I'll come out later this afternoon to see if we can make this work." Jasper winked at Penny. "I'll see you later, gorgeous."

Before she could get out a not-right-now-thank-you, Jasper was out the door, leaving her alone with Luke. She busied herself with the little knickknacks on the counter as if her life depended on getting them exactly in line.

"We going to talk about this?" Luke placed his hand over hers.

Her gaze bounced up to his and then back down. "Talk about what?"

Ignorance would save her. From what...she didn't know. She hadn't done anything wrong. She hadn't even encouraged Jasper. She just hadn't gotten the chance to say she was taken for now. And now she'd have to find Jasper to let him know that it wasn't going to happen this time.

Luke placed the card in her line of sight. "Is this why you were busy last night?"

"No." She met his gaze square on. "Of course not. I haven't seen him in over a year until this morning. Here in the shop, where we most definitely did not have sex."

"But he was the last guy you had sex with?"

"If it's any of your business, yeah. So what?" She pulled her hand back and crossed her arms.

"Do you even know him?"

"What does it matter?"

"It matters who you sleep with."

"For the last time, I didn't sleep with him. We had sex and it was good sex. There's nothing wrong with that."

"Is that all we are?" Luke flipped the card over and put it in the back pocket of his jeans. "Sex?"

"Why?" Penny threw her hands up. "What does it matter whether what I feel for you is more than sex? What is it going to change? You hate me for what I did. You know that I sleep around. That my standards are pretty low, except when it comes to you."

She felt as if she were ripping her heart open and spilling it all over the counter, but she didn't care. "We were fine apart. I got to do my thing and you got to do yours. You were only supposed to be here for the weekend."

"I'm here and I'm glad that I am." He came around

the counter and rested his hands on her shoulders. "We left some things unfinished, unsaid."

She braced herself, waiting for the anger and the accusations. Even though she felt strong on the outside, her heart felt like a brutalized piece of meat.

"I don't know where we go from here. I don't even know where here is." His hands squeezed her shoulders. "You promised me you'd try. I promise you I'll try to trust you."

Her eyes widened. She put her hands on his chest. "Trust?"

How could he say that after what she'd done to him? Kissing his own brother. Betraying every ounce of trust they had in their relationship. Making him feel like an idiot for ever believing her over all those guys.

"Yeah." His smile softened. "If you say you aren't having sex with that guy, I'll believe you. Just promise me if you decide to sleep—have sex with that guy or anyone else, you'll give me a heads-up. That way I can convince you not to."

He brushed his lips against hers, and that little fizzle of warmth spread throughout her chilled body. "Why?"

"Why would I convince you? Because you're hot and I'm horny."

She pushed on his chest. "You know what I mean."

"Because, Penny..." He kissed her and hugged her close.

Giving in to her desire, she rested her head against his chest and breathed in the freshness of him. His arms could make anything better. The day a little brighter. She wished she could stay here all the time and never let him go. "Because?"

"Because you make me feel alive. I like the way I feel

with you. I tried to forget how you made me feel by putting hundreds of miles between us. Let me be enough for you. For as long as this lasts…let me be enough."

Chapter Twelve

The next few days flew by in a haze. Penny kept busy at the store during the day and Luke showed up every night, though only for a short period before he went back out to be with Sam. Their time together wasn't just about sex anymore. They talked about everything. Her store. His medical career. The crappy stuff he had to do out at the farm. The crazy tourist with the yappy dog she'd insisted on bringing into Penny's shop.

What they didn't talk about was the past. Or their feelings. Which was fine with Penny.

Today was her day off, so she decided to drive out to the farm to check on Sam, as she promised Amber. She also planned to clean the house because the men likely hadn't had time to with everything that had to be done on the farm.

Jasper and Luke waved from the field as she passed by to turn down the driveway. Jasper hadn't shown up at her doorstep yet. Maybe Luke had told him that she was unavailable. Or maybe Jasper had noticed Luke's car in her driveway. Either way she was glad it was a nonissue.

She parked and grabbed the bags of groceries out of the back. As she walked into the kitchen, the screen door slammed behind her. Someone had tightened the spring again.

She set the bags on the counter and started to unload them. It hadn't taken her long to figure out the kitchen setup when she'd been out here with Luke and Amber.

"Oh, it's you." Sam stood in the doorway with his perma-scowl on.

"Sorry to disappoint." Penny didn't look up from unloading groceries.

Sam walked into the kitchen and sat on one of the wooden chairs.

"Shouldn't you be in a comfy chair or your bed?"

Sam rested his head on his hands. "Not you, too. How many reruns and episodes of *Judge Judy* do you people think I can take?"

Penny shrugged and grabbed the empty bags to store in the closet. When she turned back, Sam was looking at her expectantly, so she asked him, "Did you need something to eat?"

"Sure." Sam brushed his hand over his jaw. "I'd do it myself, but I'm too feeble apparently."

Penny shook her head and smiled. "Dr. Luke has you on lockdown?"

Sam nodded miserably.

"One grilled cheese sandwich coming up." She got out the bread, cheese and margarine and started heating up a skillet. She wasn't used to being alone with Sam.

His silence had always been somewhat off-putting to her; she liked to talk.

"Amber called me yesterday." Sam's voice shattered the silence.

"How's she doing?" Penny buttered the bread and unwrapped the cheese. Sam must be really bored if he was willing to talk to her.

"She's having the time of her life and trying not to sound like it."

Penny glanced back in time to catch Sam's smile. Weird.

He pulled out a farm magazine and flipped through the pages.

"I've talked to her every day, and she's always excited about all the rides. So…" Penny crossed her arms over her chest. "What's your secret?"

"What?" He stopped flipping and looked up at her.

"Before you came along, I was Amber's favorite person to hang out with. We'd order pizza, do our nails and watch romantic tween movies together." She waved the spatula at him. "Did you bribe with chocolate? Or is it the dogs? Because I got her one of those, too."

Sam scratched his chin. "I don't know. I give her chores and she asks for more. Maybe it's because I don't treat her like a kid."

Penny narrowed her eyes. "Are you sure it isn't chocolate? Because I can totally hook her up with chocolate."

"She likes the animals." Sam shrugged.

"I'm not about to install a circus in my backyard." She turned and put his sandwich in the skillet.

"Guess you won't win, then."

She spun around, but he had his head buried in the magazine again. "I wouldn't taunt the woman making your meal, Sam Ward."

"It can't taste any worse than my cooking, no matter what you do to it."

Penny laughed and turned back to the stove. "Luke used to always try to eat at my place or we'd go out somewhere. He said he'd starve to death if he had to live on what you prepared."

"I haven't starved yet."

She finished his sandwich and put it on a plate. She grabbed a diet pop and some carrots from the fridge and placed it all in front of Sam.

"Thanks."

"No problem." Penny washed the pan and the spatula and put them in the drying rack. She scrubbed down the counters and the rest of the kitchen while Sam ate his lunch and read the magazines.

"How was the sandwich?" she asked as she took his empty plate.

"Pretty good." Sam glanced up at her. "But we already know I have the taste buds of a dog."

"True." Penny smiled.

The screen door creaked as it was pulled open. They both looked toward the door as Luke came in. He stopped and the door slammed shut behind him.

His mouth opened and closed. Penny realized how close she was standing to Sam's chair and stepped back. Jasper followed Luke in.

"Penny! Long time no see." Jasper winked, completely oblivious to the tension in the room. The door slammed behind him. "What's for lunch?"

"I think I'm going to go lie down." Sam rose from his chair and headed back toward his bedroom.

Penny went to the sink and washed the plate in the water she had left from doing the pan. She'd done nothing wrong, but her stomach rolled and pitched like a boat caught in a storm.

"Guess I'll get my own lunch. You want anything, Luke?" Jasper said.

"Nah, I'm good. I think I'll go wash up some."

She knew the moment he left the room. Some of the warmth left with him.

"So you and Luke, eh?" Jasper said as he sat at the table. "I guess that means I'll have to find another lovely companion to spend my time with in Tawnee Valley."

She set the dish in the drying rack and faced Jasper. "I'm sure you'll have no trouble securing a 'companion.'"

"I don't know about that." He took a drink from his pop can. "Most of the women are looking for someone to marry them so they can pop out a few brats. Or someone to take care of the brats they already have."

"That sounds pretty bitter." She leaned against the counter and crossed her arms. "Harboring some resentment there?"

"Hardly. I just know the lay of the land. The young ones are looking for a way to get out of town. The older ones are looking for someone to hold on to." Jasper smiled. "You are definitely one of a kind."

"How so?"

"You don't want anything from guys except sex. No strings. No attachment. No having to fake I care. You get yours and I get mine and we go on our separate ways."

The way he described it, sex with her was a transaction. She'd never put much thought into it. It was a basic need like eating and sleeping. Lots of people attached significance to the act that she just didn't.

Luke walked in and she met his gaze.

Except with Luke. It was more than sex with him. Her breath caught in her throat and her knees felt as if they were going to give out from underneath her. She'd tried to keep that distance she needed, but somehow she'd fallen for him.

She loved him. It hit her like a punch to the gut. Her heart had always belonged to him, but part of her had always held itself apart. The part that knew no matter how hard she tried to stay with him, it wouldn't last. Love? She fought against the realization…and the need to breathe.

He was going to leave soon and she wouldn't be able to do anything about it. Her heart collapsed in her chest.

"Are you okay?" Concern filled Luke's blue eyes as he crossed the kitchen. He rubbed her arms.

Her head felt light and darkness surrounded her.

"Penny. Breathe."

She gasped in air.

The world spun as Luke swept her up in his arms. She linked her hands behind his head, more by instinct than by conscious thought.

"Keep breathing," he said quietly as he carried her up the stairs and into his bedroom. He kicked the door shut behind him and laid her on the bed. Sitting next to her, he brushed his hand over her forehead and her hair. "Tell me what's wrong."

I love you—that's what's wrong. Heat rushed to her cheeks. "I just got faint, is all."

"Has this happened before?" He took her wrist in his hand and watched his watch as he took her pulse.

"No." Only once. Even though she'd done it intentionally…. When she'd realized what she'd done with Sam. When she realized that everything she'd wanted was never to be hers. Because the only thing she had ever really wanted was Luke.

She'd never questioned her decision. It had been for the best. They couldn't possibly last because love didn't last. At least not for her. At some point everyone she loved went away.

Taking deep breaths, she tried to slow down her racing heart. "I'm feeling better now."

When she tried to sit, Luke gently pushed her shoulder back to the bed. "I shouldn't come over every night. You have work. You need rest."

She shook her head. She'd never needed much sleep, and having Luke was worth needing to down an extra cup of coffee in the morning. "I get plenty of sleep."

"Maybe we should cool it for a night."

She grabbed his hand. She didn't want to miss a single day with him. All too soon he'd be gone and she'd be alone. He might not have moved on yet, but he would. Luke was built for happily ever after. Just not with her.

"Luke, we don't need to cool it. I'm getting enough sleep. It was probably just the heat in the kitchen." She grasped at straws.

He brushed the hair off her forehead and smiled. "It's okay. Tonight you get some sleep and tomorrow night we'll go out on a real date. With dinner and a movie and all that crap."

She relaxed into the bed and grabbed his hand. Tracing his fingers with her fingertip, she said, "That sounds great, but you should still come over tonight."

Time alone was something she didn't need. She would have plenty of time alone after he left. She wanted the oblivion making love with him gave her. She needed it.

He leaned down and kissed her. Slow and steady. It

wasn't earth-shattering, but it was everything to her. It was the pleasure she would remember when winter came and she had to cuddle with the dog to keep warm.

Luke lifted his head. "Maybe if you are good, I'll try to make it by."

She gave a dramatic sigh and held her arm over her eyes. "Then I'm doomed because I'm never good."

"You're always good to me, Penny."

She peeked out from behind her arm. "You're the good one."

He stood and pulled her up gently, checking her eyes closely while he pulled her to sitting and then to standing. She squinted back at him.

"I'm fine, Luke." Just terminally in love.

Chapter Thirteen

Penny pulled the blanket around herself, and Flicker snuggled closer to her. The television volume was low enough that she would hear Luke's knock on her door. When she'd left the farm earlier, he'd given her a scorching kiss that felt more like a promise than a good-night kiss.

Fortunately, *My Best Friend's Wedding* was on cable to keep her occupied while she waited. Sleep was the last thing on her mind. She had to deal with the fact that she was in love with Luke, but she had pushed him away long ago by kissing Sam. Seeing that had been brutal enough to keep Luke away for years.

It hadn't hurt only Luke, though. He'd left her without asking for an explanation. Just assumed the worst and left, as she'd known he would. Luke had never been the jealous type. At least not when they were teenagers.

He had been so confident in their love. And he had

every reason to be. She had loved him with everything she had. But the thought of trying to make it in the real world—outside of the bubble of Tawnee Valley—had brought back memories of her mother.

She glanced at the time. If he didn't show up in the next thirty minutes, she would text him. She'd make up some excuse, like she was feeling faint and needed a doctor. He would show up and take her in his arms and make her feel alive.

But for how long? Could she really let him go again? Even if it would be better for both of them? He had his job at the hospital and she had her store. Three hundred miles apart. This was the one time that their lives had intersected in almost nine years. That definitely didn't boost her confidence that this could actually work.

She tried to concentrate on the story line of the movie. The future would come quickly enough without her worrying over it.

Just as she was dozing off, there was a knock at the door. Flicker lifted his head and then lay back down.

"My ferocious guard dog." Penny shook her head as she walked to the front door. Maybe she should make Luke a key. That way even if she did fall asleep he could come in and wake her up. That put a smile on her face.

"I was beginning to think you wouldn't show up." She yanked open the door and her heart plummeted. Instead of Luke on her porch, a woman about her height stood in the shadows.

Apprehension filled her as Penny flicked on the porch light. A ghost would have made more sense than what she was seeing.

"Hi, baby," Cheryl Montgomery said. Her auburn hair was streaked with silver. Her familiar brown eyes were so light they were almost tan. Her build was similar to Penny's, but her clothes were loose around her small frame. Even though it had been over fifteen years since Penny had last seen her, she would always recognize her mother.

That didn't mean that she could handle it. Her brain went completely blank trying to process this unexpected arrival. She couldn't think, let alone speak. Her chest burned as if she'd run for miles without stopping. Her hands were cold and clammy.

"Are you going to invite me in?" Cheryl looked around Penny into the house and smiled hesitantly. "From what I see you've changed some things since Mom died."

"You didn't come to the funeral." It was her voice, but Penny hadn't realized she'd said anything. She'd had seventeen years to come up with something to say when her mother finally showed up, but she'd never believed it would actually happen.

Cheryl looked down at her feet before lifting her gaze to Penny. "Do we have to talk about this on the porch? It's kind of chilly."

She didn't want her mother in this house. It was hers now. Anything she'd had as a child, her mother had destroyed, whether she'd sold it so she could buy more liquor or she'd broken it during one of her alcohol-induced rampages. Penny had never had anything until her grandma took her in. The few treasures her grandma had given her were on the dresser in her bedroom.

"I swear I'm sober." Cheryl held up a coin. "One year."

Penny wanted to scream and slam the door in Cheryl's face. Instead she stepped aside and let her in. Blood thundered in her ears as she followed her mother into her living room.

"This is so much better than my mother's decorations. She never did like much color." Cheryl moved to the wall of photos. "Is this your daughter?"

"No, I don't have any children." Penny stood next to the door frame with her arms crossed in front of her.

"That's a shame. She's a pretty girl. I'd love to be a grandma."

Don't hold your breath on that one, Mom. Cheryl would likely be the worst grandma in the world. She had definitely never received a Number One Mom mug from Penny.

Cheryl sat in the recliner and looked at Penny expectantly.

There was no way Penny was going to sit down and talk as if nothing had happened with the woman who had abandoned her. As if this was some kind of happy reunion between mother and daughter. As if she hadn't waited for her for seventeen years. "Why weren't you at Grandma's funeral?"

Cheryl sighed and clasped her hands in her lap. "I got into some trouble and had to go into rehab."

"The funeral was four years ago. You just said you've only been sober a year." It was hard to keep the accusation out of her voice. Penny didn't want her mother to matter to her. She didn't want anything to do with Cheryl at all.

"I relapsed, but I went into the program myself afterward."

"Who'd you end up in bed with?" Penny tried to keep the venom from her voice.

Cheryl lowered her eyes and took a deep breath. "You have every right to be mad at me, Penny—"

"Really? For what, *Cheryl?* Making me clean up your vomit after you'd partied all night? Or how about

how I'd have to skip school to take care of you when
you were hungover? Or how about the sleazy men you
brought into my life? Thank God you had the decency to
give me a bolt on my bedroom door. The handle rattled
enough to make me fear going to the bathroom at night
because you'd be too passed out to actually help me."

"I wasn't a good mom. I wasn't a good anything."
Cheryl lifted her gaze to Penny. "I want to make this
right. I want to start fresh. I want to be a family."

Penny recoiled as if her mother had asked her to join
a cult that worshiped goats and sacrificed bunnies for
fun. "What about what I wanted, Cheryl?"

She'd begged her mother not to leave her behind.
When they'd lived together, she'd reached out for help
for her mother's addiction and every now and then,
Cheryl would clean up and they'd be happy. Until
Cheryl let another man into her life, and it wasn't long
after that the drinking would begin again. Even though
Penny had hated cleaning up her mother's mess, she
hadn't wanted to leave her. And she'd never thought
that Cheryl would leave her behind.

*I love you, Penny. We'll be together soon. I just need
to fix myself right now.* The words had echoed in her
head for years while she waited for her mother to come
get her and for them to be a family again.

"I…" Cheryl looked confused. She flipped the coin
over in her hand and closed her eyes. Taking a deep
breath, she raised her gaze to Penny. "I can't take back
the past. All I can do is apologize and try to make you
believe that I never wanted to leave you."

Penny's lips tightened to a thin line. That was the one
thing she would never believe. She stared at Cheryl and
wondered what lies would come out of her mouth next.

Cheryl frowned and put the coin in her pocket. "I

don't know what else I can say. I'm late, but Alan says better late than never. So here I am."

"Alan," Penny spit out the name. "Is that the most recent in your train wreck of boyfriends?"

She shook her head. "He's my sponsor. He's been sober for fifteen years. He's happily remarried with kids."

"Good for him." Everything inside Penny wanted to explode. This wasn't happening. It was some sort of sick joke. Why was *she* here after everything? Where had *she* been when Penny had needed her?

They stared at each other, and Cheryl's eyes pleaded with her to understand. To forgive. But that wasn't in Penny. She couldn't just forget. Not when it had cost her everything.

The knock on the door broke their gazes. Penny took a deep breath and released it as she turned to go answer the door.

"Hey, I brought you—" Luke looked up from the bag he held. "What's wrong?"

She could feel the sob pressing on her throat. She wanted to hug him and let go of everything, but she didn't. Luke would save her because that's what he did.

"My mom is here." The words came out flat. She couldn't put any emotion behind them or she wouldn't make it through the next few minutes. *Just hold it together for a few more minutes.* That's all she needed.

Luke closed her door and set the bag down on the table. Then he took her hand in his. It was all things good and warm. She drew strength from him. He would be here for her and that meant the world to her.

She led him back to the living room. Cheryl looked expectantly at Penny and then over to Luke.

"Hello, Ms. Montgomery. I'm Luke Ward." He didn't

release Penny's hand to offer to shake Cheryl's. He stood with her as a united front.

Penny wanted to lean into him, let him take care of this situation, but she hadn't grown into a wet mop at the sight of her mother. She wasn't going to start acting like one now because Luke was here.

"It's nice to meet you, Luke." Cheryl stood. "I didn't realize Penny was expecting company."

Penny couldn't think of anything to say. She wanted her mother to leave, but that part of her that had taken care of her mother reared up. "Do you have some place to go?"

For a moment, she thought her mother was going to ask to stay with her. Luke squeezed her hand and she realized she had him in a death grip and loosened it slightly.

"I've got a room in Owen. I didn't want to assume that you would forgive me right away." She laughed awkwardly. "I hoped, but…"

Penny's heart felt as if it had been through a blender today. She shook her head as the tears pressed against the back of her eyes.

"I didn't think so." Cheryl took in a deep breath and held her head up. "I hope that you'll let me come and see you."

Penny didn't say anything but stepped out of the way so that Cheryl could leave.

Cheryl sighed and walked to the door. Once there, she stopped and turned back. "I know you don't believe me, but I love you, Penny."

Penny had never doubted that. She just wasn't enough for her mother.

"Good night, Luke."

"Good night, Ms. Montgomery."

"You can call me Cheryl." She smiled wearily. "Penny does."

With that she was gone. As soon as the door closed, Penny collapsed against Luke.

"You needed me cleaned."

"I neither knew nor cared as I pressed myself against him."

Chapter Fourteen

It had to be a cosmic joke. Penny could take only so much. Luke folded her in his arms against his chest, and she allowed the first choking sob to escape.

Her whole world had just been shaken. The pain she'd felt when her mother had left her resurfaced. How many nights had she cried herself to sleep in her bedroom? How many times had she sworn her mother would come tomorrow? How many nights had she re-packed her suitcase?

Until one day she just knew. Her mother would never come back for her. Just as her father had never wanted her. What had made her believe her mother was any different than him? Just because she was the one who got stuck with Penny? Sure, she'd said she loved Penny. But love was a deception.

"Do you want to go sit down?" Luke ran his hands over her back and brushed her hair away from her face.

"Why are you so good to me?" Penny looked up at him through the tears gathering in her eyes.

He smiled softly and kissed her forehead. "Because someone has to be good to you. It might as well be me."

Penny backed away out of his arms. She needed to give him something. Something important to her. Taking his hand, she pulled him behind her up the stairs and down the hallway. At the door to her bedroom, she stopped and turned to face him.

"This doesn't mean anything." She said the words but knew they weren't true. This was the one rule she'd held close all these years. If no one came into her bedroom, she'd be safe. She wouldn't have memories, except of herself, attached to the one place in her world that was hers. If she let Luke in, every time she entered her bedroom she'd think of him in it. Somehow forever seemed bearable when it came to Luke.

She searched his eyes for a long minute. It wouldn't matter if she looked into them for hours; she wouldn't know how to find what she was looking for, because she didn't know what it looked like. At least not as other people did. Love.

Pushing the door open behind her, she pulled him into her bedroom. As he closed the door, her heart shuddered. This was as close as she might ever come to telling Luke she loved him. The words weren't possible. Not when this all would end. She couldn't reopen that wound, but she could show him how she felt.

Her room wasn't much. Bed, dresser, lamp, nightstand. But her treasures sat arranged on a white doily on her dresser. Everything in here was hers and hers alone. No one could take them from her.

She dropped his hand and walked to her queen-size bed. Sitting down with her back against the headrest, she propped up a few pillows beside her and patted the bed. Not saying a word, Luke kicked off his shoes and joined her. Side by side.

Deep breaths. She took his hand in hers, leaned against his shoulder and let out a long sigh.

"You want to talk about it?" Luke rubbed his thumb across her knuckles.

Penny shook her head. "You don't want to hear about it."

"Don't hide yourself from me, Penny." Luke tipped her chin up and gazed into her eyes. "I care about you, and I know that had to have been painful."

She wanted to deny it. To press her body against his and take his mouth with hers until they both forgot about Cheryl's visit. But she couldn't. Her mother's visit had unlocked a dam that had been ready to burst for years.

"She left me when I was ten."

Years ago, she'd told Luke some of the story, but she wanted to get it all out now. As he listened, he held her hand in his and kept rubbing his thumb across her knuckles. His touch gave her comfort and courage.

"Sometimes it was good. It would be me and her against the world. She was fun and a little crazy. We moved a lot. Wherever she could find work. When she first started a job, we'd have a little extra money. She'd buy me gifts and ice cream. I'd go to school like a normal kid."

She closed her eyes as she rested against his shoulder. Remembering the good times was almost more painful than remembering the bad. Without the good, she would have never known that the other times were that bad.

"We'd spend the weekends like a normal family. I'd join the basketball team at school. Then mom would find a guy. She never really stopped drinking, just drank less during the good times. Things would start to get rough and she'd start drinking more. He'd get sick of her and she'd find herself at the bottom of a bottle."

"That couldn't have been easy for you." Luke put his arm around her and took her hand with his other.

"She'd start getting sick. I'd have to clean up after her just so I could use the bathroom. I'd miss school to stay home to take care of her and make sure she ate and was hydrated. She'd always go right back to the bottle, though, and bring home any guy who would have her."

A shudder ran through her. "I'd lock myself in my room those nights. But I'd always be there in the morning to help her. I thought that's what love was. Always being there. No matter what."

She shook her head. "She'd lose her job and then she'd start selling things to get more alcohol. Everything she'd bought me would be gone within a few days. I'd use any spare money I could find to get us food. Sometimes we only had ramen noodles all week. I cooked. I cleaned. When I was exhausted, I'd reach out for help."

"You were brave."

"Not brave. Scared." She struggled to form the next part into words. "It wasn't that I couldn't take care of her anymore. It was that I couldn't control her anymore. When we had no money left to buy food, I worried that she'd have to start selling herself to maintain her addiction. When she drank heavily, she wasn't my mom anymore. She didn't care about me. When she'd sober up, she'd apologize. She'd swear she wouldn't drink anymore. She'd go out to find a job and then come home drunk."

She swiped at the tear that had escaped down her cheek. "But I could handle it. I knew she loved me and I was there for her. It was us against everything. I looked into rehab, but every place wanted her to stay for a long time to get clean. How was I supposed to survive without my mom? They would have thrown me into foster care."

"What about your grandma?"

Penny scoffed. "Grandma threw out Mom when she found out she was pregnant. You remember how strict Grandma had been with me?"

She felt his nod against her head.

"She was that way because Mom had run wild. Not that I didn't, but Mom had started drinking at fourteen. Grandma had told Mom never to come to her for anything. She'd broken the rules and that was that. Grandma didn't care what Mom had to do to survive.

"So we had no one but each other. For years we made it work. I don't know what changed. I thought about it for a long time. Had she gotten sick of me? Had I done something wrong? I was always helpful. I might have talked back a few times, but that wasn't anything new."

Penny struggled to sit up straight and put a little distance between her and Luke, but she didn't let go of his hand. "When she brought me to my grandma, I begged her not to leave me. What would she do without me to take care of her? How would she remember to eat?"

Luke squeezed her hand. "Maybe she just wanted you to have someone to look out for you for a change."

"By leaving me with Grandma? By taking away everything I'd ever known?" Penny blinked away the tears. "She was supposed to come back. She promised. She said—"

Tears choked her and she couldn't hold them back anymore. Luke pulled her toward him and she fell against his chest, soaking his blue T-shirt with her tears. He gently stroked her hair and made soothing noises.

For seventeen years she'd held it inside. Pushed it down deep so that it wouldn't consume her. Forced everyone in her life away. Grandma had been easy. She had always kept Penny at arm's length. Penny had been just another thing she had to take care of, not a grandchild to be loved and cherished. It had probably been better that way. Penny would have pushed back hard if her grandma had wanted any sort of real relationship with her.

"She left me with my grandma. All alone. Maggie and I got to be friends, but for years I could never really make it real because I thought that someday Mom would come back for me. And we'd leave Tawnee Valley and start our lives together. But she never came...."

His warmth penetrated the coldness that had engulfed her when she'd seen her mother. But she still shook as the tears streamed down her cheeks.

"How could she leave me if she loved me?"

Chapter Fifteen

Luke held Penny as she released what had to be years of pent-up emotion. As the sobs diminished, he could feel her body relaxing against his, until her breath became even and slow. He grabbed a tissue from the nightstand and patted her face dry as she slept.

Everyone knew that Cheryl Montgomery had dropped her daughter at her mother's and run off. A few people remembered she'd had issues with alcohol in high school. Before Penny had been at school a month, most of their classmates had labeled her a lost cause. Probably because their parents didn't want a bad influence around them. But Penny hadn't been bad. Not at first.

After a while she seemed to become whatever they thought she should become. He wished he'd been strong enough to turn the tide. To make his classmates and the people they grew up with forget their prejudice. But he hadn't.

Of course, at the time he had a mom and dad who loved their children and who would do anything for them.

Luke slipped his cell phone out of his jeans. He texted Jasper that he'd be back later than he'd planned and asked him to look in on Sam. Jasper texted back, No problem. Luke set the phone on the nightstand and settled down further on the bed, keeping Penny close.

She was the puzzle he could spend the rest of his life solving. Even Jasper made sense once Luke got over his initial jealousy. It still bugged him that Penny had used Jasper to scratch an itch, but part of him was glad it had been Jasper, a loner without an attachment to anywhere or anyone. He would never have tried to settle down and be the man that Penny needed in her life.

Maybe *needed* wasn't the right term. Luke stroked her hair. Because any man who loved Penny would have to love her unconditionally and forgive her, knowing that something truly wild would never be true to one person.

Perhaps he should turn in his man card because of all the gushy stuff going through his mind. The thing was, as much as he wanted to be that man for Penny, he wasn't sure he could forgive her for Sam. Anyone else, yes…but Sam?

"Don't you need to go home?" Penny's voice was sleepy. She didn't even open her eyes, just stayed where she was across his chest.

"I'm good here." Because home had always been with Penny. Over the years, he'd thought of her and what she would say about what he was doing. She wasn't his moral compass—she'd always had a skewed perspective for whatever she wanted. But sometimes being a little selfish instead of selfless was just what the doctor ordered.

And right now, he wanted to be in this bed with this woman. Until she kicked him out. He closed his eyes and focused on the rhythm of her breathing.

Her eyes felt like grit paper when Penny tried to open them. They felt swollen and her chest still ached slightly. Even opening her eyes didn't help much; the room was dark. Her alarm clock read 4:24 a.m.

Luke's warm body was the only thing keeping the chill of the room from making her shiver and dive under the covers. She pressed in closer and breathed him in.

"You keep doing that and I won't be responsible for my actions." Luke's voice was low and rough.

"Thank you for listening to me," she whispered. With the darkness surrounding them, it felt safe to admit she'd needed him.

"Thank you for letting me in." He hugged her to him.

She slid off him and onto the mattress. He turned on his side to face her. Just enough light from the streetlights peeked through the curtain to let her make out his features. Her heart swelled in her chest. She wanted to tell him everything, from how stupid she had been to push him away to how much she was falling for him again.

Instead she leaned in and kissed him. Gently, exploring with just a hint of the raw passion that normally devoured them. He followed her lead, seeming to know that this time wasn't so much about fulfilling a desire but exploring the connection they shared.

His hand settled on her waist and sent intense waves of longing through her. Longing to stay in his arms forever. To be one with him. Things she'd never have, but tonight she'd cling to them and let herself dream of a future where they could be together.

"You're shaking," Luke said as he trailed kisses from her mouth to her throat. "We should get you under the covers."

"I'm not cold." Her eyes fluttered shut as his hand trailed across her belly.

"Good." He plucked the bottom button of her shirt undone.

Her breath caught and he flicked another button open. When she opened her eyes, he was watching her face. Another button and his knuckles brushed against her bare skin. Her stomach tightened and a burst of heat sparked through her system.

She reached up and ran her hand along his scruffy jaw. His cheek twitched under her fingertips. One more button loosened. She ran her fingers through his hair and brought his mouth down to hers. Kissing Luke was like Christmas and her birthday rolled into one. Excitement, anticipation, joy.

His fingertips grazed the underside of her breast and she gasped. Even though they had been more intimate previously, tonight felt like the start of something new. Or maybe it was the end of everything they had. She brushed off the dark thought and let herself be in this moment, no matter the consequence.

Her heart was already his. It always had been. It always would be. But it wasn't just her heart she was giving to him. As he undid the remaining buttons and opened her shirt, he gazed down at her silhouette. His fingers were rough from helping out at the farm as they trailed down over her white lace bra and across her stomach down to the waistband of her dark slacks.

Normally she'd be helping him remove her clothes

and his, but something about the quiet house, her bedroom and the darkness, this man, made her want to take things slowly. Luke kissed along the lace edge of her bra, making her nipples harden and beg for his touch.

He lifted his head and kissed her mouth as his hand traced along the band of her bra, then unhooked it in the back.

"I've never met anyone who ties me up in knots the way you do," he said before pushing her shirt off her shoulders. He nipped at every inch of her skin he exposed until her breath and pulse pounded.

She wanted to come back with something to take away the seriousness. But when he pulled off her shirt and slowly eased off her bra, her mouth went dry. His lips closed around her nipple. Any thought she might have had was gone in the flash fire of desire that seared through her.

Helpless to the heat flooding her, she held on to him as he took his time to explore one breast and then the other. If she bound him in ropes, he held her in chains. Surely ropes would break, whereas her chains would hold her to him forever.

Love wasn't a blessing to Penny. It was a curse that bound her to a mother who easily cast her off when she became too much of a burden and to a man who had been easily dissuaded from his pursuit. It didn't stop her from loving him or wanting to be loved by him.

When his mouth found hers again, she wished she could be more aloof and brush him off. But she couldn't. Luke had been her rock and stability in high school. They'd turned each other away from self-destruction.

His touch had always wiped away the bad. She hadn't been looking for a relationship the night at the dance when she'd approached him. With her reputation and his, she thought maybe they could raise a little hell. Instead they'd made each other better. Sure they'd done some crazy things, but he'd stopped picking fights and getting in trouble at school and she'd stopped trying to become her mother with booze and guys.

"Luke?" she said when he lifted his head.

He brushed the hair away from her face and brushed his thumb across her bottom lip. "Yeah?"

Tears pressed against her eyes. "Do you think I'm a bad person?"

"Never in a million years." He rested his head against his hand and looked down at her. "How can you think you're bad? You helped your best friend through her mother's death and helped her with her child. You took care of your mother when she needed you most. You helped your grandma and improved on her dream after she passed."

A tear slid free.

"But most of all you turned around a screwed-up teenager. Showed him what it was to be loved and how to fix his life instead of wreck it. You might want people to stay away and think that you are bad, but you are incredible." His hand reached down to her slacks and slowly undid the button and zipper.

"I never deserved you," she whispered. Her fingers played with the ends of his hair, caressing the softness.

He smiled and finished undressing her. His gaze followed her body from head to toe. The attention made her want to stretch like a cat and let him pet her until she purred.

He stood to take off his clothes. She tried to fill her head with memories for when he was gone. Tried to imagine what her life would be like once he was back in St. Louis. She couldn't begin to picture it without feeling her gut roll in protest.

Instead she held out her arms to him and drew him down to the bed. Sex would never be the same with anyone else. Just the feel of his skin against hers made her shiver with need. His kiss could steal her breath and bring her life. His hands kindled fire inside her everywhere they touched. His mouth on her skin made her melt.

No one had ever had the ability to make her burn with desire the way Luke did. She couldn't deny that what they were doing was making love. It was too intense, too emotional to be sex. He made her his and she couldn't resist.

When he entered her, she was so beyond herself that she raked her nails over his shoulders, trying to draw him closer.

He brushed her lips with his and whispered next to her ear, "Let go, Penny. Just let us be."

He moved slowly in her, building the already-raging fire into a blaze until he started to lose control and his breathing grew more ragged and his motions more intentional. Their bodies moved together, striving for release.

The edge was so near. Penny opened her eyes. Luke's face was twisted in pleasurable agony. She never wanted this to end, but she couldn't hold back any longer. Her release pulsed through her and it pushed him over.

I love you so much and you'll never know. The words rang through her mind as she slipped back into sleep.

Chapter Sixteen

Luke tried to concentrate on moving the bales of hay in the barn, but it didn't actually require brainpower, so his mind kept drifting back to Penny. How desperately she'd clung to his hand when introducing him to her mother. How vulnerable she'd been when she'd led him back to her room. How sensual she'd been lying beneath him.

"Watch out."

A bale of hay came flying down to land beside Luke. He looked up at Jasper in the rafter.

"What the hell?" Luke grabbed the bale by the strings and stacked it with the others. "You're lucky that didn't bust my head open."

"At least Penny would be available." Jasper smiled.

Luke grunted in response. The fact that Jasper still had a job out here meant Luke knew the man was teasing, but it didn't help that when he went back to

St. Louis in a few days Penny would be free to resume all her extracurricular activities.

He had no hold over Penny. She was as free as when he'd first seen her at the wedding. When he left, he would have no right to expect her to wait for him. When he left...

"Hey, I don't mind babysitting your brother so you can get some, but could you keep working so I can get out of here and hit the bars? Since you took the only hottie in town, I'm going to have to go trolling." Jasper swung down from the loft and landed a few feet from Luke.

This wasn't the first time Luke had the urge to knock the guy's smile in. Sam had insisted that Jasper would be an asset. But he'd also been an asset to Penny, which rubbed Luke the wrong way. If Penny had feelings for this guy, though, she would have said something. Wouldn't she have?

"Don't worry. You'll have plenty of time to get to the bar." Luke wiped the sweat from his forehead with a rag.

Besides, it hadn't been Jasper at her door last night and there for her when she needed someone to hold on to. She'd made a big fuss over never having anyone in her bed and never "sleeping" with anyone. Last night he'd been privy to both.

That had to count for something.

Luke climbed out of the barn and took off his work gloves. The sun was almost to midday. His skin itched from the hay and dust that clung to his sweat. He'd give his left nut for a shower, but that meant dealing with Sam.

He squinted up at the sun. It was starting to get too hot to do much, but staying outside seemed like the best defense against Sam, who couldn't seem to accept the fact that he needed to sit down and relax.

Even the dogs were napping in the shade. A drop of sweat rolled down his spine. It couldn't be helped. Luke needed a shower and everything else would have to wait until it got cooler.

"I'm heading to the house," Luke shouted back to Jasper.

"I'll take lunch after I finish this."

Taking a deep breath, Luke headed to the porch. The door creaked open and banged shut behind him. He swore.

Yesterday, Luke had readjusted the tension on the door so that it wouldn't bang shut anymore. Apparently Sam was using it as a way to know when someone was in the house and had reset it when Luke wasn't looking. Luke didn't know whether to be mad that Sam had adjusted the door or mad that he'd obviously not been sitting while he did it.

"Hey." Sam appeared in the doorway as Luke took off his shoes.

"Go lie down." Luke hung up the hat he'd been wearing. It hadn't helped to keep the hay from making his head itch.

"You guys got the bales out of the rafters?"

"Yeah." Luke had dusted off what he could outside, but hay clung stubbornly to his jeans. His dad would have dumped his jeans at the door; otherwise Mom would have yelled at him. The memory of his parents brought a bittersweet smile to his face.

"It's time to change the oil in the tractor," Sam said.

"I know." Luke glared at Sam. "You told me this morning and yesterday evening and yesterday morning."

"If it doesn't get done, you won't be able to get to the fields this afternoon." Sam's mouth was set in a stubborn line.

"I don't need to be micromanaged, Sam. I've got it covered." Luke brushed past Sam into the dining room. "Right now I need to get the hay off my skin. Unless you want to tell me how to do that, too."

"I'm sure you can handle that." Sam shuffled toward the living room.

Luke bit back anything he might have said. Sam was just trying to control a situation he felt was out of his control. It was one of the reasons he and Sam had butted heads as teenagers. It hadn't made sense to him that Sam had the right to give him punishments, but no one had been punishing Sam when he screwed up.

Sam had always been his father's favorite and got most of his attention. First Sam, then Brady, then Luke. Luke had been their mother's favorite, though. She'd always sneak him an extra cookie...for him to grow on.

He blinked back tears as he went into the bathroom. Penny's relationship with her mother was complicated— to put it mildly. But if Luke could see his mother one more time...he'd do whatever it would take.

He stripped and showered quickly before changing into fresh jeans and a T-shirt. It had been a while since he'd done so much manual labor, and sitting on his bed even long enough to pull socks on made him want to shut his eyes for a little while.

Maybe sleep would help him figure out what to do about Penny and Sam. She couldn't be trusted before. Had she really changed any? Sam hadn't changed. He was just as controlling. Just as stubborn.

Just a few minutes of sleep...

* * *

The bell above the door startled Penny into almost dropping the glass perfume bottle. Her head whipped around to see who had come in.

"Don't worry, dear. It's just me."

Penny didn't think she'd ever be relieved to see Bitsy Clemons coming through the door, but she was grateful it wasn't Cheryl, who was somewhere out there, lurking, and wanted a relationship with her. That had her on edge. That and Luke.... God, she'd been stupid last night. Wanting to cling to him as if he could ever love her again after what she did to him. She wouldn't blame him for never trusting her. But she'd wanted to believe for a few seconds that he could love her. Even if nothing came of it.

"I heard that your mother is staying in Owen." Bitsy's voice had a hint of a question at the end.

Penny decided to take it as a comment and not a question. She didn't want to acknowledge her mother's presence. She didn't want any part of the woman.

Bitsy rounded the corner and picked up a trinket off the shelf. "You wouldn't know anything about that, would you?"

Penny took in a deep breath and released it. "Yes. She came by the house last night."

Bitsy tsked and placed her hand on Penny's arm. "How are you holding up, dear?"

"I'm fine." Penny walked farther down the aisle.

"It's okay if you don't like the woman. After all, she all but left you with your grandmother—God rest her soul. You know we'll stand behind you. No matter what your decision regarding your mother."

Penny turned and looked into the serene face of Bitsy Clemons. "What do you mean?"

Bitsy smiled slightly, as if she had a secret to pass on. "Well, you didn't hear it from me, but word is Cheryl is looking at a few houses today in Tawnee Valley. Not to buy, of course, but to rent. A full-year lease."

Penny's heart clattered to a stop. "A year?"

"The Brindells' place over on First Street and the Adams' place over on Oak." Bitsy pretended to be interested in the shelf, but Penny could tell she was watching her like a hawk for the slightest reaction.

"What she does doesn't concern me." Penny straightened. "If she wants to be in our town, that's fine."

But it wasn't fine. It was terrifying, but if Bitsy saw even a hint of that, she'd tell everyone. Better to hold it in than to let the whole town know.

Cheryl destroyed everything she touched. When she was young, Penny had thought she'd been immune. That she was the one thing Cheryl had wanted to keep. Boy, had she been wrong. As she got older, Penny realized that she had just been in the way. More trouble than she'd been worth. Even though yesterday her mother had assured her that she loved her, how was that possible when she'd left her like discarded trash all those years ago?

"That's real mature of you, Penny." Bitsy glanced at her watch. "Oh, I have to run. Things to do, you know."

Most likely Bitsy wanted to go from store to store to tell everyone about their conversation. The bell rang as Bitsy went out the door, throwing a goodbye behind her as she went.

A year? Cheryl never committed to anything longer than month to month. How would she ever fit in in this small town? The nearest bar was over in Owen. Did she even have a car? A license? How did she have money to pay the security deposit on a house?

Cheryl had been pretty hard up for money when she'd dropped Penny off years ago. Hadn't she said she'd wound up in rehab because of being arrested? Or had Penny filled in that part herself?

The door rang again. Penny held her breath as she peeked around the corner. A couple, probably from out of town, walked in.

"If you need any help with anything, just holler," she said and turned back to the shelf she was reorganizing.

"Thanks," the man said.

When minutes went by and the door jingled again, she figured the couple had left. She didn't like to police her store by hovering over customers. It made people feel uncomfortable if she stood up front and stared at them while they browsed.

She went back to her register and looked over the monthly receipts.

"I love what you've done with the shop."

Penny froze, then lifted her gaze to her mother's. Her eyes darted to the back, where the couple was looking at furniture.

"Thanks." Penny didn't want her mother here. This was hers. Her safety net. Her roots. Everything her mother had never given her. It was Penny's and she didn't want her mother to destroy that. But she couldn't exactly throw a fit with customers in the back.

"I'm sorry I came over unannounced last night."

"You mean like you are doing now?"

Cheryl grinned sheepishly. "I had a feeling you wouldn't want to meet up for lunch or dinner after last night. If the only way to see you is to just pop up, then that's what I'm going to do."

"Gee, aren't I lucky?" Penny's voice might have been deadpan, but her heart was racing as if the devil himself was chasing her. The antiques store's high ceilings and large rooms seemed to close in around her. If she didn't get some air soon, she might pass out.

"Breathe, Penny," her mother said calmly.

Penny pulled in a breath and then another.

Her mother had the gall to look hurt. "I swear I didn't come back to upset you."

"You don't upset me. You don't do anything to me." She wasn't fooling Cheryl and she knew it.

"I promised to come back."

"Excuse me, but what is the price of this plate?" the woman said.

Penny pulled her gaze away from Cheryl and focused on the costumer. She put on her best smile and glanced at the plate. "That one is a 1938 Wedgwood nonhunting dog plate with poodles called March Winds. It runs around one hundred and fifty online, but I'd be willing to bargain if you are interested."

The woman glanced back at the man with a pleading look on her face.

The man shook his head but got out his wallet. "Would you take one-thirty for it?"

"For you two? Of course." Penny held out her hand for the plate.

The woman beamed. Cheryl slipped away from the counter as Penny conducted the sales transaction. Penny tried to ignore her mother's wanderings, but the back of her neck prickled.

"There you go. I added a care instruction sheet in there. Have a safe trip." Penny handed the bag to the woman, who hadn't stopped grinning.

The man put his hand on the woman's back and led her to the door as if he were afraid she might find something else.

"Thank you," he called out.

"Come again," Penny said. As soon as the door closed, the smile fell off her face.

She found Cheryl in the toy aisle. Penny kept her inventory low on these items because they weren't big sellers around here, but occasionally someone wanted something that they'd had as a child. Penny herself didn't have good memories associated with her childhood toys.

"You know, I don't think Mom would have thought of toys as antiques," Cheryl said as she picked up an old spinning top. "She always wanted this to be a classy store with only antiques from overseas."

"Classy stores don't do well in the country." Penny looked around to make sure Cheryl hadn't pocketed anything.

"She never understood that." She set down the top and faced Penny. "I know she wasn't the easiest person to live with, but she was good to you, wasn't she?"

Penny crossed her arms over her chest. "If you had cared, maybe you should have checked up on us. But then again, you just didn't care enough about me."

"I deserve that." Cheryl put her hands in her back pockets and looked down at the floor. "I wanted to come back, but I knew you were better off without me."

"How would you know?" Penny dropped her arms, walked behind the front counter and pretended to study a list of recent transactions. Her mother could run off with the whole inventory for all she cared, as long as she left.

Penny was done. This wasn't supposed to happen. Her mother had been long gone. She had no right to show up now. Penny didn't need her anymore.

"Mother wrote me."

Penny didn't look up from the figures, but they blurred before her eyes.

"She told me all about you and school and your friend Maggie." Cheryl sighed. "How could I come back and ask you to come live with me when you were clearly happier without me? How could I take care of you when I couldn't even take care of myself?"

"I could take care of myself."

"Exactly. What type of mother was I that my daughter took better care of me than I did of her? Everything you said last night was true. The men, the drinking. I couldn't control myself. I didn't want my addiction to hurt you any more than it already had." Cheryl brushed tears from her cheeks.

"Do you know how hard it was to call my mother, let alone drive back to this godforsaken town and give you to her?" Cheryl laughed bitterly. "I couldn't put you in the foster system. I was afraid I'd never get you back out of it. Plus I've heard about what happens to some kids in the system and you were already starting to develop…"

Penny pushed away from the counter. Her mother's "dates" had definitely begun to notice her development. She could still feel their hot gazes and subtle remarks.

Crossing her arms over her chest, Penny glared at Cheryl. "What do you want from me? Money?"

"No. No," she said firmly. "It took me a year of sobriety to get here because I wanted to be able to stay. I worked hard and saved every cent I made. I knew it wouldn't be easy coming back, but the only person's approval I need is yours."

Penny pressed her lips together tightly.

"I swear to you, I'm not out for anything except you. I know you don't believe it, but I love you, Penny. I've already applied for a waitressing job at The Rooster Café. I'm going to rent one of the houses in town. I'm staying—"

"Until you fall off the wagon."

"No, baby." Cheryl looked her in the eyes. "I'm staying for good."

Chapter Seventeen

"I promised you dinner and a movie." Luke held up a bag of groceries and a DVD.

"I hope you aren't looking for homemade from me because I'm no Betty Crocker." Penny stepped aside to let him in.

"I'll have you know that not only did I attend medical school, but I also learned to cook decent-tasting food on a small allowance every week." Luke started pulling out the ingredients. "Besides, if it really sucks, I've got a twenty in my wallet for pizza."

Penny smiled. "I suppose I can risk food poisoning as long as there's a backup plan."

He leaned in and kissed her. "That's my girl."

She flushed with warmth and sat at the kitchen table. This was just what she needed. No strings, no future commitment, just here and now with Luke. He wasn't pressing her to be family with him or to let him back into her life. No, it was just casual sex with the bonus of spending time together.

So what if she was head over heels in love with him? It wasn't as if that would make a difference, and it shouldn't. They could just keep having sex until he left for St. Louis.

She rubbed at the sudden ache in her chest. She needed a distraction from her crazy thoughts. "Okay, what are you going to make me?"

He wiggled his eyebrows mischievously. "Let's see if you can guess from the ingredients."

She raised her eyebrow in retaliation. "What part of 'I'm no Betty Crocker' did you not understand?"

"That's okay—I just want the saucy part of you."

"Good answer."

"I was a straight-A student."

"Mostly."

"Hey, everyone has an off year." He tweaked her nose for that one.

"I had twelve of them."

"I know for a fact you did much better your senior year." He sorted his groceries on her counter. "You can't tell me you didn't do well in kindergarten. I've seen you color. You *mostly* get it inside the lines."

Her mouth dropped open in mock indignity. "Mostly?"

"You've always been a little bit of a rebel." He winked at her.

She chuckled. "You've got me there."

He started opening and closing her drawers, pulling out a knife and then a cutting board. "I bet you would have done awesome if you'd had a fair shot at school."

Some of her lightheartedness fled at the reminder of her mother. "Probably not. Like you said, I was always a rebel."

"You know if you want to talk about it, I'm here." He glanced up at her as he cut a tomato.

"I didn't think you'd know that much about being a rebel." She touched her finger to her lip in mock surprise. "Oh, wait, you did have that one year.... How many fights did you get in? Five or six?"

"Seven." Luke set aside the diced tomato and started cutting a garlic clove. "All but two were off school property."

"And what did those boys do to deserve your anger?" She reached over and plucked a chunk of tomato off the cutting board and popped it in her mouth.

"Is it bad if I say I don't remember?" He glanced at her sheepishly, then sliced a green pepper.

She laughed. "I wouldn't believe you. That giant brain of yours won't let you forget anything."

It was what she'd counted on when she decided to kiss Sam. Luke would remember every time some guy had implied he'd banged her.

"Yeah, well," he said, "some things I wish I could forget and others I wish I remembered better."

"What do you wish you remembered?"

Luke rinsed his hands and pulled out a saucepan and a stockpot. "My childhood. My parents. Sam and Brady before our parents died. Every now and then I catch a memory, but they are few and far between. I can't remember much before I became angry all the time."

She watched him as he added his chopped ingredients to the saucepan and set a pot of water to boil. "And here I keep wishing I could forget my childhood, but that's not going to happen now that Cheryl is in town."

"Do you want wine or something else to drink?" He held up a bottle of red.

"It's definitely a wine night." When he raised his eyebrow, she added, "In moderation."

He poured them both a glass. When he brought her glass to her, he leaned down and kissed her. Sparks sizzled through her at the contact.

"I don't think I could ever forget you." Luke straightened and winked before turning back to the stove.

"I hope not," she said softly, more to herself than to him. She hoped she was as scorched into his memory as he was in hers. After the past week and a half with him she was fairly certain that he'd ruined her for casual sex. It didn't help that she'd already been losing interest in it before he arrived. She still wanted sex, just not from some random guy. Actually only one guy would do now....

"So have you guessed what I'm making you yet?" Luke glanced over his shoulder.

"Hamburgers?"

"I don't even have ground meat."

"That's probably a good thing."

"Guess again."

"Hmm...tomatoes, garlic, pepper and some stuff in a jar.... Haggis?"

Luke turned and gave her the stink eye. "Haggis?"

"You mean I guessed right?" She grinned.

"If I didn't have to make sure the food didn't burn, I'd show you what I think of your guesses." He stirred the sauce and then added pasta to the boiling water.

"I'm just surprised you don't have garlic bread. After all, everyone knows garlic bread goes well with haggis."

He very carefully laid down his spoon, then turned and headed for her.

She tried not to giggle, but a few laughs slipped out. "Spaghetti! Spaghetti!"

"Too late." He yanked her up to standing and kissed her soundly. Without breaking the kiss, he lifted her against him and walked her back toward the stove.

She squealed when he lifted her higher and set her on the counter next to the cooking food. Without a word, he walked back to the kitchen table and grabbed her wine. He handed her the glass before resuming his stirring.

She crossed her legs, glad that she'd worn shorts today. Luke's gaze dropped to her calves. Everything felt wonderful. It was so easy to forget that Cheryl was in town and that Luke was leaving. This moment could last forever for all she cared.

"Isn't using the jar sauce cheating?" She lifted the empty jar off the counter behind her.

"Rather than spend hours waiting for the sauce to get ready, I'd rather spend the extra time making love with you."

Tingles coursed through Penny at the words *making love*. It meant nothing. Loads of people used that term for sex. Just because she was in love with him didn't make him in love with her.

"I add a few things to make their sauce a little richer. You'll notice I used store-bought pasta, too. Think of all the time I saved not doing that from scratch." His eyes raked her body from head to toe and back again.

"You better watch it, or dinner will burn and we'll be stuck with pizza."

"Thirty minutes for delivery time…." He looked as if he was contemplating it.

She laughed. "Forget it. You promised me a home-cooked meal, so you're stuck now."

"Good thing this is quick to prepare. The pasta only needs a few more minutes."

When he returned to stirring, she took in a deep

breath and filled her senses with rich garlicky tomato sauce and just a hint of Luke.

"I hope you are a fast eater." Luke lifted the pot and took it to the sink, careful not to lose any noodles as he poured out the water.

"Why is that?"

He put the pot down and lifted her from the counter. The kiss he gave her was less teasing and more ravenous. It lit an answering hunger from deep inside her that had nothing to do with food. His lips tasted of the red wine they'd been sharing.

When he released her, she leaned against the counter to regain her balance. "Good answer."

He grinned. "I can't wait to ace the final."

She pulled out two plates. He loaded their plates with pasta, sauce and garlic bread—which he'd waited to unpack from the sack. She refilled their glasses and they sat at the kitchen table.

"To healthy appetites." Luke lifted his glass.

She flushed with warmth from the look in his blue eyes. "To healthy appetites."

They made it about halfway through their dinner before he moved in for a kiss. They rose from the table as one and worked their way down the hall and up the stairs to her bedroom, chucking clothes as they went.

Right beside her bedroom door, he pinned her to the wall and pressed his naked body against hers. Her breath caught in her throat as he kissed his way down her neck and along her shoulder. His hands held hers against the wall as he dipped his head to take her breast into his mouth. She was helpless against the rising tide of passion that engulfed her. When she thought she could take no more, he pushed her just a little further over the edge until she forgot where he ended and she began.

He pulled her through the doorway to her bedroom. They fell together on the bed, consuming each other with hands and mouths, finding the spots that made her moan and him gasp. When he finally lifted above her and slowly entered her, she felt as if the fire in her had always been and would never find release.

Luke made the flames burn hotter with every stroke, every touch of his hands. Finally she reached the highest point and turned to ashes, floating back down into her body. He came down with her.

With the gentlest touch, he brushed her hair away from her face. Still joined, he lightly touched his lips against hers. She'd never felt more fulfilled, more cherished. More loved.

"This isn't just about sex anymore, Penny." Luke lay beside her with his shoulder touching hers and her hand in his. She wanted this and it was terrifying.

She stared up at the ceiling, willing her body to return to normal. Fighting to hold back from proclaiming her love. She didn't say anything. She couldn't. The one person she'd never wanted to lie to... The one person she always wanted to tell everything... But she couldn't ruin his future.

"Even as teenagers, I felt it. That this could be so much more."

"This is all we'll have, though," Penny whispered because if she said it too loud it would break her heart.

"Why?" He leaned up on his elbow and looked down at her.

It was harder to hide this way, lying naked with him. It wasn't the lack of clothing, but being in her bedroom, having him make love to her, having him care for her. It was all too much.

"You can never trust me." The words barely made any sound, yet they rang loud through the room.

"Have you had sex with anyone else since I arrived?" His hand trailed over the side of her breast, down over the dip in her waist and over her hip.

"No, bu—"

"Have you wanted to have sex with someone else since I arrived?"

She stared up at the ceiling. Everything in her screamed at her to tell him the truth. To stop playing the game. She shook her head no.

"All I ever wanted was you." He leaned down and kissed her lips.

"You shouldn't." Penny shook her head.

"Why not?" Luke's voice was seductive. "You're intelligent. Independent. Beautiful."

She rolled away from him. "You shouldn't want me. There are better women out there for you. Ones who aren't so…broken."

"Let me fix you." He stroked his hand down her back.

"I can't." She wanted nothing more than to sink back into his arms, but she knew if she did, she'd never have the strength to let go. "You know the type of woman I am."

"What type is that?"

Steeling herself, she sat up and turned to face him. "The kind who kisses your brother."

She saw the light go out of his eyes. She kept her head up, but inside her world was crumbling. Her stomach knotted and her throat seized closed. He turned from her and sat on the edge of the bed. Her eyes burned.

"So *you* kissed him?" His tone was even, not betraying one ounce of feeling.

"Yeah." She'd been strong enough to do it before, and she could do it again. She could push Luke away one last time and make this one stick. And she could just tell the truth.

"Why?" He turned and lifted his gaze to hers. His question held no accusation in it, just curiosity.

In all her lonely nights, she'd wondered the same damned question. Had she just been a scared little girl? Or had there been more to it? But for him, she'd brazen it out. Be the stronger of the two of them because she knew that Luke deserved better than her. "Maybe I wanted to know if he kissed like you."

"Did he?"

No one kissed like Luke. But admitting that wouldn't help him to leave her.

"Maybe I wanted to kiss every guy in Tawnee Valley and just needed to add Sam to my list." It felt as if there was a freight train rattling down the tracks toward her and she couldn't step out of the way. "Maybe all the rumors were true. Maybe I was the town slut."

He looked away from her, and she felt the hole beginning to form in her heart. This is where he'd walk away. It didn't matter how many days he had left before he went back to St. Louis. This would be when he walked away from her again.

She should be glad. This is what she wanted. What he needed.

"Bull."

"Excuse me?" she said. Her slowing heart picked up its tempo.

"You heard me," he said as he stood. He came around the bed and stood in front of her. "Bull."

"What the hell is that supposed to mean?" She tried to recapture her breath, but when he was near, the air disappeared.

"That was years ago. If you wanted to be the town slut, you could have been. Instead you were with me. You never once looked at another guy while we were together. I knew it. I saw it. You were mine and always have been."

"You don't know that." God, she wanted him to believe that. But she couldn't let him. If he'd said this to her after she'd kissed Sam, she would have lost her resolve to push him away.

He lowered his head until his lips were barely brushing against hers. "Yes, I do. Just like I know that you are mine now."

She wanted to shake her head no and go down swinging. Instead she got lost in his eyes, picking out the flecks of dark and light blue. His mouth captured hers and she gave up. Only for tonight.

She'd start the fight over in the morning, make him see that she wasn't what he wanted. That they wouldn't have a happily ever after because she wasn't built that way.

He pressed her back down onto the bed and into the mattress. Tomorrow was definitely soon enough.

Chapter Eighteen

"Sam?" Luke came in through the screen door followed by the bang. "Sam!"

"What?" Sam came out of the bathroom, drying his hair with a towel. He looked as he always did in jeans and a black T-shirt with the faded Metallica logo. It was hard to believe he had surgery less than a week ago.

"What happened that night?" Luke came to a halt in front of Sam and searched his face for clues. It was time to learn the truth, and he knew Penny wouldn't be the one to tell him. She was afraid of something. Getting to the bottom of his graduation night seemed like his best shot at convincing her they belonged together.

"What night?" Sam threw the towel back into the bathroom. His dark wet hair stood haphazardly around his head. He slicked a hand over it and headed to the living room.

Luke followed in his wake. "The night of my graduation. I saw you kissing Penny."

Sam sighed as he sat in his recliner. "I'm surprised you didn't bring it up before."

"Why would I?"

"Because I saw you walking off when I pushed her away." Sam rubbed a hand down his face.

That answered one question. Sam knew he'd seen him. "What happened?"

"You want a blow-by-blow?" Sam lifted his eyebrow as if to say, *Are you sure?*

Luke took in a deep breath and sat on the couch. "It's been years, but I need to know."

Something about the way she reacted when her mother had come back into her life unexpectedly had reminded him of right before graduation. They'd been talking about the coming year and how he'd be at University of Illinois and she'd come with him. Or more to the point, *he'd* talked about it. Now that he thought about it, the more he'd talked about it, the quieter and more distant she'd become.

"I went into the house to get a beer." Sam reached over and grabbed his glass of water. "I was surprised to find Penny in the room when I closed the refrigerator. She glanced out the door and then kissed me."

Luke remembered that part way too well. "You kissed her back."

The tips of Sam's ears turned red. "I'd had a couple of drinks and it'd been a while.... I pushed her away as soon as I realized what was happening. She looked out the door and I followed her gaze to see you walking away. She seemed satisfied with whatever she wanted to happen, but then she just collapsed. Sank to the ground like a stone."

Luke leaned forward, concentrating on every detail.

"I grabbed her elbow to help her up. She'd gone pale and was shaking all over. She kept repeating, 'He can't know, he can't know.' I had no idea what her problem was. She was your girlfriend, after all."

Sam shook his head. "I told her you saw us and she just nodded like she was numb. I told her I'd talk to you, but she grabbed my hand and said no."

"What happened next?" Luke's mind was spinning around the details.

"She got up, said she was sorry and went out the door. I didn't see her again that night." Sam shrugged. "I couldn't find you, and you left before breakfast the next morning. That was the day Brady told me he was going to London and I lost it."

"That was a rough day." Luke remembered when he got home that afternoon. He'd still been upset at Sam and Penny, but Brady had pulled him aside. Luke said to Sam, "Brady told me to watch over you. He said you acted like you didn't need anyone, but you did."

"Leave it to Brady to make it sound like a Hallmark card." Sam shook his head and rubbed his chest.

"Do you need a pain pill?" Luke started to get up, but Sam waved him off.

"I don't need to be babied." Sam leaned his recliner back. "I just need to take it easy, like you've told me a hundred times."

Luke searched Sam's face for signs of pain or distress from his heart surgery. He'd have enough time to think about what he'd learned when he was outside working. "Why didn't you ever bring the kiss up?"

"I didn't want to deal with it. You'd broken up with Penny. Brady had left. It seemed better to just leave well enough alone."

Luke's brow furrowed. "But I barely spoke to you when I came home."

Sam closed his eyes and smiled. "But you came home."

"He's fine. I'm not sure why you still call me when I know you call him every night, too." Penny put the TV on mute and leaned back on the couch.

"Uncle Sam's not good on the phone," Amber said.

"Don't his grunts come through okay?" Penny glanced at her nails. She should paint them. It would give her something to do tonight. Who knew who would show up at her door this time? Her mother? Luke? The Easter Bunny?

"That's not funny. Uncle Sam doesn't just grunt."

"But he does grunt a lot." Penny smiled.

"Okay, he does." Amber called something out that was muffled. "Mom says we're coming home in a couple days, so I shouldn't have to call you every night...."

"You can still call if you want." Penny stared at the image of the Winchesters driving down a dark road.

"Penny says I can call if I want," Amber yelled. After a pause, Amber said, "Okay, I have to go, but Mom wants to talk to you."

"Bye, sweetie." Penny picked up the remote and pressed pause. Talking with Maggie would take more than half her attention.

Penny could almost picture her friend in a sundress in a fancy hotel room, waiting to go out with her new family. God, she missed her.

"How are things going?" Maggie said.

"Fine." Penny couldn't disguise the strain in her voice. "You're on your honeymoon. You should be having fun, not talking on the phone."

"I have a few minutes. Brady took Amber down to the pool. Now spill."

"There's nothing to tell." She was dealing with everything the best she could on her own. Maggie needed to focus on having a good time.

"Please. I know your 'fine' is never fine. Is it Luke? Sam?"

That was the issue with being best friends. They were always in each other's business. It was the best and only relationship Penny had kept.

"You asked for it." Penny looked up at the ceiling. "Cheryl is in town."

"Your mother came back! And all you said was fine. This is big. Huge. What did she say? What did you say? Is she still there? Did she leave again?"

Penny sighed. "She's here. Not here, here. But she's looking for a place to rent in Tawnee Valley. She wants us to try to get to know each other again." The last sentence left a bad taste in her mouth. No matter how many times she thought about it, her mother being here was bad. How long before she fell off the wagon? How long before she made Penny believe she was here for good and then leave?

"Is she sober?"

"Yeah, for a year apparently." Penny rubbed the bridge of her nose.

"Wow. So you guys are talking?"

"Not exactly." Penny winced because this had always been a sticking point with her and Maggie. Maggie had begged her to track down her mother. Life was short and you never knew how much time was left. But Penny didn't want to let her mother back into her life just to watch her walk away again.

"Seriously?" Maggie took a deep breath—probably

preparing for her lecture. "How many people do you have in your life?"

"Counting you and Amber?"

"Exactly—me and Amber. I know you had something with Luke and I know you still feel something for your mother. You can't keep doing this, Penny."

"Doing what?"

"Pushing everyone away. I love you. I have always been there and I'm not planning on going anywhere, but…"

"But?"

"I can't be your everything." Maggie sighed. "I wish I could be there every minute of the day, but I can't. You need more than me. You need someone who you love and who loves you and supports you in ways I can't."

Penny rolled her eyes. "That's the honeymoon and too much Disney talking."

"Weren't you the one who encouraged me to try with Brady?"

"Yeah, but that was different."

"How is that differ—"

"Because you deserve happiness. You deserve love and devotion and a great guy and a great family."

Maggie's voice was soft when she spoke after a heartbeat. "And you don't?"

"No. I don't. I deserve to grow old and die alone."

"You don't mean that."

"What else do you want me to say?"

"I want you to say that you'll try. That you'll give your mother a chance to explain. That you'll give Luke a chance to love you. Not the you who was eighteen and impulsive, but this woman you've become. What's the worst that could happen?"

Penny shook her head, pressed her lips together and

clutched at the lump in her stomach threatening to come up. If Maggie were here in front of her, she would have pulled Penny into her arms and talked her down. But she wasn't here.

"I can't," Penny pushed past her lips.

"You know I'd kick your ass if I were there, don't you?" Maggie's voice was hard, but she could hear the frustrated love behind the hardness. "You are not less deserving than I am, Penny. You deserve love. You deserve happiness. You deserve to live a full life."

Penny swallowed.

"If *you* don't think you're worth it, remember that *I* believe you are. Just promise me you'll try."

Maggie's faith in her left Penny shaken.

"I'll try."

"Now, about Luke…"

Penny could hear the smile in Maggie's voice. "We don't have enough time to talk about Luke. You need to get back to your husband and daughter."

"You're no fun." Maggie's pout came through loud and clear over the telephone.

"Well, I could tell you about the sex toys—"

"Okay, you win. I love you, Penny."

"I love you, too."

Maggie hung up the phone, leaving Penny with a lot to think about. Her mother showing up in her life upset everything. She'd broken her rule about letting guys into her bedroom for Luke. She could sit and think all night or…she could continue to watch *Supernatural*.

Hmm…life decisions or the Winchester brothers. No contest.

She punched the play button. Just when she was getting into it and Sam and Dean, the main characters, were about to face the demon, the doorbell rang. It was only six and she wasn't expecting anyone. She stopped her DVR and went to the door.

"This better be good. You're interrupting Sam and—" Pulling open the door, she met Luke's shocked face. "Hey."

"Since I just left my brother at the farm, I'm assuming you mean another Sam?" Luke came in and she shut the door behind him.

"Why would I talk about your Sam?" Taking a deep breath in, Penny turned and faced him. "Why do you care what Sam I'm talking about?"

The phone rang before Luke could say anything. She held up a finger and walked back into her living room to pick up the phone. The number was unknown, but she'd rather deal with whoever was on the other end than talk with Luke about "where they were going."

"Hello?"

"Penny?" Cheryl's voice hit her hard. It would take a while for the shock of her mother's appearance to become part of her normal. Of course, that could change at any time. Her mother was prone to leaving.

Maggie told her to try. Penny straightened. "Yeah."

"I was wondering if you'd like to get lunch tomorrow. I just signed my lease on my house and wanted to celebrate with you."

As much as her head screamed, *It's a trap to lull you into believing she'll stay,* Penny ignored it. "Sure, lunch sounds good."

Luke moved into the room behind her and her heart ratcheted up a beat.

"Oh, that's great. I can't wait. I'll come by the store at noon."

"See you then." Penny cut off the call and set the

phone down. She put her hand over her racing heart. Her hands shook and the world shifted beneath her feet.

Luke's arms went around her from behind. "Are you okay?"

She leaned back into his warmth and tried to breathe normally, but the world wouldn't stand still even with Luke holding her.

"Let's sit down." Luke helped her to sit on the couch and then released her. He pressed Play on the TV and left the room.

As the Winchesters began their fight, Penny started to relax. Her heart managed to find a normal pace again. Nothing in the room spun. She took in a breath and then another.

Luke came in and handed her a glass of water before joining her on the couch.

"Thank you," she murmured.

"No problem." He didn't take his eyes off the screen. "Sam and Dean, huh?"

She flushed. "Yeah."

"Mind if I change the channel?" Luke picked up the remote.

"Afraid of a little competition?" She relaxed into his side. Her mother and Luke were just too much to take at the same time. She was glad he was here.

"I'm here. They aren't. No competition there." Luke stopped the recording and flipped to a movie.

If he didn't want to bring up the what's-happening-with-us talk, she was more than willing to let it go. She'd made a few strides forward with one relationship today. She didn't need to fix this thing with Luke at the same time.

She settled into the crook of his arm and stared blankly at the television. Tomorrow would be soon enough to talk.

Chapter Nineteen

Penny sorted her silverware and placed the napkin in her lap. Cheryl sat across from her, looking at her expectantly. At least Cheryl hadn't tried to hug her when she'd stopped by the shop to get her for lunch at the diner. Penny was fairly certain a panic attack would have devoured her whole if Cheryl tried to touch her.

"I don't know where to start." Cheryl laughed nervously.

Penny smiled tightly but didn't offer any suggestions. She'd promised Maggie she'd try, but she didn't have to like it.

"I know you work at the shop, but did you do anything before that? Did you go to college? How was high school? Did you have any serious boyfriends? Who was the guy who came over that night?"

"Whoa." Penny held up her hands. "One question

at a time and I have the right to refuse to answer any or all of them."

Cheryl nodded. But before she could ask anything, their waitress, Rachel Thompson, came over to take their order. When she left, Cheryl folded her hands on the table.

"Okay, let's start with something easy. Did you go to college?"

"No," Penny said and looked out the window, wishing she could be anywhere else but here.

"Why not? You were always such a smart girl." Cheryl's brow furrowed.

"I didn't have the best grades going into high school and apparently all that crap they taught us in elementary school really was the basis for everything we learned later. You don't get into college taking remedial courses." Penny stopped herself from adding that her mother was why she hadn't done well in elementary school. If Cheryl didn't know that, then they were going to have more than a rocky start.

"What about the community college?"

"Grandma needed help at the store." Penny shrugged. To be honest, every time she'd thought about taking classes, she'd thought of Luke. He'd been the best tutor she could have had, and taking classes would have only reopened that wound.

"I can't change the past, Penny." Cheryl looked down at her hands and had the decency to look remorseful. "If I could have controlled the addiction, I would have. It took me a long time to realize that the addiction was in control of me and not the other way around."

"Do you still want to drink?"

"Every day," Cheryl admitted. "It's easier now than

when I first went to rehab, but little setbacks in life have a way of triggering the desire to drink."

"At any moment you could disappear or, worse, stay around and be drunk off your ass all the time?" Penny didn't hide her bitterness.

"No. That's why I go to group and have a sponsor. Someone who can talk me down when I think I need a drink." Cheryl reached her hand out, but Penny pulled hers into her lap before Cheryl could touch her. Cheryl clasped her hands back together. "I swear I'm here to stay and I know you won't believe it until you see it, but I promise you—"

"Just like you promised to come back." Penny's head was starting to hurt. It didn't take much for the pain to resurface from all those years ago. "I waited for you. I didn't even unpack my bag for a year. I was always ready for when you'd come back and get me and we'd be a family again."

"I'm sorry—"

"That's not enough." Penny glanced around the diner and lowered her voice. "Sorry isn't worth anything. You not being there meant everything was wrong. Grandma kept telling me that I'd seen the last of you and I kept telling her she'd see in the morning. You would be here then and I'd be gone. Do you know what that does to someone? To constantly be waiting for someone who never comes back?"

"No, I don't know what it was like for you." Cheryl didn't move.

"It hurts. I cried every day. I didn't make friends because I wouldn't be here long enough. Maggie was the only one who understood me. I didn't build a relationship with my grandma. I kept everyone away because I would leave as soon as you came back for me."

Cheryl pressed her lips together, but her eyes looked as if she wanted to say she was sorry.

"Do you know how hard it is to let someone in when you've kept everyone away for so long?"

"Yes, I do." Cheryl's words stopped Penny cold.

"What?"

"I know what it's like to shut down and not trust anyone. I trusted your father. He'd been my first love. Sure, my mom called me wild in high school, but I'd only been with him. When I got pregnant and Mom kicked me out, I went to him."

Penny leaned forward. Her mother had never talked about her father before. She hadn't even been aware that he'd lived in Tawnee Valley.

"We were so stupid. Or at least I was. He came with me to start a new life. We didn't get married right away, but we talked about it. We didn't have much money and I'd already started showing. We needed to save up for you, so we put it off. I was working one night and got sick, so I came home early and found him with someone else."

Cheryl stopped and took a drink of her Diet Coke. Her eyes were glazed from remembering the past.

"I tore into him. He had become my world. The only person I could trust, and he was sleeping with anyone who made eyes at him. I blew up and told him to leave and never come back."

Penny swallowed the lump that had formed. She'd never thought her father might have been bad for them. She thought he'd left because of her.

"I wasn't thinking. All these feelings had been going through me. How could he do that to me? To us? I didn't think he'd stay away. We'd had fights before, but this was different. I wasn't even sure I would have taken him back if he'd showed up." Cheryl's eyes were filled with regrets.

"Did he ever contact you?" Penny couldn't help the hope in her voice. Her father hadn't left because of her. He'd left because he was two-timing her mother. Yet he hadn't come back to be with his daughter. But it hadn't just been her.

"No. After you were born, I was sure he'd come back, but he didn't. At some point I realized he wasn't coming back and tried to date, but the only thing that made me feel like dating was the numbness of alcohol. I knew it was bad and that I was letting you down, and that made me feel worse so I'd drink more."

"You tried...." Try as she might, Penny couldn't forget the good times with her mother. When she'd get a job and drink only in the evenings. Things always seemed better then.

"I did, but it never stuck. I'd meet a guy and start thinking he'd cheat on me or leave me or both and I'd drink." Tears filled her eyes. "I wanted so badly to stop for you. But I couldn't go to rehab and take you with me. I was lucky that Child Protective Services didn't step in earlier."

Cheryl reached across the table. "I left you so that I could get help to deserve you."

Penny stared at Cheryl's open, grasping hand. How easy would it be to just accept what she was offering? Put her hand in hers and have a mom again? How much heartbreak could she stand if she opened herself up to Cheryl and she left again?

She clasped her hands to keep from reaching out and shook her head to remind herself that this wasn't real.

Rachel stopped by with their food. Penny stared down at the burger and fries. She'd been hungry before, but now with all this new information swimming in her brain, she felt too overloaded.

"Aren't you going to eat?" Cheryl asked.

"Yeah." Penny shook herself out of it. "Of course."

She took a big bite of the burger and chewed. It tasted like sawdust in her mouth.

"Did you go to your prom?"

Penny blushed and finished swallowing the burger. That night she and Luke had had every intention of attending prom, but one thing had led to another... Technically they had gone to their prom. They just never made it into the gym, where the dance was being held. "Yes."

"Was there someone special?" Cheryl looked more relaxed now that they were talking about little stuff.

Penny wished she could relax, too, but Luke was a sticking point for her. She'd loved him forever and thinking back to high school... It all had been simple until graduation.

"Yeah, I had someone." She wiped her mouth with the napkin and flagged down Rachel. "Can we get the check?"

"Sure thing."

Penny placed the napkin on the table. "I really need to get back to the shop."

Her mother set down her fork. "Of course. I wouldn't want to keep you from your business. It seems important to you."

"It is." It was the only constant in her life. Even now when everything else was spiraling out of control, the shop was still there. All her antiques were on their shelves, exactly where they belonged. And when she was in there, she could try to forget about Luke and Cheryl. It didn't always work, but she could try.

"I'm glad you have something." Cheryl smiled. "Could we try to get together again this week?"

The world hadn't opened up and swallowed her whole from this lunch. Maybe she could rebuild a relationship with her mother. Or maybe she'd be better off cutting her losses now and telling Cheryl to find someone else to make amends to. "I'll check my schedule."

Luke checked his watch. It was only nine o'clock, but all the lights were off at Penny's house. He knew he should just go home. Sam was doing fine. Instead he parked his car and walked up to the front door.

He pressed the doorbell and Flicker barked from somewhere in the house. A light flicked on in the hallway and Penny emerged in her light blue cotton pajamas. He drank in the sight of her as she made her way to the door. Her ginger hair was tousled as if he'd woken her.

A moment of worry went through him. What if she was sick? What if she was with someone else?

She opened the door after checking to make sure it was him. "Hey."

"Are you okay? Are you sick?" Luke pressed his hand to her forehead.

She scowled at him and swatted his hand away. "I'm fine. I don't need you to play doctor."

"But that's my best role." He winked.

She just rolled her eyes. "Come on in. You can watch me sleep if you want."

"I didn't mean to wake you." Luke closed and locked the door behind them. "Usually you don't go to bed until later."

"*Usually,* I don't have a man keeping me up all hours

of the night." She raised an eyebrow and quirked the side of her mouth up in a little smile.

"I can go...." He put his thumb out to point to the door.

She smiled. "Don't be silly. You're better than an electric blanket and the dog combined."

She grabbed the waistband of his jeans and pulled him down the hallway to her bedroom. "Beat it, Flicker. I've got someone who won't hog the covers."

Flicker whined and looked at her from the bed with the most pathetic look Luke had ever seen a dog give.

"You had your chance, cover hog. Get!" Penny pointed to the door and the dog huffed his way off the bed and out of the bedroom. She closed the door behind him. "Now, where were we?"

"You were comparing me to heating devices?" Luke leaned against the wall next to her dresser.

"Ah, yes. You are definitely my favorite toy. And to think you don't even need batteries, and you're water-proof." Her pajama shorts revealed her long legs and hung low on her hips. Her top barely covered her breasts.

His body twitched in reaction. "I'd like to think I'm more than just a walking heated toy."

She advanced on him like a predator. "Mmm...you are so much better than any toy I've owned."

She stopped a hair's breadth away from him. As he inhaled her sweet scent, her breasts touched his chest. Something was off, though, and it wasn't just that she'd been sleeping.

"Maybe we should check to see if you need fresh batteries." She grinned as she cupped him.

He hardened against her hand. It had never taken much for Penny to get him going, but the past few days, she'd been different. More open. More emotional. Now it seemed as if she'd bottled that back up and was using the sexpot angle again. He shouldn't mind. They had only a few days left together.

Maggie and Brady would be home the day after tomorrow, and he'd need to get back to St. Louis. And this thing between them would end. But should it? Instead of stumbling through life numb, he could have Penny to come home to. It had been almost a decade since high school, and even though they'd changed, the chemistry between them hadn't.

They were combustible when mixed. He didn't want to leave her, but would she be willing to come with him? One thing had to be cleared up first.

Penny pressed her body against his and pulled his head down to meet her lips. His arms went around her and lifted her against him for the perfect fit. Her mouth tasted of vanilla ice cream and he couldn't get enough.

Before he was completely gone, he lifted his head. "We need to talk."

"Ugh. I've talked already today." She wove her fingers through his hair and tugged his head down. "I just want to play with my toy."

She nipped at his bottom lip. As enticing as the offer was, he needed to sort this out. Their time together was closing fast.

"I'll make you a deal." He shifted his hands to more comfortably hold her against him.

"I'm listening." She stared at his lips as if waiting for the right moment to pounce.

He gritted his teeth as she moved against him. The importance of talking was slowly ebbing; his body had other things it needed at the moment. "Maybe we can do both."

"Talk and sex? How original." She rolled her eyes.

"Next you'll be showing me a new sandwich made with peanut butter *and* jelly."

Instead of answering, he kissed her. She murmured something against his lips, but then softened against him. He walked them back until they hit the bed and lowered them both to the mattress.

"Is this really what you sleep in?" He lifted his head and gazed down at her exposed stomach. He ran his palm across it and watched her quake in response. "No wonder you are cold."

"I suppose you have flannel pajamas instead." Penny pulled his T-shirt out of his jeans and inched it upward. "Mmm. Maybe you wear nothing at all."

He helped her get his shirt off, but when she reached for his pants, he stalled her hand. "Not yet."

She pouted and pressed her hand against his abs, making him tighten them in response. "I guess this is the talking part?"

"The kiss with Sam—"

"Again?" Penny flopped back against the bed and put her arm over her eyes. Her shirt rose, revealing the underside of her breast.

"I just want to understand what made you run before." He managed to keep his hand on her stomach.

"What makes you think I was running?" She lifted her arm slightly to meet his eyes.

"You went to Sam and kissed him. You knew I would see you."

She put her arm back over her eyes. "Maybe I was drunk. Why are we obsessing over something that happened almost ten years ago?"

"Because it changed us." He pried her arm off her eyes and held her hand. "I thought we were on the same page. That you were coming with me to college. That eventually we'd get married and start a family."

"Do I look like a fairy tale to you?" She raised her eyebrow.

"It doesn't have to be a fairy tale, if it's true." Luke rested his elbow on the bed and leaned his head on his hand. "Hindsight is twenty-twenty. I didn't realize then that I'd been the one doing all the planning. We were following my dream because I thought it was our dream. But the more I talked, the more you acted like this."

She pressed her lips together.

"You can't deny that you shut down your emotions." Luke ran his hand across her stomach to keep from exploring the soft skin under her shirt. "You bottle them up so tight that you practically implode. Like last night."

"I don't want to play this game anymore."

"It's not a game, Penny. It never was." Luke used his knuckle to turn her face so she'd look at him. "I love you. I always have. You're the reason I couldn't move on. Even after seeing you kiss Sam, I wanted you in my life, but it drove me crazy thinking of you with other guys."

"But that's who I am. It's who I was and it's who I became." She wouldn't look him in the eyes.

Every part of him knew she was lying. "I'd believe that if you hadn't collapsed after kissing Sam. I'd believe that if I didn't know that you never looked at anyone else but me when we were dating. I'd believe that if you were a better liar."

"You believed it then. You believed it all. That I kissed Sam because I wanted to. That everything everyone had said about me was true."

"I was stupid and afraid." Luke didn't stop looking in her eyes. "It was easier to think the worst of you than to admit that I loved you but you didn't want to be with me."

"I wanted to be with you. I've always wanted you."

"Then what happened?"

She looked away from him.

"Don't hide from me. Don't lie. I have to go in a couple days and I don't want to leave this unfinished with me always wondering and you going on the way you did after I left."

"What if the truth hurts too much?"

"Then we'll face it together."

"What if it doesn't change anything?"

"It doesn't have to. It won't change the way I feel about you." He kissed her briefly, and when she opened her eyes, he said, "I love you."

She shook her head, rejecting his declaration, but it didn't matter. It wouldn't change the way he felt about her. Or the fact that he wanted her in his life, but he knew they had to overcome the past to start building a future. He also knew that he had to go slowly with her. Something was holding her back even now.

"It doesn't matter how much you love me…you'll leave me." Her voice was even. She believed every word that passed her lips. "Everyone who loves me leaves me. My dad, my mom, you."

"I wouldn't have left you—"

"Yes, you would have." She propped herself up on her elbows. "We would have gone off to follow your dream and you would have decided I was not smart enough or not pretty enough or you just would have been done with me. And I would have been left alone in a strange town with no family and no friends."

"I wouldn't have—"

"Wouldn't you have?" Penny pushed up to sitting and

grabbed a pillow to hold in front of her. A tear trailed down her cheek. "How long did it take you to believe the worst in me after seeing me kiss Sam?"

His heart thundered in his chest. She was right. He'd made the connections quickly because she'd been distant.

"Exactly. You didn't even come to me and ask me to clear it up. You just left. You didn't even say goodbye."

"What can I say, Penny? I thought I'd lost you. I was terrified of ending up hurt and in that dark place I'd been in after my parents died." He didn't ever want to experience that again. The rage, the pain, the bleakness.

"But you didn't." Her smile was sad. "Because life without me was so much better than life with me. Admit it. You did better in school because I wasn't there to weigh you down."

"You never weighed me down. You lifted me up out of a bad situation. You always have. That night in the hospital, when you so easily could have gone home and not given me another thought, you stayed. You took my mind off what was happening with Sam. When I'm with you, I feel alive. I don't know how to explain it better."

He grabbed her hands and pressed them to his heart. "If I have to, I can *survive* without you in my life, but I can't *live* without you. I love you."

"It won't work," she said softly. "We are too different now. We both have our own lives. I have the shop and you work at a hospital. We have lives that don't intersect except for this one time. Can we just enjoy the time we have left?"

He wanted to press her. To insist that they could be more. That together they could solve any problem. But

the harder he pushed her, the more closed off she'd get.
He could see that now.

"Yeah, we can enjoy what time we have left, but I
want you to know, I would never willingly leave you."

Chapter Twenty

Penny threw down the stack of papers she was organizing and stared out her shop window. Luke loved her. How was she supposed to process that information?

If it were any other guy, she'd have laughed at him or kicked him out of her bedroom last night. But with Luke, she'd curled up in his arms and slept. Well, she slept after he'd made love to her.

Maggie and Brady came back tomorrow. Sam was feeling better every day. Between Brady and Jasper, the farmwork would be taken care of, so Luke could go back to his big-city living and find that girl who was going to keep his house and give him two point five children.

That wasn't going to be her. The sharp pain in her chest wanted to say differently, but she wasn't going to listen to it. After everything her heart had been through, Luke wouldn't be the hardest thing to let go.

She'd done it once already. Next time should be a cakewalk because, although he said he loved her, she hadn't said it back. Admitting it out loud would have been her downfall. It was bad enough that she felt it.

The bell jingled above her door, bringing her back to today. She glanced at the middle-aged woman who came in.

"Let me know if I can help you find anything." Penny picked up her papers and tried to focus on the words again. In the past two weeks or so, she'd lost her focus. First Luke coming back, which would have been fine if it'd been confined to the wedding. But he'd been here longer and every time he came to her, she couldn't help but let him in.

Worse, she'd broken the rule of letting him into her bedroom. Now anywhere she went in her house, his ghost would haunt her long after he returned to St. Louis. Him leaning against the kitchen counter with his smile and telling her about the piglets on the farm. Him sitting next to her on the couch, quietly watching a movie together. Him sleeping next to her in her bed.

She sighed and set the papers down. There had to be something else she could work on.

The bell jingled. Her mother came in, glanced around and then focused on Penny.

"I swear I wasn't planning to stop by, but I got some terrific news." Cheryl set her purse down on top of the papers. Her hair was caught back in a ponytail and she wore the uniform of the waitstaff at The Rooster Café.

"Did you want me to guess?" Penny asked after a moment. She wasn't really interested, but apparently Cheryl had the best news in the world from the smile on her face.

"No, of course not. I mean how could you guess? I

know it's not the best timing, but when is it ever. I met someone."

Penny flinched as if Cheryl had slapped her across the face. She sank into the chair behind the register and waited for her heart to start beating again. This was how it always began. Cheryl was happy with a job and a place to live and then she met someone. It wouldn't be long before she started drinking again. And that's when things got rough.

"I just needed to share with someone." Cheryl hadn't noticed Penny's reaction yet. "I wanted to share with you. You are the reason I'm here, but…to have this opportunity, when I thought I was done with men."

That's when Cheryl turned around and noticed Penny. Penny couldn't breathe, let alone speak.

"Is something wrong?" Cheryl rushed around the counter and squatted next to Penny's chair. She reached out hesitantly, as if she was going to touch Penny's hand, but decided against it. "Are you okay?"

From the pit of Penny's stomach the old pain and longing rose to the surface. She looked Cheryl in the eyes. "You left me."

"I—"

"You left me alone and didn't come back. The one person in the world I had. The one person I loved. I trusted you and you left me all alone."

"It broke my heart to leave you. I did my best. I found you a home and somewhere you would be safe. I thought if I got help I could come back to you."

"But you didn't come back."

"No," Cheryl said slowly. "So many times I tried to get clean. I wanted to. I knew it was the only way to get you back. Mother made me promise. She made me—"

Cheryl covered her mouth as tears flowed down her

cheeks. "I had to prove to her that I was worthy of you. That was the only way she'd take you in. I told her about the men, the alcohol, selling your stuff. She knew that if she didn't take you in, I couldn't protect you. It was bad enough that I was with those type of men, but if they'd hurt you, I would have never forgiven myself."

Penny couldn't respond. What was there to say that hadn't already been said?

"Every time I thought I was getting close, something would happen. I was afraid I'd never make it back to you. So I drank."

"What's different about this time? Tell me so I can believe you. Make me understand why you are waltzing back into my life seventeen years later and expecting to have some sort of relationship with me, when all I can think about is when you are going to leave me again." Penny kept her voice down; inside she felt cold and hollow.

"Don't say that, Penny-pie. Please don't say that. I'm never going to leave again. I'm never going to drink again. If it means that I grow old alone but get to be with the one thing that I did that was ever worthwhile, I can do it. I can do it for you." Cheryl brushed a strand of hair out of Penny's eyes.

"Don't do it for me." Penny grabbed Cheryl's hands and held them still. "Don't do it for me. Do it for you because you want to. Because you need to. Because I won't be held responsible for the next time you fall down that rabbit hole. I won't be responsible when you pick up a drink because you've had a bad day or week or your boyfriend isn't treating you right. I won't be responsible for you."

Cheryl straightened. "You're right. It's my fault you took on so much when you were growing up. You don't need to be responsible for me anymore. I will stay clean for me and for you, but if I do stumble, please don't shut me out. I'm not perfect. I make mistakes."

Penny felt the beginnings of a smile. "I'm not going anywhere."

"Neither am I. And if you think I shouldn't date—"

"Please, I'm hardly the authority on dating." Penny laughed and stood. "Just don't let it get bad. Make sure to end it before it gets bad."

"Promise." Cheryl walked around to the other side of the counter and leaned across it. "So let me tell you about Paul."

Penny opened the screen door of the farmhouse as the car stopped in the driveway. The two farm dogs crowded around the car and barked. Luke was already coming down from the field. Sam was inside snoring on the recliner. She wouldn't be surprised if the dogs woke him up with their insistence that the household needed to be alerted to the arrival of outsiders.

The car doors opened, and Amber was the first to be greeted by the dogs. Maggie and Brady got out while they were distracted. Penny's chest felt lighter seeing her best friend. Penny and Maggie hugged as soon as they were close enough. They hadn't been apart much in the years since high school.

"You look wonderful," Penny said. Maggie wore a sundress with a white shrug over it. She looked more than wonderful; she looked relaxed and happy.

"You haven't been eating, have you?" Maggie put her hand on Penny's cheek.

"I've been eating fine, Maggie."

"How's Sam been?" Brady asked before hugging Penny, too.

"Besides bored out of his mind, he's been fine."
Penny led them inside. Her pot of potatoes had started
to boil, so she turned down the stove a little to keep it
from boiling over.

"I'll go find Sam." Brady left the kitchen.

"So what's new?" Maggie sat at the kitchen table
and grabbed a handful of M&M's from the candy dish.

"In this kitchen, not much." Penny used stirring to
keep from meeting Maggie's gaze.

"You're lucky that I missed you and your quirky
ways." Maggie popped an M&M in her mouth. "Tell
me about your mother."

"Cheryl's fine. She's got a job, a house and a potential love interest."

"What about your relationship with her?"

"We're working on it. It won't fix itself overnight."
Penny stirred the potatoes and set the lid over them.

Maggie hugged her from behind. "I'm glad you are
trying."

"Me, too." She patted Maggie's arm.

Maggie sank back into her chair and Penny joined
her at the table. The screen door opened, and Amber
and Luke came in. Amber was talking his ear off about
some ride at Disney. Luke glanced Penny's way.

She couldn't keep her smile down, but she dropped
her gaze. She loved him, and just seeing him made her
feel warm and gooey inside. But the time to deal with
Luke was coming. She wanted to avoid it so she focused
on living in this moment. This could end only one way.

Amber ran up and tackle-hugged Penny. "I missed
you, Penny."

"I missed you, too, munchkin."

"Where's Uncle Sam?"

"I think he's in the living room with your dad." Luke

pointed in that direction and she was off. He stood there undecided for a moment.

"You can join us if you like. We're just catching up," Maggie said.

"I'd hate to be a third wheel. I'll go see what my brothers are talking about. I have to give Brady the grand tour of everything that is happening on the farm anyway and try to get Sam to sit it out."

"Good luck," Penny said.

He nodded and rubbed the back of his neck as he headed out of the room.

"So…" Maggie pointedly glanced at the door that Luke had disappeared through.

"So what?" Penny grabbed an M&M. How could she begin to talk about Luke when she didn't know what was going on herself?

"Penny?" Maggie put her hand over hers on the table. "Oh, sweetie, you've fallen for him again, haven't you?"

That's the thing that sucked about a best friend. They could see through any of the bull you put up for everyone else.

"Have you guys talked about the future?" Maggie asked with her concerned face on.

"What's there to talk about? I can't just leave What Goes Around Comes Around. I'm only just making a name for it. He's not going to give up his job at the hospital in St. Louis to come here…for what? To work in the hospital in Owen or drive all the way to Springfield for work every day."

"But you've thought about it."

"Of course I've thought about it. It's the only thing I can think about. That or my mother, and neither of them are very conducive to sleeping, eating or working."

Maggie squeezed her hand. "I bet if we put our heads together we could figure out something."

"It won't matter. What we have won't last."

"Why not?" Their heads both turned to see Luke standing in the doorway. "Why won't we last, Penny?"

Penny swallowed hard.

"Oh, I think someone is calling me." Maggie started to get up, but Penny gripped her hand tighter and gave her the please-don't-leave-me look. Maggie yanked her hand away and mouthed, "You'll be fine."

She hoped Maggie could read faces because hers was screaming, *Traitor!*

Maggie patted Luke's shoulder as she passed him. And to think Penny actually encouraged Maggie to go after Brady.

Luke took Maggie's seat at the table and continued to look at Penny, waiting for her explanation.

She opened her mouth and closed it. "We... I mean... There's just no... Can't we talk about this later?"

"When, Penny?" Luke leaned back in the chair and folded his hands behind his head. "Later today, tonight, tomorrow, or is later when I'm gone and you don't have to deal with what's going on between us?"

Heat rushed to her face. "We're just having fun while you are here."

The words sounded false to even her ears. Maybe if she hadn't said them like a question...

Luke nodded solemnly. "Sure."

The word cut into her heart. Even though she knew that's what they'd been doing, it had seemed more real than that to her. Maybe it had meant more to her than to him. It didn't matter. It had to end, and if she wanted to save her sanity, maybe now was the time to end it.

"After all—" she got up and checked on the pots on

the stove "—we were just teenage sweethearts. It's not like we could have ever made it work. Our relationship was built on rampaging hormones."

"Is that what you really believe?" Luke didn't move and his inflection didn't change to show any emotions.

"Every night we spend together is just about chemistry." She tried to make it sound believable.

"It wasn't just about sex." Luke stood up and looked out the window above the sink.

"So we had a few laughs. I cried on your shoulder. That's what friends do, right?" She walked across the room to stand as far away from him as possible when she faced him. "We're just friends."

"If you believed that, you wouldn't need to put so much distance between us. And I'm not talking about physical distance."

"I do believe it. What do you want from me?"

"In truth?"

"Yes, please tell me. I'm dying to know." She crossed her arms over her chest.

"The truth is I want you, Penny." He turned and slowly closed the distance between them. "I want you when you are laughing at a game of cards. I want you when you are mad at me for something little I did. I want you when you go sexpot on me to hide how you really feel. I want you when you cry in my arms."

He stopped in front of her and put his hands on her arms. "I want you with me. Morning, noon and night. I love you and nothing is going to change that."

Her insides felt heavy. She wanted to throw herself into his arms and say yes, but what if it all went wrong? "I can't. My shop, my house, my life…it's here."

"And no one can take those away from you."

She shook her head and pulled away. "I can't just leave. Maggie—"

"Has Brady now. You won't be gone forever."

"No." Tears flowed down her face. "No. I can't. I can't."

She stumbled to the door and jerked it open. The warm air hit her in the chest and stopped her breathing. *Turn around. Go back.*

She couldn't. She stood in the driveway with no purse and no keys. She'd have to go back in to get them, but that meant facing Luke. If he hadn't already followed her out....

The screen door screeched on its hinge and banged shut like a gun. She didn't turn. She didn't want to know. Luke had just handed her his heart on a platter and she'd shoved it back at him. How could she claim she loved him when she couldn't even accept his words?

"Hey," Maggie said.

Penny spun around and swiped at the tears on her cheeks. "Hey."

"I thought you might want these." She held out Penny's purse and keys.

"Thank you." Penny stepped closer to claim them, but Maggie held them back.

"Think about it." Maggie gave her her things. "Just think about what you really want and need. I know you're scared. I was scared, too, but this isn't just kids playing at being in love. I know Luke loves you. I've seen it in his eyes when he looks at you. And I know you love him, too."

Penny shook her head.

"Don't deny it. You might be able to hide from everyone else, but you can't hide from me." Maggie wrapped her arms around Penny.

She leaned into the hug, wishing she knew what to do.

"Whatever you decide," Maggie said, "I'll support you. You aren't alone."

Chapter Twenty-One

Luke sat on the couch and watched a show he hadn't caught the name of with Sam.

"Aren't you going out?" Sam asked.

"Not tonight." He'd considered going over to Penny's, but with the way things ended only a few hours ago, he thought it was best to let her have her space. For now.

"Penny's a good person." Sam leaned farther back in his recliner.

"I know that." Luke picked up his beer and took a swig from it.

"She's actually really responsible. I never picked up on that when you two were going out."

"I know that, too."

"She's brought in people from all over to visit her shop."

"Dammit, Sam, what's your point?"

"I can see why you like her, is all."

"Really? Wow, thanks. I was just about to ask your permission to court her." Luke rolled his eyes and stared at the cops trying to solve a case.

"No need to bite my head off. If you want to leave, I won't stop you."

"I think I'll stay right here."

"What, so she can get it in her mind that you really don't care that much about her? Can you blame the girl for being a little leery of you? After all, she kissed me once and you assumed she'd banged the entire student population. Trust is a two-way street."

"Big words from the guy who for eight years withheld the fact that Brady knocked up Maggie."

Sam held his hands up. "I have my own devils to deal with."

"Penny's just not ready." Luke shook his head.

"Will she ever be?"

"I hope so."

He was leaving tomorrow. Maggie had told her at the shop that afternoon. For the rest of the afternoon, Penny had been out of it. She caught herself staring at the door as if waiting for someone to come in.

Home alone that evening, she couldn't get settled. Not even watching *Supernatural* appealed to her. When she started to pace, Flicker barked at her.

"Screw it." She went to the bedroom and changed from her pajamas into a pair of cutoffs and a pink tank top. She let Flicker out one last time before grabbing her keys.

The drive out to the farm took ten minutes flat. A new record. She sat in her car in the driveway, wondering what her move should be. She didn't want to give Luke the idea that she was coming with him, but she wanted to be with him one more time before he left. That was all this was.

Maybe it was stupid. Maybe she should leave well enough alone.

The driver's-side door opened.

"Are you going to sit in there all night or come inside?" Luke looked down at her with the same smile in his eyes, as if nothing had changed. As if he hadn't asked her to give up everything and go with him.

He held out his hand and she took it. He kept her hand as they walked to the house and through the stupid, creaky, bangy screen door. Her heart beat in time with their footsteps as she followed him to his bedroom.

When he closed the door, she turned to face him. "This doesn't mean anything."

"Of course not." Luke sat on the edge of the bed and pulled off his shoes. He wore a pair of flannel pajama pants and no shirt.

Her mouth went dry. "I'm not coming with you to St. Louis."

"That's okay." He stood and moved toward her.

She pressed back into the wall. "I haven't said I love you."

"I know." His tone sounded as if he was trying to calm down a wild animal. He put his hands beside her head on the wall.

"I don't need you. I'm happy with my life the way it is." Her heart pounded harder with every word, knowing that he should be kicking her out.

"And I love you more for it." He leaned in.

She put a hand on his chest to hold him away, knowing he could ignore it if he wanted, but he didn't. "I don't want your love."

"But you have it." He brought his lips to hers and she gave in.

Gave in to the whirlwind of feelings only Luke inspired in her. Gave in to the fact that she wouldn't feel this way with anyone else. Gave in to the press of his lips against hers, his tongue sliding along hers, his heartbeat in time with hers.

She did need him. Her fingers wove in his hair and she pressed her body against his. The warmth of his skin penetrated through her thin layer of clothes. She wanted this night to last forever, but she knew it would end and he'd be gone. Just one last time for closure.

But in truth, she wanted to mark him as hers. Claim him one more time so he'd never forget her. Make him as insane about her as she was about him.

He lifted her shirt, trailing his fingertips across her ribs and along the sides of her breasts. She held her arms up to help him. He pressed his bare chest against hers as her shirt came off. Heat flooded her system and pooled at her core.

His hands rested on her hips as he drew her to him for another kiss. The friction of his skin against hers was setting her system on fire. His fingers stroked along the waistband of her cutoffs until he found the button.

When he rested his forehead against hers, she opened her eyes and met his blue gaze.

"I want you, Luke." *For today, for a month from now, for the rest of my life.* The love she felt for him wouldn't die when he left. She'd probably end up a bitter old woman with just her dog for company.

"There's no one I want more than you." His lips closed over hers. She let his words flow through her. It should be enough that he loved her and wanted her. But something held her back. Even as she gave her body to him fully, she still couldn't give him what he wanted. Trust. Her trust that he wouldn't leave when things got bad. His trust that she wouldn't sleep around.

She shoved the thoughts from her head. Tonight was about saying goodbye. Tomorrow would be soon enough for regrets. He pushed down her cutoffs and slid off his pajama bottoms. With their clothes in a puddle on the floor, he carried her to the bed.

It didn't matter that they'd been together so many times recently. It felt like the first time and the last combined. A hint of discovery as she found a new spot that made him moan and he found a spot that made her hold her breath. And a hint of finality when he entered her. She focused on his eyes, wanting to remember every ounce of pleasure they could wring from each other. And when she came, she cried out his name. Always his and only his. His arms wrapped around her, holding her close to his heart afterward.

Her skin still tingled and her breathing was erratic. She'd never felt more relaxed and at peace than she did in his arms. Her hand rested over his heart. The beating of his corresponded with her own. He pulled her tightly against him and tugged the covers over them.

She shouldn't sleep with him. It was another rule she'd broken for him. She loved to feel him next to her in bed, but she had to give him up in the morning. He'd become a habit that made sleeping without him impossible. She shouldn't let him have that control over her. Wouldn't it be easier to slip out now and avoid the whole scene in the morning anyway?

When she started to rise, his arms pulled her back to him. "Not yet, Penny. I just want to hold you for a little while longer."

Tears gathered in her eyes. She blinked them back. She wanted that, too. "Okay."

"Tell me you won't forget me." Luke's voice was on the edge of sleep.

"Never." Penny could feel the energy draining from her. She just needed a little sleep and then she'd drive back to her place and climb into her cold bed....

"Promise me something." He kissed the top of her head.

"Hmm?" She was so close to sleep. There was nowhere she slept better than in his arms.

"Don't shut me out."

"You're going to be gone," she murmured.

"Not forever. I'll be back." He pulled her against his body until she forgot where she ended and he began. "Promise?"

"Promise."

Luke woke with Penny still in his arms. He smiled at the ceiling. Someday this would be his every day. Penny could take only so much pushing before she closed up entirely. She needed time. He was willing to let her go for now. He could wait for as long as she needed.

She pressed on his chest and propped her head on her hand. "Morning?"

"Yeah." He brushed his knuckles across her cheek.

"I didn't mean to sleep all night." Her smile filled him with relief. Her brown eyes blinked at him, but she wasn't stumbling to get out of bed and away from him.

"I'm glad you did." He scrubbed a hand over his face. "I'd have hated not being able to say goodbye today."

Her brow wrinkled and her fingers curled into him. "I don't like goodbyes."

"How about see-you-soons?"

She pushed up to sitting and brushed her hair from her face. "It'd be better if it weren't a lie."

"It doesn't have to be a lie." He couldn't help the little push; after all, he'd already told her he wanted her to come with him.

"I can't leave here." Penny looked over her shoulder at him. "That's not why I came to see you last night."

He put his hands behind his head. "I know."

If she'd been gearing up for a fight, he didn't have one ready for her. She turned her head away from him. Her slender back was pale with a few freckles. He reached out and followed the trail of freckles with his fingertip.

"If I didn't have to get packed and do chores, I'd spend my last few hours here making love with you."

Her body shuddered beneath his fingers. He breathed in deeply of that scent that was uniquely Penny and smiled. This wasn't goodbye. Things that felt this good didn't end. He would make sure it didn't.

"Do you want me to make breakfast while you do chores?" Penny looked back at him.

In that moment she seemed so vulnerable. He wanted to reassure her that nothing had to change, but she would close up if he did.

"Breakfast would be great." He opened his arms and she snuggled into them. He hugged her to him and kissed her forehead. "Time to start the day."

She nodded against his chest and he could feel the wetness of her tears.

"I love you," he said. "I'm never giving up on you."

She pulled away and searched his eyes. When she opened her mouth—most likely to tell him to stop talking that way—he shoved off the bed and grabbed a pair of underwear.

"Breakfast in twenty?" He pulled on his jeans and a T-shirt.

"Yeah." She still sat on his bed, completely naked except for the sheet she held up.

He brushed her lips with his and left the room. As soon as he reached the kitchen, he took a deep breath in and pushed it out. As much as he wanted to keep her with him, she needed to come to terms with them as a couple first. He might be able to bully her into it with sweet kisses and long nights in his bed, but that wouldn't last.

Something was holding her back. Whether it was because he hadn't trusted her when she tried to manipulate him or whether it went much deeper, she needed to face her fears. He could only let her know that he'd be there when the dust settled.

By the time Luke finished with chores, Brady had arrived. They walked around the farmyard where they'd grown up and talked about what had been taken care of and what still needed to be done.

"So...you and Penny?" Brady pulled a weed from the field and tossed it to the side.

"Hopefully." Luke wasn't used to having his brothers around for advice. Although Brady had been the one to set him straight the summer before senior year.

"Penny's not the same girl she was in high school," Brady said.

Luke couldn't help but smile. "Nope, she's even more magnificent."

"Do you love her?"

Luke stopped and stared at the farmhouse in the distance. Inside, Penny was probably making him breakfast and trying to figure out how to leave without saying goodbye. "Yeah, I love her."

"Maggie said her mother just came back."

"It has messed with her head pretty badly. But she's been dealing with it."

"And you offered to have her come with you?"

Luke started walking toward the farmhouse. "Of course. I love her."

"And what are you giving up for her?"

He stopped dead in his tracks and turned to face Brady. "What do you mean?"

"Love isn't about follow me or don't. It's about finding a happy medium ground. It's about talking through what is best for both your futures. Because it's not just your dreams anymore. It's what you can achieve together."

"I have to finish my rotation—"

"But what about after that? You can't expect her to blindly follow you. I almost lost Maggie by doing that. I thought the only way things would work out was if she and Amber came to New York with me. But the worst thing was going back alone and knowing I'd only get to see them some of the time."

Brady clapped him on the shoulder. "She's got her shop, her best friend and her mother in this town. What are you offering her?"

Brady strode toward the farmhouse, but Luke couldn't move yet. He had done the same thing he did back in high school—made plans for them without realizing that maybe she had plans, too. How stupid could he get? He might as well have drawn a line in the sand and said either come over here with me or stay over there.

Dammit. He needed to fix this now before he lost Penny.

Chapter Twenty-Two

Bacon and eggs and toast. The day was just starting to warm up as Penny stood over the stove. She'd pulled her hair back with a rubber band and used the toothbrush she kept in her purse. She tried her best to cover up the redness around her eyes but kept the rest of her makeup to a minimum.

Luke was leaving again. This time she'd get to say goodbye and good luck. She hoped whoever he ended up with would make him happy. She felt hollow on the inside, but maybe that was for the best. No emotions meant no one could hurt her.

"Morning." Sam came into the kitchen and sat in his chair as if they did this every day.

She plated the over-easy eggs, a couple strips of turkey bacon and two slices of toast. She put it in front of him with a cup of coffee. He grunted.

She was tempted to watch his face when he bit into

the turkey bacon to see if he'd notice the difference, but Brady walked in.

"Hi, Penny." He came over and gave her a one-armed hug, which she shrugged off. "How are things?"

Brady wasn't normally the cuddly type. Because the only thing happening today was Luke leaving, he must be trying to comfort her. Which she didn't need or want.

"Fine." She grabbed a plate and loaded it up for him and shoved it at his chest. "Go eat."

He chuckled and sat at the table.

She finished making two more plates and was about to set them on the table when the door opened. Luke looked out of sorts as he headed for her. She put the plates down and opened her mouth. He grabbed her hand and tugged her after him.

"Breakfast will get cold." She followed after him as he pulled her into his room and shut the door.

"Let it."

"Cold eggs? Not the breakfast of champions." Penny wrinkled her nose.

"Please sit down. I'll make you more eggs." He raked his hand through his hair and paced the room.

She sat on the edge of the bed and waited for whatever he needed to say. What if he was going to try to convince her to go with him? "If you are going to try to convince me to go with you—"

"I'm stupid." He sat next to her.

"Okay. Is that it? We can still make those eggs work…."

"Why do we do this? Every time?" He put his head in his hands.

She rubbed his back. "Whatever is eating you, let it out. I can take it."

He met her eyes. "You can, can't you? Here I was

thinking you needed time to change your mind, but you are the strong one. I get so one-track that I can't see all the other options."

"What are you talking about, Luke?" Her hands trembled as she clasped them in front of her.

"We need to work this out together if it's ever going to work. I can't demand you come to St. Louis with me. We need to make that decision together." He put a hand over hers.

She stood and walked across the room, holding herself tight. "What are you saying?"

"I want us to be together. We can figure out a way to make this work if we really want it."

"Is that what you want?" she said, nervous of what his answer would be and what that would mean to her.

"More than anything."

When she looked into his eyes, she could tell he was being honest, but was it enough?

"I kissed your brother because I knew you'd leave without me." The truth burst out of her before she could stop it. "I knew the rumors of me with other guys bothered you and I hoped you'd believe them if I kissed him. I tore us apart because you will leave me. Everyone I love leaves me."

"I'm not going any—"

"For how long?" She couldn't stop the tears flowing down her cheeks. "A month? A year? Until one of your colleagues gets handsy at the Christmas party? Would you believe me if I said it wasn't my fault? Or would you blame me because I flirt too much?"

"I love—"

"Love isn't enough. You need to trust me."

He grabbed her shoulders and forced her to look up at him. "I trust you. I will believe you always."

"How can I know that?" she whispered.

"I'll spend the rest of my life proving that I trust you, if you'll let me."

She searched those blue eyes she'd always loved. She wanted to believe him. To forget her fears. To not end up alone.

She shook her head. "I can't."

She turned and walked out of his room. She grabbed her purse and said goodbye to Sam and Brady before heading out the door. It closed with a final bang.

Maggie had tried to talk to her about Luke for the past few days, but Penny walked away every time. She just needed to get over him. A few months and she'd be back to her old self and out at the bars, dancing and flirting. Maybe not picking up men....

As she stared out the door of her antiques shop, she rubbed the ache in her chest that had been her constant companion since Luke had left. He'd left himself everywhere she looked. Leaning against the counter while she worked. Teasing her down the aisle while she dusted. Asking her for the story of an old glass bottle.

It wasn't any better at home. Her couch, her kitchen, her dining room, her bedroom. He was everywhere she turned. Every night she'd wait for the doorbell to ring to let her know he was there. But it never did. She lay awake in her bed for hours, trying to ignore the cold spot beside her that still smelled like him.

Penny sighed. It wouldn't be so bad if business weren't so slow. All she had were her thoughts to spin constantly back to Luke.

When the bell over the door rang, she stood and walked around the counter, ready for any distraction.

"I hadn't heard from you in a while." Cheryl walked

over to the counter, all smiles. "I thought I'd pop in and check up on you."

"I'm here." Which was part of the problem. She sank down into a chair.

"What's going on?" Cheryl sat in the chair next to her. "I know I'm not your most favorite person, but I've got a world of experience to share. You can talk to me."

"I don't know what I'm doing." Penny stared out the door at the cars going down Main Street. "I don't know why I can't get over him."

"Man troubles. Was this that handsome man from the other night?" Cheryl leaned back in the chair and crossed her legs.

"Yes." Penny was not at all certain she wanted to talk to Cheryl about this, but maybe she was the best to understand. "I made him leave."

"Why?"

"I hate to blame my messed-up childhood but..." She waved her hand as if she had presented something to her audience.

"It has to be more than that." Cheryl sat quietly for a moment.

Penny wasn't ready to fill in all the blanks.

"Do you love him?"

"Yes." With every fiber of her being.

"Then what's the problem? Doesn't he love you?"

"Yes." Penny stood. "Don't you get it? He loves me and I love him. When he leaves me, I'll be crushed. Alone."

"How is that different than now?" Cheryl said softly.

"I left him! So he couldn't leave me. The first time I made him leave, and this time I left him." She buried her face in her hands.

"If you love him, why did you leave? Was he bad for you? Into drugs? Gambling? Alcohol?"

Penny shook her head. "He would leave me."

"Why, Penny?" her mother pressed.

Penny spun around. "Because you did. Because everyone I ever loved and who claimed to love me leaves and they don't come back."

Cheryl looked down at her hands and took a deep breath. "I'm back now."

"But how can I trust that you won't leave me again? He left me before, so how can I trust he won't do it again?"

"Oh, baby." Tears welled in Cheryl's eyes and trailed down her face. "You have to have faith and let go of your fear. If you don't, you'll just shut everyone out. Wouldn't you rather have a year more with him if it meant you were happy for that year?"

Fear? Faith? "What if he doesn't want me?"

"That's just fear talking." Cheryl stood and put her arm around Penny. "You can't let fear speak for you. Wouldn't it be worse to never see him again? I know I hurt you, Penny. I can't make up for the past, but don't let my problems and my regrets make you not live your life."

"But how do I know?"

Cheryl smiled at her. "You already know. You wouldn't be miserable if you thought you'd done the right thing."

Her mother was making sense. Luke had been pressing her to reveal more of herself, and every fear she'd shown him, he'd held her through. "What do I do?"

"Call him, go to him, get him to come back here or go be with him." Her mother smiled. "I'll be here when you come around."

"But my shop—"

"Won't die without you."

"You won't leave?" The ten-year-old girl inside her needed to hear the words.

"I'm never leaving your life again. No matter what you throw at me. I'm here to support you and need to be part of your life. Even if we aren't in the same town." Cheryl hugged her again, and this time Penny opened her arms and returned the hug.

"Well, then," Penny said, wiping the tears from her eyes, "I need to call Maggie."

Chapter Twenty-Three

Luke finished up his notes in his patient's file. It was quarter past one in the morning, but he knew sleep wouldn't come easily. He'd been back at the hospital for a week, and in that time he'd worked more fiercely than ever to keep his mind from dwelling on Penny.

His first days off weren't for another week, so he couldn't do anything until then. He'd already made plans to go back to Tawnee Valley for that weekend. He wanted to check up on Sam, but mostly he wanted to convince Penny that they belonged together whether it was here or there or anywhere in between.

He scrubbed his hand down his face and stared at the hospital-green walls. He should go home and try to sleep. He was supposed to scrub in on a surgery in the morning.

Stacking his paperwork, he scooted back in his chair,

then grabbed his keys. As he headed to the elevator, a nurse called out to him.

"Doctor Ward?"

Luke walked toward the nurse. "What is it?"

"Someone's here to see you." The nurse glanced down the hallway.

"At this hour?"

She nodded. "I put her in room twenty."

"Thanks." Luke grabbed a cup of coffee from the nurse's station and went to the room she'd indicated. "How can I hel—"

Sitting on the bed was Penny. "Hi."

Luke closed the door and crossed the room to stand before her, but he didn't touch her, afraid she wouldn't be real. "What are you— When did you—"

"Cat got your tongue?" Penny swung her crossed leg. "Never thought I'd make Luke Ward speechless. Where are your color-coded index cards when you need them?"

"I missed you." Luke's pulse raced. She'd come to him.

"I missed you, too." She pushed her hair behind her ear. "So, *Doctor,* I've been having these pains right here." She pressed her hand to her chest.

"Is that so?" He wanted to reach out and touch her so badly, but he held himself back. If he touched her, he wouldn't stop until they were both naked.

"It started before you left." Her brown eyes held his gaze. "I don't think I ever stopped loving you. I was so scared that you would leave me that I didn't want to give you that power over my heart. You left so easily the last time—"

"Because I was scared, too. I loved you so much it hurt and seeing you with Sam did a number on me.

But I think you knew that. Otherwise you would have picked any other guy to kiss."

"I'm sorry."

"I don't need you to be sorry. I need you to have a little faith in me and trust that I won't ever intentionally try to hurt you."

"I couldn't help trying to drive you away this time, too...."

"It didn't work. I was planning on coming back to you every chance I got. Even if it was just to get inside your bedroom for a day or two, I knew eventually I'd win you over. You make my life fun and sexy. You remind me of the man I am when my logical side wants to take over. I want you with me for as long as you'll have me. If I thought you'd say yes to marrying me, I'd fly us to Vegas on the next flight out."

She smiled and reached out to hold his face. "Someday on the marriage thing. First, let's try to make this work. You make the fear worthwhile. You make it easy to forget to be afraid. Are you ready to trust me?"

He lowered his mouth until just a hair's breadth was between them. "With my life and with my heart. I love you, Penny."

"I love you, Luke." She pressed her lips to his, sealing their love with perfection.

* * * * *

LET'S TALK

Romance

For exclusive extracts, competitions
and special offers, find us online:

 facebook.com/millsandboon

 @MillsandBoon

 @MillsandBoonUK

Get in touch on 01413 063232